BRUMBACK LIBRARY

D0331177

$24.95

F   Black, Daniel Omotosho
BLA   They tell me of a
    1/06 home

THE BRUMBACK LIBRARY
OF VAN WERT COUNTY
VAN WERT, OHIO

They Tell Me
of a Home

They Tell Me
of a Home

Daniel Black

St. Martin's Press New York

THEY TELL ME OF A HOME. Copyright © 2005 by Daniel Omotosho Black. All rights reserved. Printed in the United States of America. No part of this book may be used or reproduced in any manner whatsoever without written permission except in the case of brief quotations embodied in critical articles or reviews. For information, address St. Martin's Press, 175 Fifth Avenue, New York, N.Y. 10010.

www.stmartins.com

Design by Phil Mazzone

Library of Congress Cataloging-in-Publication Data

Black, Daniel Omotosho.
    They tell me of a home / Daniel Omotosho.—1st ed.
      p. cm.
    ISBN 0-312-34187-3
    EAN 978-0-312-34187-9
     1. African American families—Fiction.   2. Conflict of generations—Fiction.
   3. Parent and adult child—Fiction.   4. Children—Death—Fiction.   5. Young
   men—Fiction.   6. Arkansas—Fiction.   I. Title.

    PS3602.L267T47 2005
    813'.6—dc22   2005044137

First Edition: October 2005

10 9 8 7 6 5 4 3 2 1

To my sons: Toundi and Ryan

To my nieces and nephews: T.J. (Karanga), Michael (Osobiyii), Mark, Ben, Jonathan, Anna, Andre, Imani, Malcolm, Elijah, Malika, Tyler, Darnell, Jamelle, Terrance, Cherelle, Chelsie, Celeste, and Makala

To my grandchildren: Rami, Isaiah, Amari, Josiah, Kamia, Austin, Ever, Tacuma, Elijah, Kemet, Kai, Trevan, Iyanna, Shania, Mark, Marquez, Kendryana, Sha, Diallo, M'kai, Ramia, and Zuri

This is your heritage.

Acknowledgments

To my literary elders: Sonia Sanchez, Michael Eric Dyson, Melvin Rahming, James Baldwin, Paule Marshall, Toni Morrison, Randall Kenan, Jonathan Franzen, Percival Everett, John Edgar Wideman, Ayi Kwei Armah, Zora Neale Hurston, Ernest Gaines, and Jeffrey Woodyard. You have blazed the trail upon which I now travel. Thank you for clearing the way.

To Tony Clark, my literary agent: Thanks for laboring on my behalf, brotherman.

To all the descendants of Blackwell and Happy Bend, Arkansas, especially my parents, Mr. and Mrs. Harold Black, and my siblings: Together, our history and memories make this novel possible. I hope I've made you proud.

To Akino Aeikbns, The Nation of Ndugu and Nzinga: Your healing power and love kept me sane when I thought I was losing my mind. Don't worry about others' evaluation of you. Everyone who ever changed the world was first thought strange. Thank you for saving me, and now let's save the universe.

To the Norments: A crown awaits you in the kingdom of God.

To the members of First Iconium Baptist Church: Thank you for providing a place wherein my creative gifts could bloom. I pray that my presence has enlarged the body, and I give thanks for the embracing so many of you provided.

To the Clark Atlanta University family: The literary training I acquired while an undergraduate planted the seed for this achievement. Now, as a faculty member, I thank all of you for the support you've given. Thanks, Dr. Liddell, for encouraging me to write when this project was still an embryo. For your wisdom, Ms. Maolud, I am eternally grateful.

They Tell Me
of a Home

1

"Excuse me, sir," I said apprehensively to the Greyhound bus driver. "Could you let me off at the big oak tree about a mile up the road on the right?"

He studied me through the rearview mirror and frowned, confused.

"See, if you let me off there"—diffidence colored my words—"I won't have so far to walk. My parents' house is just on the other side of those woods." I pointed out the big tinted windshield of the Greyhound bus toward a gathering of trees some distance away. Most would have thought the area uninhabitable, for there was no sign of a human dwelling anywhere in the midst of those trees. Yet the origin of my beginning lay nestled quietly among them.

"I see," he affirmed as he nodded. "I believe I can do that. You's a country boy sho' 'nuff, ain't chu?" He laughed heartily.

"I guess I am," I responded less enthusiastically.

"Boy, dat sun gon' bake you black as coal! It's got to be a hundred degrees or better today. I hope you brought a hat, 'cause if you didn't, you liable to have a sunstroke 'fo' you get home."

"I forgot how hot Arkansas is in the summer," I said, more to myself than to the driver.

"Well, you 'bout to be reminded."

I reclined in the seat, preparing myself mentally to walk the two miles I once had walked, years ago, with ease. "Lord have mercy," I mumbled as I grabbed my bags. One of them contained my clothes—three African dashikis and matching pants, two plain white T-shirts, two pair of shorts, some underwear, and some dress shoes—while the other carried books. Armah's *Two Thousand Seasons* had captured me only days earlier, so I couldn't leave it behind, and I had been reading *Some Soul to Keep* by J. California Cooper simply too long. A friend recommended *Song of Solomon* fervently, and after the first couple of pages I saw why. There were others I hadn't started, like *The Outsider*, but my mind was already cluttered with too many characters, so I decided to finish at least one book before I started another. Leaving things incomplete was a habit I couldn't get rid of, but I had a feeling coming home was going to force me to do so.

The bus pulled off of Highway 64 onto the dirt space in front of the big tree.

"Well, here you are, son," the driver said as he opened the door for me.

"Thank you so much, sir," I returned as I stepped off the bus Saturday afternoon. "I really appreciate this."

"Oh, it ain't no problem," he yelled down to me. "Hope you enjoy yo'self. Tell yo' folks hello fu' me."

"I sure will, sir. Thanks again."

The bus disappeared into the heat wave. I glanced at my watch and murmured, "Two sixteen," as the blistering sun welcomed my deracinated spirit home. It was hotter than any day I could remember. The whirlwind of dust, which the bus left behind, consumed me in a ball of humidity, making breathing practically impossible. It was the kind of heat that pastes clothes to skin during the day and disallows a cool breeze at night. A nice, cool shower would have been divine, but it never helped much in Swamp Creek since, after a moment or two, the sweat returned, even in the shade.

I dropped both bags and, with my hands, shielded my eyes from the scorching sun. Everything looked the same. The Meetin' Tree stood broader, like a great elder watching over a flock of children. We called the tree the Meetin' Tree because that's where folks gathered to socialize and gossip. Every Friday night, people came and listened to John Lee tell lies or watched Miss Liza Mae strip naked as the liquor took effect. As children, my friends and I caught lightning bugs in the field next to the tree as the grown folks told their stories. Sometimes we'd listen, too, but always from a distance. Children didn't sit with elders back in those days.

Uncle James Earl's old abandoned house, on the south side of the highway, was more weathered than it once had been. It leaned now like an old man without a walking cane. Sideboards were sinking inward, causing the house to emit an aura of depression. Rust had completely consumed the tin roof in the last ten years, and in a few places the roof had blown away. The house resembled a person in mourning over the loss of a child. The crumbling porch, barely hanging wooden screen door, and broken windows all reminded me that I hadn't been home in a very long time. Even the famous fruit trees, which once framed Uncle James Earl's house, appeared frail and desolate. It wasn't always this way. One day, when I was about twelve, my cousin Darrell and I sneaked behind Uncle James Earl's old house and prepared to steal some of those juicy peaches. Darrell whispered, "If we get caught, we gonna get a whoopin'!"

"Who gon' catch us?" I murmured intensely.

"Hell, I don't know! You know what they say 'bout dis house." Darrell was starting to tremble.

"Man, be cool. We can get what we want and be outta here. Don't start trippin' now."

"I ain't the only one trippin'. You sound like you fixin' to start crying or something."

"No I ain't, nigga. I'm just tryin' to think while you acting like a li'l bitch!" I was scared as hell and Darrell knew it.

"What if the house really is haunted by Uncle James Earl's spirit?" Darrell asked more earnestly than I had ever heard him.

"You don't believe in all that shit, do you?"

He hesitated for a moment and then said, "I don't know. I might."

I didn't say anything more because talking about it was weakening my confidence. We were squatting in the high grass behind Uncle James Earl's house, and our knees were about to give way as we spent an eternity contemplating what we were so sure about an hour earlier.

"We gon' do it or we ain't?" I asked, trying to force the fear out of Darrell.

"Yeah, OK," he responded with a tone of great uncertainty.

"Well, let's go."

We jumped up and ran to the first peach tree we saw. Never had I tasted anything so delicious. We were about to load our sacks when someone hollered, "Git on 'way from dat tree, boys! You knows better!" We looked around excitably but didn't see anyone. "Did you hear me, boys?" the voice said again. This time, when we looked around, we saw an old man walking toward us. He had a cane and wore a badly tattered straw hat. One strap of his overalls was unbuckled, and his hair was white as snow. "Run!" I yelled to Darrell, and he obeyed without complaint. We ran to Grandma's house and told her everything.

"Y'all ain't seen nobody," she chuckled.

"Yes, ma'am, we did," we protested. "We saw Uncle James Earl!"

"You boys ain't seen no James Earl! He been dead almost five years."

"I know, Grandma," I was screaming, "but I swear it was him!"

"Well, even if you did see him, you ain't got to holla 'bout it. He can't do too much harm to nobody. Dead folks ain't neva been no bother. It's the livin' you betta worry 'bout." And that's all Grandma said about the matter. Darrell and I never spoke again about seeing Uncle James Earl.

I shook my head and laughed as I remembered how crazy Darrell and I used to be. We would get whoopin's every day for something one of us talked the other into doing. Those were precious days.

I turned northward and noticed the pond in Old Man Blue's field glistening like it did when I was a boy. We fished in that pond every chance we got. Grandma would get out her almanac and tell us whether the day was a good fishing day or not, and if it was, we would get our cane poles, dig up some worms, and pray for luck. Sometimes we caught catfish or bream or perch, but most times we simply watched the water.

"You ever seen a girl's thang?" Darrell asked one day while we were fishing.

"Yep," I said proudly without facing him.

"You a lie, boy!" Darrell screamed excitedly.

"No I ain't. I done seen a girl's thang before. For real."

"What does it look like?"

"It's kinda hard to describe."

"Try anyway!"

"OK, OK. Damn." I wanted to sound as grown and unmoved as possible. "I guess it sorta resembles a little hairy bootee. It's right down in between a girl's legs and it's got a split in it. It's got hair all around it, and when she gets ready to have sex, it gets all moist and stuff."

"How you know?" Darrell asked with great inquisitiveness.

"Don't worry 'bout how I know, nigga. Dat's my business!"

Darrell resumed watching his cork in the water as he nodded his head in the "Oh, I see" fashion. Actually, except for watching Grandma wash herself in the kitchen Saturday nights, I was completely naive about a woman's genitalia. Yet what I had seen was enough to make Darrell believe I knew more about girls than he did, and of course that was the point.

My memories made me feel as though home were an ancient place. I arrived back in Swamp Creek ten years after I thought I had seen it for the last time. The day after high school graduation, I left

Arkansas, promising never to return. People bred hatred in me as a child concerning everything about Swamp Creek. Daddy worked me to death and said, "Dat's life round here, boy." So I had to leave. Hay fields, pea patches, cotton picking—I had had enough. I didn't ever acquire a nostalgic love for the place. What I did enjoy, though, was how people learned to sing their troubles away. Mother Berthine, Miss Iza Lou, and Old Man Blue could line a hymn on Sunday morning and even have sinners calling on the name of the Lord. They would moan and holler as they worked out the angst in their souls and then come the following Sunday and perform the ritual all over again. Miss Iza would cry when she sang, pleading for the Lord "not to move the mountain but to give her the strength to climb." I felt sorry for her because the relief she wanted never seemed to arrive. Yet for some reason she persisted in seeking. I anticipated seeing these old soldiers on Sunday if they were still living.

Ten years and there I was again. I had received a Ph.D. in black studies a month earlier and felt compelled to return to the place of my origin. Exactly why I didn't know, but for some reason I felt the need to go home. My heart, or my head, had begun to twist, to beg for familial clarity, in the last several years, and maybe, I hoped, Swamp Creek could help. Or maybe I dreamed of returning and finding a picturesque family into which I could safely place myself. Whatever the reason, I had a feeling as I stood in front of the old tree that home was going to be anything but sweet.

I walked over and sat underneath the Meetin' Tree. Even there, the air was muggy, but a little shade provided minimal comfort. Grateful to be released from the sun's torturous grip, I threw my head back and noticed that the tree's billions of leaves together took the shape of a beautiful dancer with arms stretched wide and legs perfectly straight beneath her limbs. I remembered years ago how the leaves moved in choreography at the wind's command. Darrell and I stood underneath the tree when it rained and watched the water fall all around us. We were fascinated that fragile leaves could totally block such heavy downpours. "The tree likes us," Darrell proclaimed. "It's kinda like a big umbrella." We would play chase or tag beneath the tree, grateful we could do so and stay perfectly dry in the midst of a storm.

However, the Meetin' Tree didn't do me much good the Saturday I arrived, for even in the shade, I was still dripping with sweat. The long bus ride from New York to Swamp Creek had only added to my frustration, and the growling of my stomach kept me reminded that, on top of heat exhaustion, I was starving. I heard a car race by, and when I turned my head to observe, the glare from the sun made me squint my eyes until they hurt. "Good God!" I said aloud, fishing through my bag for a notebook with which to fan myself. It did no good. Cool air had completely abandoned Swamp Creek. I was sure the sun was laughing at me for having hoped, somehow, that summer in Arkansas wouldn't be blazing hot.

I sat a long time on the old wooden church pew beneath the tree because I needed to assess what my return to Swamp Creek might mean. My sudden reappearance would surely cause some kind of disturbance, although such was not my intention. I had hoped a ten-year hiatus would provide my family and me with sufficient distance for old wounds to heal. Deep within I knew better. Time doesn't heal old scars; it just makes them bearable.

More than anything, I dreaded the encounter with my father. We had never been close—a vulnerability Southern black men rejected—but I had a feeling my unexcused absence might ignite in him unimaginable rage. Fear was what I felt whenever he was around, and somehow he exacerbated my inadequacies without ever saying a word. "I'm a grown man," I reminded myself aloud, but Daddy certainly wouldn't agree. His children would be children forever, at least in his eyes, and his job to feed and clothe us was the only obligation he had embraced. The day my oldest brother, Willie James, ran away from home, Daddy was clearly unmoved. Momma told him, "Somebody need to go find dat boy, Cleatis." Daddy continued eating casually and returned, "Then you go." I was stunned. The third night, Willie James returned battered and worn. "We got to plow dat field tomorrow, boy," Daddy announced as though Willie James never left, "so you betta take yo' ass to bed 'steada sittin' up watchin' dat damn TV."

Daddy's work came before anything else. Always. He believed, at the expense of everything, a man ought to work by the sweat of his brow, and Daddy upheld this conviction. He was obsessed with physical labor, afraid that one moment of rest would automatically prove him lazy, and Daddy would never allow anyone the opportunity to call him lazy. This was a principle he lived by and one he made all the rest of us live by, too.

"That boy has got to go to school," Momma said one evening at the dinner table.

"He ain't got to do nothin' but what I tell him," Daddy responded, clearly talking to both Momma and me. "First thang he got to learn is how to work. All dat readin' ain't gon' put no food in his mouth. How a man s'pose' to make a livin', sittin' round on his ass wit' a book in his hands?"

"We ain't living in dem old times no mo', Cleatis," Momma said sternly. "He can't go to school off and on like you makin' him do. He miss too much lesson and be behind and can't catch up. He goin' to school. You may as well get that through yo' thick skull!"

Momma continued eating, confident she had won the battle. Daddy chewed slowly as though planning his retaliation. No one asked me anything.

In public, Momma acted as though my love for reading brought her great joy. Her hope, she proclaimed, was that one day "one of my children make somethin' out of theyselves." I would read anything I could get my hands on. Newspapers, cereal boxes, TV guides, obituaries, and almanacs composed my makeshift library. Momma contradicted herself, though, because she never bought books for me. She wanted a smart child in order to elicit praise in the community. She really didn't enjoy my intelligence, I presumed, for she reminded me constantly of my unwelcomed analysis. "You think you know so damn much," she sneered any time I offered my opinion. Grandma told me not to worry about her. "You jes keep on keepin' on, baby," she said. Usually, the only time I got books was when Grandma brought them home from the white lady's house in which she worked.

Grandma surprised me on my fourteenth birthday. She called me over to her house and said lovingly, "Here, boy," and handed me a battered copy of *The Complete Poems of Paul Laurence Dunbar*. "Grandma! Oh my God! A book by Dunhar! How did you know? I've always liked Dunbar! Thank you!" I danced around her small living room with a treasure I had never dreamed of possessing. In school, we had read only one Dunbar poem, "We Wear the Mask," but it was enough to convince me of his exceptional literary talent. Grandma smiled as I hugged her, and said, "I wanted you to have yo' own copy so I asked Miss Ruth if I could have this book for my grand-baby. She said OK. I saw how you was lovin' dat other poetry book I brought home, so I thought I'd find a way to git chu one by a black man. Don't let dat book git you in trouble wit' yo' daddy." I knew what she meant. "No, ma'am, I won't," I said and ran out to the barn to read. I was supposed to be feeding the cows but decided I could read awhile before they starved to death. I nestled between two bales of hay and arbitrarily opened the book to a poem called "The Lesson":

> My cot was down by a cypress grove,
> And I sat by my window the whole night long,
> And heard well up from the deep dark wood
> A mocking-bird's passionate song.

> And I thought of myself so sad and lone,
> And my life's cold winter that knew no spring;
> Of my mind so weary and sick and wild,
> Of my heart too sad to sing.

But e'en as I listened the mock-bird's song,
A thought stole into my saddened heart,
And I said, "I can cheer some other soul
By a carol's simple art."

For oft from the darkness of hearts and lives
Come songs that brim with joy and light,
As out of the gloom of the cypress grove
The mocking-bird sings at night.

So I sang a lay for a brother's ear
In a strain to soothe his bleeding heart
And he smiled at the sound of my voice and lyre,
Though mine was a feeble art.

But at his smile I smiled in return,
And into my soul there came a ray:
In trying to soothe another's woes
Mine own had passed away.

"My God!" I cried. Dunbar's words had brought healing to my young heart and convinced me that a black man could have feelings and express them without shame. I jumped up and ran all the way to Darrell's house and declared, "Man, I got to tell you something! You ain't never heard nothin' like this!"

He cast me a suspicious eye. "T.L., what do you want?"

"I want to read you somethin' incredible, man. It's gon' change your life forever!"

"Change my life forever? Is you crazy?"

"Naw, I ain't crazy. Just listen for a minute." My excited anxiety made it difficult to hold the book steady. I threw my head back, Martin Luther King, Jr. style, and recited the poem with all the drama I could muster. My eyes bulged and narrowed at the right points, and the inflection of my voice made Darrell laugh several times.

"'But at his smile, I smiled in return,'" I read, and then grinned broad enough to show all my teeth at once. "'And into my soul'"—I tapped my chest—"'there came a ray.'" With eyes closed and face grimaced in preparation for the imminent theatrical moment, I clutched the book to my bosom and whispered the final couplet slowly and intensely: "'In trying to soothe another's woes, Mine own had passed away.'" A tear formed in my right eye but stood there stubbornly. I wanted it to fall to convince Darrell of the power of poetry, but it remained a watery glaze, too stubborn to obey.

"Is that it?" Darrell frowned.

"Man, you must be a fool," I said, disappointed.

"The poem was OK, but it wasn't great."

I turned and walked back to the barn, depressed that my joy had not been contagious. "He just don't get it," I resolved. I had almost gotten over my frustration when the barn door opened and Daddy's angry eyes pierced mine. My usual quick wits failed me, so I fidgeted and said, "I'm 'bout to feed the cows."

"Give me dat book," he demanded. I obeyed, fearful he was about to destroy it.

"Who de hell is Paul Dunbar?" he inquired with a tone of frustration.

"He's a black man who lived a long time ago who wrote poems and stuff," I answered, hoping my response would encourage interest.

"Well, de next time you run off and leave dese cows unfed you gon' need Dunbar to come rub yo' sore ass." Daddy tossed the book onto a nearby bale of hay and went out.

Relieved, I fed the cows quickly and returned to the barn, reading half the book before I went to bed that night. Most of the poems moved me to tears. I didn't understand how Dunbar did it, yet I knew then I wanted to be a writer when I grew up. The power of his words captured and healed my heart, and that's what I wanted to do for others. To know that I could construct a poem in Arkansas and it soothe the soul of someone in California or Budapest was absolutely intriguing. I knew I'd have to leave Swamp Creek to do it, though, because my hometown offered very little room for a man whose occupation was the cleansing and nurturing of human souls.

However, my escape plan must have backfired, for there I was again, sitting under the Meetin' Tree sweating, unable to explain to myself exactly why I was there at all. I had risen to start walking home when I heard an engine coming down the road and glanced to see who it was. I didn't know what to say to anyone, but not to say anything was completely unacceptable. Whoever it was would definitely speak. Swamp Creek folks have always had that principle.

The little pickup truck pulled off the highway onto the bare dirt spot in front of the tree, and out stepped Old Man Blue. "Hey dere, young fella!" he said, obviously not recognizing me, beneath the brim of my hat. "You from round dese hyeah parts?"

"Yes sir, Mr. Blue," I said, smiling. He was shocked I knew his name, and the frown in his eighty-year-old wrinkled forehead exposed his desire to know who I was.

"Seem lak to me," he said, shifting from one bad knee to the other, "you looks rat familiar." He took a handkerchief out of his overalls to wipe the sweat from his shiny jet-black face. "I jes' can't place you." He hobbled a little closer to where I was standing and looked down from his six-five frame directly into my eyes. His hair, which used to include a few black strands here and there, now stood short, stubby, and completely gray. Even the hair in his eyebrows was gray, as was the hair on his right knuckles that held the homemade walking cane.

Suddenly Old Man Blue's eyes bulged and he gaped at me. "Lawd have murcy," he murmured. "T.L., is dat you?" His voice trembled.

"Yes, sir. It's me, in the flesh. It's been a while, huh?" I reached to shake his hand, but Old Man Blue grabbed me and hugged me violently.

"Lawd have murcy Jesus!" he kept repeating. He had caught me off guard, really, because menfolk in Swamp Creek didn't hug each other, at least not while I lived there.

"Boy, folks thought you might be dead somewhere. Ain't nobody hea'd from you since befo' Momma died. You jes' disappeared, seemed lak to me, and all we knowed to do was pray."

He slapped my shoulder and grinned, apparently unashamed of the two lonely teeth in his mouth.

"Where you been all dis time, boy?" Old Man Blue asked, both for information and to reprimand.

"I went away to college and then decided to get my doctoral degree. I've been doing a lot of studying and writing, so I haven't had much time to . . ." I knew this excuse was lame even before I offered it.

"Folk where you went to school ain't got no telephone or post office?" He hesitated and wiped his brow again, frowning from the glare of the sun. He had trapped me and he knew it.

"It's a long story, Mr. Blue. Hopefully I'll get a chance to come by and sit and talk before I go back. I ain't been home yet, so I guess I'd better be gettin' on that way. I just stepped off the Greyhound bus a few minutes ago."

"Lawd, boy, yo' momma gon' have a tizzy when she sees you! I 'speck yo' daddy might shout, too, don't chu thank?"

"Yes, sir," I said, wondering why both of us were lying.

"Well, hop on in and I'll take you home." Old Man Blue began to drag his bad leg back to the driver's side of his truck.

"Oh, no sir. Thank you, though. I'm just sitting here enjoying the breeze and catching my breath. I'ma walk so I can take my time and look around."

Old Man Blue chuckled, a sign that he knew something was wrong, especially since there was absolutely no breeze to be found anywhere in Swamp Creek that day. "Well, help yo'self," he said as he struggled to climb back into the little beat-up Toyota. "I'ma git on down de road heayh. I'll see you in de moanin' at church, won't I?"

"Oh, yes sir," I said emphatically. And he would see me. You don't sleep in my momma's house and not go to Sunday school on Sunday morning.

He began to drive away slowly. "If you run into my folks, before I do," I yelled from the shade, "don't say anything about seeing me, OK? I want to surprise them."

"Oh, I ain't gon' say a wurd! But I'm sho' is gon' thank de Lawd that you's in the land of the livin'!" He raised his extra-long arthritic left arm and waved. "I'll see ya."

"Good-bye, Mr. Blue," I said too softly for him to have heard. He was always such a nice man, he and his wife, Ms. Polly. Willie James and I used to go to their house and eat fried pies every chance we got. We almost got a whoopin' one Saturday morning because Ms. Polly begged us to "come on in hyeah and git you some o' dese old pies, boys. Yo' daddy ain't gon' mind," she said convincingly. Still, we knew better, but we went in and ate the pies anyway. After a moment, we heard Daddy calling us.

"We gon' get it now," I told Willie James.

"No you ain't," Ms. Polly intervened. "Cleatis better not touch you. I gave y'all dem pies 'cause I wanted to, and he better not say nothin' 'bout it. Shit, he used to eat 'em all de time hisself!" I don't think Ms. Polly realized she had said a bad word. Willie James and I laughed, hopeful that Ms. Polly's clout as an elder would cover us.

"Ain't I told y'all 'bout eatin' at other folks' houses?" Daddy said when we exited Ms. Polly's front porch.

"Ah, you hush, Cleatis Tyson!" Ms. Polly scolded. "You can't say nothin'. You done ate enough of dem ole pies to fill a barn! Now let dem boys alone!" She winked at us as she turned to reenter her house. We chuckled from the joy of watching Daddy get put in his place for once. I had never seen him submissive. Even the hardest men bow down when an elder speaks. The smart thing, I realized, was to be on the side of the elders—always. So I started speaking to all the old men and women at church, and they began to adore me. "That T.L. is somethin' else!" Mother Berthine used to tell Momma proudly. "He gon' be great one day. You mark my word!" I loved hearing Mother Berthine prophesy about me.

Momma didn't. She would give a patronizingly fake smile and say, "Yes, ma'am," but her tone did not confirm the sentiment. I don't know why. As I got older, I began to think she didn't like me, but I could never think of a reason why. I had decided, in fact, to ask Momma one day why she hated me, and, from the looks of things, that day had finally arrived.

It was ninety-five degrees in the shade with no relief in sight; therefore I saw no reason to prolong the imminent confrontation. I took a deep breath, grabbed my bags, and began the long, slow walk home.

2

I had forgotten the walking distance between the Meetin' Tree and our house, but the heat reminded me. Sweat drenched my face and back, and my hands were too moist to hold my bags for more than four or five steps. I had to stop, dry my palms, and continue the journey, which seemed much longer than I remembered. "Good God!" I proclaimed aloud, wiping my brow in disbelief of the heat. The sun was beaming down on me hard, like a parent standing in authority over a recalcitrant child. Even when I passed beneath the few trees along the road, the shade proved irrelevant. I concluded this was what hell must be like, or at least this was my preparation for the hell I was about to encounter.

In some ways, I was most anxious about seeing Sister. She was only nine when I left home, a youngster who certainly wouldn't have understood why her favorite brother hadn't stayed in touch. She was my baby girl, I used to say. Maybe she would understand, for we always shared a special connection. Any time one of us cried, the other cried. When we laughed, it was always about something both of us thought was funny. She and Grandma were the center of those rare moments of happiness I knew as a child. Sister and I used to sneak and sleep with each other, joking and laughing all night long. I knew I'd get a whipping in the morning if Momma found out. She said it wasn't right for girls and boys to sleep together, yet when I asked why, she scolded me for questioning her and threatened to whip me if I didn't obey. I didn't care. Hell, whippings came my way almost every day. However, the boy-girl argument didn't hold, because any time we had company, Momma would tell Sister to get in bed with Willie James and let the company use her room. Sister didn't like sleeping with Willie James, though, because he snored monstrously. Yet if she ended up in my bed, we would be in trouble by morning. Usually we took our chances.

"Scoot over, girl," I whispered late one rainy night. Thunder caused the old house to shake freely.

"I'm scared, T.L.," Sister said and grabbed my arm, leaving fingernail marks. "Is God mad again? Dat's what Grandma say when it thunders like dis."

"Naw, God ain't mad," I consoled her. "Thunder is the result of electrical properties—" And as I offered a scientific explanation of thunder, a fierce clap sounded, causing both of us to jump into each other's trembling arms.

"God's really mad at somebody, T.L.!"

"Maybe He is," I said, rubbing Sister's head gently. My explanation seemed insufficient and ineffectual, so I dropped the whole thing. "Who could God be mad at?"

"Mean people," Sister murmured confidently.

"Mean people are everywhere. It would thunder all the time if God was mad at mean people."

"No, sometime people are real mean. And maybe that's when God make it thunder real hard." Sister looked squarely in my eyes to see if I agreed. Our faces were close enough to have kissed simply by puckering our lips.

"I don't know, girl," I said. I brought her head deep into my bosom and rocked her back to sleep. I must have fallen asleep, too, for in the morning Daddy's voice woke us abruptly.

"Ain't I don tole you two 'bout sleepin' togetha!" he screamed vehemently.

I mumbled a weak, "Yes, sir."

"So y'all gon' do what chu want to! You ain't gon' mind me!" Daddy revealed a belt he had concealed behind his back.

"We gon' mind, Daddy! We promise! We gon' mind!"

The declarations fell on deaf ears. "I done tole you, boy, 'bout thankin' you grown and ain't gon' do what I say. You gon' mind me or either git kilt!" Daddy stood over me, striking my body like one chopping wood for a fire.

"Don't hit T.L., Daddy! Don't!" Sister pleaded on my behalf, but there was nothing she could do.

Daddy whipped me and left welts all over my body. Blood oozed from some of the wounds, but that didn't deter him. Indeed, the blood fueled his anger, for he struck me harder as it flowed, to assure I never slept with Sister again. I did, though. My time with her was about the only fun I had in childhood, and even Daddy couldn't take it away.

Sister and I used to run in the woods behind the house and mock old Reverend Samuels's whoops and laugh at him for hours, bless his heart. He said he was called to preach at fifteen, yet Daddy said he should have let the phone ring, "'cause Samuels is a no-preachin' wonder!" They didn't say this to him, however, because he was an old man who had to be respected. Folk didn't disrespect elders in Swamp Creek.

Sister and I had Reverend Samuels down pat! I would jump up on a log, creating a raised pulpit structure, and say, "Good moanin', bruthas and sistas! We'se gathered here dis chere beautiful day to heayh a wurd from de Good Lawd. He's done brought us from a mighty long way."

"Amen, amen," Sister would say, cracking up with laughter.

"See, if you thanks about how good Gawd is, you ain't gon' be able to sit there lak you's doin' now. 'Cause, see, the Lawd didn't have to wake you dis moanin', but he did. Yes, He did! Oh yes, he did!" I would whoop, and jerk my head back like Reverend Samuels. While Sister rolled on the ground, hysterical.

"You ain't got no sense, boy!" she would scream repeatedly. After she got herself together, she would begin to mock Miss Josephine's puppy shout. "Yes! Yes! Yes! Yes! Yes!" Sister would shout in her highest soprano, saying the words fast as she could. She would then dance like Miss Josephine and shout simultaneously. You talkin' 'bout funny! That child had Miss Josephine down! If Momma had seen us, oh Lawd, what a beatin'.

The prospect of seeing Sister again made me smile. In fact, the heat cooled a bit the more I thought of her. She had been a cute child with profoundly kinky hair. Momma washed it in the kitchen sink, with Sister laid out on the countertop like a dead corpse. She would complain the entire time about Sister's "damn woolly hair" as she scrubbed it like a hardwood floor. Once clean, the hair was wrapped with a towel until it dried partially. When the towel was removed, Sister's hair sprung out into a massive black bush. Sister would walk around the house shaking her 'fro like Tina Turner. She would laugh and pose for me, her photographer, and I followed her excitedly every step of the way. "Lean your head a little more to the right," I would say, trying to sound professional. I'd drop to my knees with the imaginary camera in my hands. "Sex! I need sex!" I'd whisper to Sister, and she would fling her arms wide and throw her head back, Diana Ross style. Momma would get mad and make us cut it out.

I heard a tractor engine coming down the road. I started to hide because I wasn't ready to deal with Daddy yet. "Hell, whatever," I said instead, and braced myself. Around the bend came my brother, Willie James, bobbing up and down on the old John Deere tractor with the bush hog attached. As he got closer, he gazed at me real funny, like he suddenly saw the dead. Then he nodded his head slowly and chuckled sarcastically, making sure I heard him. Without saying a word, he turned off the tractor and stared at me with confusion in his eyes. I wasn't sure what to say, so I simply stared in return.

The sun's brightness blinded me and made me shield my eyes with my hands to break the glare as I looked up into my brother's face.

"Hey, boy," I said wimpishly.

Willie James didn't respond. He brought to mind an old man who had lived a life of regrets. He was five years my senior, but I was sure he could pass for my daddy. His face had patches of hair where a beard started to grow, and he was thinner than I remembered. In fact, he was at least fifty pounds lighter. Only the baseball cap gave him any appearance of youth. He kept examining me, trying to discern the image the puzzle would be if he had all the pieces.

"Hey, kiddo," I said again desperately. I was starting to feel like shit.

"Where you been all this time?" Willie James said, sitting on the tractor.

"I went to college. Remember?"

"Oh yeah," he patronized. "You left here right after you finished high school. I didn't know college took people ten years to finish."

"It's a long story, man. I'm sorry. I had to get away. I couldn't stay here, Willie James."

"OK, fine, but why didn't you call or at least write? You always liked to write."

"Let's not start this. It's too hot out here to argue."

"We ain't startin' nothin'. You started this ten years ago."

"OK! I'm sorry. I didn't know what else to do. I needed a break from Daddy's tyranny and—"

"Tyranny? Why can't you talk plain?"

I breathed heavily to control my frustration. "I had had enough of Daddy's beatings and working me to death in the fields."

"So that's why you left? Daddy?"

"Well, no, not completely. I'd rather not talk about it right now, Willie James. I'm tired, soaking wet, and starving. Are you gonna come down from the tractor and hug your little brother or what?"

Willie James descended the antique and came over to where I was standing.

"You looks good, little brother. Life must treat colored folks pretty good wherever you stayin'."

We shook hands, but his demeanor clearly rejected the possibility of a hug.

"New York. I've been in New York City. Well, I first went to Atlanta and graduated from Clark. Then I went to graduate school in New York."

"Well, good for you. Did you finish? Graduate school, I mean?"

"Yeah, I did. I graduated last month with my Ph.D."

"Whaaat? That's incredible. A doctor in the family," Willie James said with a tone of causticity. "Dr. Tommy Lee Tyson. I 'speck dat's what folks call you?"

"Only my students. My friends still call me T.L."

Willie James shook his head up and down and wiped the sweat from his forehead with his sleeve. "A lot done changed around this place, little brother. A whole lot."

"Really? I bet things are pretty much the same."

"Well, they ain't."

"Talk to me. What's happening?"

"Momma'll tell you everything. I gotta get on over to Miss Pearlie Mae's place. Her chillen comin' home soon and she wants the field behind her house cleared befo' dey gets here. You know how she is."

"Does she still give you a dollar or two for a full day's work?"

Willie James and I chuckled. Miss Pearlie Mae was good for pleading with us to come do some work and, in the end, giving us two whole dollars. We said we hated her, but really we hated her miserly nature. Yet Daddy kept sending us back, teaching us, I suppose, how a community takes care of its elders.

"I'll see you later?" I asked.

"You will if you don't run off befo' I git back," Willie James offered. I suppose I deserved the comment. He climbed back onto the tractor and paused. "It's been ten years since I last seed you, T.L. You was wrong fu' dat. I b'lieve you had good reason and all, but runnin' away wasn't the way to deal with it. I know you thought nobody round here cared about you 'cept Sister, and you mighta been right. Yet why didn't you at least stay in touch with *her*? When you left, she talked about you night and day. She really loved you, man, and you ran off and left her. Why, T.L.?"

Unable to find the right words, I said, "Man, look. My sorrows were bigger than me. I was about to die. If I hadn't left, I might have killed myself—or Daddy."

Willie James didn't know what to do with such talk. "I'm sure she'll be glad to hear from you now. I wish you had stayed in touch with her though."

"I did," I blurted without thinking.

"What?" Willie James said angrily.

The letter was supposed to be a secret, but it wasn't any longer. "I wrote Sister a long letter about three years ago. I told her where I was and why I had to leave. She already knew, but I felt the need to tell her anyway. I knew she was checking the mailbox every day in hopes of hearing from me. I had been contemplating writing her, but I didn't want Momma or Daddy to know where I was. One day, I got up the nerve and did it, and in the letter I made her promise to destroy it after she read it and not to tell any of you she had heard from me."

"Well, she sho' kept dat promise," Willie James said, very tight-lipped. "We all thought she stopped checking the mailbox 'cause she gave up on you. Come to find out, she got exactly what she wanted."

I had nothing else to say. Neither did Willie James. He put the tractor in gear and drove off with vengeance in his eyes.

The dust, which rose from the earth like a cloud, left a bad taste in my mouth. It was dry Arkansas red dust that covers everything in the summer, including people, giving them a red, Indian-like hue. "Is Sister home now?" I turned and yelled to Willie James, but he was too far gone to hear me or too angry to answer. I continued my march home.

I wondered if Willie James remembered the painting I had given him in sixth grade. The assignment was to paint a picture of a natural object and present it to a loved one. I knew better than to give a painting to Daddy or Momma because they hated sensitive, mushy stuff, and since Sister was too young to appreciate it, I decided to give it to Willie James. At first I doodled around, unsure of what to paint, but then out of a nearby window I saw the most beautiful butterfly suspended in midair. It was bright red and yellow with black around the edges of its wings. I stared at it in awe, for it seemed a bit exotic in Swamp Creek. Suddenly it disappeared as quickly as it had come, and I had to depend solely upon five seconds of memory to create my masterpiece. When it was complete, I felt proud and anxious to present it to Willie James.

"I have something for you, Willie James," I told him before we went to bed one night.

"What is it?" he asked nonchalantly.

"You can't laugh at me if you don't like it, OK? I think you'll like it, though."

Willie James smiled and opened his palm to receive the gift. I asked him to close his eyes and not to open them until I told him to.

"OK. You can look now."

Willie James gasped in amazement. "Oh my God, boy!" he said, taking the painting from my hands. "This is really good." His approval boosted my self-esteem more than I cared to admit. He hung the painting on the wall over his bed, where it still hangs today, I suppose. Late one night, Daddy came into the room and, noticing the picture, he asked Willie James, "What's dat bullshit?" and Willie James told him I had painted a picture for him. Daddy grunted something insulting and left. I promised myself that night not to stay in Swamp Creek a day longer than I had to.

I decided to take a shortcut through the Williams place and snagged my pants on the old, rusty barbed wire fence. "Shit!" I said. I knew better than trying to cross those old country fences with two bags in my hands. I suppose I thought I could do things now that used to be impossible. The fence put me in my place.

I was disgusted. Sweaty, hungry, frustrated, and mad my one good pair of khakis was ruined, I walked on in misery. I saw some old-looking cows and recalled the story about when Ms. Henrietta was kicked crazy. At least that's what everybody said.

"Dat cow kicked de shit outta Henrietta," I overheard Mr. Blue tell Daddy one Saturday night at the Meetin' Tree.

"Did?"

"Hell yeah. She was callin' hu'self milkin' dey old milk cow in a hurry. Dey say she was rushin' to git ova and see Billy Ray Henderson, so she was jerkin' dem titties like she was tryin' to pull 'em off!"

Daddy and the other men spilt beer all over themselves as they laughed. Their mingled voices sounded like a chorus of deep, long, guttural cries. Darrell and I snickered, too, but we remained quiet in order to hear the rest of the tale.

"Bad thang about it, Billy Ray wun't stuttin' Henrietta. He wonted Jophelia Mae Walker!"

"Is dat right?" Daddy said, adding fuel to the fire.

"Sho' he wonted her. He couldn't stand Henrietta. Every night de Good Lawd send, he was draggin' his stankin' ass ova to Jophelia's, lookin' like a ol' bug-eyed possum!"

The laughter sounded like thunder. Mr. Blue was the most incredible storyteller I had ever heard.

"Henrietta still wonted his no-good ass anyway. She thought she could steal him 'way from Jophelia Mae. So late dat evenin' she was milkin' de cow too fast and too hard and 'fo' she knowed anythang ole Bessie hauled off and kicked hu' right dead in hu' right jaw."

"Oh no. Dat's terrible!" others mumbled sincerely.

"She ain't neva been right since. Hu'mouth got a little betta, but it ain't neva been back right. Dat's how come she talk out de left side o' hu' mouth right now."

"I bet she don't drink much milk, neither!" somebody joked.

"Oh, dat's ugly!" Mr. Blue repeated, laughing unashamedly. Darrell and I slipped from the company of the men into the dark and never talked about Ms. Henrietta's twisted face. The story wasn't funny to us, maybe because she was lonely and depressed and we felt sorry for her. We offered to do work for her around her house, but she said, "No thank you, boys. I 'speck I betta do it myself," as though surrending to a divine punishment. We shrugged our shoulders and moved on. The other reason we never made fun of Ms. Henrietta was because Grandma told us, "Whoever you laugh at, you gon' get the same thang they got." We believed her, at least enough not to laugh at most folks.

I chuckled to myself about how strange folks were in Swamp Creek. Some of that craziness I must have inherited, I admitted. Little did I know I was about to find out how much.

3

The sight of the house unnerved me. It seemed smaller for some reason. Daddy or probably Willie James had painted it white, although it was once a dull blue. That's one of the reasons I hated it. The color simply represented the cloud of depression that hovered over our family. The moments of fun and laughter we shared inside that house were few and never allowed to last long. More than anything, we were a family of people who despised our own blackness and complained incessantly about never having enough. Not until I went to college did I understand how hair relaxers and skin lighteners reinforced a self-perception of ugliness. While I was growing up, everyone teased me about liking the brown-skinned little girls with hair that didn't require a perm. Of course everyone in my family had bad hair, so we searched elsewhere for models of beauty. When Sister was born, she had straight, silky hair and Momma rejoiced in having given birth to a "good-hair" child. Over the following year, though, her hair coiled until it was too tight to comb. Momma was pissed off. "We black and we can't get around it," Daddy told her.

Grandma's house, across the field from ours, looked the same. It had been my refuge. She was my best friend, and her house was the place I went whenever I felt lonely and dejected. Born in 1910, she died my senior year in high school at age seventy-three. On her deathbed she said, "Sonny"—that's what she called me—"de Lawd done blessed me to see you grow into a fine young man. You de one dis family been waitin' on. I ain't stuttin' dem ignut-ass folks you livin' wit'. I'm talkin 'bout you, boy. You got to fugive folks and go 'head on or dat hatred'll kill you. I know you tries hard and you dos yo' best. Keep dat up. But don't treat yo' folks lak dey treat you. De Good Lawd'll handle them. Don't never thank He won't. He got His ways and He got His time. You jes' keep yo' head in dem books and make somethin' outta yo'self. Now I ain't gon' live to see all this, and don't chu go to cryin', neither, but I'm still gon' be wit' cha. Ain't gon' never be a time when I ain't wit' cha. You remember dat, you hear?" I said, "Yes, ma'am," and burst into tears. Most eighteen-year-old boys would have been embarrassed for crying in front of their grand-mother, but I wasn't. I could express myself any way I wanted in front of Grandma. During my back porch performances of Shakespeare she applauded like I was the best actor she had ever seen. When I started memorizing excerpts from black writers, Grandma said, "Amen! You comin' on home!" She loved my Dunbar recitations best. His dialect poems made her laugh and cry simultaneously. After she gave me the first Dunbar book, she started getting me black books every Christmas and made me promise to read them and recite parts of them to her. I never failed. When she died, I knew one of my greatest connections to Swamp Creek, Arkansas, was gone forever.

Grandma was a tall, burly woman. She could whip any man's ass, folks said. I never saw that side of her. What I saw was a woman who loved to hum church hymns and rock in her rocking chair, piecing quilts. She had a slight hump in her back, which reduced her normal six-foot stature to a modest five-nine. She told me once that her dream had been to be a gourmet cook. People came from miles around to taste her desserts, and Grandma always feigned rejection of their compliments with, "Chile, please! I messed this batch up!"

Cookies, muffins, pies, cakes, and cobblers were her specialties. I was the sampler. "Taste all right?" she would ask, and I'd offer sarcastically, "I didn't get a good taste. After I eat some more, I'll know." Grandma would smile and say "Uh-huh," and I knew not to eat another bite.

Someone's car was parked in front of Grandma's house, but of course I didn't know whose. For a moment, I felt a sense of protective jealousy overcome me, and I contemplated walking in there and telling someone to leave my grandmother's house. Of course I had no right to do so, especially since I hadn't been home in ten years, but even the idea of someone else in her house troubled my spirit. Grandma and I had created a sacred space there, sharing secrets and crying tears together, and I simply didn't want anyone else in her house. The truth of my childishness confronted me, however, and I was forced to let it go. "Oh well, whatever," I mumbled in resignation.

Momma walked out of the front door. She didn't see me, though, because I was standing behind the large cypress, which stood alone in the field in front of the house. For an instant, I felt the urge to run and yell, "Momma, I'm home!" but I decided against it. "Just take your time, T.L.," I whispered to my unsettling nerves. I took a deep breath and, for the first time, wondered if, in fact, coming home was a good idea. Of course I couldn't turn back, so I walked the last few steps slowly, trying to prepare myself for the encounter. She had checked the mail and was about to reenter the house when I approached her and said, "Hi, Momma."

She turned quickly and froze, statuesque. Her eyes narrowed intensely and she examined me from head to toe with an expression at once painful and refreshing. She knew it was me, for she kept staring and nodding her head, the long-established sign of her unexplainable irritation. I immediately noticed she hadn't changed much: newly pressed hair, yellow flowered dress, size 9. I was actually startled, for she seemed to have stepped out of time for ten years in order to pick up where we left off if I ever came back home. She was a rather pretty woman, everyone in Swamp Creek agreed. Her baby smooth skin and hourglass shape had been maintained since high school, folks said, and no one—including her children—had ever seen her hair undone. I see why Daddy married her, I thought.

Finally she smiled seethingly and said, "So you came back."

"Yes, Momma. I came back."

"Why?"

"Why?" I asked in return, trying to buy time.

"Yes, why? You hadn't needed to befo'."

"True"—I was beginning to stammer—"but I needed to now. I didn't want to live the rest of my life estranged from my own family." I hated how I sounded, and I wished to God I hadn't said "estranged."

"You came to start confusion."

"No, Momma, I didn't come to start confusion. I came—"

"Did you take the bus?" Momma cut me off, not wanting me to explain myself clearly. Clarity left no room for conflict.

"Yes, ma'am. I stepped off the Greyhound bus about an hour ago."

"Dat's good. Come on in de house and set yo' bags down." She turned and led the way with an amazing lack of sincerity.

I followed Momma into the house. The tension was so thick it made me restless. I set my bags down in the living room, noticing Momma's rearrangements over the years. The piano, which she had hoped Sister would play, faced the wall opposite the front door. As far as I know, Sister never touched the thing. I was the one who played it, much to Momma's chagrin. I was a boy, and boys who played the piano were usually "funny," she said. I knew what she meant, but I didn't care. The piano was fun and therapeutic for me. I ended up being the musician for a number of local churches and made some nice spending change playing for weddings and funerals. The piano soothed my troubled soul, although Momma often tired of hearing me practice. Some days, she wouldn't let me play at all.

I noticed there was carpet on the living room floor. Folks in Swamp Creek didn't have carpeted floors when I was growing up. I also noticed it was a little—and I mean a little—cooler inside because of the fan Momma had running in the living room window. This didn't feel like the house I remembered. I felt like a guest who knew his days were numbered.

I went into the kitchen, where Momma was cleaning fish in the sink. The house was totally silent.

"What's been up, Momma?" I said, leaning on the countertop casually, hoping to initiate a healthy dialogue.

"Nothin'," she offered coldly.

"Everybody round here doin' all right?"

"Yeah," Momma said, expressionless.

"Why aren't you glad to see me, Momma?"

"I am glad to see you," Momma lied as she wrapped fish guts in newspaper and placed them into a nearby plastic garbage bag.

"You could have fooled me," I said sarcastically.

"Well, you fooled me ten years ago," Momma said, gaining the upper hand.

"Momma, you know why I left. Don't act like you don't."

"Yeah, I know why you left, but I don't know why you stayed gone so long."

"What would I have come back to? What was here for me?"

"Your sister," Momma said with a demeaning smile. I couldn't say anything to make her understand.

"Where is that girl anyway? I know she's grown," I said in an effort to lighten the mood.

"She's out back," Momma said, scaling more fish. "She's been waitin' on you a long time."

Momma was not going to let up, so I decided to go see Sister. When I exited the back door, I immediately saw the tombstone:

Cynthia Jane Tyson
1970–1987
"loving sister and daughter"

I fell to the ground in shock and horror, screaming at the top of my lungs, "Sister! Sister! No!" I rolled on the ground with snot pouring from my nose and tears streaming from my eyes. "Oh God! Sister, no! Please, Sister, no! Oh God, no! Not you, Sister! Please, Sister, not you!" I was slinging my arms, kicking my feet, and throwing my head from side to side, bellowing, "Sista! No! God, no!"

I heard Momma come from the house and say, "She's been waitin' on you. You were the last person she asked for. We had nothin' to tell her, although whatever she wants to know, you can tell her yourself. Now." She turned and reentered the house.

My heart was pounding like I had run a marathon. "Oh my God, oh my God!" I kept mumbling. "What the hell is this?" I felt like I was losing my mind. I embraced myself tightly and screamed even louder in agony, "Sister! This can't be true! You can't be dead! Sister! *Sister!*" Momma or Willie James should have prepared me for the truth. Their vengeance alone was the only explanation for their deception.

Sister was dead. My last joy, my childhood friend, my spiritual confidante, was gone. She had been my only reason, over the past ten years, for wanting to stay connected to these folks who obviously had no commitment to me. I could not hold her, touch her, hear her laughter, or see her make fun of Miss Josephine again. Sister was simply gone, and there was nothing I could do about it. I rolled around in despair, screaming, "No, Sister, not you! No, Sister! Please not you, Sister." I tore my shirt in anguish, and my pants were covered with red dirt stains. "Please come back to me, Sister. I need you. Oh, Sister, please," I cried. I began to lose my voice. Why had Momma done this to me?

Suddenly I jumped up furious and stormed back into the kitchen, screaming and crying profusely.

"What happened, Momma?" I yelled loudly. "Did y'all kill her because I loved her? Did you and Daddy decide to fuck up my entire life by taking the only thing about this godforsaken shit hole I enjoyed?"

"You betta watch yo' mouth in this house, boy," Momma whispered intensely.

I ignored her warning. "How did she die, Momma?" I screamed even louder, shaking and trembling and wiping snot from my nose.

Momma said nothing. She simply kept cleaning fish.

"Momma, if you don't say something to me, I swear to God . . ."

"Not in this house you don't!" She stabbed the knife into the cutting board violently. Her anger brought me back to reality.

"How did she die, Momma?" I asked slowly with my eyes closed.

"I don't know. She just died one day, boy."

"What?" I was yelling again. "What kind of nonsense is that? People don't fall over dead arbitrarily! Not at seventeen! What the hell happened, Momma?" My tone was totally disrespectful and I knew it.

"You 'bout to make me mad, boy," she said, smiling softly.

"Fine! That'll make two of us!" I retorted. I was really losing my cool.

"I 'speck you betta watch yo'self befo' you git in a heap o'trouble wit' dat damn mouth." The smile had evolved into a tight-lipped grimace.

"Momma!" I screamed. "You got to tell me more than simply she died. How did she die?"

"I don't know, boy. We found her dead in her bed one evenin'. The bed was full of blood." Momma was whispering. "Nobody knew what happened, so we just buried her."

"What?"

"You heard what I said. She died; we buried her. Dat's what you do wit' dead folks." Momma rolled up the last of the fish guts and put them in the same plastic bag with the others.

None of this made sense to me, but I decided to try a calmer approach. I certainly wasn't getting anywhere yelling.

"Momma, wait," I said more quietly, hoping my diplomacy might elicit more information. "I'm sorry for cursing. I really am. But to come home after ten years and find my sister dead is outrageous—"

"That's right, ten years," Momma interrupted. "That's yo' fault. If you hada kept in touch with us, you woulda knowed."

"Momma, I can't change the past! I'm asking for an explanation about Sister. Why is that so difficult?"

"Because your presence here is difficult."

I appreciated her honesty, although it hurt badly. "What do you mean?"

"When I saw you today, it took everything in me not to slap the shit out of you."

The feeling's mutual, I thought.

"You were Sister's hero, T.L. Her dying hope was to leave this place and go find her brother. She told us we ran you away. Said your leaving was our fault. 'Y'all were too mean to him,' she would say. You know Sister said what she thought. 'I woulda left, too, if Daddy beat me like that,' she told me one day. I told her to hush up her mouth 'cause she was talkin' business she didn't know nothin' 'bout. But, yeah, you were her man. And you didn't love her enough to send a card."

Momma didn't know about the letter, and telling her wouldn't have made any difference.

Hearing about Sister's love for me reignited my hysteria. "Momma, please! What the hell happened?"

"Why do you keep asking me the same question over and over again?" Momma began to get a little louder. "I told you everything."

"No, you didn't. I don't know how she died!"

"Well, hell, I don't, either!" Momma screamed, and walked out of the back door with the bag of fish guts.

I sat at the kitchen table with my head in my hands in utter disbelief. How could this be? Sister was dead and Momma had no explanation. My emotions changed from sadness to confusion. None of this made sense to me. Momma was acting like her daughter's death was regular, ordinary, simple. My level of trepidation had not moved Momma's peace one bit. I began to feel almost apologetic. This was insane, so I returned to the grave.

"Sister, Momma's not telling me the truth. I know you wouldn't leave me without seeing me first. You knew I would come back for you, didn't you?" I was crying as I gently rubbed the petals of the artificial roses, which framed the tombstone. "How did this happen? Did Momma or Daddy hurt you?" I laid my head on the ground next to the headstone. I thought that maybe if Sister felt my tears she would respond. "Sister, tell me who did this to you. I don't believe you died suddenly one day. You weren't sickly as a child. Please tell me, Sister, and I promise—" I didn't know what I promised. I was too disheveled, distraught, and disgusted to recognize any immediate recourse. A song came to mind I thought might soothe my lamenting heart, and I sang it loudly for Sister without shame:

> "I come to the garden alone,
> While the dew is still on the roses.
> And the voice I hear falling on my ear
> The Son of God discloses.
> And he walks with me and he talks with me,
> And he tells me I am his own.
> And the joy we share as we tarry there
> None other has ever known."

I was there at least an hour or two, telling Sister secrets about me she probably already knew. I told her about my experiences traveling the world and meeting all different types of people with tons of different ideas. I even mentioned the time I tried to kill myself because my past had overwhelmed me. She understood, I think. I felt better. I tried to explain it to her in detail, but I knew Sister and I never needed words to communicate.

"Git up off that ground, boy, and come git yo'self somethin' 'teat," Momma called from the kitchen window, ignoring both Sister's grave and my pain.

I rose and reentered the house from the back porch. The reality of it all struck me when I saw Momma again.

"Momma, why is Sister buried in the backyard?" I asked, not realizing how crazy this was until I spoke the words themselves.

Momma said nothing.

"Momma? Why is Sister not buried in the graveyard at the church?" I was beginning to worry severely. Everything about her death was extraordinary and strange.

"'Cause I wanted her near me," Momma said as though this explanation made perfect sense. "You had her in life; I have her in death." Momma was losing her mind. She was losing her goddamn mind.

"After Shelia died, I wanted a little girl more than anything. One whose hair I could comb and who I could dress in pretty little dresses and send off to Sunday school. I wanted a little girl who all the boys wanted and who all the other little girls envied. And I got a little girl, but she didn't want none of what I wanted for her. All she wanted was you. What could I do besides let her go? And once you left, I knew I'd never have my baby girl because her memory of you and her hope of your return was bigger than you had ever been. I couldn't compete. But once she died, I decided I was gonna have what I wanted."

"Momma, that's crazy!" I said, astonished and bewildered.

"Maybe it is," Momma wailed, "but when you ain't neva had nothin', you do what chu can to hold on to the little bit you got. Dat's why you left here. You was always searchin' for things to hold on to, somethin' that could be yours by yo'self. Wunnit no readin' and writin' jobs for no black boys round here, so you left."

I wanted desperately to correct her poor reasoning, but she was on a roll and I didn't stop her.

"I never got a chance to have nothin'. A woman can't do nothin' but mind her man and have his babies. Dat's what de ole folks believed and I believed it, too. When Scooter drowned, I thought I was gon' die from the pain in my heart, but I didn't. I learned how to live without givin' my heart away. He was my baby, and I couldn't figure out why God took him back. Then God took Shelia, too. I didn't have nobody but Willie James left. Momma told me it's all part of being a woman. I decided I'd better learn how to lose and still have peace of mind. Then you came along."

Momma started setting the table. I think she was crying, but I couldn't tell. I didn't know what to say.

"Sister was a pretty baby," Momma continued, placing forks and glasses next to the plates in perfect proximity. "She never did cry. All she did was smile. I used to tell folks she knew a secret she wouldn't tell nobody. A pretty baby girl seemed like a welcome gift to me. I started makin' her cute little dresses and I'd plait her hair real nice, but she never liked any of it. All she wanted to do was play wit' chu. She didn't care nothin' 'bout no lady things. No, no. She wanted to fish and swim naked in de pond and read all dem damn books. She didn't want nothin' to do wit' me. That's why I gave up. I quit trying to make her my little girl. She wanted you, so I let her have you."

"I didn't know Scooter drowned," I said. "I thought it was epilepsy."

"Lot of stuff you don't know. More stuff you don't know than stuff you do." Momma put the fish and salad on the table. She placed her hands on her hips, leaned back in exasperation, and proclaimed, "Ten years is enough time for a whole lotta stuff to happen. You jes' got to catch up wherever you can. I don't know what happened to Sister, and if I did—"

"You wouldn't tell me, would you?" I interrupted with a sharp edge.

Momma wasn't moved by my tone. "I don't know. If you didn't care about her in the last ten years, I ain't too sure she means much to you now."

"That's not fair, Momma."

"Fair? Ain't nothin' been fair in my life, boy. Shit. I done worked hard for damn near fifty years and still ain't got nothin' to show for it and you talkin' 'bout fair? I done buried three children, lost one," I guessed she was referring to me, "and been married to a man thirty-five years who loves what I do—not who I am. Don't I deserve somethin' fair? You ain't the only one who want a life of pleasure and joy. You ain't hopin' for somethin' nobody else in the whole world ever wanted. Don't fool yo'self. I been wishin' all my life for what you jes' thought about a few minutes ago. Don't show up after ten years and start talkin' to me 'bout what's fair and what ain't."

Momma walked away from the table toward the bathroom. She seemed satisfied she finally said what she had been hoarding for years. I had never heard her speak so matter-of-factly. She seemed more human to me than before. Yet I still didn't know what happened to Sister.

4

A grave in the backyard. Who had heard of such a thing? My visit home was becoming more than I ever imagined. I had spent every day of those ten years longing to hold Sister again, waiting to laugh at people with her again, and when I get home she's buried in the backyard? This was crazy to me. Momma walked around the house—and the yard—tranquil about Sister's death to the point of being numb. She hung clothes on the line out back, amid the tombstone, with a contentment at once disturbing and fascinating. I looked at her, at the house, at the peace of the woods, trying my best to figure out why I was the only one troubled. Of course there was no need to confront Momma again, for she had said what she was going to say. For the possibility of my return—she knew Sister's spirit would summon me—Momma had undoubtedly rehearsed exactly what she'd say to me. My questions, which she had not anticipated, she simply circumvented. She definitely wouldn't dignify me with a discussion.

I left Momma in the house eating fish. It was about seven o'clock and beginning to get dusky. I walked outside, trying like hell to find some meaning, some logic, to this madness. I noticed three or four of

Daddy's cows grazing in the field east of the house. They looked peaceful, unconcerned. I wondered if they had known Sister. I thought maybe she had fed them a time or two and had petted them tenderly in her sweet way. If she had, they would have remembered her soft touch and mourned her sudden disappearance. I wanted to ask them what happened, if they had seen or heard anything strange. They seemed to read my mind, for they began to survey me intensely, although having no words by which to express their thoughts. I walked closer to the fence that separated their world from ours. Leaning there, I hoped for some type of revelation, but I got nothing.

I walked around the edge of our land like a lost fawn trapped and seeking a way out. It was still hot, though a bit cooler than when I had arrived. The sky was transforming into a dark, ominous purple, suggesting rain. The wind was strong, and pollen lingered in the air. I saw the garden where Momma and Daddy had planted peas and okra and potatoes and collard greens. The cabbage heads were shaking excitedly from the wind. I stood there and stared at the big collard green leaves, which, bunched together, trembled intensely and resembled a church choir on Sunday morning rocking with the power of the Holy Ghost. Yet I could not hear them. I sensed the urgency of their message but received no communication. I felt chill bumps cover my skin. What was going on in Swamp Creek?

I walked onto Grandma's back porch and sat down. I didn't know who lived there, but at the moment I didn't care. It was beginning to rain. The rain would bring some relief from the heat although no relief for my heart. Tree limbs were swaying in the wind like old women in church, listening to a good sermon. Dust was flying in the air, covering everything in sight. I sat with my knees to my chest, feeling the cool breeze and praying for an answer. I knew Daddy would be coming down the road any minute and I would have to deal with him, but for the moment I was simply trying to regroup.

Grandma's back porch had been my refuge, other than the barn. It was nothing elaborate. Old mason jars, a rusty garden hoe, an old gas can that no one ever used, some battered work shoes from thirty years ago, and an outdated push mower. It was more like a junk house than a back porch. As a child, I would go there to sit and think or read or get away, and when I left, I felt prepared for battle once again. The hay barn was my other respite from the world, but I didn't want Daddy to catch me off guard, so I sat on the steps of Grandma's back porch instead, watching the rain and awaiting his arrival.

"I like rain," I told Grandma one day as we shelled purple hull peas.

"You do?" she responded nonchalantly.

"Yes, ma'am. It makes me think of Noah and the flood in the Bible when it starts raining. Think it'll ever rain like that again?"

"Naw, boy! De Lawd done promised us it wouldn't never rain like dat no mo'. De rainbow is de sign of de promise."

"What if God doesn't keep His promise?"

"Is you a fool?" Grandma said sternly. "God don't neva break no promise." She kept staring at me wild-eyed.

"Maybe God changed His mind. Ain't that possible?"

"No!" Grandma screamed, jumping up spilling the bowl of peas. "You must ain't got good sense, boy! De Lawd don't neva need to change His mind 'cause eva'thang He do is already perfect! He ain't got to rethink nothin'! He done planned out what's gon' happen in de world and dat's what's gon' happen! Ain't nothin' you can do 'bout it and He ain't gon' change His mind to fit you!"

I was on thin ice, but I pushed ahead anyway. "If God done planned out everything, what's the use in praying?"

"'Cause you don't know what God done planned out!"

"It doesn't matter! According to you, if God done planned it out, it can't ever be any other way, so what's the use in asking?"

"'Cause prayer changes things, boy!"

"Oh! God might change His mind after all if we beg Him hard enough?"

Grandma glared at me silently for a second, carefully planning her response, then suggested, "God already knowed what you was gon' pray for befo' you was eva born. He done already took yo' requests into account when he was planning de world."

"What if I pray for something different from what God thought I would?"

"It ain't possible, boy! You can't neva do nothin' God didn't already know about befo' it eva happened."

"That doesn't sound like free will to me, Grandma. 'Cause if it was truly free will, God got to wait to see what I'm gon' do and say."

"God ain't got to wait to see nothin' from you, fool! Who you thank you is?"

I let it go at that point. I wasn't going to win, and too much was at stake for Grandma to lose. She was trembling. I suppose I tugged at the very fabric of her beliefs, although I hadn't meant to. I was trying to resolve some of the conflicts I had after church service on Sunday mornings. Pastor would always say at least one thing that simply didn't make sense to me, especially his belief that "to understand de Lawd, you can't use yo' mind." What kind of nonsense is that? On the way home one Sunday, I asked Daddy how a man was supposed to understand God if he didn't use his mind and Daddy said, "You too damn smart fo' yo' own good." I didn't understand that, either. If indeed God was smarter than everybody in the whole world put together, how could my little intelligence be too much? I didn't ask this out loud. Daddy had made it clear he didn't want to hear any more of my intellectual bullshit, as he called it.

Momma never entertained my childhood wonderings. She simply shook her head and mumbled, "You idiot," and walked away. Therefore, the only person I knew to go to was Grandma. However, after seeing her extreme anger, I kept all my questions about God to myself.

The rain had stopped. I knew it wouldn't pour down long enough to run the heat away permanently, but I had hoped for more than a mere dust-settling shower. Arkansas summers were famous for gathering black clouds together and blowing 25 mph winds yet delivering ten-minute rains. Rethinking Momma's words, I realized her jealousy of me. She wanted a relationship with Sister like the one I had with her. Maybe if I had known, I would have encouraged Sister to pay Momma more attention. Maybe not.

The end of the rain disappointed me. Generally, storms gave me a hiding place and hours of quiet contemplation, and, the day I returned home, I needed both. Thunder and lightning disturbed me as a child because Grandma associated storm with the announcement of God's apocalyptic wrath. Yet, in later years, I grew to appreciate the beauty of a storm. The whistling of the wind, rain beating diligently upon the rooftop, clouds colliding nervously into one another, and the darkening of the sky together formed a tapestry of nature both exhilarating and soothing. In the midst of storms, I enjoyed watching the rain fall, imagining each droplet as a tear that fell from my own eye. That's why I cried when it rained. The earth's cleansing provoked my own and served as catalyst for the release of baggage and pain lurking in my soul. My friend George asked me, as an adult, why I liked rain so much. I tried to explain how it allowed me to purge my heavy heart and make room for a new day, but he said my explanation made no sense. George offered an argument about the depressing nature of rain and the cloud of gloom it left behind. Hence rainy days contributed nothing to the union of our brotherhood.

I met George Thornton in New York City, and he quickly became my best friend. Our relationship was strange from the inception because we shared an intimacy unusual for black men. We wore each other's clothes, wrote weekly letters—we lived in the same apartment building—and wept openly together without shame. We were definitely more than friends, although I never found the word or category to describe adequately the extent of our bond. We were committed to meeting each other's needs and making sure nothing happened to each other. For a while, we were roommates, but the level of our comfortability often resulted in our insensitivity toward and even disrespect of each other. So I got an apartment next door. It worked out really well. When I was broke, George fed me, and when he didn't have food, I fed him. We nurtured each other through our relationship blues and retreated into our secret hiding place whenever our girlfriends pissed us off. George offered to go to Arkansas with me, but I refused him. "T., man, you might need some support from a brother after yo' folks get through cussin' yo' ass out," George said jokingly. I knew then not to take him. He clearly didn't understand fully the seriousness of my return.

George was an actor and a good one, too. He did mostly off-Broadway shows, although occasionally he landed a small part in a Broadway hit. Acting was his natural-born gift, but acting was also his problem. He feared reality. He didn't know what to do with life outside of the theater. I was his closest friend, and even I didn't know anything about his family. He simply wouldn't talk about it. I asked him about his mother once and, through tearstained eyes, he told me never to ask him again.

He kept a diary under his bed. I know because, well, let's just say I know. I started to steal it and read it one day, but I decided against it. Any man who would reveal himself to a book before he would another human probably had some heavy shit to deal with, and if I read it, I would feel responsible for the truth of his life. Ain't no way I was about to assume that responsibility. Yet, even with his idiosyncrasies, George Thornton was my dearest friend. It's sad more brothers couldn't hang like George and me.

When I first got to New York in September of 1987, I bumped into George at La Guardia Airport.

"Excuse me, sir," I said shyly.

"Sir?" he cackled.

"Well . . . I mean . . . I don't know your name . . . so . . ."

"My name's George Thornton Junior," he stated abrasively, examining me from head to toe and laughing the entire time.

"What's funny, Mr. George Thornton Junior" I inquired curiously.

"You must be from down south somewhere, huh?"

"I am. Arkansas. How'd you know?"

"Because nobody in New York would ever call me 'sir.' They hardly say 'excuse me,' either."

"Oh," I returned, relieved that this stranger wasn't laughing at me.

"What are you doing in New York?" he went on.

"I'm going to graduate school."

"Is this your first time in the city?"

"Yeah. It's my first time up north actually."

"Good! Welcome to crime and poverty and one-thousand-dollar studios!"

"One-thousand-dollar what?"

"Studios. It's a glorified name for a small room with an even smaller bathroom and kitchen. Most of them are about as big as first-class areas on airplanes."

"For a thousand dollars a month?"

"This is New York, baby!"

"My God. I had no idea."

George sensed my apprehension and said, "You'll do fine. Country boys know how to survive. Most of my friends from the country aren't very materialistic, so New York won't kill y'all."

"I hope I like this place," I said to lighten the conversation.

"You will. You already have one friend. Come on. I'll show you around."

George took one of my bags and started walking with me as though we had been friends for years. He told me about the World Trade Center, the theater district, and the Schomberg Center for Research in Black Culture. He went on and on about how dynamic the clubs were in New York and how he was the quintessential party animal.

While we were waiting for a cab, I asked, "Are you sure you have time to show me around? I mean, I know you probably have a job to get to or things to do. Please don't rearrange your schedule for me."

"Why not? Aren't you worth someone rearranging his life?" George glared at me and smiled.

I didn't know what to say. "I've only known you a few minutes, and I don't want to consume your time."

"I do with my time what I like. And I like you."

"OK," I said slowly as George opened a taxi door for me.

"Don't worry. I'm not some crazy person out to rob you. I could use a friend in my life and I think you could, too."

The taxi sped off and into more traffic than I had ever seen. For whatever reason, I felt absolutely comfortable with George. He seemed independent, self-assured, hilarious, and completely open. We spent the whole day together. Toward nightfall, he asked, "Do you already have a place to stay?"

"Actually, I had planned to search today for a room or an apartment, but you consumed all my time." I smiled.

"Well, I guess you'll have to stay with me. Poor me." He hung his head, feigning sadness.

"Oh, shut up!" I said, poking him in the shoulder playfully.

"By the way, what's your name?"

"Oh my God! I'm sorry. I've known your name all day and I never told you mine. I'm Tommy Lee Tyson." I extended my hand to shake his.

"I don't need to shake your hand, Tommy Lee. I've been with you all day!" We both laughed at the realization.

"Call me T.L.," I said after the laughter subsided. "No one ever calls me by my full name."

"That's why I'll call you Tommy Lee. I want to call you something no one else calls you. Is that cool?"

"Yeah, if you like. It doesn't matter to me."

"I do like. Come on; we'll go home."

My first night at George's house turned into a six-month stay. He treated me like a king, cooking practically every night, paying for the two of us any time we went anywhere, and never making me feel indebted to him. I couldn't have asked for a better situation. The only problem was that I hadn't been raised to accept such charity, and George had been charitable longer than my dignity usually allowed. I moved at the beginning of the seventh month. George understood. We talked every day thereafter, telling each other everything about ourselves, even the most risky information. That's why I'd never let him go. We went places with each other I'd never been with anyone.

Yet George Thornton was not my main concern that evening in Swamp Creek. I was still trying to figure out what had happened to Sister. As I thought about it, I suddenly remembered Sister's picture was missing from the living room wall. Momma once had pictures of all of us plastered throughout the house, but I didn't recall seeing Sister's picture earlier that day when I walked inside. Or mine, for that matter. I didn't take note of their absence at the time, but they were definitely not on the wall.

Momma had every right to be a bit beside herself. Yet that was the funny thing—she wasn't beside herself. She was the same calm, unmoved woman I had known all my life. She had worn one hairstyle for thirty years and still cooked fish on Saturday. I could never figure her out. If she was depressed and unsettled, why didn't she leave Swamp Creek? She deserved happiness, too. Why didn't she go somewhere and find the source of her joy? I didn't understand. Why wouldn't she tell me what happened to Sister? And how did it make sense for Momma to bury the girl in the backyard in order to keep an eye on her? Where did Momma think Sister was going? "*Dead* means 'immobile,' Momma," I wanted to say.

I had an acute suspicion Daddy knew what happened. He would never have had Sister's grave in the backyard without his wanting it there. It definitely wasn't his idea, but he had to have agreed. However, it wasn't the grave that troubled me most. It was the logic of it all. Didn't folks who came by the house tell them this wasn't right? I mean, surely Mr. Blue or Deacon Payne had seen the tombstone and asked Daddy about it. They attended the funeral, I was sure, and didn't they wonder about the place of interment? The more I thought about it, the crazier it became. When Daddy or Willie James mowed the lawn, didn't Sister's grave leave them discomposed? How did they ever get past the agony of Sister's death with her body lying only a few feet away? Had folks gone absolutely insane in Swamp Creek?

I got up and began to walk back to the house. It was practically dark. I had thought Daddy would have been home by now, but, as luck would have it, he was late. I had wanted to meet him on the road in hopes of our encounter being eased by the chirping of birds or the slightest evening breeze, but now I had no choice but to encounter him within the confines of our small family room, and I had a feeling it wasn't going to be pleasant.

I reentered the house. Momma had finished cooking and, because of the rain, was sitting in the dark quietly. No lights, no sound. Folks in Swamp Creek unplug everything electrical in the house except the icebox when it begins to rain. I never really understood it. I guess I didn't need to, though, for my lack of understanding certainly didn't stop anybody from unplugging their appliances.

"Where you been?" Momma questioned me.

"Walking around," I said and took the nearest chair.

"What you find this time?" she asked sarcastically.

"Momma, why are you doing this to me? You knew Sister's death would devastate me, and you make a joke of it?" I felt empowered in the dark. Momma couldn't see me and I couldn't see her, but we certainly felt each other.

"I'm not makin' a joke. I was jes' askin' a querston. Yo' whole life you been lookin' for stuff, and I was jes' askin' if you had done found any of it."

"Momma, why won't you tell me about Sister? And please don't say that same shit—I mean stuff—again."

"I done told you all I know, boy. Now stop worr'in' me 'bout dat damn girl."

"Momma, she was your youngest child and you don't even know how she died?"

"No."

"I don't believe that for a moment."

"Well, you ain't got to."

Willie James walked into the dark house, presumably soaked from head to toe.

"You seen T.L., Momma?" he probed without searching the room.

"He sittin' right dere."

Willie James turned his face in my direction but said nothing.

"Why didn't you tell me about Sister?" I asked with more than an edge of ugliness.

He walked on into the kitchen and asked Momma what she had cooked.

"You know what she cooked. It's Saturday. Why are you ignoring me?"

Momma rose to turn the lights on and replug the TV. She was more relaxed with Willie James at home.

"Miss Pearlie Mae sho' is one' o'nry ole lady. Ain't nothin' neva right and she always complainin' 'bout how hard it is to git good help. She too cheap to pay anybody. Lawd, soon's I got dere, here she come talkin' 'bout—"

"Stop it, Willie James. *Stop it!* What the hell is wrong with you? I asked you about Sister!" I was standing, ready to fight if it came to that.

"I don't know nothin' 'bout Sister," Willie James mimicked. "Don't ask me again!"

"Your own sister dies and you tellin' me you don't know anything about it? Oh, come on, man! I ain't no fool."

"I done told you I don't know nothin'." Willie James began to walk toward the bathroom, but I wasn't giving up that easily.

"Willie James, what the hell is wrong with you?" I walked up on him, peering into his eyes deeply. "Don't you think I deserve to know?"

"I don't think you deserve shit," Willie James whined resentfully.

I couldn't take it any longer. I punched him in the stomach, and the war was on. We were scrapping in Momma's kitchen. Willie James put me in a headlock and slung me onto the kitchen floor. I raised my right foot and kicked his shoulder like I was trying to break down a door. Instead of hurting him, I only infuriated him. Willie James grabbed the broom and began to beat me like an old dirty, dusty rug. He was clearly overpowering me, but I grabbed the end of the broom and plunged it up against his throat. We continued fighting until I was simply exhausted. Willie James stood over me with that do-you-want-some-more-of-me expression and, since I didn't, I said very softly, "Sorry."

"You damn right," he said furiously, and proceeded to the bathroom.

I peeled myself from the kitchen floor and noticed Momma had not moved the entire time. She simply watched us in excitement to see which son would overcome the other.

"Momma, what's wrong with y'all?" I asked helplessly.

"We the same thang we always been," she insisted.

Having no response, I dragged myself to the back bedroom and fell across the bed in tears. I had never felt so nihilistic in my entire life. Traditionally, Momma and Willie James weren't allies, but I guess things do change over the years. She had the ability to consume people, and Willie James had fallen victim to her venom. Like the time Grandma got sick, it was Momma who decided she should stay with us. People praised Momma for being the committed daughter, the one who honored her mother enough to take care of the latter in her old age. Yet even back then, I knew Momma's actions were not centered in love for Grandma. Momma treated her like an old sofa she couldn't figure out how to get rid of. She told Grandma when she could move, eat, shit, and when to keep her mouth closed. However, in public, Momma acted like she was bearing the burden of her mother with love. People would ask, "Marion, how ya' momma doin'?" and Momma would fake exasperation and say, "Momma's doin' pretty good. I tries to make sho' she got ever'thing she needs." People would

then extend their hearts in sympathy, admiring Momma's commitment to an ailing mother. I wanted to tell everybody what was going
on for real, but Momma would have destroyed me had I exposed her
charade.

I rolled over on the bed and gazed at the wall. That's when I noticed the butterfly picture was gone. The nail on which it hung was
still in place, but the painting had been removed. Of course I knew
who had moved it, but I didn't know why. No need to ask that
question, though. "No one around here knows anything," I mumbled.

Momma called me to come eat, but I didn't want any fish. I
wanted her to tell me what happened to my baby sister. I lay there
and acted like I didn't hear her and decided to write George a letter.
Fumbling quietly until I found pen and paper in my bag, I wrote desperately:

Dear George,

*This is more than I bargained for. You wouldn't believe it if I told
you. People in Arkansas have gone absolutely crazy. I found out that my
sister died almost two years ago, but nobody knows how. That's right.
Momma and my brother say they don't know what happened, and I
haven't had a chance to ask Daddy yet. This is some strange shit, man.
Can you imagine? I mean, you go home anxious to see your sister and
find out she's dead? And the way I found out—well, I'll have to tell you
in person.*

*I'm an emotional wreck. I jumped on my brother a few minutes ago
and got my ass kicked. My anger got the best of me. This house, these
people, this place, is making me crazy. It's hard to believe I lived here
once. Harder to believe I got out. Why did I come back, George?*

*I wish I had let you come with me. I could use your strength.
Man, just being close to you would do me a world of good today. I
can't really explain it to you because I don't understand it myself. All
I know for sure is that I've got to see this through. I have too many*

questions, especially about my sister's sudden death. No need to write back because I'm not staying long. Just pray for me. I need you worse than you know.

Your friend,
Tommy Lee

5

I heard Daddy come through the door about fifteen minutes after I finished my letter to George. Daddy told Momma he got caught in the rain and took shelter in Chicken's shed house. Chicken was Daddy's best friend since childhood. He and Daddy were born three days apart, and because Chicken's momma's breast milk wasn't any good, she asked Grandma if she would feed her baby, too. Grandma agreed. Mr. Blue told me Daddy was on one of Grandma's titties and Chicken was on the other. People called him Chicken because, as a baby, he was little and thin and resembled a frail baby hen. Grandma said she knew he'd be all right after he suckled her breast for a couple of months. She had some good milk, she bragged. In other places, folks might have found this arrangement bizarre, but when folks in Swamp Creek said children belonged to everybody, they meant it.

I didn't hear Momma mention my name to Daddy, so I prepared for another intense collision. Emerging from the bedroom, wracked with nerves, I approached Daddy with his back toward me. I had no choice but to speak first.

"Hey, Daddy," I said, sounding like a toddler.

Daddy turned around, and, for the first time in my life, I saw emotion in his face. He actually appeared moved to see me.

"What chu doin' here, boy?" he asked after gathering his composure.

"I came to see how everybody's doin'." I didn't know what else to say.

"Well, it sho' took you a while to git heayh. You musta been a long way off for it to take you ten years to git back."

Daddy started fixing his plate of fish and fried potatoes and onions. Tears gathered in my eyes again because I knew Daddy was about to give me hell, yet before they fell I blinked them away, trying to stay strong and focused before Daddy's overwhelming energy crushed my ego.

"How's the farming going?" I asked, fixing my plate. I needed something tangible to hold on to.

"Oh, 'bout de same," Daddy stated coolly and sat at the head of the table. I took the seat at the opposite end. Tension lingered between us thicker than homemade molasses. Daddy started smacking on fish and glancing at me in a way that made me uneasy.

"I . . . um . . . hope you're not angry with me, Daddy. I know it's been a while. I just . . . didn't really think . . . um . . ."

"You neva did think. You was s'pose' to be so damn smart, but you couldn't think. Ain't that funny?"

"No, it's not funny," I said, frustrated.

"Well, I think it's funny." Daddy laughed in mockery. "I think it's real funny that a man who s'pose' to be so smart can't even think. Yeah, dat's funny to me." He roared in a way clearly meant to demean.

"See! That's why I left here! How was I to grow and thrive with you tearing me down every chance you got?" I screeched.

"No, no, Son. I didn't tear you down. If I had tore you down, you wouldn't ever be able to build yo'self up again. I don't half-do nothin'."

Daddy stared at me contemptuously. I knew coming home wasn't going to be easy, but I didn't think it would be this hard.

After a moment, I said, "Daddy, I'm sorry if I ever dishonored you." I kept my head bowed in fear of his retaliation.

All he said was, "Um."

I had come a long way to resolve old family issues, I reminded myself, but I must have left my diplomacy in New York, because nothing was getting resolved.

The staring left me unable to chew. Every time I raised my head, Daddy searched my face desperately for the truth of why I had returned. His eyes were squinted narrowly, allowing me to see only his pupils, which never moved the entire time we sat at the table. Daddy's bodybuilder frame intimidated me into a submission that disgusted me.

"What chu really heah fu'?" he asked softly after a while.

"I came to figure out some stuff about myself. And all of us." I felt a trickle of urine run down my leg.

"What chu tryin' to figure out? Ain't nothin' deep 'bout us."

"Well, I beg to differ. There are a lot of things about us that seem very deep to me. Like this grave in the backyard."

"That ain't deep."

"What?"

"You heard me. I said that ain't deep. 'Cause it ain't."

"Your own daughter's death ain't deep?" I probed, feeling my courage return.

"Nope. People die every day."

"Not like she did!"

"You don't know how she died, so what chu talkin' 'bout?"

I couldn't argue. Instead I said, "Why don't you tell me how she died and then I'll know."

Daddy dropped his head and continued eating, ignoring me perfectly. I would have to work on him much longer, I concluded, before he yielded any information, if he yielded any at all.

"Daddy, she was my sister!"

"I know who she was." He raised his head slowly.

"Am I missing something here?" I purposely dropped my fork onto my plate. "This is all supposed to make sense to me?"

"You done missed ten years o' shit, boy. You got a lotta catchin' up to do. I 'speck you betta keep yo' mouf shut and yo' eyes open. Never can tell what you might see."

"What? Why can't you tell me what happened? I know I've been gone a long time, but that doesn't mean I'm not supposed to know. She was my best friend!" I pleaded desperately.

"She wuz? Well, I hope I ain't neva yo' best friend, 'cause you sho' don't talk to yo' friends very often."

I almost told Daddy not to worry because he would never be my best friend, yet thinking the statement rude, I kept it to myself and bellowed, "Why I left here is not the point right now. I need you to tell me what happened to Sister!"

Nobody said a word. Daddy appeared rather amused at my insistence, thinking, I believe, that I was challenging him to some sort of game, which he certainly intended to win. He began to giggle.

"Did I miss the joke?"

"You are the joke," Momma volunteered. She wore a smile on her face of vengeance and evil, a sign she and Daddy had conspired to create the whole ordeal. I would have to get Daddy alone before I could manipulate any information from him. I backed off and thought to change the subject, but Daddy beat me to it.

"I guess you done finished school by now."

"Yes, sir."

"What chu take up?"

"Black studies."

"You mean to tell me you went to school all dis time to study black folks? You didn't need to go to school fu' dat."

"There's a lot about black people we don't know."

"We? I knows colored folks better'n I knows anythang."

"But there's a lot about our history most black people don't know."

"Like what?" Daddy asked, surprised at the possibility he didn't know something about his own people.

"Like how we used spirit to survive the Middle Passage."

"The Middle what?"

"The Middle Passage. It's more correctly called the Maafa. That's the boat ride we endured to get from Africa to America."

"I know we was slaves, boy. You ain't teachin' nobody nothin'. Everybody know we came over here on boats. You gotta do better'n dat."

"What you might not know is exactly what we endured along the way. First of all, many African villages were hundreds of miles from the Atlantic coast. How, then, did they get to the boats?"

"Dey walked, shit!"

"What if they had to be there in the next couple of days?"

Daddy didn't respond.

"The slave catchers would march them for fifteen hours a day until they reached the boats. This period of the process is known as the Long March. Thousands died on this part of the journey from exhaustion or physical abuse. Children and elders were usually murdered on the spot, and pregnant women often lost their babies. All of this happened before we left Africa. When history books speak of how many died during the Middle Passage, the numbers must be horribly incorrect, because most scholars don't even count those whose blood was spilled on African soil before departing."

"OK," Daddy conceded. "But when dey got to de water dey was loaded up and brung here. I know dat much."

"No, sir. It didn't happen that way."

Daddy examined me with bucked eyebrows, outraged by my gall.

"Most often, slaves had to wait weeks before they were herded aboard ships. They waited in what became known as slave pens. These holding places of filth and unbearable stench claimed the lives of thousands more of our people. They were located all along the western coast of Africa, and millions of people died in them before any boat departed. Tourists go to Africa today to view them as historical landmarks. Isn't that funny?"

"No, it ain't funny," Daddy said. "It's crazy."

"By the time they were actually taken aboard ship, they defecated upon themselves, vomited upon one another, and died chained together as people were forced to watch their brother's or sister's body rot. And there was nothing any of them could do. They were shackled aboard deck, despondent, weak, and depressed. Many of them simply decided to die."

"You can't je's decide to die and then die, boy."

"Most people can't, but some of our people did. They pulled upon their own spirit and resolved they would rather dwell in the land of their ancestors than live in captivity with white strangers. Hence they closed their eyes and died. They commanded their spirit to move from the realm of the physical into the realm of the spiritual. Everybody didn't possess such mastery of spirit, of course, but many did."

"Uh-huh," Daddy mumbled.

"That ain't all. On those ships is where African people began to hum melodies and cry out to God in moans and hollers we use in churches today. Because they were in the same condition, the humming gave room for everybody to participate in the lyrical moment even though people of different languages were often bound together. Journals of slave traders speak of the noise belowdecks being loud at times, to the point where white traders became horrified at the energy of the sound. Our people were enslaved, but their spirits were not."

"Dat's how come we do so much hummin' and moanin' now?" Daddy asked, surprised at the connection.

"Yes, sir, it is. The moans and humming keep us from having to depend upon language to communicate with God or each other. Of course, most of us speak English, but the moaning tradition has a power we've not been able to replace."

"Maybe you did learn somethin'," Daddy said, signaling I had said enough.

He continued eating supper. A moment of silence ensued wherein I felt horribly awkward. I wanted to ask about Sister again, but the time wasn't quite right.

"How's everybody doin' round here?"

" 'Bout de same."

I was trying to think of other questions to ask, but I couldn't, so I sat there and nibbled on my piece of fish, too.

Daddy finally said, "Well, you back." He didn't look at me or raise his voice. He never was one for small talk. Any time he said anything it was the bare minimum, and he meant what he said.

"Like I said, I wanted to see how everyone was doin'." My voice floundered a little.

"You done seen. How come you ain't gone?"

Daddy had a way of asking questions that left one paralyzed. I took a deep breath, found courage in my heart, and said, "Daddy, I needed to come home again and find answers to some questions."

"Questions like what?"

"Like why none of us ever loved each other, or why you beat me like you did." I didn't believe I had said it.

Daddy became silent and continued eating. He discovered slivers of fish between bones most people would simply have discarded. I examined Daddy's face, waiting for him to respond to my statement, but, once again, Daddy ignored me. After a while, I knew he wasn't going to engage me. Instead, he asked, "What chu doin' dese days? You workin'?"

"No, sir, not yet. I graduated last month with my Ph.D. I'll be teaching at a university somewhere this fall."

"Good for you," Daddy said smugly.

"Colleges need young professors," I offered in my own defense, "so I'm sure I won't have a problem finding a job."

Daddy wasn't interested in hearing about my future. He wanted me to explain why I had reappeared after ten years. He probably had a guess, but he wanted to hear me say it.

I held my peace. He finished his first piece of fish and got another. Every now and then he glared at me and shook his head up and down slowly, thinking thoughts he would never share. I felt immobilized by his authoritative presence, and Daddy knew it. Since childhood, I was afraid of the sound of his voice. He would yell at me and cause sweat to break out all over my body, even in the winter. Whenever he was around, my equilibrium was shot, because I couldn't hold anything steady or speak without stuttering heavily. To one extent or another, he affected everyone in the family this way. Years ago, we had to wait for Daddy to finish eating before we could leave the table, even if we finished before he did. I never knew why, and, of course, none of us were bold enough to ask. So, reminiscent of old times, I sat at the table wondering what the next few hours of my life would bring.

Upon closer scrutiny of Daddy's face, I realized he shared features with James Evans from *Good Times*. The broad, flat nose, high cheekbones, and shiny black complexion gave Daddy a warriorlike aura. He would have been a handsome man had he cared about grooming, but Daddy was totally divested of form or fashion. When I was a child, he had one church suit and the rest of his wardrobe was work clothes. I was sure he hadn't bought anything since I had been gone. He didn't need to. Women talked proudly and boldly about Daddy's deep-set eyes and his thick, bushy eyebrows. "Girl, dat's a fine ole country boy!" I overheard Ms. Mae Helen tell Ms. Helen Faye one day after church. "Dem wide shoulders and dat thick ass could keep a woman warm on a cold Arkansas night!" They chuckled to themselves, thinking no one heard them. I felt proud, actually, that my daddy was attractive to women. I never could see it, though, probably because my eyes were blinded by my fear of him. His loud voice, big hands, and protruding lips intimidated me into a silence I never outgrew. Daddy enjoyed the power he wielded, even as we sat at the dinner table that day, although he was a bit nicer than I remembered. It may have been my own maturity that softened his presence, or it may have been his own aging process. Either way, I wasn't totally frightened of him anymore. For that I was grateful, because over the next several days I would need all the courage I could get.

After what seemed like an eternity, Daddy rose, put on his hat, and headed for the door. "A man oughta spend his time outdoors, boy," he used to tell Willie James and me. "The house is the woman's territory. Bible'll tell ya dat." Daddy only came inside to eat and sleep. He used the bathroom outside, napped outside, entertained his buddies outside, and made Momma stay inside.

I rose and followed him. Although Daddy was direct, he never said all he wanted to say at once. I decided to join him outdoors in hopes of learning more about what happened to Sister. He went to the barn to get a bucket of feed for the cows, and I grabbed a bale of hay and walked slightly behind him into the field.

"Ole Bessie dere is 'bout to have a calf, boy," Daddy announced out of the blue.

We fed and watered the cows and returned to the barn. Daddy put the bucket back in its place and began to sharpen the garden hoe.

I sat on a bale of hay like a naughty child awaiting reprimand. This is ridiculous, I thought to myself. I am entirely too old to be afraid of this man. However, my fear kept my thoughts from ever being expressed.

"Ms. Swinton is down low sick," Daddy reported nonchalantly. I think he spoke simply to relieve me. Maybe Daddy could be kind.

"Is that right?" I said, honestly moved. Ms. Swinton was the teacher at Swamp Creek School. The only teacher. I guess we didn't need but one, since we only had a one-room schoolhouse. Swamp Creek was far enough from the next county that, years ago, black parents convinced the local school board to let them keep their one-room school instead of busing black kids thirty miles to the nearest white school. The board didn't want Swamp kids integrated with white kids anyway, so everyone was happy with the decision. Ms. Swinton simply had to report attendance and test scores to the Pope County school board every six weeks. Other than that, white folks couldn't have cared less whether we learned a damn thing.

Ms. Swinton cared about us, though. She was an incredible

teacher who taught every subject masterfully. Her aim in life was to help black children learn in order to love themselves. She started teaching in Swamp Creek in 1948, and rumor had it that she has given every child she's taught pure hell. Daddy said she came when he was in the first grade and assumed every child was an Einstein. She read with such eloquence and emphasis, her students boasted, that they would sit and cry as they listened. Sometimes she would cry, too. She had a love for teaching most people can never fathom. How she managed to teach all elementary grades alone was phenomenal, but Daddy said, even in his day, no one was bored or misbehaved. She was immaculately clean every day, rain or shine, and when she wrote on the board, students marveled at her calligraphic penmanship. All the boys had a crush on her, and all the girls envied her. Everyone loved her.

When I started school, she gave me extra books to read and required my papers to be longer than other students'. I thought she was mean at first, but later I discovered she really perceived me as brilliant. Her applause of my intelligence meant the world to me. The possibility Ms. Swinton believed in me made me frantic to prove I was worthy of her admiration. By my senior year in high school, Ms. Swinton said she was tired of the classroom. She had taught for thirty-five years and was ready to give it up. I knew she'd never quit, though—not Ms. Carolyn Swinton. The classroom was her domain. She would walk around in our little schoolhouse like a queen in a castle, her head held high and her high heels tapping the floor with a remarkable precision. She would die before she stopped teaching, and I was afraid that was about to happen.

"Yeah, ole Doc Sanders say she prob'ly ain't gon' be wid us too much longer."

Daddy loved Ms. Swinton. He talked about her all the time. His eyes would light up whenever her name was introduced into conversation, and he never failed to affirm how smart and exceptionally pretty she was. She loved Daddy, too. She told us stories about how

Daddy would come to school late, huffin' and puffin', running from the fields. She would make him stand in the corner for fifteen minutes as his friends snickered and jeered at him. She knew his lateness was not his fault. He couldn't help it if his daddy made him do field work before school hours. Yet she was never one to accept excuses, regardless of whose they were. She said Daddy was probably the smartest little boy she had encountered, but he missed too many school days to be consistently bright. After his fourth year, he assumed the role of class clown, apparently without knowing how much Ms. Swinton abhorred aberrant behavior. She took him home one day, Daddy said, and told his folks his coming to school was a waste of time. He was absent two or three days a week, and consequently, he had simply given up the desire to catch up. Grandpa didn't mind, Daddy said. He needed help in the field. Grandma, on the other hand, didn't like the idea of her son not getting "somethin' in his head," but she took what Ms. Swinton said as a sign that Daddy was not school material. Many people in Swamp Creek drew similar conclusions about their children.

I wondered how old Ms. Swinton was. She'd have to be at least seventy, since she had taught in Swamp Creek as long as anyone could remember. She was the only glimpse most of us got of culture, protocol, and class. Momma said Ms. Swinton was full of herself and ought to come back down. "Down to what?" I wondered. She dressed nice and her language was impeccable. That's probably why Momma couldn't stand her, "walkin' round tryin' to talk like white folks." Ms. Swinton was my idol, and I loved everything about her. She taught me things and exposed me to ideas, which have stayed with me a lifetime. I never will forget the day she told me to stay after school. I thought I was in trouble. I didn't remember anything I had done, but any time Ms. Swinton kept a student after school, everybody knew he was in trouble.

Once the other children left, she told me to bring a chair and place it next to her desk. I was both disquieted and anxious. "What did I do, Ms. Swinton?" I asked very softly, about to cry.

"You have done nothing wrong, Thomas Lee," Ms. Swinton pampered me kindly. I had never heard her take a motherly tone with any of us kids. I felt warm. "I asked you to stay because I have something for you."

Ms. Swinton went into her desk drawer and pulled out a brand-new book. I began to sweat.

"I know how much you like to read, and I see how hard you work. Take this book, read it, and keep it for yourself. Don't tell anyone you have it. It's our secret. In fact, why don't we start reading it together, if you have time?"

"Sure," I said, grinning like a Cheshire cat. I knew I didn't have time because Daddy was in the field waiting on me. He'd simply have to wait, I decided. I might get a whoopin', but this was worth it.

The book had a shiny, bright green cover. This was the first brand-new book I had ever seen. All our books at school were used ones the white school had thrown away, and this new book belonged to me!

"This is your birthday present, Thomas," Ms. Swinton declared as I pulled my chair next to hers. I knew she was lying. She never gave anyone birthday presents because she didn't bother herself with such trivialities. My fifteenth birthday simply offered her the opportunity to give me the book without showing favoritism.

"I think you'll enjoy this book a lot," Ms. Swinton concluded as she handed it to me and asked me to start reading aloud.

The book was titled *Go Tell It on the Mountain*. I liked the title because it reminded me of the song we sang at church during Christmastime.

"Yes. This is the story of a young man, much like you, who has some difficulties in his life that he must overcome."

"Is he black?" I asked excitedly.

"Yes, he is black, and the other characters are, too."

I dropped the book from sheer excitement.

"You must take good care of this book, son. New books are hard to come by in Swamp Creek."

"I'll take care of it, Ms. Swinton. I promise!"

I began to read. Every word was like medicine for my wounded spirit. I would read a page and Ms. Swinton would read a page. We read for about an hour until she suggested I go home before my folks came after me.

"Finish the book whenever you get a chance. The sooner the better, for then you won't forget what we've already read."

"I will, Ms. Swinton. I will!"

In my excitement, I jumped up from my chair and hugged her tightly. I released her abruptly, however, when I realized I had invaded her personal space. No one ever hugged Ms. Swinton. She just wasn't the touchy-feely type. Yet, much to my surprise, she giggled and hugged me in return.

"Get on out of here, boy," she said playfully, and tapped me on my behind. If I could have married her at that moment, I would have.

I stayed up all night and finished the book. John, the main character, and I had similar lives. His daddy beat him just like mine beat me. "Why are black daddies mean?" I wondered aloud to myself.

Concerning our mothers, however, our lives were very different. John had a momma who loved him. She hugged him and told him he was special. He had an auntie, too, who gave him some relief from his daddy. What troubled me most, though, was how his daddy claimed to love God passionately yet treated John like dirt.

I woke up the next morning too tired to hold my eyes open. "I tole you to take yo' black ass to bed, boy," I remembered Daddy threatening. And I wished I had, but I couldn't stop reading. The stuff in the book about church, God, singing, and hypocrisy made me realize I wasn't alone in my confusion.

"I 'speck you might wanna go see Ms. Swinton befo' you go," Daddy requested, interrupting my memory.

"I will. For sure."

He kept sharpening the hoe. Clearly he wasn't going to volunteer any explanations unless I proceeded with my questions.

"Daddy, what's wrong with us?"

"Wrong wid who?" he quizzed without making eye contact.

"Us. Our family."

"I didn't know anythang was s'posed to be wrong."

"Come on, Daddy." I was beginning to get frustrated again. "My memory of this place hurts. I think about how we abused each other and how we'd go for weeks without speaking a word to each other."

Daddy remained silent. I had probably hurt his feelings, but I had to say what I felt. Otherwise, I never would.

"I'm sorry, Daddy," I apologized after a brief pause. My eyes were beginning to water.

"Ain't nothin' to be sorry fu', boy. You jes' sayin' what you needs to say, I guess." Daddy glanced at me briefly and raised his brows.

"Daddy, don't make this harder for me than it already is."

"I'm listenin' to you, boy."

"I don't need you to listen to me; I need you to speak."

"What chu want me to say?" Daddy asked loudly.

I began to pace around the barn. "I need you to tell me about some things."

"Thangs like what?"

"Like what happened to Sister."

Daddy gazed into space, probably wondering how he could avoid this confrontation.

"I don't know what happened," Daddy responded, and resumed sharpening the hoe.

"Stop it," I screamed. "How can you tell me you don't know what happened?"

"Because I don't know, boy. What I do know is dat you on thin ice hollerin' at me like dat!"

"Fine. Forgive me. But, Daddy, your own daughter dies, *somebody* buries her in your backyard, and you don't know anything? Is that what you're saying, Daddy?"

"Yep."

"You expect me to believe this?"

"It really don't make me no diff'rence if you b'lieve it or not. It's de truth. And if you was here, maybe you'd know fu' yo'self."

"Well, I wasn't here and you know why. Does that mean I don't deserve to know what happened?"

"I told you I don't know nothin' 'bout what happened to dat girl. I came home and dey had done already buried her."

Daddy rose to hang the hoe back on the barn wall. He had that don't-ask-me-no-more-questions expression on his face, but I ignored it.

"You came home and saw your daughter's grave in the backyard without knowing she had died?"

"Somethin' like dat."

"What do you mean?"

"I mean dat yo' momma said she found her dead in her bed early dat mornin' right after I left for the fields, and wunnit no needa waitin' till I got home to bury her, so they buried her right then."

"They who?"

"I don't know. She said a coupla folks gave her a hand."

"Daddy, there was no funeral or anything? This is the craziest thing I've ever heard of in my life!"

"I done tole you what I know."

"No, you haven't."

"You callin' me a lie, boy?"

This was getting a little out of hand. Of course I was calling Daddy a lie, but I couldn't admit it to his face.

"No, sir," I acquiesced, a bit more softly.

"I knowed you and yo' sista was close, and dat was good. But I can't tell you no mo'."

"Can't or won't?"

"Boy, don't make me mad, hear?"

"Daddy, I come home after ten years and find my baby sister dead and nobody knows how she died? This can't be real."

"Well, it *is* real. Sister was sweet, but de Lawd called her home."

"Oh, don't give me that bullshit."

Daddy swung and hit me in the mouth with the back of his hand. "Don't chu neva cuss at me as long as you live, boy! Is you done gone plumb damn crazy?"

I was lying on the ground with Daddy standing over me breathing hard. My teeth were still in place and nothing was bleeding, so I pushed my luck.

"No, I ain't crazy, but y'all are!" I jumped to my feet.

"Well, we might be, but it ain't got nothin' to do wid you. You ran away from dis place ten years ago. You ain't got nothin' to say far as I'm concerned."

"I'm not trying to run anybody's business, Daddy. I'm trying to find out what happened to my sister. Is that too much to ask?"

"From me it is, 'cause I don't know. Don't ask me again!" Daddy stormed out of the barn.

I sat down on the feed bucket and tried to make sense of it all. Daddy said he didn't know anything and Momma didn't, either. Of course, both of them were lying. Who could I turn to? Tears came to my eyes as I felt a warm trickle of blood flow from my bruised lip. If I had left at that moment, my folks would probably have been glad. But I didn't leave. I couldn't. Not yet.

6

Sunday morning was bright and shiny. I awakened to the smell of smoked ham and eggs and knew everyone was up except me. I rose, washed myself quickly, and dressed for church. When I emerged from the bathroom, I realized everyone had already eaten. We exchanged phony "good mornings," and I sat at the table praying church would be as good as it had once been.

The family waited on me to finish eating. Sitting at the table alone, I could feel their disdain for my lateness and their disgust at my interruption of the normal Sunday morning flow. Consequently, I ate hurriedly, although I didn't eat fast enough to pacify their impatience, for moans, grunts, and nasty facial expressions confirmed they were about to leave me if I didn't hurry. Choosing not to face their wrath, I left my plate half-eaten, and we got in the car and headed on our way. As we approached the church, I could hear Miss Odella singing "I Woke Up Dis Moanin' wid My Mind Stayed on Jesus." That was her favorite song. Every time Deacon Tilman asked somebody, which meant anybody, to lead the congregation in a song, Miss Odella would jump up and start singing her song. Grandma commented, "The song is fine and all, but Odella know she lyin'! If hu' mind was stayed on Jesus, she wouldn't have hu' ass in the honky-tonk on Saturday nights." Miss Odella loved to party and drink, although nobody really minded, I guess, because no one ever said anything directly to her about it. Grandma used to titter and say, "That woman oughta be 'shame' o' hurself. Ain't no way she woke up dis moanin' wid hur mind on Jesus. She ain't neva been to sleep!"

Daddy parked the car in the same place he had parked it for thirty years. We got out in reticence and prepared for the ritual. Daddy had on his one navy blue suit, although people had given him others in hopes he might experience change for a moment, but no luck. Momma wore a pink two-piece dress that I didn't like, and her hairstyle was exactly as it had been since I was born. Never anything different, never a risk. Convention was Momma and Daddy's theme. They walked into church first, suggesting at least the appearance of love and order in our home. Willie James followed in his black slacks and white shirt. These were his "meetin'" clothes, and any time he dressed up, I was sure, this was his attire. I asked him once if he wanted some other clothes and he said, "Why would I?"

I concluded the Tyson family processional in a pair of khaki shorts and a dashiki. Daddy said I reminded him of something straight out of the African jungle.

When we entered the church, I laughed aloud at the sound of the old piano. It had been out of tune for fifty years. Mr. Jared, the pseudo-musician, played in a kind of juke-joint style, producing a "plunkety plunk, plunk, plunk" rhythm that made every song sound alike. He had not learned one new chord in ten years. If I had asked him about it, he probably would have said exactly what Willie James said: "Why would I?"

The congregation saw me and immediately began to cheer the prodigal son's return. I smiled at everyone and took my seat.

"Good moanin', good moanin'," Deacon Blue burbled cheerfully. "This sho' is a gred day!"

"Yes, it is, brotha' superintendent!" Ms. Polly confirmed.

"We see dat de Good Lawd done seed fit to brang one o' our own back to us."

Daddy and Momma didn't say anything. They beheld everyone as though wishing we'd get on with the business at hand.

"Come say a word to us, T.L., befo' we opens up fu' Sunday school."

A chorus of loud "Amens" reinforced the request and left me positioned behind the old wooden podium in front of the small congregation.

"Praise the Lord, saints," I began. Everybody was glad to see I hadn't lost Jesus.

"Praise the Lord," they returned.

"It's been a while, huh?" I snickered, embarrassed.

"I'm tellin' you!" folks said as they nudged one another.

"Well, the Lord has been good to me. I went away to college, and now I have a Ph.D. in African-American studies. I attend church regularly and I work with young people in my community. Seems like every time I planned to get home, something came up. This time I refused to let anything get in my way. It's good to see all of you, and I ask that you pray for my strength in the Lord."

Most of what I said was a boldface lie, but it was what they wanted to hear. While returning to my seat, I could tell folks had more questions than I had answered. Miss Odella turned around, pinched me endearingly, and whispered, "Where you been at, boy?" She patted my leg affectionately, a sign she wasn't finished with me yet.

Sunday school was hilarious. Deacon Blue misquoted "Stripture," called Elijah "Isaiah," and said Deuteronomy was in the New Testament. I barely held my peace. The Sunday school lesson was called "A New Creature." It was based on II Corinthians 5:17, which says: "Therefore if any man be in Christ, he is a new creature: old things are passed away; behold, all things are become new." Deacon Blue's explanation of this verse sent me to the bathroom.

"See, what de Lawd is sayin' here," he explained self-righteously, "is dat we got to get rid o' all dat old stuff in our houses. Somma y'all got clothes and little ceramic stuff you been had fu' fawty years. Dis Stripture is tellin' us we got to get rid o' dat. All yo' old stuff you got to th'ow 'way!"

He stepped back from the podium, proud of his assumed profundity. I couldn't hold it any longer. I started coughing to keep from screaming, and I ran to the restroom before I embarrassed myself irreparably. Had Sister been there, she would have known exactly why I was laughing. In fact, she would have followed me a few seconds later, and we would have laughed together back in the church kitchen. Yet Sister wasn't there. The thought of her stole my ephemeral joy. I sat on the commode thinking, instead, about the time I had spent in that old church. I had been the musician, once upon a time, learning new songs from the radio and attempting to teach them to the choir. Folks couldn't sing parts, thought notes were too high, and wanted to know what was wrong with the old songs we sang. Forget it, I said to myself. Progress simply had no luck in Swamp Creek.

I suppose I was the problem because I wanted more than a mediocre country existence. I was never satisfied with the bare minimum or with things being the way they had always been. Rather, I wanted to experiment with new foods and creative forms foreign to Swamp Creek culture. My goal as a teenager had been to birth some new ideas in Swamp Creek—like reading for pleasure—and to question the validity of long-held traditions, the meanings of which no one knew. As an adult, much of what I once believed I didn't anymore, but had I exposed this truth at church, I might have been crucified. Homefolks would certainly say I had lost my salvation. Like the time I objected when the church voted to excommunicate Ms. Janey and Ms. Pauline. I knew even back then the church was dead wrong, but Momma and everyone else said the two women had to go because they were "funny" and God didn't like that. Whether they were funny or not, both women were kind to me. If they loved each other, I thought, they'd done better than any of us. "Maybe the Bible is incorrect on this matter," I suggested boldly when the church met for the vote. Daddy shot me a glance more threatening than an automatic rifle, so I shut up and complied. I wasn't afraid to disagree with church folks, but I was scared to death to defy my father.

I saw an old fan on the bathroom floor with the name Mosley Funeral Home across the top. That was the mortuary that had buried Grandma years ago. I had dreaded seeing her in a coffin. However, when Mosley finished with her and opened the casket at the funeral, she simply looked as though she were asleep. She wasn't ashen and stiff, as I had feared. Actually, I remember thinking how pretty she was. Old Man Mosley and his son had dressed her in pink, her favorite color, and I asked them if I could cornrow her hair. It was a strange request, I know, but Grandma loved it when I braided her hair, so they let me. In the morgue, I told her things I had never told anyone.

I returned to my seat in church as Sunday school was about to end.

"Seem lak to me," Deacon Blue said, "we oughta git T.L. to come on up heayh and review dis lesson. He done gone and got all dat learnin' and I sho' would lak to heayh him talk."

"Amen, amen," said everyone except my folks.

I stood, a bit unsure, because I had not studied the Sunday school lesson, but soon calmed, for it didn't take much learning to do what they were asking.

I spoke for a few moments, inserting a little drama here and there, and then resumed my seat. "Dat boy sho' can talk, can't he, Louise?" I heard Ms. Peggy say as she grinned proudly. Ms. Louise nodded her head repeatedly.

"Dat's what dat schoolin' do fu' ya!" proclaimed Deacon Blue, returning to the podium. "I been tryin' to git mine to go and git some learnin', but seem lak dey don't wanna do nothin'. But chu cain't make nobody drank water. All you can do is hold de glass."

"Dat's de truf," the congregation returned in chorus.

"T.L., it sho' is good to see you back round here. Dese chillin needs somebody like you to come and tell em how to go 'bout. I tries all de time, but dey don't wanna lissen to no ole man. You talk to 'em while you's heayh, OK?"

"Oh, sure," I said, knowing I planned to break town as soon as I got a chance.

Sunday school dismissed and church began. Aunt Cookie opened with "I Shall Not Be Moved." I sat there, very still, trying not to cry, but I couldn't help it. "Just like a tree, planted by the waters," she bellowed from the pit of her soul. That woman could sing for me any day!

They did the announcements, took up collection, sang another song, and Reverend Dawson got up to preach. To this day, I don't have the slightest idea what he said. He started somewhere in Genesis, and by the time he got to hoopin' good, he was in Revelation. I tuned him out after a while. Since folks in Swamp Creek obviously enjoyed—or endured—him, I decided to roll along. I said amen occasionally, simply out of respect. His entire sermon was filled with trite clichés and lines from old Baptist hymns. It was funny, really, how people could go to church their entire lives and listen to the same sermons week after week. When black folks drop the fear of critique, I thought, our liberation can come.

Church ended and we headed home. Again, no one said anything. I sat behind Daddy, staring out of the car window at the open land that used to be full of trees. "Who cut all this down?" I asked.

"Willie James," Momma sighed, probably hoping I wouldn't ask anything else.

We arrived home and the first thing I saw when I exited the car was Sister's grave. I instantly recalled that no one had said a word about it at church. Daddy, Momma, and Willie James walked by the tombstone and into the house unmoved by its presence. I shook my head in disbelief, walked over to the mound, and sat like a zombie. Momma peered at me through the kitchen window.

"Sister, I don't understand," I confessed softly, staring into oblivion. "What the hell is going on? Something is horribly wrong! Everyone else is fine, while I'm the one traumatized! Are niggas crazy? This doesn't make any sense. What happened, Sister? What happened?" I rocked myself back and forth with my arms folded as the sun beamed down hard on me. "Girl, girl, girl!" I cried as rivers of tears meandered down my face.

Then, wondering whether I had lost my mind, I wailed, "This doesn't seem crazy to anyone but me?" Momma was still surveying me with a devious smile. Her ability to witness my pain without reaction was uncanny. I rose to my feet and rubbed the tombstone gently. "Sister, is this real?" I searched back and forth from the grave to the house, totally bewildered. "I must be in the Twilight Zone," I crowed, walking into the house.

"What's so funny?" Willie James asked. He had changed into his overalls and was sitting at the kitchen table waiting on the rest of the family to sit for Sunday dinner.

"Man, I must really be crazy. I mean, for real. Do you see that grave, Willie James?" I pulled back the curtain from the kitchen window.

"T.L., please!" Willie James whispered intensely.

"Please what? Man, what's wrong with y'all? This shit ain't crazy to you?"

"Yeah, it is, little brotha, but I cain't say nothin'. You oughta jes' leave it alone."

"And how am I supposed to do that?"

"By keepin' yo' damn mouth shut."

"Man, fuck that!"

"See? You still talk too damn much. You always thought you knowed everything. You never listened to nobody long enough to learn nothin'."

Willie James was implying he might talk later; so I humbled myself and whimpered, "Sorry."

"Trust me when I tell you dat you don't want to know what happened to Sister. It ain't a pretty picture."

"I don't care how ugly it is! I want to know!"

The kitchen table vibrated from our vicious murmuring. I was trying to get what I could out of Willie James before Momma and Daddy got to the table.

"The only thing I can tell you is that she was on her way to see you."

"What?"

"One Thursday night, Sister came to my room and said, 'I'm leavin' tomorrow, Willie James. I ain't stayin' here anotha day. I'm goin' to find T.L. I think I know where he is.' 'How do you know?' I asked her. 'Trust me,' she said as she sat on the edge of my bed and started cryin'. She was desperate and hurting bad. 'I gotta go. I can't take it no more. Tell Momma and Daddy not to worry.' 'You got money?' I whispered. 'Yeah, I got some. I got enough, anyway.' We hugged each other like we knew it would be the last time. She asked me if I would give her a ride to the bus station about five o'clock the next morning, and I told her I would. I was jealous she loved you more than she did me, but wasn't nothin' I could do about it. I wished her well and told her to take care of herself."

Willie James stopped talking. "Go on!" I demanded.

"Ain't nothin' else to say. She died that night before she got a chance to leave."

"She died? That don't make no sense, man! How did she die?"

"That ain't yo' business, boy," Daddy blazed sternly. His voice startled both of us. We glanced up into the face of a man who would have killed had we spoken another word. I gazed at Willie James, frustrated he feared Daddy enough to deny me the information I wanted.

The only other time, years ago, Daddy warned me about minding my own business was the situation dealing with the banishment of Ms. Janey and Ms. Pauline from the church. Momma said it was a disgrace and a damn shame, two women sleeping together. I didn't see what was wrong with it. Ms. Janey and Ms. Pauline had set up the college fund at church for any youngster who wanted to get a college education. God was glad about that, wasn't He? Yet if He was, folks in Swamp Creek didn't care, because they expelled Ms. Janey and Ms. Pauline anyway. It was ugly.

Deacon Blue got up in church and said he had an announcement to make: "It hath been reported that some of our members is funny." Immediately everyone began to look at Ms. Janey and Ms. Pauline. "We all know God don't like dat. De Bible say homosexials is goin' to hell."

"Amen," people chimed.

"The Bible say fornicators are going, too," Ms. Janey said defensively and stood to her feet. "So if I'm goin', Blue, I'll definitely see you there!"

Everybody knew, back in the day, Deacon Blue had been a ladies' man, and Ms. Janey was making sure Deacon Blue understood God's judgment to affect every life. Her case didn't carry her far, though. The church voted unanimously to excommunicate them. Ms. Pauline was silent the whole time, having anticipated the judgment.

To quell my dissent, Momma said, "They started that shit years ago, and what's done in the dark got to come to de light." I told her, if I were they, I wouldn't have been doing anything in the dark. I would have done it in the light from the start. She told me I didn't know what I was talking about and to keep my mouth shut about the matter. That's what I did.

Ms. Pauline was a retired schoolteacher who came home to bury her daddy and decided to stay. He had left her plenty of land, and her retirement pension left her financially stable. She was tired of running the rat race in Chicago, she told Grandma upon arrival, so she shipped all her things to Swamp Creek and took root once again. She had grown up there and moved away at eighteen. Grandma said she acted shy and aloof even back then, especially when boys approached. Whenever girls asked her what was wrong, she would say softly, "Pardon me, but I don't share your male obsession." The girls would snicker at her, because of both her response and the structure of her language. Ms. Pauline didn't pay them no mind though, Grandma said. As long as she had a good book, she was fine. She wasn't nasty, ugly, or mean; she just wasn't consumed with men.

As a child, I watched her in church pull out some thick novel and read it as Reverend Samuels preached. One day I asked her why she read in church and she said, "No need to waste good reading time! If he were saying something substantive, I'd listen." "Why come at all?" I asked in return. "Because every Sunday I hope he'll say something worth hearing." Ms. Pauline had an answer for everything. I loved to hear her talk because her words sounded clear, crisp, and smooth like church bells. Grandma said the woman had enough books to make a school library. I never saw the books, however, because Daddy said he'd whip my ass if I ever went inside Ms. Pauline's house. I'd walk by there and wave vigorously, trying to tell Ms. Pauline I liked her but was forbidden to visit. She would wave with the same energy, confirming she knew my hesitation was externally driven. At times, I contemplated whether to go inside against Daddy's command, but Ms. Pauline would smile sadly and I knew not to invite the battle.

Ms. Janey was a different story. She was loud, boisterous, and definitely wasn't one to take any crap. Born and raised in Swamp Creek, Ms. Janey never left. She married Old Man Jake Harris and treated him like a dog, Grandma proclaimed. She wouldn't cook or wash his dirty draws, and she definitely wasn't giving him any pussy. I overheard Grandma tell Momma that Ms. Janey and Mr. Jake had their own bedrooms and Mr. Jake wasn't allowed in Ms. Janey's room. She just married him to keep folks from talking. Everybody already knew she was "funny." When she was sixteen, somebody caught her and another girl out behind Mr. Blue's barn doing something sexual. Exactly what they were doing is apparently irrelevant, because people filled in the blank themselves. Ms. Janey didn't care. She kept on living like nothing had happened. Youngsters mumbled ugly comments at her, Grandma explained, and she would whisper lively, "Wish you were there, don't you?" She smiled and walked away with her head held straight up in the air. Grandma mocked her demeaningly and asserted, "Ms. Janey Harris was a pistol!"

Folks said she and Ms. Pauline had always been lovers, but when Ms. Pauline left Swamp Creek, Ms. Janey was depressed and decided to marry Jake. People knew she was still in love with Ms. Pauline. Grandma said Mr. Samson, the mailman, delivered mail to her from Ms. Pauline and told everybody in Swamp Creek Ms. Janey got a letter from her lover. When Ms. Pauline came home to bury her daddy, Ms. Janey was right there the whole time consoling and cooking for her. It was wonderful, I thought. I was about twelve years old and I remember thinking how great it would be to have a friend who loved me that much. I knew they weren't blood relatives; thus the commitment seemed all the more amazing.

Momma and Grandma didn't agree with me. "Janey Harris oughta be plumb 'shame' o' hu'self," Grandma argued. "She got a man at home and she runnin' afta anotha woman. Lawd, don't strike us dead!" I smiled and said, "Isn't it great how they take care of each other? I mean, that's what Jesus would do, isn't it?" That's the only time Grandma slapped me in my mouth. "Go play, boy, and stop actin' so damn grown!" she yelled.

After Ms. Pauline's daddy's funeral, Ms. Janey moved in with her. I walked by the house the day she was moving in, on my way to the fishing hole, and asked them if they needed any help. "That's mighty kind of you, T.L. We could use a strong man for a minute or two." I started taking Ms. Janey's things off the truck. Suddenly Daddy came by on the tractor and summoned me angrily. I met him on the road and that's when he told me never to let him catch me at those women's house again. I started explaining they had been very kind to me and I was only giving them a hand because some of Ms. Janey's things were quite heavy. He didn't care. He wanted me to stay away from those damn dykes, as he called them.

The day they were banished from the church, I wept. Ms. Janey cussed and accused everyone of being judgmental. She didn't deny anything they said about her; she simply wanted to know why she had to leave the church, but all the other sinners didn't. She said, "We ain't teachin' dese children nothin' but hypocrisy. Some of them exist today because y'all was in the wrong bed. Might as well tell de truth and shame the devil!" Folks got beside themselves and began to grumble loudly. That's when the deacons physically threw Ms. Janey out the front door of the church. They weren't thinking about her sin anymore; they were afraid she was going to tell the truth about their lives. Of course, they weren't willing to suffer exposure. Truth and church folk never got along too well in Swamp Creek.

Ms. Pauline sat and cried softly. She watched the deacons throw Ms. Janey outside and accuse them of things no one could possibly have proven. She was no coward, though. She rose to leave, knowing everyone was waiting for her to do so. Before she reached the door, she turned and pronounced, "I'm glad I met God before I met you." I never forgot that moment. Ms. Pauline had taught me indirectly that God doesn't think like people do. I didn't agree with the church's decision, but I was only a child, and children have absolutely no power in Swamp Creek. Daddy reminded me later that the church must have standards. "We can't allow sin to live in the church and do nothin' 'bout it," he avowed. I wanted to ask him what we were going to do about the sin in his life, but he would have beaten me. Everyone in the church had committed transgressions against God, but I would never have told them God didn't love them. I also knew in my heart God loved Ms. Janey and Ms. Pauline. Kicking them out of church was supposed to be a clear sign to me that God didn't love them, but I never believed it. More important, I didn't understand how God wouldn't love them. They were the most righteous people I knew. Anytime someone died, they were ready to assist the family. If the church sponsored a program, they gave the most money and dedicated the most time to assuring its success. When I got ready to leave for college, Ms. Pauline slipped me a brand-new hundred-dollar bill and a note that read: "Study hard and do well, son. Education will take you anywhere you want to go. If you need anything more, just call." My own folks had not given me anything. Even when Ms. Pauline and Ms. Janey were abused and talked about, they kept their commitment to righteousness. And these were the people Swamp Creek citizens sent to hell for their sins?

7

Before Sunday dinner was served, I escaped the house long enough to gather wildflowers for Sister's grave. The makeshift bouquet made the reality of her death more comprehensible. I begged Sister to speak to me, to give me a sign she knew how much I loved her, but I got nothing. Placing the flowers at the foot of the tombstone very carefully, I decided to call the area around her grave Eden. She was my first love and the only paradise I'd known, so to think Sister was resting in Eden comforted me.

Willie James called me to supper. Not wanting to eat but trying to avoid turmoil, I rose and entered the house.

The food smelled good and looked pretty on the table. Momma was famous for making ordinary things appear extraordinary. I sat down and Daddy said the blessing.

"Lawd, thank You for dis food we 'bout to receive for de nourishment of our bodies and the benefit of our souls. Amen." We each mumbled a Bible verse and began to serve ourselves. Meat loaf, green beans, okra, potatoes and onions, and baked sweet potato pie. The food was scrumptious, but the company was sour. Everyone's head remained bowed throughout the meal like disciples saddened at the lost of their Savior. No one dared speak. Sunday dinner had been the kind of ritual in our home where one's presence was required yet one's voice undesired. It was the time during the week when we reminded ourselves, in our attitude, how much we disliked one another. We chewed our food quickly, enduring the moment only because our flesh demanded it, and retreated into our own private worlds where we preferred to live. Once, Sister and I glanced at each other and burst into laughter. Daddy never raised his head, but Momma warned us, "Y'all better stop all dat damn clownin' at de dinner table!" Daddy told me later, "Men don't giggle, boy. That shit's for women. Next time, I'll slap de shit outta you." I think my folks were afraid joy might come along one day and demand they relinquish their love for hatred.

I was about half-finished with my plate when Daddy queried, "What chu puttin' dem weeds on dat grave fu'? She can't smell 'em, can she?"

"Yes, she can," I defended. "Only her body's gone. Her spirit is still alive."

"Is dat so?" Daddy snickered.

Joking about Sister's death and her grave angered me. "How can you belittle your own daughter's death?" My tone infuriated him.

"Don't start dat shit today, OK? I ain't in de mood. It's Sunday anyway."

"What's Sunday got to do with Sister? I keep asking you what happened and you won't tell me anything. I've been here a day and none of you have tried to explain the specifics of her death to me. You know how close we were. Why are you torturing me?"

Daddy ignored me and kept eating, Willie James refused to make eye contact with me, and Momma acted as though she hadn't heard anything.

"Will someone tell me what happened?" I implored after a moment or two of silence.

No one replied.

"I'm not leaving here until I get some answers."

Momma glared at Daddy. My persistence hadn't troubled her; the possibility of my extended stay was what worried her.

"T.L., all I know is—"

"Shut up, boy," Daddy told Willie James emphatically.

"Why shouldn't I know, Daddy? You don't think I deserve to know what happened to my own sister?" I slammed my fork on the table and gawked at Daddy with the meanest expression I could muster.

"Don't get beside yo'self, boy. I'd hate to have to whip yo' ass, especially since you thank you grown and all." Daddy's eyes assured me I did not want to push him. "Finish yo' supper, and I don't intend to deal wit' chu about yo' sister no mo'."

"I'm supposed to let her go? Just like that?"

"Don't be a fool, boy," Momma patronized me. "Yo' daddy don't want to talk about it, so let it go."

"Momma, please! Whatever Daddy says, you just go along with it."

"Is you disrespectin' yo' momma, boy?" Daddy yelled. He stood up. "I'll kill you if you disrespect yo' momma again in my house!"

"Sorry, Momma," I submitted quickly, more to satisfy Daddy than to honor her. "I didn't mean to disrespect anyone. I'm trying to discover what happened to Sister."

"We done told you we don't know!" Daddy screamed, and pounded on the table.

"But y'all do know! How can you expect me to believe otherwise?"

"I don't expect you to do nothin'. I didn't expect you to come back to Swamp Creek, I didn't expect you to amount to much, and I don't expect you to keep worryin' me about Sister! Now leave me the hell alone!" Daddy resumed his seat and continued his meal.

Tranquillity subsumed us again. Whenever we approached the point of real communication, we reverted to silence. Strangely enough, we used to go for days and not say a word to anyone. The beauty of verbal expression was never welcomed in our home. Sister's death seemed, somehow, to contribute to the family vow of silence, and since the taciturnity was larger than me, I said nothing further.

After dinner, I followed Willie James out to the barn as he prepared to feed the cows and slop the hogs. That was once my job. I
hated it, but come slaughter day, I didn't mind.

"Why you followin' me?" he interrogated.

"I don't know, really. Maybe I was hoping we could talk."

His eyes met mine. "About what?"

"Oh, whatever." I was making a complete ass of myself.

"If you came out here to ask me about your precious little sister,
keep it. I ain't got nothin' to say." He filled the buckets with feed and
proceeded into the field toward the cows. I ensued.

"I didn't come out here to ask you about Sister," I lied. "I came to
ask you about you."

"What about me?"

I hesitated a moment, then asked, "Why did you stay? I mean, you
could have left."

"What makes you think I wanted to leave?"

"Why wouldn't you? Every man wants to explore the world. I
knew how you felt about the limitations of Swamp Creek. I remember you cursing these fields and these animals and talking about how
much you hated Daddy."

"I never said that."

"Oh, come on! At least let's tell the truth to each other, Willie
James."

"Well, maybe it wasn't as easy for me to leave as it was for you. You
had the ability to walk away from things, you know."

"What are you trying to say, Willie James?"

"I'm saying I was never as free from Daddy as you were. I was the
oldest son and I was supposed to stay by his side, right?" His tone suggested regret.

"But, big brother, what about you? Is that what you wanted for
yourself?"

"Nobody gets a chance to want anything for theyself around here.
You know that. Ain't that why you left? In order to have something
all to yourself?"

"I suppose," I pondered. "You didn't have to stay all your life, did you?"

"I ain't never knowed nothin' but Swamp Creek, and I guess I never will. It crossed my mind to leave a couple of times, but I didn't. Daddy needed me."

"For what?"

"To work in the fields. You left and Sister was threatening to leave, and I felt I'd better stay so Daddy would have somebody."

"He has Momma, doesn't he?"

"Momma don't belong to him. He didn't create her. He needed to see somethin' which wouldn't exist if he didn't. That was me."

"Why are you so committed to keeping Daddy alive and feeling good about himself?"

"I ain't. I'm tryin' to keep Momma alive."

"I don't understand."

He continued, "You know how Daddy feels about women. He'd just as soon rape one as tip his hat. He got mad with Momma when you disappeared. Said you probably wouldn't have left if she had been doin' what she was s'pose' to. Whatever that was." Willie James paused and then said, "Everything what done gone wrong in this family Daddy blame on Momma. I know you and her ain't neva been friends, but I kinda feel like I oughta stick around for her sake."

"What about your sake?"

"What about it?"

"Are you gonna let Momma and Daddy consume all of you? I mean, when are you gonna stand up and claim your own existence?"

"I ain't got nothin' to claim, T.L. I was never smart like you, I ain't neva been too good-lookin', and God ain't seen fit to give me too many breaks in life. Look like to me I ain't got no choice."

"But you do, Willie James. You do. You got to insist upon your own happiness, on your own terms. You're beautiful if you think you are. And you are smart. You never did too well in school because you didn't try hard."

"You wrong there, little brother. I tried real hard. I gave myself headaches trying to memorize poems and learn algebra. It wouldn't come to me. I acted like I didn't care 'cause I was failin' and couldn't help it. I didn't wanna be a failure, not unless I chose to be one. It's OK, though. I'm gettin' by."

"But gettin' by ain't good enough, Willie James."

"It's gon' have to be. You got somewhere I can go?"

I did not. I wasn't even sure what I was doing with my own life, much less his.

We finished feeding the cows. I wanted to say something profound to inspire my brother to take control of his own life, but I found no words. Once we left the field, we returned the buckets to the barn, and as we walked back toward the house, Willie James said, "I'm glad you left, T.L. I was hoping one of us would get out of this hellhole and live to tell about it."

"Well, here I am." I held out my arms like an actor at the close of a play.

"Yeah, here you are," said Willie James with a fake smile. "Here you are and there she is." He pointed to Sister's grave.

I did not understand Willie James's meanness. "Why are y'all doing this to me?"

"OK, I'm sorry. But I think you could have done better, at least by her. Now that she's gone, ain't no way for you to make things right. And just in case you were planning to ask me, no, I don't know what happened. I really don't."

"How do you expect me to believe that?"

"It don't really matter what you believe. I came in out of the field one day and saw the fresh grave. I ran from the tractor and asked Momma what was going on. She stared at the mound and said nothing. I kept asking and finally she screamed, 'Yo' sista done gone and killed herself! We buried her right away. I didn't want you and yo' daddy to face no funeral. She would have wanted it that way.' I was going to argue, but I didn't see no need. I couldn't bring her back, so I parked the tractor and fed the cows. I knew Sister didn't kill herself. But since I didn't have any other explanation, I left it alone."

"Why didn't you keep asking Momma until she told you the truth?"

"Because I ain't like you, T.L. I can live without knowing some things."

"But can you live without knowing how Sister died?"

"I been doing it, ain't I?"

"Yes, but that doesn't mean you can do it for a lifetime."

Willie James wanted to say something badly. "Momma had a strange look in her eyes that day. She kept saying, 'My baby, my baby.' I tried to ask her what happened. I was cryin'. I knew somethin' was wrong, really wrong, but she wouldn't say nothin'. She was drippin' with sweat and rockin' herself back and forth like she was in another world. I tried to grab her and ask what was wrong, but she wouldn't budge. She just kept sayin', 'Yo' sista's dead, boy. Yo' sista's dead.'"

"Why don't you believe she committed suicide?"

"Because Sister had a plan of how she was gonna leave here. She was sure about it, T.L. She didn't kill herself. I know she didn't."

"I don't think she would have, either, but you don't have even a guess as to what really happened?"

Willie James studied my eyes deeply and said, "Daddy know somethin'. I know he do. But, T.L., he'll kill you 'fo' he tell you. I ain't asked him nothin'."

"Then how do you know he knows something?"

"'Cause he come home and saw the grave and acted like it's been there his whole life."

"What?"

"It didn't move him at all. I knew he was gon' flip and trip out on Momma and act like a madman 'cause his baby girl was dead, but all he did was nod his head when he walked by the grave. Dat's why I think Daddy know what happened. Plus, don't nothin' happen round here 'less Daddy give the OK. You know dat."

"Man, I must be losing my mind. All this seems normal to you?"

"No, it don't. But who I'm gon' question? I ain't neva been bold as you, T.L."

"I got to question somebody. I can't live like this. Maybe you can, but I can't."

"Maybe you ain't got nothin' to lose."

"What do you mean?"

"I live here. I got to live here, 'cause I ain't got nowhere else to go. I can't stir up shit and leave. I got to walk easy, man, or my life will be a livin' hell every day."

"But you grown now, Willie James. We ain't kids no more. You ain't got to bow to Daddy like you his slave."

"Maybe I ain't his slave, but I sho' ain't free."

"You got to make yourself free, Willie James."

"How you do dat?"

"By declaring your freedom."

"I wish it was that easy, little brother, but it ain't." Willie James halted. "I was seein' this girl about two years ago named Arbella. We wuz courtin' pretty hard. I brought her home and introduced her to Momma and Daddy one evenin'. They wuz nice and all—you know how they do—but after I came back from takin' her home, Daddy asked me, 'Is dat de best thang you can find to fuck?' I thought she was pretty. In fact, she was beautiful to me. But Daddy said she looked homely. He told me to find someone better so I broke up with her. I ain't found nobody else, though."

"You mean you left her because Daddy thought she was ugly?"

"Yep. I didn't want to hear his mouth, and I didn't want him to hurt Arbella's feelin's one day. I was scared Daddy would be rude to her and tell her she was ugly to her face."

"Willie James! You can't give Daddy that much power."

"He already got it. I ain't got to give him nothin'."

"His power only worked because we were kids!"

"No, it works right now. I know I could have stayed with Arbella and married her, but the hell Daddy would make her pay wouldn't be fair. She said she didn't understand my fear of him and I told her she never would, but I couldn't ever see myself confronting him."

"Why couldn't you? You're a grown man, Willie James!"

"Ain't nobody grown to Daddy but Daddy. Since I don't know nothin' 'bout no other life, I felt like I didn't have no choice but to please him. He told me a pretty girl would come along one day, but I ain't met her yet. I think I ain't goin' to."

"Willie James, are you crazy? Go find Arbella and marry that woman! Love is too hard to come by in this life to let it go easily."

"I didn't let it go easily. Man, I cried for days about Arbella. It tore me up to let her go without a reason I felt in my heart. But I didn't have no choice."

"Why didn't you get your own place and start your own family?"

"Wit' what? I ain't got no money 'cause I'm workin' for Daddy and you know he don't pay. Food and shelter is 'bout all you git, and wit'out some education, I couldn't git no good-payin' job. I guess doin' what I been doin' is gonna have to work."

"Are you satisfied with that?"

"I'm tryin' to be."

"You don't have a dream, Willie James? You're OK with Daddy ruling you like a little child?"

"I got to be 'cause I ain't got no other choice. It's all right, though. The Good Lawd'll keep takin' care of me."

I abandoned the discussion when I realized it was going in circles. Willie James put the feed bucket on the ground next to the barn door.

"Is you free, T.L.?" he posed out of nowhere.

I didn't quite know how to answer him. I had never thought about the possibility that I wasn't.

"Of course I'm free, man. I wouldn't have it any other way."

"Why you come back here then?"

I was stunned. "I, um, thought I needed to come back and find out some things."

"What difference would they make if you already free?"

I couldn't answer the question. Willie James was making too much sense.

"To be perfectly honest, I don't know. Maybe I ain't as free as I thought I was."

"Seem like ain't nobody free really. We all tied to somethin' or somebody."

"Maybe you're right."

"Yep."

Willie James and I investigated each other's faces and raised our eyebrows knowingly. For an instant, I wished I could have taken him away from Swamp Creek long enough to show him the world. He would be amazed, I thought. He was the obedient child, the one who never rocked the boat. He deserved to know he didn't have to succumb to Daddy's demands. Yet what would I do with him afterward? His loyalty to Daddy and Momma would leave him with guilt bigger than anything I could handle.

"How long you stayin'?" Willie James sought to lighten the mood.

"I don't know. Until I find out what happened to Sister, I suppose."

"Stay awhile, T.L., if you can." Willie James's voice sounded like that of a man in need. "If you can't, I understand, but if you can, it'd be nice." He nodded his head and left the barn.

I didn't say a word.

8

Had Willie James told me how Sister died, I would have left Swamp Creek that Sunday. After our little chat, however, I knew it wasn't going to be him. He was scared to death of Momma and Daddy and afraid to think of what life would be like without them. He was also terrified of what they might do to him if he told me what happened. I couldn't blame him for his silence. Our family had always reverted to silence when speaking threatened to annihilate our comfort zones. Willie James knew no other way to bear the weight of Daddy's authority. At times, I felt like Willie James wanted to tell me, but since he couldn't imagine a life on his own terms, he had no choice but to follow Daddy's edict. I could tell my agony moved his heart, yet, again, his compassion was certainly not greater than his fear. So he kept his distance from me and probably prayed that I wouldn't confront him again.

Walking back to the house, I thought about my older sister, Shelia. People implied our extraordinary similarities. She was pretty and smart as a whip, Ms. Polly said. Her kindness and exuberant spirit were rare, even eerie, for a child. Folks said she drowned in Ole Man Blue's pond a week after her fifth birthday. I overheard Daddy years ago talking to Mr. Blue on the phone about it. Daddy said Shelia had been missing for days and everybody in Swamp Creek stopped what they were doing to look for her. It was mid-November and folks were hopeful that, wherever she was, she was inside. After three days, Daddy said, he stopped searching. "If a five-year-old child can't find her way down de road and back, she a fool anyway." Shelia loved to eat, so he was sure hunger would make her reappear. He was wrong. A week went by and no word from Shelia. He said he wasn't worried. "De Lawd's will be done." Then, one day, Old Man Blue was out checking on one of his cows, Daddy said, and noticed a red object floating in his pond. He didn't think anything of it at first, but then he remembered Momma had told Ms. Polly that Shelia was wearing her red coat the last time they saw her. He walked over to the pond, waded in a short distance, and, sure enough, it was Shelia. He trembled in horror, for her body was floating faceup. This is what Ole Man Blue told Daddy. She had a big grin on her face and her arms were stretched out like she had been crucified. He wasn't sure whether to pull her from the pond or leave her as she was. He hesitated a moment but then took her body to his house and immediately called Momma and Daddy. When they got there, Shelia wasn't smiling anymore. Privately, they concluded Ole Man Blue was probably in a state of shock and didn't know what he was talking about, but Daddy said Ole Man Blue insisted, "She was smiling, I tell ya! When I laid her in dat bed she was smiling. I know she looks pale and frowned now, but just a few minutes ago, she was smilin'. I ain't crazy. I know what I saw. I had enough sense to drag her out of the pond, didn't I? What make you think I ain't got enough sense to know how she was lookin' when I dragged her? She was smilin' big and any minute I thought she might open her eyes and tell me everything she wanted me to know. Soon as y'all come, though, she stop grinnin'. I can't explain it, but it's sho' de truth." Momma and Daddy probably didn't say anything else. I suppose they thanked Ole Man Blue and Daddy carried Shelia's body back to the house.

I asked Ms. Janey about the funeral. She said everybody cried except Momma and Daddy. They sat in church as though required to be there against their will. As soon as the funeral ended, Ms. Janey said, Momma and Daddy accompanied the casket to the graveyard, covered it up, and never mentioned Shelia's name again. I wouldn't have known I had another sister if I hadn't overheard Daddy's conversation. Of course, I told Sister about it. She was surprised but accepted, quite easily, the reality of another sibling. Yet Shelia's death puzzled me for a long time. I seemed to have all the details, but I wasn't at peace about it. I asked Grandma, but she didn't know any more than I did. Then, one day, it hit me. It wasn't Shelia's death that was troublesome; it was the funeral. The way Ms. Janey described it didn't fit the conventions of a Swamp Creek homegoing. I went through some of Momma's old papers to reexamine the obituary, but I didn't find it. In fact, I realized Momma didn't even have a copy. She had kept no record of the passing of her daughter from life to death. Maybe she wanted to rid herself of all memory of Shelia. I remembered what Ms. Janey had said: "Marion was fine. It was the rest of us who were crying. She never shed a tear." Momma undoubtedly told them, "Oh, don't cry, baby. Shelia's all right." I couldn't figure out why, but there was another reason Momma didn't have Shelia's obituary. I went to Ms. Janey's house and asked, from the porch, to examine her copy. Everything was normal until I got to the poem Ms. Janey said Momma told everyone Shelia had written before she disappeared:

> I play hide-and-seek
> with myself sometimes.
> "Ready or not, here I come."
> But then I can't find myself
> And the game ceases to be fun.

"What?" I exclaimed aloud.

"Your mother said Shelia wrote it. It seems a little bizarre to me, too, son."

I knew I was on to something. Ain't no way a five-year-old could have written a poem that complex. If Shelia didn't write it, who did? And, more important, why? No one lived in Swamp Creek who was literary enough to care about poetry, except Ms. Janey and Ms. Pauline. And of course, Momma wouldn't have made any such concession on their behalf. I didn't understand. I pondered for weeks, trying to piece together some sort of explanation, but nothing materialized. Eventually, I let it go.

Instead of going inside, I turned abruptly and decided to walk down to Old Man Blue's place and visit Ms. Polly. The house was dark except for a lamp burning in the living room window. I was usually scared to walk those dark dirt roads alone, yet for some reason, I wasn't scared that evening. I suppose Sister's death made me immune to fear. I heard hoot owls and all kinds of rustling in the grass next to the road, but the sounds didn't bother me at all.

I stepped onto the porch and stood there a moment. The house was nothing grand. It was made of two-by-fours and had a tin roof. There were only four rooms—a living room, bathroom, kitchen, and bedroom—but the house had always been squeaky clean. I hesitated a moment because I thought about how content Mr. Blue and Ms. Polly were. They were old folks who owned few worldly possessions and had no desire for them. They didn't have a brick home, a fine car, or a heavy bankroll, although people said Mr. Blue had a coupla thousand dollars hidden away. Their kids sent them money every month and he sho' ain't spent it on nothing, others said. The things that brought them joy were children, honeysuckles, and fresh catfish. They didn't care about mink coats or forty-dollar Stevie Wonder concert tickets. Their health seemed to be their joy.

I knocked hard because Ms. Polly's hearing was bad even when I was a child.

"Come on in," she said without moving from her rocker.

"How y'all doin'," I said loudly as I entered the front room.

"Oh Lawd, chile, come on in heayh and sit down! I'm sittin' up heayh half-noddin'. I'm sho' is glad you done made it back home."

She grabbed the arms of the rocker and began to rise, offering me her seat.

"Oh, no ma'am, I'll sit right here on the couch. I came by to holler at y'all since I told Mr. Blue I would."

"Well, I'm sho' is glad you seed fit. Go'n in de kitchen thar and fix you a plate. Got some roast and cabbages and collards, and you can have one of dem fried pies if you wont it." She started grinning because she knew that's exactly what I wanted.

"No, ma'am, I just ate. But I sho' will have one of those pies."

"Help cho' self, boy."

That fried pie almost made me hurt myself. The crust was extra flaky, crumbling heavily every time I took a bite. The cinnamon, nutmeg, and brown sugar made my mouth water like a salivating canine's.

"Ms. Polly, your fried pies are the best!" I exclaimed.

"Oh, boy, hush yo' mouth. I throwed dem thangs together dis moaning when I was half-'sleep." She chuckled.

"What cho' momma nem doin' dis evening?"

"Sittin' round watchin' TV, I guess."

We both smiled at each other like we were about to speak, but neither of us did. Mr. Blue said nothing more than, "How you doin' dis evenin', boy?" the entire time I had been there. The silence was becoming awkward so I decided to direct the conversation.

"How are your children, Ms. Polly?"

"Oh Lawd, chile, dey's jes' fine. You know dey calls me every weekend and lets me talk to my grandchi'ren. Dey wears me out on dat phone, chile!"

Ms. Polly knew if her children didn't call every Saturday night she would have a fit. All the fuss about being worn-out was simply drama.

"I sure am glad to know they all doin' fine." I couldn't say much more than that because I hadn't called my own mother in ten years.

"You sho' looks well, boy! You done gone off 'way from heayh and got right handsome. Jus' as tall!"

Ms. Polly grinned at me as she spoke. I was grateful for her attempt to make me feel good, but I was neither tall nor handsome.
Both of us knew it.

"What chu doin' back round dese parts?"

"I'm not sure. In my heart, I felt the need to come home."

"What for?"

"I don't know, Ms. Polly. I been tryin' to define my life, and, somehow, I ended up back in Swamp Creek."

Mr. Blue rocked in his rocker, seemingly oblivious to our exchange.

"Well, you back now. What chu done found out?" Ms. Polly asked
curiously.

I could tell she didn't mean to ask that question. At least not yet.
Her mouth twitched, both from the desire to retrieve her words and
from the frustration of knowing she could not.

"Ms. Polly, you've been like a mother to me. Can you please tell
me what's going on round this place? No one will tell me anything."

"I don't know what—"

"You know 'zactly what he mean, Polly," Mr. Blue said softly. He
neither raised his head nor said anything more.

"Baby, that thang done troubled me since it happened, and I still
ain't got no understandin'. I walked ova theah early one afternoon
and saw yo' momma diggin' like a wild woman. I stood beside that big
oak out from the yard and watched her. I didn't say nothin' 'cause I
didn't want to disturb her. She looked frantic and panicky. I started
gettin' scared 'cause I ain't neva seen nobody act like dat befo'." Ms.
Polly shook her head from side to side sadly. She continued, "All a
sudden she dropped the shovel and ran into duh house. I started to
follow her and ask her what was duh matter, but my spirit told me not
to. I stood dere, tryin' to make sense of all this. A minute or two later,
I saw her draggin' somethin' big out of duh house. It seemed like a
body wrapped in a sheet, but I wasn't sho'. The sheets were bloody
and dirty. I covered my mouth to keep from hollerin'. I still didn't

know what was goin' on, but I knowed it was bad news. I turned to run and go get somebody, but I decided to wait and see what cho' momma was gon' do next."

Mr. Blue gazed at Ms. Polly, warning her not to say too much.

"Yo' momma took what she was draggin' and throwed it in dat hole she dug. Then she started coverin' it up real fast like she was scared. In a minute or two, the hole was full of dirt again. She stared at it real hard and walked away real slow like she was satisfied. She took the shovel back to the barn, I guess. I don't know fo' sho' 'cause dat's when I left. I was scared, chile; I didn't know what to do. I come home and started readin' my Bible and askin' de Lawd to give me understandin'.'"

"You didn't tell anybody?" I asked.

"Not for 'bout three days. Blue keppa astin' me what was de matta wit' me, but I didn't say nothin'. Then I got up one morning and he told me he heard yo' baby sister had died and she was buried in y'all's backyard. That's when I couldn't keep it no mo'. I told Blue everythang."

"Is that all you know, Ms. Polly? Is that everything?" I leaned forward in desperation.

She studied Mr. Blue's face before she proceeded. "Well, I don't really know if I oughta be the one tellin' you this, T.L.," she said skittishly.

"Ms. Polly, please! My family won't tell me anything. I deserve to know! You know how close Sister and I were." I was about to scream.

"Yeah, Lawd, I remembers you two runnin' round heayh like y'all ain't got a care in de wurld. I'd see y'all and jes' go to grinnin'. Y'all was really somethin'!"

I knew she was evading the subject. I dropped my head to make her feel bad. It worked.

She was silent for a moment; then she said, "After ya' momma dropped dat bundle in de hole she throwed somethin' else in dere, too."

I waited for Ms. Polly to go on although I could tell she didn't want to.

"It looked like framed pictures. One of them I saw pretty clear 'cause she dropped it on de ground. When she bent ova to pick it up, she jes' happened to be holdin' it wheres I could see pretty good."

"Was it me?" I asked slowly, already knowing the answer.

"Yes, T.L., it was a picture of you. I believe de other one was yo' sister, but I ain't sho'. I couldn't believe what I was seein'. It didn't make no sense."

Mr. Blue had been unusually silent the entire time. He sat in his rocker like God, overseeing things. Ms. Polly proceeded.

"Like de day yo' daddy brought you home."

"Polly!" Mr. Blue hollered. He surged upward and gleamed at her, a sign she had committed a crime.

"Ms. Polly, I don't understand. What are you talking about?"

Ms. Polly realized Mr. Blue's objection. She had said far too much. Now she was praying God would take back her words, but He didn't.

"Mr. Blue, please tell me what Ms. Polly's talking about." I had no idea what they were about to reveal.

"Son, we ain't the ones oughta tell you this," Mr. Blue despaired.

"I was sho' you already knowed. Lawd have murcy!" Ms. Polly was about to cry.

I simply waited for one of them to speak. I wasn't leaving until they told me the truth, and they knew it.

Ms. Polly began to mutter methodically, "Yo' daddy brought you home when you wunnit nothin' but two or three days old. You was born in de winta and he had you wrapped up tight like a Christmas present. Blue saw him walkin' down de road and went out to meet him. He knew what yo' daddy was carryin'. Everybody knew. Blue said he peeked in dat blanket and yo' eyes was wide open and you was jes' grinnin' like you knowed eva'thang."

"Where was he bringing me from? I still don't understand. If Momma jes' had me, how could I be—"

Then I knew. Daddy had been with someone else. Oh my God.

"Son, I swear we thought you already knowed! I mean, I can't see why yo' daddy ain't told you de truth by now!" They knew they had said too much. I was weeping.

"Yo' daddy told me on de road dat it didn't make sense to try to act like you wunnit his. He said he was gon' raise you de bes' way he could and he was gon' ask Marion if she would be yo' momma. He said he knowed he done wrong by bein' wit' dat otha woman, but he couldn't do nothin' 'bout it. I told him I'd pray for him and his family, and if he needed me, to let me know. I watched him walk home and shook my head 'cause I knowed dat household was gonna have a rough time. But de next day yo' momma startin' braggin' 'bout dis baby she had when she ain't neva been pregnant! Folks went along and acted like dey was surprised, but dey knowed de truth. Everybody knowed."

"Except me, huh?" I was trembling all over. "Who was the other woman?"

Mr. Blue and Ms. Polly wouldn't say. "That's for yo' daddy to tell you," they said.

I got up to leave. The pictures of their children plastered on the walls made me envious of their familial unity. I saw baby, graduation, and wedding pictures. Such closeness only exacerbated the unrest in my heart concerning my own family.

"T.L., I am so sorry, baby. I didn't know you didn't know. I mean, you's a grown main. Yo' daddy oughta be 'shame'a his self not tellin' you." She rose to hug me. "You's still my boy, and don't chu neva fugot dat!" Ms. Polly was trying to comfort me, but it wasn't working.

"I need to go," I whined.

"Come back and see us again befo' you go, won't chu?" Mr. Blue invited awkwardly.

"Sure," I said, simply to be nice. I walked through the front door and onto the porch. Tears were still streaming down my face. I turned, prepared to holler, "Thank you," for the fried pie and the information, but I realized the two were standing right behind me.

"Thank you, Mr. Blue and Ms. Polly. You've helped me out more than you'll ever know. I came home for answers and you've certainly given me a few." I chuckled; they didn't.

I stepped off the porch and began to walk out of the yard as Ms. Polly said, "T.L." I turned. "Go with God." She was crying, too.

It took me over an hour to get home that night. It was hot as hell, but the heat was irrelevant. I was trying to ascertain how I could have been so stupid. I should have guessed my questionable maternity years ago. Momma never claimed to have loved me. Her contempt for me should have been my first clue. All mothers love their children, don't they? All my life, Momma had been courteous to me, careful to make sure my clothes were clean and my food prepared. However, she was also careful never to touch me or say a kind word to me. She had distinguished meticulously between love and civility. I suppose Daddy made her take me—she never would have done it otherwise—but he couldn't make her love me.

My tears flowed freely, blinding me, as I walked down that pitch-black road, and now I could see clearly why Momma never loved me. I was a bastard child, the living proof of Daddy's infidelity. I just didn't know it. I always felt unloved and rejected, and finally I knew why. I went out of my way sometimes to please Momma—clean the house, cook, whatever—in hopes that she would accidentally hug me, but she never did. Because I was not of her womb, I could never enter her heart. I didn't know why as a child, so I kept trying to make Momma love me. Anything I thought would make her happy I did. However, my efforts only angered her. She accused me of trying to "outdo" Willie James and Sister and told me my biggest problem was that I needed too much affirmation.

Finally, after twenty-five years of wondering, I understood why she hated me. Yet why did Momma blame me for Daddy's indiscretion? She should have resented him. He was the one who had committed adultery and had insulted her by asking her to embrace his sin and his son. He was the one arrogant enough to lay his crime before her and ask her not for forgiveness but for understanding. It was Daddy's patriarchy that allowed him to assume that Momma's commitment to him was unconditional while his commitment to her was ephemeral. Why was I made to carry the weight? In fact, Daddy asking Momma to raise me was like asking Momma to celebrate his extramarital exploits. I suppose that's why Momma couldn't despise him. She had accepted him and everything that came along with him, including his patriarchy, sexism, and self-assumed superiority. Consequently, she couldn't fault him for the same reason she had married him. Momma embraced all men as the same. If a woman was to have a man at all, and every woman needed a man, Momma said, she would simply have to tolerate his shit, and there was nothing she could do about it. I found it funny as a child that Daddy got all kinds of breaks while Momma was told to endure or get the hell out.

Momma took her vengeance out on me because I didn't know any better. Ignorant to the rules of gender and patriarchy, I was the only male she could abuse and exploit safely. She needed to do this to make at least one male in the family feel her resentment of men.

Walking home, taking the smallest steps possible, I noticed the night was more silent than usual. I heard no crickets, owls, or birds fluttering in the trees. It was as though nature had stopped to see what I would do or say. However, I had nothing to say, no drama to offer. I wanted to scream, to kick Daddy's ass, to wake up everyone in Swamp Creek and ask why I was the last to know. Yet I didn't have the strength. I was tired from being home—home can be a job—and a show at that hour of the night would have been senseless. I prayed I'd do the right thing with the truth I had found.

I reached the bend in the road and could see a small light in the house. I began to shake my head in disbelief. I chuckled out loud at the madness of all I had learned. How would I find out who my momma is? Daddy would never tell and certainly I wouldn't ask

Momma. Telling me would give her too much pleasure. I chuckled again. This was too much damn drama for such a small place.

The sweat rolling down my neck exacerbated my irritation. I wanted to say "fuck y'all" and go back to New York, but I couldn't. I had come home for answers I couldn't live without.

I stopped walking long enough to regain my composure. My eyes were full of tears, but I decided I didn't care to feign stability by wiping them away. Hell, my momma didn't care to know me, so I wasn't going to stress myself over her. But what if she did love me? What if she wanted to tell me, to embrace me as her own, but Daddy forbade her? The thought made me want to know her all the more. "A mother of my own," I said aloud. One who would love me, cuddle me, and be there for me regardless of what the world said about me. It was unimaginable. I was getting excited thinking about it. I really did care. I needed to. In addition to discovering the details of Sister's death, finding my mother became the hope that justified my continued stay in Swamp Creek. I didn't know where to begin searching, though. I couldn't think of anyone Daddy would have been sleeping with had he been offered the opportunity, and my fear of him kept me from being able to ask him. "I'll find out, though," I promised myself. "If I have to turn this backward-ass place upside down, someone's gonna tell me who killed my sister and who my momma is!" I laughed aloud. "Who am I screaming at?" I murmured, wiping tears from my eyes.

Passing Sister's grave, I said, "Girl, you wouldn't believe it if you heard it yourself! Lotta shit goin' on in Swamp Creek, and it ain't pretty."

I had reached the back door of the house. I decided not to let my folks know I knew the truth although I was determined to discover who had birthed me. I wouldn't leave Swamp Creek until I knew.

I walked into the house and Momma asked me where I had been.

"Down to see Ms. Polly," I said.

"How she doin'?" Momma asked, unconcerned.

At that moment, I considered telling her everything but resolved to hold my peace. "She's all right," I said.

I sat down for a moment, hoping Momma might be ready to talk about Sister, yet after a second she rose and went to bed without saying a word.

9

Monday morning came much too quickly with a bright, beautiful sunshine beaming through the paper-thin curtains and blinding me in bed. I felt like I had only been asleep an hour. My restlessness stemmed from both my inability to guess my maternal origin and my unwillingness to discontinue probing the family about Sister's death. I must have slept, however, because I recalled bits and pieces of dreams from throughout the night. One I remembered distinctly. A lady hugged me real hard and cried as she rubbed my head affectionately. She was beautiful, thin, tall, and walked with a divine eloquence. When she gazed into my eyes, I knew her, I felt her, I connected with her in a way only a son can with his mother. But I couldn't speak. I remember trying to tell her I loved her, but no audible sound emitted from my throat. All I knew to do was to hold her and pray she would never leave me again. Yet when I woke up, she was gone.

I crawled out of bed and dressed hurriedly, embarrassed for not having risen with the rest of the family. I didn't know what time it was, but I knew it was late because the sun was high in the sky. Swamp Creek folks didn't think much of people who slept past rooster crow.

I peered out the window and saw Momma working in the garden. "Good," I said jovially. "Maybe I can put this letter to George in the mailbox without anyone noticing." I ran out of the house quickly, hoping to complete my mission undetected, yet when I turned away from the mailbox I saw Momma staring at me through narrow, slanted eyes. Attempting to ignore her, I walked to the garden casually, strolling like a tourist in an exotic land.

"Good morning," I said cheerfully.

"Mornin' been gone, boy," Momma returned. She was picking peas, so I followed suit.

"Where are Daddy and Willie James?"

Momma feigned exasperation and said, "Cuttin' hay over in the other field."

"Why didn't Sister have a funeral, Momma?" I asked out of nowhere.

"Don't know," she said lightly.

"Why don't you?" I asked. "When people die—"

"I don't know, boy," Momma repeated, and kept on picking peas. She had on a big straw hat and an old floral-pattern dress that blew at the slightest breeze.

"Are you glad I'm home, Momma?"

"Are you glad you home?"

She had caught me off guard. "Um, yes," I said much too slowly. "And now I wish you'd tell me what happened to Sister. I don't understand why her death is such a big secret."

"It ain't no secret," Momma maintained. "Everybody know she dead."

"But everybody don't know *how* she died."

"Everybody ain't suppose' to know that. It ain't everybody's business."

"But it's my business, ain't it?"

"Nope." Momma glared straight at me.

"Why ain't it, Momma? She was my sister!"

Momma shook her head, perturbed, and put peas in a #3 tin tub she used for a basket.

"Come on, Momma! Tell me. Please."

"I can't tell you nothin' 'cause I don't know nothin'."

Momma studied my face like she really wanted to speak but then dropped her head and continued working. Suddenly, she cackled aloud, glanced at me in the next row, and declared, "You come back here after ten years and think folk oughta stop what they doin' and answer all yo' questions. You always was full o' yo'self." Her boisterous laughter frightened me. Indeed, she kept laughing as though she had heard the funniest joke. There was nothing I could say. I knew I was being patronized, and no one could do it like Momma. I finished the row hastily and told her I was going to help Willie James. She dazed at me blankly, obviously uninterested.

I took my time getting to the other field. My memory of farming in Arkansas was everything but nostalgic. When I arrived, Willie James was surprised to see me. He turned off the tractor engine and walked over to where I was standing under the big cypress tree.

"You come to work or to stand around?" he asked, wiping sweat from his brow.

"I can help you out if you want me to," I said.

"Well, there's plenty to do round here," Willie James said and surveyed the land.

"Before I do anything, can I ask you a question?"

"It ain't about Sister, is it?"

"Yes, it is."

Willie James's entire countenance changed. "T.L., why you keep bringing that up? I done already told you I don't know nothin'."

"Oh, come on, Willie James! I'm not crazy. Of course you know something. At least give me one detail. You know how close we were and how this is hurtin' me inside. Help me out, big brother."

Willie James stagnated and stated, "I shouldn't tell you nothin'. You ran off and left Sister like you didn't care nothin' 'bout her. All she did was cry 'bout you. Every day she would ask me if I thought you was all right. I said of course you was. You was strong and smart, too."

"We've been over this, Willie James," I intoned. "I was trying to save myself."

"Well, you did that."

Willie James made me feel like my entire life had been one gigantic mistake. I felt selfish, self-centered, and thoughtless.

"I overheard Momma tell Daddy that Sister was pregnant," Willie James announced, and began to walk back toward the tractor.

"Pregnant?" I screeched.

"That's what Momma said. They thought I was out in the field somewhere. They were yelling at each other like little children. Daddy couldn't believe Sister was pregnant while Momma was sayin' it like it was no big deal."

"How could she have been pregnant?"

"How do most folk get pregnant?"

"You know what I mean."

"That's all I know. She couldn't have been far along 'cause she wasn't showin'. Or maybe she was carryin' small."

"Who was the father?"

"How in the hell would I know? Plenty of boys round here her age."

"Oh my God." I covered my mouth in disbelief.

"Well, now you know. Don't ask me no more questions."

"Thanks, Willie James," I said.

He nodded his head. "Do I still get the help?"

"Sure," I said, approaching the old John Deere tractor. I dreaded every moment of handling that antique contraption, which boasted of neither power steering nor air-conditioning, but I couldn't renege on the promise. Mounting the tractor, I said, "This certainly brings back old memories."

"I'm sure it do," Willie James jeered. He left me cutting hay in the field and went to fix the broken fence where the cows had been getting out.

As I bobbed up and down on the ragged tractor, my mind wouldn't let go of Sister. Pregnant. Wow. She was only seventeen, which was certainly old enough to get pregnant, but it didn't make sense. Sister having sex was a notion I never imagined. Sex was simply a reality that I didn't associate with her, probably because she was a child when I saw her last. Still, Sister and sex collided in my mind to the point where I had probably made a eunuch of her. I never wanted to think it possible that another man would enter her most intimate space without my knowledge, yet I was forced to admit not only the possibility but also the fact of his entry. I wanted Sister to provide me details from the grave about this baby she had conceived and how the process of lovemaking had gone wrong. I could hear her in my head say, "It's not what you think, T.L." Nevertheless, I wanted to know who had violated my sister.

I had gotten to the end of the field and prepared myself for the fight to turn the old, rusty tractor around. The brakes were older than me. Somehow I managed, though, and soon felt sweat walking proudly down my back. It had to be one hundred degrees or better, and dust was flying like white folks around money. I started singing to myself the way I did years ago to pass the time more quickly:

> "I found Jesus, yes I did, and I'm glad!
> I'll never, no never, be sad, my Lord;
> I've tasted his love divine,
> He's with me all the time,
> I found him, I found him, I found Jesus,
> And I'm glad!"

Swamp Creek's church choir sang this song at least three times a month when I was growing up. It was the only song the choir knew well so we sang it often. For many, we sang it too often. In fact, Grandma said God was sick of hearing it. Plus, God found us, she said, 'cause we were the ones lost, not Jesus.

I surveyed the field and admitted to myself I'd be there until sundown. I didn't remember the field being that broad. I was dying of thirst, coated with dust and sweat, and thoroughly miserable.

I determined to ask every young boy in Swamp Creek if he had slept with my sister. Of course, they probably wouldn't tell the truth. Yet, honestly, I wasn't as concerned about the sexual act as I was about Sister's mental state before she died. Was she happy? Depressed? Did she talk about me?

These wonderings frustrated me until I had to stop pondering them. I sighed deeply, tired from handling the old tractor, which was whipping my ass, and sang another song:

> *"Oh, they tell me of a home,*
> *where my loved ones have gone;*
> *Oh, they tell me of a land,*
> *so bright and fair—*
> *Oh, they tell me of an uncloudy day!"*

This had been Sister's favorite song. Although she was young, she would get to hollerin' the notes and folks would get to shoutin' and church would be on fire all day long. Sister would glance at me and smile 'cause she knew her singing had moved me beyond words. I was her accompaniment, and every time she sang, I cried.

One day after church she told me, "We gon' be famous one day, me and you. We gon' go round de whole world singin' and makin' folks happy. Jes' me and you."

"Oh really?" I laughed.

"Really! When I git big, we gon' jes' leave one day and never come back. We can do it. I know we can."

"What about Momma and Daddy? You ain't gon' come back and see them?"

"Nope," Sister proclaimed confidently.

"Why not?"

She was hesitant.

"Don't you think Momma nem gon' worry about you?" I asked, curious to hear her response.

"Yeah, but—"

"But what?"

"They ain't gon' worry 'bout you. And if they don't like you, I don't like them."

I smiled. She was too young to be involved in the tension between my folks and me, although clearly she understood more than I had thought.

"Sure, we'll go sing around the world. Me and you."

We joked about headlines featuring our names and about all the money we'd make. We agreed to buy us an island where no one would live but us. Those were great days.

Sister was a smart child, analyzing things and figuring out stuff well beyond her years. For instance, I noticed her observing a caterpillar one day.

"What cha lookin' at?"

"Jes' this caterpillar."

"What's wrong with it?"

"Nothin'."

"Then why you starin' at it like that?"

" 'Cause I'm gonna watch it turn into a butterfly."

I laughed hysterically. "You can't watch a caterpillar turn into a butterfly, girl."

"Why not?"

"Because it takes too long."

"I'll jes' have to wait."

"You'll be out here in the yard for days."

"I don't care. I wanna see it."

"It's not that easy."

"Then I'll take it in the house and watch it."

She scooped the caterpillar in her hands, placed it in a mason jar, and set the jar underneath her bed, afraid Momma might throw it

out. After a couple of days, Sister didn't understand why the caterpillar had not become a butterfly. I didn't have the heart to tell her that
the caterpillar had died from suffocation in the tightly sealed jar and,
now would never become a butterfly. Still, Sister kept her fingers
crossed. Every day she would wake up hopeful her caterpillar had
transformed, but after examining the jar, she would drop her head,
disappointed. One morning, I heard her scream.

"T.L.! It's a butterfly! It's a butterfly!"

"A butterfly?" I said to myself. "That's not possible." I ran into her
room.

"Here," Sister said, crying tears of joy.

I studied the jar, but all I saw was the dead caterpillar.

"I don't see no butterfly, girl."

"It's there! It's invisible, but it's there!"

She began to dance around the room happy she finally got what
she had been waiting for. I was worried; there was no butterfly in the
jar. Nevertheless, Grandma told me not to fret. "Sometimes folks see
what they wanna see," she said. Maybe Sister did see a butterfly, I
concluded. She saw a lot of things thereafter, like imaginary friends,
spaceships, and angels. Her imagination was incredible for someone
her age.

"Heaven is like a big church meeting," she told me later the same
day. "The angels sing all day long and never stop. And people shout
and cry and dance and just be good all the time. You're on the piano,
T.L."

"How can I play the piano in heaven and be down here at the
same time?"

"It's possible," she insisted. "God preaches every day to make sure
everybody stay nice. I'm the choir director." Sister stood and flung her
arms wide. "Heaven got flowers everywhere! There is a lot of tall trees
and green grass and it's the most beautiful place you ever seen. The
animals sit in church with the people and listen to God. Some of
them sing in the choir, too."

I didn't argue.

"But everybody ain't in heaven. All the mean people live with the devil."

"Who are the mean people?"

Sister hesitated. "A lot of white people." I was about to respond when she added, "And some black people, too."

"Do you know who they are?"

"Yes," she said sadly, about to cry. However, to avoid emotional trauma, Sister simply dropped the subject altogether and resumed her original focus. "I like heaven better. There's a whole lotta food, and Grandma don't mind cookin' all day long. Angels tell her, 'Ma'am, you sho' can cook!' And Grandma say, 'Oh, git on outta heayh!'"

I roared exultantly. Somehow, Sister's voice had metamorphosed and sounded exactly like Grandma's. Sister was not simply imagining things; rather, she was living a life all her own, with ideas and possibilities she had designed. As a child, she knew she needed a life other than the one Momma and Daddy had given her, so she created her own world and it became her constant dwelling place.

Around noon, Willie James summoned me to come get lunch. He had gone to the General Store and bought bologna, crackers, potato chips, and two peach Nehi sodas. We sat underneath a grove of small trees at the back end of the field as we ate.

"It's hot as hell today, man," Willie James protested, breaking the awkward silence.

"Shit, this is crazy!" I confirmed.

"Folk have heatstrokes behind this kinda heat."

"I know! I don't remember it being hot like this when we were kids. Was it?" I sulked.

"It probably was. We jes' didn't pay no 'tention."

"It's deep, what you start paying attention to when you get grown."

"Yeah, it is." Willie James passed me a soda and broke out in uncontrollable amusement.

"What are you laughing about?" I was giggling, too, primarily because he was.

"Remember the time Daddy sent you to the store to get some nigga toes?"

"Oh, shut up! Daddy made me make a complete fool of myself!"

"Did you really ask dat white man to sell you some nigga toes?" Willie James was crying with glee.

"Shut up!" I said, pushing him playfully.

He bellowed merriment from deep within. "What did he tell you, T.L.? I forgot."

"Man, you ain't forgot! You jes' wanna make fun of me!"

"No, no, no! For real! I forgot! What did he say?" Willie James struggled hard to appear serious although suppressed mirth contorted his face.

"He told me, 'Son, you don't need to buy no nigga toes. You got ten of 'em!'"

Willie James lost control of his faculties and spilled soda all over himself. He rolled on the ground laughing unashamedly and tried unsuccessfully to regain his composure.

"Man, dat's the funniest thing I ever heard in my entire life!" he said, resuming a position next to me. "Daddy shoulda been 'shame' o' hisself, sending you to dat white man talkin' 'bout some nigga toes! You didn't know dat nigga toes is Brazilian nuts?" Willie James started rejoicing all over again.

I chirped along. When I thought about it, it really was hilarious.

"What about the time you cussed out Ms. Sandidge, Willie James, when you thought she wasn't listening?"

"Who told you about that?" Willie James shouted.

"Grandma."

"Man, I got a whoopin' you wouldn't believe!"

"What did you say, Willie James?" I asked delightfully.

"You know what I said, fool!"

"No, I don't! I wasn't there!"

"But you still know! You said Grandma told you!" Willie James was trying his best not to retell the story, but I wouldn't let up.

"Ah, come on, man! I never knew exactly what you said. You know Grandma didn't tell it exactly like it happened!"

"OK, OK."

I was attempting to listen attentively, but my jubilation wouldn't be contained.

"We were standing behind the church. Scooter had jes' got a whoopin' 'cause he sucked his teeth at Ms. Sandidge. She was the Sunday school teacher for the kids, and everybody knew she didn't hear too good. Anyway, she asked me to stand up and read Hezekiah, chapter ten, verse five. I stood up and searched desperately for Hezekiah in the Bible. Suddenly, Ms. Sandidge screamed, 'There is no such book as Hezekiah in the Bible, young man! Now sit down! If you read the Bible as you should, you wouldn't be so stupid!' That's when I mumbled under my breath, 'I ain't as stupid as yo' stupid ass.'"

Willie James and I split our sides.

"Well, Ms. Sandidge heard me. The other kids did, too, but they acted like they didn't hear so I wouldn't get in trouble. 'What did you say, young man?' she asked me real slow. 'I ain't said nothin', Ms. Sandidge,' I said, scared to death. 'Oh yes, you did!' She grabbed me by the ear and took me out behind the schoolhouse and tore my ass up! I swear she beat me for about thirty minutes. She came back in and acted like nothin' happened.

"When Sunday school was over, Carol Ann, Ole Man Blue's granddaughter, came outside to find me. I was sitting on the old well behind the church steaming mad. 'You all right, Willie James?' she whispered.

"Why was she whisperin'?" I asked Willie James to evoke his drama.

"'Cause she didn't want me to jump on her and whip her ass 'cause I was so angry! I'm tellin' you, T.L., the fire in my eyes woulda scared anybody."

Willie James made the ugliest face he could to represent what he felt that day. "Anyway, I started tellin' Carol Ann 'bout how I was gonna whoop Ms. Sandidge's ass good. I said, 'I'ma catch dat bitch by herself one day and snatch dat wig off her head and kick her ass like I'm stompin' roaches. Goddamn deaf ho'! She always pickin' on me! Keep on fuckin' wit' me.' All of a sudden, Carol Ann's eyes became real big. I wasn't paying her no 'tention, though, because I was too mad. 'Who de fuck she think I am?' I went on. 'Some goddamn child? Hell, dat ho' don't know me. Muthafucka. I bet I kick her ass, what chu bet?' I looked up to see if Carol Ann was listening to me, and boy, you woulda thought I saw a ghost. Ms. Sandidge had been standing behind me the entire time! 'Oh no, Ms. Sandidge! I was jes 'trippin'! You know I was trippin'! Me and Carol Ann was shootin' de breeze and talkin'. You know how it go.' Ms. Sandidge didn't say a word to us. She told Momma and Daddy."

"You have to be lyin'!"

"Naw, I ain't lyin'! She told them every single word I said. When Daddy whooped me, he made me scream out a cussword real loud every time he hit me. I screamed, *Bitch!* Daddy hit me again and I hollered, *Muthafucka!* Daddy struck me again and I yelled, *Ho!* Daddy kept this up until I shouted every word I had called Ms. Sandidge!"

We rolled on the ground, crying, like two helpless little boys.

"Willie James, you were a straight fool! That beats any story I've ever heard!"

"Yeah, I was crazy. Me and Scooter." Willie James calmed. "Dat was my man. Me and him stayed in trouble. He was cool until it came time to get de whoopin'. He'd get real quiet 'cause he couldn't stand to get no whoopin'. Most times, he'd stand there and take de beatin' without ever sayin' anything. He was pretty amazin'. I miss ole Scooter."

"I wish I had known him. And Shelia, too. Did they look alike?"

"Yeah. Jes' alike. Most identical twins do."

"They weren't identical, Willie James. They weren't the same gender."

"I don't know how you explain it, but they were exactly alike. I mean *exactly*. People confused them all the time. Momma and Daddy, too."

I didn't dispute his testimony because I wasn't there, but the prospect he was right troubled me.

"Momma said they was identical twins in every way," Willie James maintained.

"What?"

"I took her at her word and went on 'bout my business. You best do de same."

I grunted but held my peace.

"Yeah, I miss ole Scooter," Willie James reminisced again. "He was great, but he was too fragile. Dat's why he shot hisself."

I turned my head suddenly toward Willie James. "Momma said he drowned."

"I know what Momma said, but it ain't de truth. Scooter shot hisself. I know 'cause I was there. We was out rabbit huntin' one evenin' alongside de river and Scooter started cryin'. I didn't know what was wrong, so I asked him. He said, 'I been thinkin', Willie James, 'bout dyin'.'

"'Why you thinkin' 'bout dyin', boy?' I asked him.

"'I don't know. I jes 'got a feelin'.'

"'You ain't fittin' to die, is you? You too young.'

"'You ain't neva too young,' Scooter said, gazing off into space.

"Since I didn't know what else to say, I didn't say nothin'. I spotted a rabbit a few minutes later and followed him, hoping to have him for dinner. I heard a shot behind me. I turned and saw Scooter on de ground and de snow around him soaked with blood like a red snow cone. I screamed, but nobody heard me. We was too far away. At first, I hoped some other hunters mighta shot him by accident, but after a moment of panic I knew. I put his head in my lap and rubbed his forehead as I cried. He was tryin' to tell me he wanted to die, but I didn't want to hear him."

"He was six years old talking like an old man?" I asked, amazed.

"Yeah. Him and Shelia was some unusual twins. They was like old people in little children's bodies."

"I wonder why Momma told me he drowned?"

" 'Cause that's what I told her. She had already lost Shelia the year before and I didn't want her to hurt no more than she had to. I told her we was huntin' back by de river and Scooter slipped in, hit his head on a big rock, and drowned. It wasn't true. I put his body in de water and held it under for a minute so his clothes would be wet, making it look like he drowned. I struck him in de head with a big rock so Momma and Daddy would think he hit his head when he fell in. They never knew he shot hisself in de head."

"Do you ever intend to tell them the truth?" I inquired, horrified.

"Nope. I did them a favor and I'd do it again."

Willie James's confidence forced me to drop the issue. I sat there, trying to ascertain how he had carried this secret for a lifetime.

He stood up and stretched, a sign it was time to return to the field.

"Ole Scooter's in a better place than we are, li'l brother."

"Amen," I stammered guardedly.

"I'll see you back at the house this evenin'. Thanks for the help."

"Sure," I mumbled as he walked away. "Thank you for the truth."

10

By sundown, I was exhausted. I despised farming, and now I knew exactly why. The last ten years had removed me far enough from the fields of Arkansas that I forgot what manual labor felt like. I had become a laborer of the mind, one who theorizes about the world and writes books to share those thoughts. More particularly, I had become a fiction writer. Nothing intrigued me more than to tell stories of how black people survived and how we created laughter in the eye of the storm. I wanted my words to heal hearts, incite joy, evoke tears, and initiate change. As a freshman at Clark College, I realized the magical power of literature and marveled that a person could take language and alter my existence without ever knowing me. I wanted such power in order to get on the inside of people and help them fix things. My dream was that, one day, one of my poems or short stories would make people cry or love themselves into their own liberty.

So, when I left Arkansas, I started writing. The stories people told at the Meetin' Tree became my text and gave me foundation for understanding the art of good literature. Students from all over the world gathered at Clark, and many of them made great additional characters for my stories. I started writing poems first, however, because I wanted to see if, in a few words, I could achieve profundity.

"What are you doing?" my friend Marsha asked one day.

"Writing a poem," I returned casually.

"What's it about? Can I see it?"

I wasn't feeling very secure. "Maybe later when I finish it."

She left, only to return moments later.

"Well, can I see it now?"

I was sitting in the Brawley Hall lounge. It had gotten dark and I had not bothered to turn on the lights. She didn't, either.

"I bet it's goooood!"

"You might be disappointed," I whimpered timidly.

We decided to go outside under the streetlight since the weather was nice.

"I'd rather read it to you myself, if you don't mind. It's kind of rough and I've made some marginal changes."

"Go for it," Marsha encouraged excitedly.

"It's called 'The Black Bouquet.'" I faltered a moment and then began reading:

> "I am that flower you picked and vased,
> Cut off from roots as such debased;
> No seed to come again next year,
> Turn brown and die alone in here—
>   you call me beauty
>
> "Arranged among the other ones,
> My friends the rose, the chrysanthemum,
> Placed on mantle high and bright,
> Our death will come soon one fortnight—
>   and still you call us beauty
>
> "Bouquet you call us in this vase,
> And look on us with prideful face;

As though you've done a wondrous thing
To rid us of our petaled wings—
  and dare to call us beauty

"Tossed in the trash with no remorse,
Dismissed, forgotten, no recourse;
'There will be more next year,' you say,
But we'll not ever see that day—
  and still you call us beauty"

"Oh my God!" Marsha clamored. "That was incredible!"

I was afraid she wasn't going to like it.

"That was the most beautiful poem I've ever heard in my life!"

She hugged me tightly, with tearstained eyes. "You're a writer, Thomas. I can't believe it! You are a real-life, bona fide writer! Write something else right now and let me hear it!"

"It's not that easy, girl," I chuckled. "Poems come to me when they get ready. I can't simply grab a sheet of paper and decide to write one."

"Why not?"

"It doesn't work that way. At least not for me."

"As soon as you write another one, let me know. I'll be glad to listen." Marsha stood there studying me.

"What's wrong?"

"I can't believe it." She threw her head back and examined the sky as though searching for understanding. "You are so good, Thomas. Your poem went all through me. It rhymed and flowed like Langston Hughes or Sonia Sanchez. You're gonna be famous. I can feel it."

"I doubt that," I said, hoping she was right.

"No, I'm serious. Sometimes I feel things before they actually happen, and this is one of those times. I'm serious! I can feel this. You're like a caterpillar waiting to transform into a beautiful butterfly. You know what I mean?"

I gaped at Marsha, dumbfounded, as I remembered Sister's jarred caterpillar under her bed.

"Wait and see." Marsha walked off nodding her head.

I didn't know whether I'd be famous or not. I merely wanted to write. Finally, I had moved a human being with my own words and experienced what God must have felt when He made the world—a sense of sheer ecstasy for having created a universe of possibilities out of nothing. I wanted to write again immediately, but my mind was blank. Instead, I sat under the streetlight watching other students go by, wondering what their lives were like, what they longed to do, to become. A pretty, mocha-complexioned sister waltzed by with her head hung low and I wanted to reach out and touch her and ask what I could do to make her life better. I didn't, though. Maybe she would read one of my poems one day, I hoped.

The day I arrived back in Swamp Creek I had several of my poems with me. I had intended to read them to anybody who cared to listen, but after getting home and discovering levels of impending drama, I dropped the idea. Swamp Creek was not a place for writers. People there loved words, but they weren't interested in changing their ideas. I didn't tell Momma or Daddy I had become a writer. They would have wondered why I got a Ph.D. if all I wanted to do was write.

By the time I got home from the field, night had descended. I parked the tractor by the barn and began strolling toward the house.

"That field ain't no joke, is it?" Willie James was leaning against Daddy's 1960 Chevy smoking a cigarette and drinking a Corona. I hadn't seen him standing there.

"Boy, you scared me to death," I said, startled.

"Didn't mean to scare you. Jes' wanted to speak."

We were silent for a moment.

"Yeah, that field wore me down, man. Bobbin' up and down all day drained me dry."

"I do it for a living."

"I'm glad I don't," I said, immediately wishing I could retract my words.

"It ain't bad after a while. You gets used to it. Ain't nothin' else to do."

"There are a lot of other things you could do, Willie James."

He sighed heavily. "Like what?"

Mosquitoes were in attack mode, and although we were losing the battle, our valiant fight was admirable.

"You could always go back to school."

"No, I can't. I wasn't good the first time. You know school was never my thing."

Yes, I knew, but I thought the suggestion alone might boost his self-esteem.

"Maybe you could start your own business then."

"Doing what? And with what?"

"I don't know, Willie James. I'm trying to help."

"I never said I needed help."

"I know. I thought maybe you needed something else."

"Something like what?"

"Like a life."

"Who said I ain't got a life? I ain't got yours, but mine is OK with me."

I thought to apologize but instead became silent and let it go.

"I'm gon' be round heayh the rest of my days, I believe," Willie James asserted after several minutes. "When you leavin' anyway?"

"Saturday. The Greyhound bus comes through Swamp Creek around five in the evening."

"Oh! We can get a lot more work outta you befo' you leave, huh?"

"Don't start!"

We both grinned, although we knew working those fields was no joking matter.

"I guess you done seen a lotta things and people from all ova de world."

"Yeah. The world is amazing, Willie James. People are different in some ways yet very similar in others."

"Tell me about it."

"About what?"

"The rest of the world." Willie James's eyes were glued to the ground. He sounded like he wanted to cry. "What's it like when you leave this damn place?"

I didn't know where to begin or exactly what to say. "The world is beautiful, big brother. People speak differently depending on where they come from. They think differently; they do things differently; they believe differently. Some people believe in God, some don't; some people love the opposite sex, some love the same sex; some people speak, some never say a word; and some spend their entire lives trying to determine who they are."

Willie James frowned. "How you gon' be alive and not know who you are?"

"Easy, actually. I don't mean they don't know their names or who their folks are. They're trying to understand their individuality, trying to discover what's unique about themselves. In truth, they're searching for that thing about them no one else can boast. It's what some people call personal identity."

"I see," Willie James said curiously. "It's wild. I ain't never been outside this old place. I been to town and back, but that's 'bout it. Maybe I'll get to see some of the world one day."

"Yeah, maybe."

Both of us knew better. Willie James would never leave Swamp Creek even if he had the chance. It was his comfort zone, his cocoon.

The mosquitoes were about to carry us away, so we got a couple of old tires and set them ablaze to ward off the little black vampires.

As the smoke ascended, I asked Willie James, "What's the one thing you wish for more than anything?"

He seemed to be ignoring me until he said, "I wish our family was a family."

I didn't expect that response. I didn't think he cared much about family love and unity, especially ours.

"I wish we could talk to each other real nice and stand up for each other like we suppose to. I wish we loved each other. I wish you didn't ever leave. I wish Sister was still here."

Willie James was more vulnerable than I had ever seen him. Maybe the beer helped loosen his otherwise reserved, inhibited nature.

"We got to do better, T.L. We ain't got nothin' but each other. You, too. I guess that's why you come back. Even with them degrees, you still ain't got shit if you ain't got family."

"I wouldn't quite say—"

"It's the bottom line, though. Don't feel bad. It's true for everybody. That's why God don't let you choose yo' family. You got to work with who you git. And you sho' got to work with 'em, 'cause ain't nobody gon' stand by you like yo' own folks."

"Family doesn't always mean blood relatives, Willie James. Family is those people who choose to love and support one another."

"OK, but blood mean somethin', don't it?" Willie James asked desperately.

"Yeah. It means those are the folks you come through to get here. That's about it."

"Who chooses which folk you'll be kin to?"

"God, I'm sure."

"I can't wait to hear God explain this one," Willie James mumbled.

"I want God to explain a lot of stuff," I concurred under my breath.

Willie James scoffed. My tone disturbed him and made him change the subject.

"You found out anything interestin' 'bout yo'self since you been home? You say dat's why you came, right?"

"Yeah, that's what I said all right." I started to tell him about Momma not being my mother but decided against it.

"You know what they say: if you look long enough you can find anything."

Instantly I changed my mind and resolved to take a risk and tell Willie James. I didn't have anything to lose, and neither did he. "Actually, I did discover something. It's kinda complicated, though, man, and I don't know if you truly want to know."

"Try me," Willie James prompted sluggishly.

"I was talking to Ms. Polly and Mr. Blue Sunday night and Ms. Polly told me—"

"Momma ain't yo real momma," Willie James completed my sentence after taking another gulp of beer.

"You knew?"

"Yeah. Everybody in Swamp Creek know."

"Why the hell didn't I know?"

" 'Cause you wasn't supposed to."

"Why wasn't I? It's my mother we're talking about here, isn't it?"

"Calm down, man. Shit. Ain't nothin' you can do 'bout it now. It don't mean nothin' noway."

"Who my mother is does mean something!"

"No, it don't. You said blood ain't deep, didn't you? Plus, you still the same person anyway."

"It's the truth I'm after, Willie James. Telling me Momma isn't my mother shakes the foundation of my personal identity."

"Why?"

"Because what I thought was my lineage ain't. I'm searching for the origin of my beginnings in the wrong woman."

"Not true. It's the woman who raised you who influenced you the most. This other woman simply carried you."

"Carrying a child is a sacred thing. There is a bond established between mother and child in the womb that lasts forever. The truth of this bond can never be erased."

"You sayin' you been feelin' this woman yo' whole life?"

"No, not exactly. Yet I have had a feeling I didn't belong here, you know what I mean?"

Willie James nodded.

"Since we were kids, I felt like Momma didn't like me, but I never knew why. Maybe it ain't important to you, but it is to me," I said contemptuously.

"Do what chu gotta do, but don't let the truth kill you. Bible say it'll set you free if you let it." Willie James finished the beer, then retrieved another from a cooler in the bed of the truck.

I investigated the stars and asked, "How long have you known?"

He shrugged his shoulders and said, "Long time. Folks used to talk about it all the time. How they kept it from you is a miracle."

"How did everybody else know? Daddy or Momma surely didn't tell."

"Who told you?" Willie James posed sarcastically.

We laughed. Whatever Ms. Polly knew instantly became known throughout Swamp Creek.

"To tell you the truth, there's a better explanation of why everybody knew," Willie James said, peering deep into my eyes.

"What is it?" I questioned curiously.

"The fact that Daddy was a ladies' man. He kept company with plenty of women other than Momma."

"Get out of here!"

"Shit, man. There's a lotta stuff you don't know. Remember Ms. Hazel?"

"Yeah."

"Folks said Daddy was fuckin' her all the time she was livin'."

"Ms. Hazel?"

"Hell, yeah! She had a pussy, too! I know she was sweet and all, but she wunnit no angel!"

"Well, I'll be damn'."

"Yeah. That's just the tip of the iceberg."

"What do you mean?"

"Daddy done been wit' half de women in Swamp Creek! At least dat's what folks say. I ain't actually seen him wit' nobody, but all the rumors can't be lies. It ain't unbelievable, though. You know how he is. Gawkin' at women and huggin' sistas at church and comin' home long after dark. It make sense."

"Daddy don't seem like the romantic type to me," I remarked, a bit puzzled.

"Not to *you*," Willie James reinforced. He lit another cigarette and inhaled like he was taking his last breath. As I watched him, he snickered from time to time, glancing at me with a this-is-crazy-ain't-it? expression.

The more he drank, the more his disappointment surfaced. I wanted to fix his worries instantly, to tell him how wonderful he was inside and to comfort his fragile soul, but no words came. I thought about telling him that there were people all over the world waiting to befriend him. People who would let him be himself and never ask him to work all day to prove his love. However, I didn't say any of this. It would have been very unreal to him. Honestly, it was rather unreal to me, too.

"Big day tomorrow. Guess I'll turn in before these mosquitoes carry us off," Willie James said, practically inebriated. I think he wanted to say more but decided against it.

"It's really good seein' you again, big brother," I sounded corny. "It really is."

Willie James chugged the last of his third Corona, examined me for a moment, and then embraced me so tight I couldn't breathe. "Thanks," he whispered into my ear as he rubbed my head gently. "I love you, li'l brotha. Don't chu neva fugit dat." Willie James wouldn't let go.

"I love you, too, man," I said, and Willie James finally loosened his grip. He grabbed my right hand and held it endearingly, patted me on the back to affirm the moment with his left, and turned and walked away.

I drank the last beer alone.

11

A Federal Express letter from George arrived on Tuesday. I had forgotten I gave him the Swamp Creek address and phone number in case of an emergency, yet I had a feeling the letter was more drama than trauma.

T.L.,

Man, I miss the hell out of you! I hope you're having a great time in Arkansas, and I hope your folks ain't trippin' like you thought they would. I know you and Sister are having a ball! I wish I could come check you out and meet the folks. They probably ain't ready for me though, huh?

I saw your girl, Nzuri, yesterday. She said to tell you hello and that she has been trying to call you. Lying bitch! She claims she's been working sixteen hours a day and hasn't had time to come by. Do you believe that story? I certainly don't. I told you that ho' didn't want you in the first place. But no, you had to pursue her anyway. Be careful what you pray for, my mother used to say.

New York is what it is was when you left it—fabulous! I've seen a couple of plays lately and been to a few good fun parties. Jami had a *gig at his apartment Saturday night that was incredible. Cuties for days.*

I'm reading a very intriguing book called Billy. It's by this new brother, Albert French, who writes about southern culture and black folks in the late thirties. His writing style is nice. Of course, he ain't as good as you, but I like him. I bought this other book, too, called A Gathering of Old Men, by a cat named Ernest Gaines, but I haven't read it yet. Have you? I hope it ain't boring.

How are you, man? I felt in my spirit that your heart was bleeding right about now and needed my special touch. I'm praying for you, doc. Remember to do what you told me: when times get tough, hide in the bosom of God. I know I'm not a big churchgoer and all, but I do believe in God. And though I don't testify all day like some people, I do call on God when I need to. Today, you might need to.

I love you. I always will. Please don't forget that. I can't imagine my life without you right next to me. You are my best friend, my confidant, my everything. I joke around a lot and I guess I can be a bit obnoxious at times, but if you ever need anything, I'm the one to call. Maybe I'll surprise you and show up in Swamp Creek. Psyche! But if I don't, I'll wait on you here. Anxiously.

Yours,
George

What a friend, I thought to myself as I folded the letter and slid it into my pocket. Most folks wouldn't have understood my relationship with George. I loved him more than anybody I knew, except Sister, of course. He reminded me of Anthony Barnes, a boy who lived across the hall from me at Clark. Anthony watched out for me, and after the first week or two, we were inseparable. We took classes together, partied together, and told each other absolutely everything about ourselves.

"You tell me a secret you've never told anyone and I'll tell you one," Anthony suggested one night as we studied biology in his room. Because his roommate went home weekends, Anthony's room soon became our weekend hideaway. I thought the request a bit bizarre at first, but then I complied. It could be fun and intimate, I told myself.

"OK, but you go first, since this game is your idea."

"Cool." Anthony sat up on his bed and began to think. The room was dim, with only the two study lights shining above the study desks. He turned his off and squirmed on his bed for a moment, a sign of discomfort, I thought.

"You don't have to say anything serious if you don't want to," I said, beginning to feel a bit uncomfortable.

"Oh no. I know what I want to say. I'm not too sure how to say it, though." Anthony glared at me, seeking permission to continue. I glared back.

"Well, see . . . um . . . um . . . one time . . . I . . . um . . ."

"Come on, man. Say it," I blurted out impatiently.

"OK. I kissed this guy once."

"What?"

"I didn't mean to, T.L. Damn! Don't start trippin' and shit."

"Oh no, I ain't trippin.' You just caught me off guard."

To tell the truth, I had never met a man who had kissed another man before. I didn't tell Anthony, though, because he would have thought I was naive and sheltered, coming from Arkansas and all.

"It wasn't a big deal," Anthony justified. "He was my cousin and we were playing house. Although I was nine and he was twelve he said he'd be the wife if I wanted to be the husband. I told him I wasn't going to play if I couldn't be the husband, so he had to be the wife. He agreed and we played."

Anthony believed this synopsis sufficient, but I pried further.

"How did the kiss happen?"

"Curious, huh?" Anthony smiled at me accusingly.

"Oh no, I was simply trying to understand."

"It's OK. I was kidding with ya anyway."

For some reason, I felt guilty.

"I was playing like I had been at work all day," Anthony continued, "and when I came home, I said good evening and he said, 'When a man comes home, he's supposed to kiss his wife,' so I did. At first I wasn't going to, but I did. He acted like nothing happened. In fact, he made it clear I had done what any good man would do. I thought nothing more of it."

"Was that the only time you kissed him?"

"My, my. You like this story, don't you?" Anthony laughed. I didn't. "I kissed him many times."

I didn't ask any more questions. I had heard enough. People had taught me all my life that homosexuality was wrong, and although I didn't agree, I didn't want my homophobia to disturb my relationship with Anthony. I didn't think he was gay, yet because he had kissed a boy I had no other category in which to place him.

"You ever kiss a boy?" Anthony asked me in return.

"Nope," I whispered as sweat beads blossomed all over my body.

"Wanna try it out?"

Suddenly the fire alarm sounded. Both of us jumped up, grabbed our books, and flew out of the room faster than we needed to. I learned later than some idiot had pulled the fire alarm as a prank. God works in mysterious ways, I thought.

Anthony and I lived across the hall from each other the following semester. He wanted to be roommates, but I didn't. He could be overbearing at times, and I knew better than to live with him. Nevertheless, we still shared clothes, shoes, books, papers, ideas, personal secrets, fears, and anything else we possessed. We declared each other soul mates and resolved to be friends for life.

Yet my relationship with Anthony was not all fun. He would correct me incessantly and criticize me for being wimpish. He got on my nerves, but I still loved him dearly.

George's resemblance to Anthony made our union easy. Actually, George and Anthony were mirror images, only George was nosier, especially concerning my friend Nzuri. She and I were more acquaintances than mates, probably because I didn't love her quite like I said I did. George told me to leave her alone because she wanted more than I was willing to give, but I pursued her anyway. We weren't exactly girlfriend and boyfriend, since she hated labels and I hated commitments; thus ambiguity served us well. I loved her though. I wasn't in love with her, but I didn't believe in such notions anyway. She was sweet, kind, smart, independent, African centered, and cute. Yet we weren't right for each another. I had more shit in my personal life than I could deal with and Nzuri loved being with me more than anything in the world. Quite frankly, I didn't feel like being bothered half the time. She wanted to be in my presence every chance she got, but I told her I wanted a companion, not a child. She got the message. Nzuri pulled back and started doing her own thing. She might have been seeing another man, one who could be more of what she needed a man to be. More power to her was my sentiment.

Nonetheless, when I needed someone, I called her and she would come to my rescue. Nzuri said she was my friend because she had decided to be, not because she needed to be. She came to me by choice, not obligation, and I was too fuckin' stupid and self-centered to appreciate it, she claimed. Nzuri knew she was in control of the relationship, and it didn't matter if I knew. We stayed together, ultimately, because neither of us could find anyone else willing to tolerate our crap.

George couldn't stand her. He was jealous of our intimacy and thought she wasn't good enough for me. He was protective of me in a motherly kind of way and felt that she was coming between us. Truth be known, Nzuri didn't like George, either. She said he was possessive and a pitiful excuse for a man. One night, after Nzuri and I had sex—she said I had sex because she never got aroused, much less climaxed—she tried to convince me George wanted more from me than brotherly love, but I wouldn't hear of it.

"Of course you don't agree," she said blankly. "Like most men, you like having a girlfriend and a lover. It confirms your patriarchy."

"How am I patriarchal?"

Nzuri smiled disingenuously and said, "This arrangement allows you to use a woman for what a man can't do, while you still get to spend your most valued time with the one you love most."

"I love you most, Zu," I purported unconvincingly.

"No, you don't, and I'm not mad at you for it. Western society does not teach men to love women. It teaches men to love what women can do."

"Bullshit!" I hollered.

"No need to get defensive. Believe me when I tell you I'm not upset. This is not peculiar to you; all your brothers share in the fruits of patriarchy. Men love the notion that women enjoy being support systems for them. What could a woman want more than to stand next to a loving, strong man, right? Yet what most women don't know is that men are excited by the use of our biology, not the potential of our company. Like when a man needs an heir, he searches frantically for a woman to bear him a child. The fact that she *can* bear a child is what he loves most."

I chuckled and shook my head.

"Laugh if you please, but I think I have a point. Answer me this one question: If men could have babies and society wasn't homophobic, do you think men would still seek women to bear their children?"

"Let me make sure I understand you right," I said, buying a little time because the question troubled me. I thought of how George and I got together when we were tired of being with our lady friends, and I knew Nzuri had a point that I could not counter. "You're saying men would rather procreate with other men than with women?"

"Absolutely."

"You're crazy!"

"No, I'm not. See, the only reason the proposition appears ridiculous is because most men are homphobic."

"No, the reason the proposition appears ridiculous is because men can't have babies!"

"Yes, but what if they could? Do you think most men would tolerate women if they could reproduce themselves without us? No nagging, no fussing to endure, no one to explain themselves to. Think about it, T.L. Most men, when they simply want to chill and relax, find their brothers and hang out. They don't kick up their feet with a can of beer and search for girlfriends to chill with. Most men enjoy the company of men more than the company of women."

"I disagree! Most brothers I know love chillin' with sistas."

"Only because every sista is a potential sex partner. If we had no pussies, I wonder how many men would even speak to us."

"This is insane. If a woman had no pussy, she wouldn't be a woman."

"See! There's the proof right there of my argument!"

"What?"

"That you can reduce the definition of a woman to nothing but a pussy proves that men value women for what they have. In other words, what you've actually said is that the essence of a woman is her vagina. And that pussy can be used to make your dick happy as well as serve as the avenue through which your children come. Hence, no pussy, no woman. All I'm saying is if y'all could reproduce without us, you would. You need us, essentially, for pussy, housework, and babies."

"I don't agree."

"Argue then."

"I will," I said emphatically, although I had a feeling I was about to lose this one. "I think some men use women for what they can get, but women do the same with men. And most brothers I know like kicking it with a sister on a Friday night."

"No, they don't, T.L. They like taking a sister to the movies in hopes of the possibility of having sex later. Maybe not later that night, but certainly at some point they hope to reach the pussy. Therein is the point of the mission."

"I don't agree."

"I don't expect you to. You can't afford to. Agreeing would be too much like telling me you don't respect me, and you can't take such a risk. Your game would be blown."

"No, I don't agree because, well, I just don't."

After a moment, Nzuri went on, "T.L., when you want to chill, relax, and take a break from the world, you call George. If you're funky and dirty, it doesn't matter because you don't have to impress George since you're not trying to get pussy from him. You can be yourself. There is no ulterior motive, conscious or subconscious, that would disturb your ability to coexist equally with him. However, every time we chill, you bathe and put on clean clothes or want to take me to dinner in order to please me. Why? Not because you love me, for you love George, too, and you don't do these things. It's because I have a pussy and George does not and you are always in pursuit of it. If George had it, you could stop the game altogether with me and chill with George and get your pussy and babies, too. See, if both men and women could have babies, what sense would it make for a man to endure a woman's madness because he wanted to procreate with her? Go ahead and procreate with the one you chill with and cut out all the drama. Doesn't that make sense?"

"No!" I screamed, more because I had no counterargument than because I disagreed.

"Sure it does," Nzuri noted coolly. "The idea only appears ridiculous because most men are sufficiently homophobic never to consider it. Yet if homophobia disappeared and men could carry a child, I have no doubt, even if women could still have babies, most men would much rather reproduce without having to tolerate a woman's shit, as y'all call it."

"OK. You have a point, but God didn't give men the ability to have babies."

"And most sistas I know are glad She didn't 'cause they know they would have little value to men if She had."

"If men didn't have penises, women wouldn't want us, either." Somehow I knew this argument wasn't going to fly.

"Not true at all. Women believe maleness to be divine in and of itself. Most sistas would love to have relationships with men without having to worry about the sex element. Don't get me wrong. Women love sex, too. Yet most of us don't want sex with every male we befriend. In fact, we don't even want the possibility to arise in most instances. Actually, most women I know argue they get along better with men than with women. They aren't saying the sex is better; what they're saying is they revere male company over female company. This is no surprise in a patriarchal society, for everybody prefers the male, men and women. Being in his presence alone allows women to share in his divinity."

"Share in his divinity?"

"Yes. Men are seen as agents of the Most High God, made in His image, and given the responsibility and privilege of governing humanity. Yet not humanity alone. The Bible suggests God gave males dominion over the entire universe! Fish, fowl, beasts, and women are supposedly under their command. Who wouldn't want to be in the presence of one who boasts such divinely ordained power? Women having babies is simply a service rendered unto earthly gods called men."

Nzuri studied my face, challenging me to a brawl. I threw my hands up in surrender, but she wouldn't let up.

"Let me ask you this: How many women friends do you have whom you have never had sex with and never wanted to?"

"A lot!"

"Like who?"

"Like Jasmine."

"You don't find Jasmine physically attractive?"

"Yes, but so what?"

"Isn't she someone you *would* have sex with, whether you actually do or not? Who are the women you don't find physically attractive with whom you are friends?"

"Why is it necessary for me not to be attracted to them?"

"You have male friends you're not attracted to, right? I'm trying to find their female equivalents." Nzuri smiled sarcastically.

"Opposite-gender relations are different from same-gender relations."

"My point exactly. I'm trying to explain how they're different. It's like this: the only thing I can do George can't is give you pussy and have your babies."

"That's not true! I love you for your female energy alone."

"George has as much female energy as any woman I know."

"Here you go criticizing George again."

"No, no. This isn't about George."

"Somehow, everything we talk about concerns George."

"And why is that, you think?" Nzuri asked derisively.

"I know what you're implying and I'm not going to entertain it."

"That's fine," she laughed confidently. "Let's get back to this 'female energy' thing."

"Don't you think women have a different cosmic energy than men?" I asked desparately.

"No, I don't. Energy and spirits are not gender constructed. If there is such a thing as 'female energy,' then I believe some women have it and some men have it. I believe the same for male energy. I also believe for us to appropriate our gender categories and limitations onto the spirit realm is an act most arrogant and juvenile. When a little girl is born, for example, I do not believe she is born with the propensity to be dainty, emotional, and everything else people perceive as feminine. I believe she is born with the propensity to be whatever she was carved out to be in the spirit realm. However, the way a spirit gets constructed in the spirit realm has to do with the necessity of what the world needs spiritually, not whether or not the spirit is going to come via a male or female body. For instance, if the world needs love—"

"All right, Diana Ross!" I hollered, throwing lots of imaginary hair over my shoulders.

"I'm being serious."

"Sorry."

"Like I was saying, if the world needs love, I believe a spirit will be sent to bring love, regardless of whether the body is male or female. I do not believe God disperses spiritual missions dependent upon gender. Every soul that comes to the earth is here to complete a spiritual task. The categories and dichotomies into which people and characteristics get placed are not spiritual but socially constructed because of humans' limited sight and our inability to comprehend spiritual ideals outside of social dogma. This notion of 'female energy' is another way of keeping women in a place that ultimately serves the interests of men. Ironically, even women believe in it. Phrases like 'boys will be boys,' spoken by mothers across the world, are simply another way of saying boys will be allowed parameters girls won't get."

"Oh, come on Zu! You're interpreting the statement incorrectly! All it's saying is boys do things differently from girls."

"Only because we teach them to! Most boys would play with dolls if they weren't taught they shouldn't. A boy with a doll is a social taboo, not a spiritual one that boys bring with them from the divine realm! I agree with you in your insinuation of the differences of spirits, yet those differences are not gender based."

"Why not?"

"Because gender is not a spiritual phenomenon; it's a social one. Most humans can't conceive this possibility, since gender colors everything we do and conceptualize."

"Are you saying gender has no place or function in the world?"

"I've implied no such thing! Gender could help people understand the differences between male and female in both a biological and a socially productive way. As it is, however, gender teaches children to honor maleness over femaleness and results in social and spiritual hierarchies that often leave women oppressed. My point is that gender is a social thing—not a spiritual one."

"You do agree that men and women are different?"

"Don't insult my intelligence, T.L. Any fool knows the differences between males and females. I know, for example, the average man is taller than the average woman and the fastest man is faster than the fastest woman. These are biological differences that, if we were smart, could be utilized to make all of us better by assigning tasks unto people based upon their physical capabilities. I am also clear women can carry babies and men can't. Yet, again, that's a biological issue. This does not signify women are better parents than men or women love children more than men or women are natural nurturers."

"Some people believe the mother is more critical to the child's physical and emotional development in the formative years than the man." I had thought this at one point, but I sure wasn't about to admit it.

"How ridiculous! Sure, the mother breast-feeds, so this makes her biologically necessary, but this function, or any other, does not make her more critical than the father to the child's spiritual development. The problem is we try to correlate biological differences with spiritual ones and the juxtaposition does not work. In a patriarchal society, seeing the spiritual as merely a reflection of the physical is necessary to justify and help sustain the oppression of women. For example, when a girl grows up playing with boys she is called a tomboy, and will tell others later in life that she was a tomboy. She often speaks of this reality very nostalgically. No one dismisses her for this and, indeed, she is believed to be tough and strong because of the experience. However, if a boy grows up playing with girls he is called a sissy or fag or some name demeaning to his character. He never proclaims with pride that, as a child, he was a 'sissy.' Heaven knows the repercussions of his experience will haunt him the rest of his living days. Male experiences and characteristics are valued in Western society while female influence in anyone but a female is frowned upon greatly. To be sure, female influence is tolerated in women because we supposedly can't help it. However, for a man to be feminine is an insult to other men because he had the choice to be greater."

"Honestly, I never thought of it that way."

"It takes lots of analysis to put all the pieces together, but when you do, the picture is pretty clear. The bottom line is that we, as humans, have created lots of definitions and categories that we use as the basis of our spiritual understandings. Unfortunately, we have put words and concepts into God's mouth and God's realm that don't belong to God. We will never understand spirituality until we relinquish our own limitations and accept God's wisdom and insight. The first step, I believe, to knowing God's wisdom is abandoning our own homemade exegesis, and most people simply won't do that. We use God to confirm foolish thinking by devising spiritual equivalents of our social and personal limitations. We'll have to answer for it one day."

"To God?"

"No. To each other."

12

I decided not to go to the field on Tuesday. The old tractor had whipped my ass the day before, and I wasn't in the mood for more torture. When Willie James asked me if I would help him again, I told him I couldn't because I had to go see Ms. Swinton. She was real sick, I said, and I was afraid to postpone my visit any longer. Willie James gazed at me pitifully. He knew I was lying.

Actually, I hadn't planned to see Ms. Swinton until Wednesday, but since she was the excuse I gave, I decided to go see her Tuesday morning. She lived off of Highway 64, about a mile west of the Meetin' Tree, in the nicest house in Swamp Creek. I had to walk because Daddy was already gone in the truck, and I could hear the sun laughing as it prepared to bake me, again, two or three shades darker.

After grabbing my writing journal and hat, I set out walking down the road. The air was scorching hot and dusty. Every now and then a breeze would come by, but, for the most part, I sweated profusely. I saw a fawn along the way and wondered how great life must be without worries. Yet the possibility that the fawn was running from a predator put into perspective how everybody's life is up for grabs. All living beings are hunted, or at least haunted, by a foe or a memory that has the potential to kill them. Often, the best we can do is run. I wished the animal the best and continued my journey.

By the time I saw Ms. Swinton's house, I was dying of thirst and miserable from the heat. The house had a gloom resting upon it that startled me. It had once been my dream mansion. As a child, I rode by her big, beautiful yellow A-frame house and dreamed of owning such a dwelling with lots of books, flowers, and floral-print curtains in it. At times, I would see Ms. Swinton walking around inside, dressed like she was going to church, as she tended to things very meticulously. In the spring years ago, her house looked like a picture in a *Better Homes and Gardens* magazine. Jonquils covered her yard and outlined her porch impressively. In the evenings, she moved among her flowers angelically, watering them and singing in her highest soprano "Let There Be Peace on Earth, and Let It Begin with Me." Like a conscientious mother, she fertilized her babies regularly and gave them the attention they needed in order to prosper. The yellow paint on her house never weathered because Old Man Blue painted it annually, whether it needed it or not. The white picket fence that separated Ms. Swinton's yard from her neighbor's served as the dividing line between manicured perfection and a failing attempt at such. Potted marigolds, geraniums, and abenas decorated her front porch in a reverie of purple, red, orange, and magenta. People drove from miles around in the springtime to admire the proud blossoms standing perfectly erect and aligned in rows like soldiers. Sometimes folks would park and ask Ms. Swinton if they could takes pictures of themselves with her flowers in the background, and she usually obliged, warning them not to pick or step on any of the blooms. I often slowed my walk as I passed, amazed at Ms. Swinton's ability to transfer her academic standards to the maintenance of a flower garden. Her long, wide porch supported two white lounge swings that swayed constantly, even if there was no breeze. Grandma said ghosts swung in them, keeping watch over the house, for Ms. Swinton was the diva of Swamp Creek.

However, Tuesday morning when I saw her house, my anticipated joy waned. It had lost its luster. The paint was peeling a little and the window shades were drawn, giving the house a mournful aura. Most of the old flower beds were weed infested, although a few blooms managed to survive, and neither swing was moving. They appeared frozen in time. I studied them, hoping to make them sway via mental anguish alone, because I needed some memory of home to remain constant. Yet the stillness of the swings confirmed a lot had changed since I was a boy.

I rested for a moment on the front porch, attempting to prepare myself and my heart for a deteriorated Ms. Swinton. Failing inordinately, however, I resolved to knock on the door and face whatever fears I had conjured.

"Come in," a voice called weakly from a distance.

I shoved the heavy mahogany door open and stepped into a literary gold mine. There were books everywhere. I found myself gawking around the room in awe, amazed to see books on the floor, on the sofa end tables, on shelves, and on the dining room table. I had never seen a million books in one room in my life. My mouth was open like a child at Disney World for the first time. I saw *Native Son*, *The Street*, *Banjo*, *Their Eyes Were Watching God*, and *Invisible Man*. I noticed on the floor the entire canon of James Baldwin and smiled to remember her having given me *Go Tell It on the Mountain* years before.

"Who calls?" Ms. Swinton asked in a whisper.

I followed the voice and discovered her lying in the most beautiful bed I had ever seen. It was covered with a snow-white lace bedspread, several big throw pillows, and an overhead canopy, which gave it a dreamy appearance. The bed accented beautifully the hardwood floors, which would have shined more resplendently had Ms. Swinton had her strength. She was much thinner than I remembered, but her spirit was very much the same.

"It's me. Thomas," I said, beaming at her.

She gasped at me in total shock. Her mouth was agape and her eyes were three times their normal size.

"Precious Jesus!" she hollered, and reached for my hand. Ms. Swinton pulled me next to her on the bed and began to cry softly.

"Lord have mercy! No one informed me of your return, Thomas. I had determined I'd see the Lord before I saw you again." She was patting my hand, very motherly. "My, my, my. You're all refined and polished now. What a handsome young man you've become." Ms. Swinton endeavored to sit up, but her strength failed her.

"Take it easy," I urged sincerely. "I don't want you troubling yourself because I'm here. I thought I'd come around and surprise my favorite teacher."

Ms. Swinton smiled as her grip on my hand loosened.

"You have a beautiful house, Ms. Swinton. And all these books! Maybe I'll have such a collection one day," I said, feeling overwhelmed with even more books in the bedroom.

"First of all, this is a home, Mr. Tyson—not a house. You remember the difference?"

I laughed aloud, for Ms. Swinton had taught us as children that a home is where people live. A house, on the other hand, is a structure meant for human dwelling.

"Yes, ma'am, I remember. Actually, I remember almost everything you've ever taught me."

"Almost is not sufficient, young man," Ms. Swinton admonished lovingly. "You must remember every lesson in order to endow your students with your best."

I gasped, surprised. "How did you know I teach?"

"I knew you'd be a teacher and scholar when I first met you. Your intellectual acumen and zeal could lead you to nothing else."

"You were right," I yielded. "I finished my Ph.D. in black studies a month ago and am anxiously anticipating joining a prestigious faculty this fall."

"Marvelous! Congratulations, Dr. Tyson. Go conquer the world!"

Ms. Swinton started coughing and couldn't stop. She signaled for me to pass her the glass of water resting on the nightstand, and I did so, although my unsteady hand resulted in a teaspoon of water being spilt on her bed. Motioning for me not to worry about it, she swallowed the tepid water and recuperated arduously, her head falling back on the pillow like a heavy weight. "I shall surely miss this old home," she commented after perusing the room slowly. "It has brought me great joy and comfort for almost forty years. I ran out of bookshelves years and years ago, so I simply placed books wherever I was when I completed them. Usually my home does not resemble a jungle, but poor health has brought the unusual."

She began to cough again, this time more violently. I braced her back as she drank more water. My misty eyes almost spilled over as I remembered how much I adored Ms. Swinton and her once-statuesque form.

"We shall all go one day, son," she whimpered and relaxed onto the pillow again. "And my day approaches."

"Ms. Swinton, don't worry. You'll be fine. You ain't goin' nowhere," I lied. I couldn't find anything comforting or truthful to say.

She smiled weakly and corrected me, "You mean aren't. And of course I am going somewhere. You'd better hope I'm going to the right place." Her hand touched mine affectionately.

I couldn't hold back the tears any longer. I had promised myself not to usher gloom and sadness into the room, but they overcame me.

"Why do you weep, son?" Ms. Swinton asked compassionately. "This is God's will. I never expected to be here forever, and I hope you don't, either."

"I know, Ms. Swinton, but—"

"Aw, it's OK, baby. Tears are signs of love. I've always known you loved me."

The frog in my throat was relentless. "You meant the world to me as a child, Ms. Swinton." My head, like a shy puppy's, dropped diffidently between my legs.

"Raise your head, boy," Ms. Swinton insisted. "I've taught you never to hide anything, including your feelings. Black people are a proud people, and we surrender our dignity to no one."

"I know, Ms. Swinton, but I can't help it. You believed in me and loved me. You made me work hard because you saw brilliance in me everyone else ignored. You wanted success for all of us and you demanded the best. I would never have made it without you."

I leaned my head on her shoulder and cried freely. I was a grown man, but I felt no embarrassment. I wanted her to know what she had meant to me, and I had a feeling this would be my last chance to tell her.

Regaining my composure, I apologized.

"For what?" she asked, sounding truly puzzled.

"I don't know," I muttered. "I've missed you terribly in the last ten years. I can't even explain how much."

"I've thought of you often as well, but I knew you were doing fine. I knew it." She smiled as she blinked slowly. "I also know why you left."

The statement didn't surprise me. Ms. Swinton knew everything.

"I didn't think I'd ever see this place again," I said as I rose and paced the bedroom floor.

"Oh, I knew you'd come back. You had to. I only hoped it would be before my time was up."

"Why were you sure I'd return?"

"Because you had no choice. A tree can never escape its roots. The day it does, it dies, and you weren't about to die. You had too much life in you. Oh yes, I knew you'd return."

She coughed again, but this time less impetuously.

"See, son, all that abuse, heartache, and pain you carried away from here is part of you. These country folk, these trees, and those chitterlings you love so well all combine together to form your identity. And a person can never escape his identity. Indeed, a smart man learns to embrace his, the good as well as the bad. You had to come back to connect with the people and the place that shaped your initial identity. You can't find it anywhere else because it does not exist anywhere but here. When you left years ago, you were running too hard to come to terms with yourself. But then I thought about it awhile and knew you were too smart to let your folks strip you of your self."

Ms. Swinton's insight was astounding. My subsequent silence resulted from an inability to comprehend how she could possibly have known the workings of my heart, and, more significantly, why she cared.

"You're right," I surrendered, "but also I came to see Sister. And the rest of my folks, too." I was definitely lying.

"No, you didn't," Ms. Swinton whispered emphatically, struggling to sit up in bed. "You came back because the world never gave you what you were looking for." The cough languished to a wheeze, allowing Ms. Swinton to continue. "You thought you would leave Swamp Creek and, eventually, the memory of it would evaporate. You tried hard to repudiate this place and forever be free. But, Thomas, freedom never comes to anyone. Freedom is a creation, and the first step in creating it is knowing and embracing your past. You had no choice but to come back here to do it."

Ms. Swinton was reading me. She knew the outline of my entire personal evolution and was speaking about me with an authority usually reserved for a parent. Actually, the ease with which she described the complexities of my life implied her knowledge of me to an extent most remarkable.

I didn't argue. Instead, I stood in the middle of the floor with my head bowed like a man on trial without a jury.

"Look, baby, it's all right. I ran, too. I escaped Swamp Creek at sixteen and didn't come back until I was twenty-six. I refused to tolerate the intellectual indolence of these folks. Reading was a disease to be strictly avoided back then, and a good, well-informed discussion hardly ever came to fruition. Leaving was my only option. Yet I didn't stay away. The people and things I had to come to terms with were here. I knew they weren't coming to me, so I had to come back to them. Because it took me more than ten years, however, to establish a viable identity, I never left again."

Her pitiful stare comforted me. She then closed her eyes and attempted to regain strength as she afforded me time to digest her words. Illness did not suit Ms. Swinton, for lying in bed weak, she had lost her pizzazz and enormity. I never imagined she could be vulnerable and dependent.

"I want to have peace of mind, Ms. Swinton," I said vehemently and resumed my seat beside her. She reached for my hand and I gave it to her. "I didn't come home to start confusion like my folks think. I simply wanted to see Sister and ask Momma and Daddy some questions. That's all." I hesitated a moment and then inquired, "Did you hear about what happened to Sister?"

Ms. Swinton nodded affirmatively. "Yes, I heard. It doesn't make sense to me, either. I didn't ask anyone any questions, though, due to fear of impropriety. I prayed that, when you learned the truth, it wouldn't crush you too badly. I know how much you loved her."

"Yeah. I loved her a lot."

Ms. Swinton squeezed my hand harder and said, "Thomas," but then stopped.

"Yes, ma'am?" I responded curiously.

"Oh, forget it. It can wait."

"Are you sure?" I pressed, wanting to hear what she had to say.

"Yes, I'm sure."

She took a deep breath, a sign exhaustion had returned, but she tried to smile anyway.

"Thomas, the Lord has answered my prayer today. I asked Him to send you back to me before I die. I wanted to see you, hold your hand, and know that your life is abundantly blessed."

Ms. Swinton's physical affection frightened me, although less than her fervid heart. Within me, I would have to make room for her character to be other than that of the stoic woman of my childhood.

"I guess I'd better be getting home. I've been here awhile now and I don't want to drain you. I only wanted to come see you and to let you know I was back home. Also I wanted to thank you for all your kindness and help over the years."

I hugged her very gently and struggled to rise, but she held on to me and would not let go.

"Stay a little while longer, son," she beseeched. "I don't have company too often and you always were my favorite student. I want to study you real good"—her eyes squinted—"so I can take you with me when I go home."

I obliged, of course, continuing to hold her hand as she rubbed mine amiably. Honestly, the woman was scaring me. Her plea for my presence forced the realization that, indeed, she was dying. Now, more than ever, I needed her to speak to me and say whatever would set her spirit free, but, instead, she lay silent in bed, rocking herself slowly and lamentably, dealing with me more as a memory than a real person. I had no choice, it seemed, but to endure, for Ms. Swinton was in her final hour. Her quietude and inner bliss were at once admirable and ominous. She manifested absolutely no fear; rather, her heart's desire, it seemed, was to transition while I held her hand. I didn't know how much time she had, whether days or moments, but it wouldn't be long. My arrival, I was afraid, had been the defining factor.

I gazed at this irreplaceable legend of a woman. Everybody in Swamp Creek had a story about how Ms. Swinton whipped them in school until they "got their lesson out" or how she slapped their hands with a ruler until their penmanship was impeccable. She had given her students her best. Yet never once did I consider whether Ms. Swinton felt loved and appreciated. People's reverence for her never left room for me to consider her pain or loneliness. I assumed her heart was always satisfied. I never knew she, too, had left Swamp Creek in search of a life more abundant.

"Thomas," Ms. Swinton said, barely audible.

"Yes, ma'am?"

"I have a favor to ask of you."

"Sure, ma'am. Anything. You need water or food or—"

"No, son. It's much more serious than that."

"Whatever it is, just ask," I said. I saw no need for reservations.

"Fine. I want you to know, though, I've thought this through thoroughly and I know it's right," Ms. Swinton whimpered intensely.

I began to worry. She sounded more serious than I wanted to entertain.

"I want you to take my position as Swamp Creek's schoolteacher."

"What?" I screamed, jerking my hand from hers.

"No one else is as qualified as you, Thomas. You know the people, you know the territory, you have the education, and you have the intellectual savvy. I recognize this is a lot to ask from such a young, brilliant man, but there is no other choice."

"I can't do that, Ms. Swinton! I'm sorry." The fire in my eyes was disrespectful, certainly, but I had no intention of entertaining what she had requested, even in further conversation. She pressed on irreverently.

"I know the children will love you," she complimented me, ignoring me perfectly. "They are eager to learn and full of life. You'll have to be strict and firm, for Swamp Creek parents don't value education very much. The money isn't very good, but the reward comes when you see the children transform."

I wasn't even listening anymore. "Ms. Swinton! I can't do that! I can't live here again! It's out of the question."

I stood, preparing myself to go because Ms. Swinton had angered me. How dare she ask me to take over the school and move back to Swamp Creek permanently! I was seething with wrath and exuding irascibility well beyond my comfort zone.

"Yes, you can do it, Thomas," she declared calmly. "You must. There is no one else."

"I'm sure there's someone else somewhere! I know lots of recent black college graduates who might like a small country school. I'll get in touch with a few and see what—"

Ms. Swinton cut me off. "It must be you, Thomas. These children need to know who they are. I've done my best, but my day is over. You know enough black history to transform these children's lives completely. The Harlem Renaissance, the Negritude Movement, the Scottsboro Incident, the Berlin Conference of 1850 where Europe divided Africa like a puzzle and decided which European country would colonize which part of Africa . . . these children need to know these things. You, T.L., could explain to them why they loathe their own black skin and despise nothing more fiercely than beautiful kinky African hair. And, most important, you could show them the connection between their own rural black culture and elements of traditional African cultures so they would be proud to be African instead of fighting not to be. You've traveled the world and seen people and places most of them will never see. Furthermore, they can relate to you. You and the children are cut from the same cloth."

It was my turn to cut her off. "I'm sorry, Ms. Swinton, but I can't. I already have a job," I lied, "a home, and other things I want to do that I can't do here. I'm flattered you'd ask me—really, I am—but I'm sorry."

I began walking toward the door.

Ms. Swinton yelled, "Do not walk as I'm talking, boy!" I froze, feeling like a third grader again.

"I know this seems unfeasible, Thomas, but we need you." She paused. "And you need us. Pray about your answer before you give it." She breathed wearily and then turned her head to examine me. "You may go now."

Distraught and disillusioned, I had begun to walk out of the bedroom when she stopped me abruptly.

"Thomas?"

I said nothing. I kept my back turned toward her.

"Thomas Lee Tyson?" Ms. Swinton called more emphatically.

"Yes, ma'am?" I mumbled.

"Look at me," she insisted. Tears stood fragilely in her eyes. I could hardly behold her.

"Thank you. And . . . I love you." She expelled a weighted sigh, obviously relieved of a very great burden.

"Ms. Swinton, I'm flattered and all, but—"

"Do not insult me, young man!" she roared, then gasped deeply to regain her strength. "This is not about flattery or your ego. This is about the salvation of black children in Swamp Creek. They need your brilliance, Thomas. No one else is going to believe in them like I know you will. That's why it must be you."

She hesitated, in order to catch more breath, and continued. "I envision you rising proud and strong," she proclaimed with a smile as she closed her eyes, "leading the students in '*Lift Every Voice and Sing*' until they know it perfectly. They'll beam at the power of your voice, T.L., and seek nothing more earnestly than to match it. I'll be so happy!" Her voice broke and tears formed rivers down her cheeks. "You'll tell them about Frederick Douglass, Ida B. Wells, lynching, Black Codes, and the Little Rock Central High Integration Incident. Or maybe you'll read *The Bluest Eye* and teach them the dangers of black people embracing European standards of beauty. Or maybe you'll study *Native Son* and contextualize black rage so they won't think African people in America are livid for no justifiable reason. Whatever you study, the children's lives will be changed forever. They'll never forget you because you showed them that their savior is a real-life black man who shares their genesis. Consequently, they'll finally believe that, maybe, they, too, can save another's soul. See, T.L., you know things most college graduates do not. I'm sure of this. You left here with a thirst for knowledge and you were not going to be satisfied until you learned enough to see your own beauty. And it's that beauty you must teach these children, son. They're dying constantly. They think they're too black and too stupid to be of any value. Unfortunately, their folks inadvertently reinforce such notions, and I am too old to fight the battle any longer. But you're not."

"Ms. Swinton, I'm sorry. This is more than I can handle."

"No, it isn't."

"Yes, it is! Do you know what you're asking of me?"

"Of course I know. That's why I'm asking you. I asked God for a sign you were the one to do this, and today I'm staring at the sign."

"I'm not the one, Ms. Swinton. I promise you, I'm not."

"Oh, you're undoubtedly the one. No need to be volatile, Thomas. You'll do splendidly. When I glance down from heaven and see those children loving themselves and believing in themselves, I'll put in a good word for you!" she chuckled.

"This is not funny, Ms. Swinton. I can't help you this time. I'm sorry, but I can't. I'm only here until Saturday."

"Then you'll go get your things and come back to where you belong."

"No! I don't belong here anymore. I grew up here, but my life is elsewhere. New York feels good to me, and I have a girlfriend whom I can't simply abandon without notice. I am really honored you would think of me to walk in your footsteps, but I have to decline the offer. I'm sorry."

I was trying to go, but Ms. Swinton wouldn't release me.

"You can't decline it, son. It's your destiny, your heritage. You can never get away from that."

"I'm not trying to get away from anything! I simply refuse to relocate back to Swamp Creek. There's nothing here for me anymore. I need a life, things to intrigue me. Don't misunderstand me, however. Swamp Creek is good for whoever wants to live here, but it's not for me."

"It's not about you anymore, son," Ms. Swinton announced soothingly. "It's about what you can give, what you can do. This alone will be your joy and your satisfaction. When you see these poor black country children ascend and declare their own history and their own beauty, therein will be your pay sufficient. Give your all and you shall be great."

I opened my mouth to protest further, but I knew I could not dissuade her. I wasn't sure what more I could have said anyway. What I knew for sure was that I was not living in Swamp Creek ever again.

"Good-bye, Ms. Swinton," I said attitudinally.

"Good-bye, Thomas," she said with her eyes still closed and a slight smirk on her face. "And thank you. You will not be sorry."

13

When I left Ms. Swinton's house, I paced the woods for hours contemplating her request. Never had it crossed my mind to live in Swamp Creek again. Escaping from it was the achievement, and God knows I had absolutely no intention of returning to it permanently.

Daddy was leaning against his pickup truck when I got home. As I approached, he fidgeted like one preparing himself for an uncomfortably imminent encounter. He was dusty brown from working in the fields, and his slight grimace caused him to resemble Morgan Freeman, especially when his brows furrowed at the feigned clearing of his throat.

"Where you been all day?" he asked.

"I went to see Ms. Swinton," I droned with my head bowed.

"How she gettin' 'long?"

"All right."

"All right? How a woman gon' be all right who dyin'?"

"I don't know," I whimpered, about to cry.

Daddy frowned and asked, "What's wrong wid chu?"

I didn't want to divulge the source of my turmoil, but I did anyway. "Ms. Swinton wants me to take her place as Swamp Creek schoolmaster."

We observed silence for a very long time. Then Daddy asked, "Well, what'd you say?" He began to move toward the barn.

I followed him. "I told her I couldn't do it."

If I hadn't known Daddy better, I might have thought he was disappointed.

"So what chu cryin' fu'?" Daddy asked, pouring the cows' feed.

"I don't know."

I filled the other bucket and we walked to the cows' trough in yet more silence. The sun was setting, and the blue, orange, and purple in the sky were incredible. I didn't remember Arkansas sunsets as breathtaking. When the cows heard the feed hit the trough, they came running. Daddy and I backed away quickly to avoid getting trampled. We stood there examining the cows because neither of us could figure out what to say next.

"Folks round here sho' is gon' miss dat woman," he asserted, and turned to walk back to the barn. "Specially dem kids."

"I'm sure someone will come along who is just as good as she was," I stated. "No one is absolutely indispensable."

"Yeah, I guess so," Daddy replied, more to himself than to me. Then, peering into my eyes he asked, "You couldn't see yo'self livin' back hyeah with us crazy backward country folks, huh?"

He had caught me out on a limb.

"Oh no, it's not that," I fumbled. "It's just that . . . um . . . well, I . . . um . . ."

"I don't blame you, boy. Dese hyeah folks ain't got much sense and they sho' ain't tryin' to hear from a youngun like you."

"Living here again wouldn't be a big problem," I said as Daddy walked out of the barn and into the evening dusk. Again I followed, disgusted with myself for not having the courage to speak truth to my own father. His broad laughter, however, exposed the lie I was trying desperately to conceal.

"I 'member de day I told myself dat I was leavin' this old country place. I was 'bout sixteen." He chuckled again, at what I don't know. "I wunnit nothin' but a li'l bitty fella back den. The days was long and hard. We chopped cotton from mornin' dark till evenin' dark. Wunnit no such thang as goin' shoppin' or sittin' down readin' a book. We had to work, boy. The only time you wunnit workin' you was sleepin'." Daddy shook his head slowly.

I was trying to discover why he was talking to me. Daddy and I had never had an extended conversation, and this one felt unnatural. I didn't say anything, though; I kept listening.

"You thank you de only person eva had a hard time?"

I knew the question was rhetorical, but the pause left an awkward silence momentarily.

"Well, you ain't. Plenty folks done had hard times, boy. I sho' done had my share."

Dusk evolved into night and I wondered how long Daddy was going to talk. I wasn't about to interrupt, however, for although mosquitoes in Arkansas have no mercy, I was still a boy to him. In other words, I knew when to speak and when not to speak.

"When I was a boy, we had to git up 'bout five every mornin' and do our chores. Feed the hogs, gather cookin' wood, milk de cow. Wunnit no such thang as sleepin' late. Hell, six o'clock was late to us. We ate breakfast, which wunnit nothin' usually but some fat meat, grits, biscuits, and molasses. We was grateful to git it. Some mornin's we just had de biscuits and molasses. Then we'd load up on de back of de truck and make our way to de cotton field. It'd be black as midnight, but we didn't have no choice. We had to eat. Didn't nobody have no high education where dey could get no good job. All we could do was sweat like damn slaves. Every coupla hours de water boy would come round and give everybody a sip o' piss-warm water dat didn't do nothin' but make you wanna whip his ass. You couldn't fault him, though. He had de hardest job in de field. Runnin' from de well to de workers all day made you 'preciate dem long rows a little better."

Daddy cackled, but I knew he hadn't meant to be funny. His story was intriguing, so I continued listening much more earnestly.

"If you didn't work fast enough, de old folks would tear yo' ass up rat dere in front o' everybody. Dey meant for you to pick at least two hundred pounds o' cotton a day. Some folks was good at it and some wusn't, but you sho' betta make like you was killin' yo'self or either you was gon' git a good whoopin'."

Daddy suspended his tale, surveying the stars in seeming awe and wonder. Whether the beer or his nostalgia softened his countenance I could not ascertain, but, for some reason he was impetuous about my knowing his life saga. How it would empower me I didn't know, yet I was clear Daddy was trying painstakingly to bequeath something to me.

"I had enough whoopin's for a lifetime, boy. My grandpa would catch me playin' when I wuz s'pose' to be workin' and start beatin' me like a carpenter beats a nail. I would scream and holla, but it didn't make no difference. I thank he liked it. I don't know why, though. I tried to cry enough to convince him dat he was killin' me, but dat's when he started hittin' me harder. I thought I hated him till I got grown and knowed betta."

A mosquito landed on my arm and Daddy shooed it away protectively. He had never told me the specifics of his past before. All I ever heard about was how people worked hard all the time and never had enough. It was ironic, to say the least, that he began telling me this after I told him about Ms. Swinton's *request*.

"Didn't you hate this place?" I asked, seeing the pain on Daddy's face.

"Naw, I ain't neva hated it. I always loved it, to tell you de truth. The land, the cows, the fishin', the farmin' . . . I'm a country boy at heart. I just hated how we lived back then. Hard times make hard people, boy."

Daddy reached into the bed of his truck and got another beer. He handed me one, too, and although I didn't want it, it didn't seem right to refuse the truce.

"You ain't neva had no hard times, boy. You always knowed you was gonna eat somethin'. It might notta been what you wanted, but you knowed you was gonna git somethin'. When I was comin' 'long, we wusn't sure if we was gon' eat sometime. If we didn't find some berries or muscadines or fruit on somebody's tree, we woulda been up shit creek. Or sometimes we'd find a old fishin' pole and go down to Blue's pond and see couldn't we catch a mess o' fish. If we didn't, then we'd just be hungry. Folks was too proud to beg, so we starved and smiled about it."

He gulped the beer greedily. I still didn't understand what I was supposed to do with all this information. I was leaving in a few days and failed, quite frankly, to see the relevance. Then Daddy shocked me.

"When you come along, I promised myself dat my kids wusn't gon' have to work theyselves to death for no white man or no other man. I told Momma dat she was crazy if she thought I was raisin' another generation of cotton-pickin' colored people. She told me not to talk too fast, but I didn't listen. I meant what I was sayin'. My kids gon' go to school and learn theyselves somethin' and be somebody. But I saw pretty soon dat I wasn't nobody, so dat's what I raised y'all to be."

"You are somebody, Daddy," I protested, unable to look him in the eye.

"I wanted one o' y'all to be a lawya. I heard 'bout how dey talks in cote and makes a whole lotta money. You come 'long and like to talk so well, I thought it might be you. But I guess you can't make nobody be nothin'. You got to live fu' yo'self. But see, boy, I didn't have no life to live. Dem cotton fields and all dat damn work had done took my life. I was hopin' thangs I didn't have no business hopin'. I neva could go to school too long 'cause de folks needed me to work. So by de time I had my own kids, I knowed dat I wasn't gon' neva be nothin'. I 'speck dat's what kept my mouth stuck out all de time. I seed you learnin' and readin' dem books and how Ms. Swinton went on 'bout how smart you was. And I was proud. Real proud. But I was mad, too, 'cause dat was s'pose' to be me. You didn't seem to want it like I wanted it, and it came to you so easy. It just seemed lak you was gittin' my life."

"Why didn't you leave here and go find what you wanted?" I asked empathetically.

He gaped at me and burbled sadly, "Leave here and go where? Wit' what? I didn't have a quarter to catch de bus to town, let alone travelin' to anotha city. I neva finished school, so I knowed it didn't make no sense thankin' 'bout no college. I wunnit no dummy now; don't git me wrong. But I knowed I couldn't catch up to de other chil'ren. So I stayed right heayh.

"It's all right, though. A man can make a livin' anywhere. He just got to know what he doin' and know how to do without sometimes. But every now and then, he thanks about what he was s'pose' to be or what he coulda been and he might drink a little bit to help ease the memory."

Daddy was trying to make me feel guilty, I decided. This was absolutely not the man I had grown up with. He sounded like he had a heart, a dream, a desire for more than he could see. This wasn't my father. He had always been an angry man, one who knew how to reduce the world and the people in it to manageable terms. This new man was one who sensed another existence belonged to him. He spoke now of peace and familial joy that was beyond the man who had raised me. I was confused.

"Don't be too surprised," Daddy declared, reading my mind. "You ain't the only one who thought about leavin'. You just had enough nerve to do it."

"It wasn't because I hated the place, Daddy."

"Yeah it was. That's exactly why you left. You hated everything about Swamp Creek, and I don't blame you. I just thought I'd let you know dat you ain't de only one thought 'bout escapin'. When you left, I knowed you wunnit comin' back. Fu' what? Wunnit nothin' here fu' ya. Even Sista wunnit enough. I always knowed dat. I thought she'd leave here, too, and find you somewhere. But I knowed you wunnit comin' back. I wouldn't have come, neither."

It was pitch-dark. Only the night-light emitted a shadow sufficient for Daddy and me to see each other. Its burning hot surface euthanized flies, mosquitoes, gnats, and lightning bugs as they danced too closely, tempting a deadly foe. I watched excitedly until Daddy interrupted.

"You might wanna thank about what Ms. Swinton asked you. It ain't about you really; it's 'bout de rest of dem kids. They really needs somebody what knows somethin' more than readin' and 'rithmetic. Maybe you de one."

"And maybe I ain't," I muttered a bit too loudly.

"Maybe you ain't. But since you left here without havin' enough dignity to say anythang to anybody, seem like to me you could at least thank about it. Ms. Swinton carries on 'bout you so you'd thank you was God."

"I love Ms. Swinton, too, Daddy, and I've already thought about what she asked. I'm flattered and all, really I am, but I can't do it. It's not my calling. My life is elsewhere now, and anyway, I don't want to lose the modicum of peace I've found by coming back here."

Daddy glanced at me quickly.

"I didn't mean it like that, Daddy."

"Yeah, you said it right. You said it just like you meant it."

"No, I didn't. What I meant was that I don't know how to live here anymore. I can't pretend and ignore truth the way we've always done. I need compassion and honesty in my relationships."

"If you could get that, would you stay?"

What I wanted to say was no because I also needed a lucrative job and a life personally fulfilling to assure me all those years of study would eventually pay off, yet, somehow, this sentiment felt arrogant.

Croaking bullfrogs kept the silence between us from being deafening, and the cacophonous chirp of crickets confirmed there would be no easy solution.

"I need change, Daddy. New things, new ideas, you know?" I shuffled a little, demonstrating my discomfort, grateful for the shield of the dark night. "I can't go on in the world ignoring truth like you and

Momma, I can't watch abuse and simply turn a blind eye, and I can't allow white folks to keep oppressing our people without fighting back."

"White folks ain't got nothin' to do wit' you comin' back here or not."

Daddy was right. I didn't have anything else to say.

"Well," Daddy announced, and began to walk away.

"Like this whole Sister thing," I intruded boldly. "How do you expect me to live with this? I come home and my sister is dead and you claim not to know anything? That's the kind of shit—stuff—I can't live with here in Swamp Creek."

I applauded my boldness. For the first time, I saw myself as a man before Daddy. His back was turned toward me, suggesting he might walk away at any moment. The darkness made it impossible for me to read his body language, so I had no choice but to wait him out. He started kicking a rock nonchalantly, preparing, it seemed, to confront me in a way he hadn't contemplated thoroughly.

"There's always mo' to it than what you thank you know," Daddy proclaimed slowly. "I done told you what I knows 'bout yo' sista and dat's all I can say. It don't make no sense to me, neither. Of course you mad, but I can't help you none."

"That's what doesn't make sense, Daddy. You were here the whole time. How is it possible Sister died, *somebody* buried her in *your* backyard, and you know nothing about it? I might not be God, but I sho' ain't no fool."

"Maybe you ain't no fool now, but you sho' was one. When you left heayh you gave up all yo' rights to know anythang 'bout dis heayh fam'ly. Now, I ain't sayin' I'm mad wit' you. I'm just sayin' dat when you left heayh, you left a whole lotta stuff. Like yo' right to know what goes on in my house or how yo' sista died. Some of dat you pro'bly didn't mean to leave, but you did. And now you mad about it."

What could I say?

"If you could do it all over again, maybe you wouldn't leave like you did. Maybe you would. I don't know. But what I do know is dat you ain't got no right comin' back heayh talkin' loud to folks 'cause you got somethin' you needs to know."

Daddy started walking toward the house. "Do you love me?" I asked fearfully. My trembling voice denied whatever daring defiance I thought I had mustered.

He giggled lightly and turned, revealing a dumbfounded expression. "Are you crazy, boy? If you don't know dat by now, ain't nothin' I can say to make you know it."

"How would I know it, Daddy? We've never been a close-knit family. This is the longest you and me ever talked! We lived in the same house and ate food at the same table for eighteen years, but you never said you loved me. Was I to assume it?"

I was shooting blows from the heart. To my chagrin, I sounded like a rejected child begging for his father's approval. Indeed, that's exactly what I was.

"I always tried to say de words," Daddy admitted with his head hung low. "I just didn't know how. When I wuz comin' 'long, folks had kids and just clothed 'em and fed 'em. I know now that it's mo' to bein' a good father than that, but since I didn't know it then, I did what I knowed to do. I got married at seventeen and had my first child at seventeen. I thought raisin' a child meant beatin' his ass when he didn't do right, puttin' food on de table, and keepin' a roof ova his head. But dat ain't de same as lovin' no chil'ren, is it, Son?"

The mistake of my life would have been to engage Daddy's question.

"I don't know what else there is to it, but I know dat ain't enough. I shoulda told y'all I loved y'all, but I didn't know how to say it, especially to you. You was soft and sensitive, and God knows I didn't know what to do wit' a boy like dat. So I beat you, thankin' I might toughen you up a little bit, but I guess not."

"I was already tough, Daddy. I simply wasn't like you and Willie James," I dissented, resenting his insinuation.

"Yeah, but I didn't see it lak dat. Now that I looks back, I guess I woulda done a whole lotta stuff dif'rent. You can't change the past, though. You jes' gotta keep movin' on, even when you see dat you done fucked up real bad. See, ain't no use in us clownin' now 'bout what happened yestiddy. Ain't nothin' you can do 'bout it noway."

This was the father I remembered. He peered at me fiercely, making sure I understood what he was saying. "You got to take yo' burdens to de Lawd and leave 'em there. Once you done done dat, let 'em go."

"What if that ain't enough? What if God tells you to fix your own problems since you created them? That's why we got a mind, Daddy, in order to think for ourselves and stop complaining to God all the time. I'm not asking you to be the all-American father. I only want to know what happened to my sister. I wasn't here, but I still have a right to know. She is my sister, isn't she?"

"What chu tryin' ta say, boy?"

"Don't get angry, Daddy. My aim is not to insult you. More than anything, I'm trying to get you to see how much my sister meant to me. That's all. And it would really help if you told me the truth."

"I done already done dat."

Daddy disappeared into the night. I heard the screen door slam behind him, reminding me he would always have the last word. Only the mosquitoes and crickets remained. I gazed at the night-light again, wishing it were another planet where I could escape and start a whole new life. Yet a hoot owl brought me back to reality and caused my fantasy to fade. I paced the yard deliberately, searching for memories of Daddy that would help me understand him. The old family car standing in the field, overgrown by grass and probably snakes, symbolized his divinely ordained position as head of the family and reminded me that, in whatever direction the family evolved, it was Daddy's life we were following. Grandma's neat little shotgun house made me imagine Daddy as a kid opening his Christmas bag of peppermint and fruit, content, ultimately, to have a gift not scarred by a previous owner. Somehow, with Daddy at the helm, the Tyson family had survived death, hunger, emotional dependency, and enough self-hatred to annihilate us. Yet, because we survived, I realized Daddy had a sacred, adhesive power to hold people together stronger than anything for which I had given him credit. In some ways he was a very great man, and in other ways his greatness I had missed altogether.

Yet, with all of this, he still didn't say he loved me. Or did he?

14

I didn't sleep well that night. Indeed, I had had many sleepless nights in my parents' house. Nightmares haunted me incessantly as a child, resulting in hours of early-morning reading time as I awaited the dawning of a new day. Sister and I thought ghosts dwelled in our house and were determined to get us. Sometimes we would hide under the covers holding hands, praying our collective strength was sufficient to ward off evil. By morning, we would rise joyfully, relieved the previous night had not been our last.

However, I must have fallen asleep at least briefly, for I remember having had the strangest dream. I was seventy or eighty years old, walking with a cane down a dusty dirt road. The sun was shining resplendently, and suddenly I found myself entangled with a host of beasts. The first was big and red, with one eye. He had alligator skin and tigerlike teeth. The monster stood at least nine feet tall and weighed well over a ton. I was swinging my cane with all my aged might, but the red beast was clearly my physical superior. Fatigue consumed me, but I refused to abandon the fight. The beast's razor claws sliced my arm into layers of flesh and blood. I bellowed curses unmentionable and conjured virility enough to pick up a nearby rock and fling it at the monster's eye. It hit the creature, but it did not hurt him. He roared loudly, frightening me, and then charged me ferociously. He was about to devour me when another beast appeared. This one was forest green, with no head. She had one eye the size of a watermelon in the middle of her head. Her breasts were hairy, firm, clearly distinguishable, standing upon her chest, like grassy mountain ranges. She, too, roared vivaciously, but, much to my astonishment, she attacked the red creature. She was a little smaller than him, but no less fierce. Frozen in the moment, I was unable to run or scream. The beasts' intertwined bodies made it impossible to ascertain which of the two was overpowering the other. Both shrieked wildly when the other struck intensely, and neither appeared the worse for it.

After a moment, the fighting ceased. The creatures stared at each other as though wondering why they had ever been contentious. Then, suddenly, they turned on me, approaching cautiously, having prepared themselves, it appeared, for this confrontation. The green female grabbed my arm and began to jerk it violently. I wasn't going to die easily, I resolved. Gritting my teeth, I screamed, "Bitch," and kicked her mightily, although to no avail. She twisted my arm out of its socket and threw it over her shoulder like one discards a chicken bone. Her subsequent laughter incensed me. In fact, she laughed hysterically and fell to the ground. In my distraction, the red male grabbed me from behind and squeezed my stomach until pus issued from my mouth and ran down my cheeks onto my shirt. That's when I noticed laughter coming from every direction around me. The beasts had multiplied, and each of them examined my bizarre one-armed form as they mocked me. There were hundreds of them. I kept turning in circles, and everywhere I gaped I saw a beast jeering at my accursed lot. Since I could neither run nor hide, I stood there trying to scream but emitting no sound. Unexpectedly, the red male exposed a penislike extension of himself, exuding from his right side. He began to beat me with this long rubber tube, and I had no defense against such extreme force. I tried to catch the rod with my one hand, hoping somehow to tear it away from him, but the monster was quicker than me. In the midst of this battle, the green female was further humored. She laughed heartily, unable to regain composure, as blood ran from her nose. However, I couldn't concentrate on the female very long, for the thick tube was leaving welts all over me. Blood covered my body, and I knew if I didn't destroy this red beast soon I was going to die. So, without thinking about it very long, I charged the monster. My confidence only fueled his anger. With one arm, I knew I couldn't do much damage, but I knew I wouldn't get a second chance, either. I aimed my head at his right kneecap, hoping the impact would cause him to lose his balance and fall. My plan worked. When he fell, I bit his leg and ripped away a mouthful of flesh. He threw his head back and released a scream that sounded like a thousand elephants. Immediately the female stopped laughing. She rose and came to where I was standing, then knelt down and gazed at me with her gigantic eye. I was trembling, wondering if I were about to die.

To my utter surprise, the female extended her hand to me, offering assistance. The red male was still hollering in agony, for the wound to his leg disallowed mobility. I can't explain why I trusted her, but I took the female's hand, and she stood me aright again. I noticed that the long tubelike extension on the male's body had retreated back into the monster and left no sign of its existence. The green female let go of my hand and began to walk away with slackened, hunched shoulders and a countenance of defeat. She waltzed clumsily and lazily, dragging her incredible frame to God knows where. Perplexed and exhausted, I was too afraid to speak or move.

I woke up. The sheets were soaked with sweat and my body was quivering. For a few moments, I lay still, trying to calculate the meaning of the dream. Nothing came to me except fear of the unknown. I rose and went inaudibly to the bathroom to splash my face with cold water. Hoping to confirm my sanity, I studied my reflection in the mirror, but it only frightened me further. My rose red eyes and dilated pupils testified to a night of horror I sought desperately to forget. I turned the light off and returned to bed, although never to sleep. Lying on my back, gazing into absolute darkness, I prayed the dream would never come again or, if it did, its meaning would accompany it. Grandma always said dreams were signs sent from God to inform us about our life's destiny. Most people circumvent the truth, she claimed, in order to avoid personal and spiritual accountability. On second thought, I prayed never to know the meaning of the dream.

I sprang up and went to the kitchen in search of a snack. The digital clock on the stove read 3:12 a.m. "Great," I muttered, retreiving from the refrigerator a wax paper package of souse meat. This was the nastiest lunchmeat in the world, but it was the only thing available, so I ate it. I sat at the kitchen table inconspicuously, miserable because it was three o'clock in the morning in Swamp Creek and I was awake with nothing to do. I dared not turn on the TV and wake the folks lest I invite a brawl in the midnight hour. Thus I sat there eating souse meat and crackers, hoping a little food would sit heavy in my stomach and make me sleepy again. After several minutes, I returned the crackers to the cabinet above the stove and the meat to the refrigerator. While tiptoeing pass my folks' room back to bed, I overheard Momma hiss, "You gon' have to tell dat boy somethin'. He ain't leavin' hyeah till you do."

I stopped abruptly and leaned my ear to the door, listening arduously.

"I ain't got to tell him nothin'. Shit, I'm de daddy round dis place. He ain't runnin' nothin', includin' me!"

"Stop talkin' so loud, man," Momma admonished intensely. "You gon' wake him up and then we'll have to hear his mouth all night long."

Their voices hushed considerably. I couldn't move. I wanted to hear everything they said, especially about me, but I didn't want them to know I was outside their door. Therefore, I quietly lay on the hall floor and put my right ear next to the open space between the floor and the bottom of the door.

"Cleatis, listen. We can't jes' keep tellin' de boy we don't know what happened. He gon' figure it out sooner or later."

"I don't care what he figure out," Daddy threatened. "He ain't gon' know de truth 'cause we ain't gon' tell him, and don't nobody know but you and me. So you betta not say nothin' to him."

"How can we jes' keep walkin' round like we don't know nothin'? T.L. ain't stupid."

"Well, dat's exactly what we gon' do till I say dif'rent."

There was a short pause wherein I imagined Daddy's grimace, and thereafter Momma said, "I got a mind to tell him everything. If I do, I can be through with all this shit."

"I'll kill you first," Daddy whispered boldly.

"Maybe that's what you gon' have to do, 'cause I can't live with this forever."

"You'll live with it long as we need to."

"Fine, Cleatis, don't tell him. But at least tell de boy who his momma is. He got a right to know."

"You his momma and dat's all to it."

"No, I ain't. I ain't neva felt like I was his momma. I neva shoulda told you I would be."

"Well, you did, so now ain't nothin' you can do about it."

"Dat's where you wrong. I can tell him who his real momma is, and dat's exactly what I intend to do."

"I thank you betta be cool, woman. You 'bout to git yo'self in a heapa trouble."

"Trouble?" Momma responded turbulently. "I ain't scared o' nobody. De truth is jes' de truth. I ain't neva been scared o' de truth before and I ain't scared of it now."

"If you tell dat boy anythang, I sware 'fo' God you gon' regret it."

"What chu scared of, Cleatis? T.L. can't do nothin' to you. He can't change nothin', neither. All he can do is know what everybody else already know."

"But he ain't gon' know 'cause you ain't gon' say nothin'."

"I can't promise you dat no mo'. He come back here searchin' for de truth and I think he oughta get it. He oughta know who his momma is and he oughta know why dat girl's grave is in de backyard. He ain't no li'l boy no mo'."

"He a li'l boy to me and I say he ain't to know nothin'. It wouldn't do nothin' but make thangs worser'n dey already is."

"How could things be worse than dey already is, Cleatis?" Momma screamed quietly.

"'Cause soon as T.L. know, dey whole world gon' know. He neva did know how to be calm 'bout nothin'. Everythang he do is full of a lotta goddamn drama."

"Everybody already know I ain't his momma! He oughta know de truth, too. What he do wit' it is his business."

"No, it ain't, woman. It's our business. We du ones in de middle of dis shit."

"In de middle of what?" Momma asked through clinched teeth. "I ain't done nothin' I got to be 'shame' of. Is you?"

"You know it's not dat simple, woman." Daddy sounded exasperated. "If we tell him what happened to Sister he might lose his mind or somethin'. You know how frail and weak he is."

I was offended, although I finally knew Daddy's perception of me. Muthafucka, I mouthed.

"T.L. might fool you, man. He's not as weak as you think. But even if he is, he got to learn to be strong fu' hisself. And how he gon' learn dat if he don't neva have to walk wit' de truth?"

"I don't know how he gon' learn and I don't give a damn. Dat's his problem—not mine. What I got to do is keep on livin' de way I been livin' and not let dis boy come back here and disturb my peace."

"Well, somebody oughta disturb yo' peace, 'cause you disturbed mine thirty years ago when you went and decided to fuck somebody else."

"Is you gon' ever let dat go? Damn!"

"Naw, I ain't gon' let it go 'cause it wasn't right and you ain't fixed it yet."

"How I'm s'pose' to fix it, huh? Tell me dat."

"By tellin' dat boy de truth. You done let him live his whole life believin' I was his momma. I neva could love him right 'cause I knew he wasn't mine. I tried to act like he belonged to me and sometimes I convinced myself he did, but, in de end, I knew he didn't."

"So why ain't you told him yet? You had every chance in de book."

"'Cause dat's yo' job and yo' responsibility. It's de only way you can make right what you messed up. I been waitin' on you to be right for de last thirty years and it ain't come yet. I ain't waitin' much longer."

"So I'm s'pose' to jes' go in dere and tell dat boy everything about me and Ms. Swinton? Is dat what you want me to do?"

"No, dat ain't what I want you to do. Dat would be too easy. What I want you to do is sit him down like a man and tell him de truth of what you and Carol Swinton did. Tell him how it happened and why. Let him see yo' sorry ass for what you really are."

"I ain't tellin' dat boy nothin'. It ain't gon' make no dif'rence noway. He love dat woman too much to tell him dat. She over dere on hu' deathbed right now, so it don't make sense for me to stir up some mo' strife."

"You mean to tell me, Cleatis, you'd let dat woman die befo' you tell yo' own son dat dat's his real momma?"

"I ain't got no choice, woman! She gon' die and T.L. gon' leave hyeah in a few days. It don't make no sense to start a bunch o' shit 'bout what happened thirty years ago. It wasn't s'pose' to happen noway."

"But it did! And you wanted it to happen. Dat's why you used to go over there every chance you got. You think I didn't know you had a thing for Ms. Swinton? Come on, man! Everybody ain't as stupid as you thank dey is."

"I ain't neva said you was stupid, woman."

"No, you ain't said it, but you act like it. You acted like it back then, too. What sense did it make for a grown man wit' children to be hanging round a teacher woman's house when he couldn't even read? What did you think people would say? You made up some lame excuse every day to go over there. I knew you thought she was pretty, and she *was* pretty. I jes' neva thought you'd take it so far."

"Woman, will you let it go? I done apologized to you every day of my life. How much mo' can I do?"

"Oh, is that what you been doin'? Tryin' to convince me dat you sorry? Well, you can let dat go right here and now 'cause I forgave you the day you brought T.L. home. What I'm fussin' 'bout is dat you ain't neva corrected yo'self. And de only way to make right what you made wrong is to tell T.L. de truth. If you ain't gon' do it, I will, 'cause since both of us know, I guess we both wrong and I ain't gon' be wrong wit chu no mo'. I done been wrong long enough."

"Then we gon' be wrong some mo', 'cause you ain't sayin' nothin'. Did you hear me?"

"I done said what I needs to say. You gon' do what de hell you wanna do anyway. That's what you been doin' ever since I knowed you, so ain't no need in me thinkin' you 'bout to change now. But I'm gon' do what I gotta do, too. I done lived with you, but I ain't got to die with you, too."

Momma must have turned over, for her words ended the conversation. I arose from the floor dazed, went to my room, and sat on the bed in the dark. "Oh my God!" I whimpered. "Ms. Swinton? How could it be? She and Daddy? I don't believe it!" Yet I had no choice. The truth was the truth, and I simply had to accept it. I never thought of Ms. Swinton having sex, though. Of course, she, like other women, has a vagina and breasts, but I never associated sex with her. "My mother?" I couldn't make sense of it. "Ms. Swinton is my mother?" I kept whispering it over and over, hoping my words might make the truth more bearable. "Why didn't she tell me?" I wondered. All the special attention, books, and extraordinary love made perfect sense now. She was loving her own son. But, again, why didn't she tell me? Was she embarrassed by her actions? Having a child out of wedlock was certainly a no-no in Swamp Creek fifty years ago, but I thought certainly times had changed.

I leaned back on the bed and peered out of the window. The moonlight and a few stars glistened brilliantly in the clear night, exposing shadows of things once very familiar to me. The old barn, the cows, the junk cars in the field all functioned like stage props placed there to help me remember bygone days. But remembering the past has never been difficult for me; forgetting it is my struggle.

"Ms. Swinton?" I marveled again as I released the curtain and resumed my place on the bed. It was beginning to make sense. There were days at school when she would scrutinize me constantly and I couldn't understand why. I would glance up and she would smile lovingly but then shake her head briskly, as though exiting a fantasy. Whenever this happened, she would ignore me the rest of the day. I would have my hand raised, either to ask or answer a question, and she simply disregarded me. I thought she was affording other children a chance to participate, but maybe she was trying not to illumine her bias toward me. Or maybe she was trying to keep from getting overwhelmed in a public place. One thing for sure, I would never have guessed she was my mother. I began to cry. "Why me, Lord? Why is it always me?" I retracted my body into a fetal position and held myself tightly. Trembling and hurting badly, I didn't know what to do and I didn't have anyone to talk to. Grandma always affirmed that Jesus was a "friend in the midnight hour," so I began to pray:

"Lord," I droned through snot and tears, "I don't get it. I don't understand why nothing is ever right in my life. Did I do something wrong? One thing after the other keeps taking my joy away. You know how much I longed for a mother to love and hold me, and the day I find her, she's dying. This doesn't make any sense. I come home and find a dead sister, a terminal mother, and who knows what else! Is this my punishment for sins unatoned? If it is, I'm sorry, Lord. I'm really, really sorry. Please forgive my transgressions against you. You know how much I love you, Lord, so please don't hold my weaknesses against me. Hear my cry, Jesus, please, and help me understand what you're trying to show me. I know you don't put more on a person than he can bear, but this is too much for me, Lord! I'm losing it. Please help me! How can Ms. Swinton be my mother? This is asinine, God."

I reached despairingly toward the heavens and dropped my arms back down in powerless surrender.

"Am I not supposed to understand? Am I to wait until death before I see things clearly? If so, Lord, give me comfort in the interim. Please don't leave me. Send me a balm in this, my weakest hour. Don't let the devil get the best of me. Be my strong tower, Lord, and take me into your bosom. Sometimes I can't see why things have to be the way they are, but I know your wisdom is perfect. If this is a test to make me stronger, give me the strength, Lord Jesus, to endure. Do me like you did the woman at the well, Lord, and forgive my sins even before I recount them to you. Stand guard over my soul, Master, and as I walk, let me walk close to thee."

I cried myself back to sleep.

15

Wednesday morning I awakened like I did every other morning at home, exchanging fake pleasantries and talking about the beauty of the day. I didn't want either of my parents to know I had overheard them the previous night, yet I sat at the breakfast table and ate with a contentment that should have left them suspicious.

"You sleep all right, boy?" Daddy inquired as I finished eating. His loud smacking on salmon patties and fried potatoes irritated me more than years before.

"Yes, sir. Quite fine. Slept like a baby."

Momma glared at me incredulously. I smiled in return, hoping to anger her before she ascertained what I knew.

"Lotta work to do round hyeah today," she said. "Willie James could use a hand in the hay field."

I didn't respond immediately. Momma had a habit of speaking in parts, and I waited for her to continue. However, she remained silent. I hated the way Momma left herself enough room to backpedal if necessary.

"I'll see what I can do," I avowed, and moved away from the table.

Then I remembered Ms. Swinton's request. "Did Daddy tell you what Ms. Swinton wants me to do, Momma?"

"Naw."

"She wants me to take over the school." I was standing at the sink washing my plate. My back was turned toward Momma and Daddy at the table.

Apathetically Momma asked, "Is that so?"

"Yes, ma'am. She says I would make an excellent teacher for the local children because I'm from here and I know everybody and everybody knows me."

"Don't nobody know you," Momma declared sarcastically.

"Well, you know what she means. They know y'all and since I grew up here, she thinks I'm pretty well connected to the place."

Momma kept eating like I had not said a word. I continued washing my plate over and over again, trying to bide a little more time.

"It's flattering and all, but I told her I wasn't interested. I do like it here, but I think I would be a poor replacement for someone as smart as Ms. Swinton."

"Say you ain't gon' do it and leave it at that. Them other reasons is jes' a waste of breath."

Momma's words sliced me like a razor. I had no defense when she leveled her critique, and attempting to convince her I was sincere would have been futile. I dropped the subject and left the kitchen to go get dressed.

While in the bathroom, I heard Daddy tell Momma not to forget the family reunion next month.

"A house full of niggas again," she muttered back.

The first family reunion had been a blast. I was sixteen and eager to meet my extended family because most of them had moved away from Arkansas long before I was born. I met aunts, uncles, and cousins I never knew existed. And they were crazy! Uncle Jethro, my grandfather's brother, was drunk the whole time and cursed people vehemently for absolutely no reason at all. He has ten boys and all of them are preachers except the baby. His name is Thomas, too. Thomas went crazy after his momma died, people said. He was only fourteen, but folks say the day of her funeral, he returned home in the afternoon and put on his momma's apron and started cooking supper like she had done every day. His brothers whispered about his behavior, but they were so damn greedy, folks said, they actually enjoyed the home-cooked meal more than they worried about who cooked it. In fact, Thomas handled all the housework like his momma had taken over his body and come back to life! Uncle Jethro was so confused about his boy acting like his wife that he started drinking heavily. Before Aunt Cil's death he didn't touch the stuff, Grandma said. But the day Cil died and his son became the wife and mother of the house, Uncle Jethro took to the bottle, and he's been inebriated every since.

Rumor had it that Uncle Jethro never confronted Thomas. He remained completely unmoved as he watched his son piddle around the house in his mother's clothes. At mealtime, he fixed his father's plate and placed it before him like Cil did. At least, that's what folks said at the family reunion.

"I b'lieve he and Jethro wuz sleepin' together, too," Uncle Roscoe, Daddy's oldest brother, added with a smirk on his face.

"You lyin'!" an older cousin proclaimed.

"Naw, naw! If I'm lyin' I'm flyin', and I sho'ain't got no wings! I was ova there 'bout three or four days after Aunt Cil passed and saw that boy prancin' round in her old housedress. I asked him was he all right and he said, 'Yeah, I'm all right. Why wouldn't I be?' He looked at me like I was the one crazy. He offered me some lemonade and somethin' to eat and said, 'Don't you mind me none now, Roscoe. I got to git dis house in order 'fore dese mens get in here from de field.'"

Cousin Remmy interrupted, "What that got to do with them sleeping together?"

"I was jes' 'bout to tell you dat, muthafucka!"

People roared with laughter. These two were like a tag-team comedy show.

"I asked Thomas if he wanted some help with his house chores and he said, 'No, no. I jes' 'bout got eva'thang done. I jes' got to git in dere an' clean our room.'"

"*Our* room?" Cousin Remmy hollered.

"Ain't dat what I said? Then he froze and shut right up like he had done said somethin' he didn't have no business sayin'."

"Dat nigga said *our* room?" Cousin Remmy repeated even louder.

"He sho' de hell did! And I knowed he was talkin' 'bout Uncle Jethro's room 'cause he nodded his head toward it. Ain't no tellin' what kinda shit goin' on in dat house, I said to myself. But jes' then Uncle Jethro came stubblin' in de door drunk as a skunk. He acted like everythang was normal, so I didn't say nothin' else. I jes' nodded my head and left."

"That's why dat boy didn't neva leave home," Cousin Remmy stated. "Jethro told all de rest of 'em that they had to find dey own place, but not Thomas. He got to be 'bout thirty, thirty-five by now, ain't he?"

"Hell, dat nigga damn near fawty! Shit, dat was thirty years ago when I was ova dere!"

Uncle Roscoe was the king of exaggeration. Everyone loved that about him.

"I hope he ain't still livin' dere now," Cousin Remmy instigated, pretending he didn't know the truth.

"Shit yeah, dat nigga still livin' dere! He been cookin' and cleanin' for Uncle Jethro ever since his momma died and he ain't neva stopped. He got on one of Aunt Cil's dresses now. There he go! Jes' look at him!"

They all turned and gawked at Thomas as he continued a conversation with another relative. Dressed in a soft pink spaghetti-strap dress with black high-heel shoes, Thomas laughed daintily, waving his hands dramatically. He wore a wide-brimmed floral-print hat that was a bit too much for such an occasion, especially since he stood at least six-four, yet he walked around the family reunion in complete peace. He was known to speak to everyone in a friendly manner, hugging them longer than most appreciated.

"How come Uncle Jethro ain't put his ass out?" Cousin Remmy agitated further.

"'Cause he miss Aunt Cil too bad," Uncle Roscoe answered. "See, Thomas remind Uncle Jethro of Aunt Cil, prancin' round de house doin' for him. And he like havin' somebody wait on him, specially somebody what remind him of his wife. He been in love wit' her all his life."

We waited for Uncle Roscoe to swallow the last gulp of his beer so he could continue.

"Uncle Jethro had been tryin' to get Lucille ever since dey was young folks. Well, when he finally got her, he thought he was in heaven. Least this what folks told me. But when she died he jes' couldn't neva git hisself back together. Now when Thomas come home and start actin' like his momma and doin' what his momma did, Jethro felt kinda grateful, I guess. It kept remindin' him of her and kept him from missin' her so bad. That oldest boy of Jethro's say Thomas used to sing in falsetto round de house, soundin' jes' like dey momma. I think it messed up Jethro's head. He probably thought Thomas really was Cil all over again."

"Aw shit, man, ain't nobody dat damn confused!" Cousin Remmy asserted.

Uncle Roscoe shook his head compassionately while saying, "Sometimes people don't neva recover from death. Dey jes' go on actin' like the person is still here. I guess dey can't let go."

"Roscoe, shit! You know well as I do dat that ain't no reason for dem two to be sleepin' in de same bed!'

"Maybe he got some pretty legs!" Uncle Roscoe teased.

Standing boldly and fanning himself with his worn-out fishing hat, Cousin Remmy exclaimed, "I don't know what he got! But he ain't got what a woman got!"

"You don't know dat, Remmy! He might!" Uncle Roscoe yelled, leaning on Cousin Remmy to keep from falling over with laughter.

People howled at this insinuation. I wanted to ask someone why they didn't talk to Thomas and ask him whatever they wanted to know. My position was too obvious to be right, however, so I laughed along.

Uncle Roscoe was the ringleader at family gatherings. He could tell stories and embellish the truth magnificently. People would sit and listen to him for hours tell tales about things that couldn't possibly be true, although he always swore they were. He was always in the right place at the right time, ironically, to witness every strange event that ever occurred, and he would just happen to be the only witness.

"Come ova heayh and hung yo' uncle, boy!" he would holler any time he saw me. "You ain't dat damn grown yet!" And he would squeeze me until I couldn't breathe. "You 'bout to git big as me, nigga, shit!" Of course, that couldn't possibly be true, for Uncle Roscoe has weighed three hundred pounds since I've known him. He used to tease me about being named after Uncle Jethro's Thomas.

"It's just a coincidence, Uncle Roscoe," I told him at that family reunion.

"Oh, OK. If that's what you think, I'll let you think it."

"Leave the boy alone," Cousin Remmy prodded. "Ain't no need in you messin' up somebody else's life wit' yo' shit."

"Whose life I done messed up, muthafucka?"

And they were off to war. When I got older, I realized their battles were actually games of verbal signification. They had lived together for years, and whenever you saw one, you saw the other. I finally admitted to myself that I belonged to a family of people who liked to talk shit.

The family reunion was held in the field behind our house. That's where most of the older ones grew up, so that's where the reunion ought to be, they argued. Uncle Roscoe decreed, "We sho' ain't givin' no white folks no money to rent no space. Shit, dat's why we havin' de family reunion. To remind us who in de family." The argument made sense to all who mattered; thus they decided to have it on the "old home place." "We can barbecue, fry fish, make potato salad, roast coon, and whatever else we want. Shit, jes' have a good time!" encouraged Uncle Roscoe. So that's what we did. Days before the event, Daddy made all of us pick up trash, mow the lawn, and get the land ready for all the crazy niggas comin'. And when they came, I mean they came! I had never seen that many people in one place in all my life. Illinois, Michigan, New York, Kansas, and California were among the license plates I read as people parked on the side of the dirt road and got out. They were clean, too, wearing suits, dresses, and hats that must have cost hundreds of dollars. "These niggas ain't shit," Daddy mumbled as he exited the house to greet them.

They had all been born in Swamp Creek, Uncle Roscoe said. "Nothin' but a bunch of country-ass po' black people who love to eat and love de Lawd. That's who you come from," he told me.

I stuck my chest out pridefully.

"Did yo' daddy tell you 'bout de time him and Chicken stole the teacher's spelling book?" he asked me, cackling.

"Roscoe, stop lyin', man," Daddy warned playfully.

"I ain't lyin' and you know it, Cleatis!"

Daddy hadn't told me this story, but whether he had or not, it didn't matter. Uncle Roscoe was going to tell it again anyway.

"Where Lizzie Mae? She know!" Uncle Roscoe glanced around, feigning a brief search for Cousin Lizzie who could corroborate his story.

"What happened, Roscoe?" Cousin Remmy prompted, knowing he had heard the story a thousand times.

"Well, see, Cleatis and Chicken hadn't studied for de spellin' test. So dey come up wit' de idea dat they gon' steal de teacher's spellin' book and change de spellin' words to make her call out words they knowed they could spell."

"Roscoe, you oughta be 'shamea yo'self lyin' like dat," somebody said.

"This de God's honest truth," Uncle Roscoe declared with his right hand stretched toward the sky. "Chicken was 'spose' to write out a list of words him and Cleatis could spell 'cause Chicken had pretty handwriting jes' like Ms. Swinton. See, she had about fifty spellin' lists, and she would choose whichever list was on top to give out for that day. All Chicken had to do was sneak in her drawer and put a new spellin' list on top and then the words she called out would be the ones they could spell. Cleatis's job was to stand guard at de door and make sure Ms. Swinton didn't catch 'em in the act.

"Dey switched 'em and thangs went real good. About eleven thirty Ms. Swinton told everybody to get out they writin' books 'cause they was 'bout to have the spellin' test. Chicken and Cleatis looked at each other and went ta grinnin' 'cause they was sure they was gonna make a perfect sco' on the test. Ms. Swinton told everybody to number they paper from one to fourteen. Now, this seemed strange 'cause Chicken had only wrote ten words on the paper he left in Ms. Swinton's drawer. They didn't think too much about it, I guess, 'cause they was real happy they was 'bout to make one hundred on the spellin' test."

"Roscoe, kiss my ass, nigga!" Daddy said while laughing along.

"Then Ms. Swinton—" Uncle Roscoe was laughing uncontrollably. "Ms. Swinton said, 'The first word is . . . *shit*.'"

People's screams sent chill bumps up my arm. Uncle Roscoe's laughter echoed in the woods behind the field.

"Then, she said, 'Number two: *pussy*.'"

Cousin Remmy fell out of his chair wailing and spilt wine all over himself.

" 'Number three: *dick*.'"

I had never heard anything more hilarious in all my life. Uncle Roscoe stood up and tried to sound proper and refined like Ms. Swinton. His antics really made it funny.

"She went on down the list, givin' out every curse word you could think of, until she read to number ten. After that, she surprised everybody and said, 'Number eleven: *Cleatis*.' Everybody looked around the classroom confused. 'Number twelve: *Chicken*.' Couldn't nobody figure out what was goin' on. Ms. Swinton smiled like a Chess cat and said, 'Number thirteen: *ass* and number fourteen: *whuppin'*!'"

The earth trembled from people's uproarious laughter. I looked at Daddy and saw he was laughing, too. He didn't deny the story, revealing that it must have been true. I had heard tales of him and Mr. Chicken doing all kinds of wild stuff, but this one was the best yet.

"Ms. Swinton tore our asses up, too," Daddy offered after the laughter subsided a bit. "My mind tole me to check dem damn words Chicken was puttin' in her drawer, but for some reason I didn't. Dat boy used to git me in trouble all de time!"

"Y'all was some crazy fools," Uncle Roscoe confirmed.

Relatives shook their heads and laughed for about thirty more minutes, until Uncle Roscoe requested everyone to make a gigantic circle in the middle of the field.

"For what, man?" people asked irritably.

"You'll see! Shit!"

Folks didn't appreciate his bossy nature, but he was too big to argue with, so everyone began to form a big circle in the middle of the land. It took seemingly an hour. Folks kept laughing and talking and clowning around until Uncle Roscoe said, "All right, niggas! Let's go now. Y'all movin' like dat ole tired mule we used to have!" and the family circle finally materialized.

"We gon' give thanks for everybody in the family who done passed on," Uncle Roscoe explained. "We gon' go round de circle and give everybody a chance to call de name of any family member that done died. Say de name real loud for everybody to hear. Dese chil'ren need to know who dey is and where dey come from."

I loved the idea. It also gave me a chance to count the number of people who had come to the reunion. We resembled an African village, I remember thinking proudly. The whole scene reminded me of *Roots*.

"We gon' start with Wizard Lee and go right round de circle till we git back to him. If you don't know nobody you ain't got to say nothin', but try to remember, specially you older ones. I'm gon' git dis boy heayh to write down all the names so we can make a list for next time, jes' in case we start forgittin'."

I ran into the house and got my notebook and came back anxious to hear the names of people I was related to but surely had never known.

Wizard Lee began with, "Aunt Mae Helen," screaming like we were fifty miles apart.

"Snuke James," said the next person.

"Uncle Buddy Epson."

"All right, all right," mumbled Uncle Roscoe as he remembered people from way back.

"Aunt Trucilla Faye Nealy," the next person said.

"Eloise Tyson and little baby Joyce." I had heard of them. It felt good to hear someone's name I recognized. Eloise was Daddy's oldest sister, who died in childbirth. Minutes later, the child stopped breathing, too. Nobody knew why.

"Uncle T-Bone Jones."

"Daddy Jake Tyson," said Uncle Fred, my daddy's other brother. Uncle Fred's real name was Alexander, but they called him Fred because he looked liked Red Foxx. He acted like him, too.

"Mother Lucille Tyson," one of Uncle Jethro's boys called out.

"Aunt Mary Francis."

"Uncle Nimrod Tyson."

"James Earl Anthony." That was another name I knew. I remembered him because he must have been the sweetest man I had ever met. He would sit around and cry tears of joy all day. Folks said he was weak and got on their nerves, but I adored him. He came to visit one summer and I saw him crying so I asked him what was the matter. "Oh, I'm jes' fine, son," he replied enthusiastically. "Then why are you crying, sir?" I asked, bewildered. "'Cause it's jes' good to be alive!" he exclaimed. I sat down beside him and he put his huge arm around my shoulder and I cried too. I don't know why.

"Andre Morris."

"Janie Mae Reed."

"Uncle Lang Hughes."

"Aunt Joe Ester."

"Grandma Bertha Tyson." My daddy's grandmother.

"Priscilla Ray Barnes."

"Cousin Catherine McDaniel."

"Boy and Girl Williams." These were twins who died of crib death before they were named. Grandma told me about them.

"Princess Tyson." Daddy's second-oldest sister. Her husband killed her because he thought she slept with another man, Uncle Roscoe told me. People always spoke of her as the prettiest woman anyone had ever laid eyes on. She was rather tall, I understand, five-eight or so, and jet-black. She was thin, but not too thin to be fine in the country. I wished I had met her.

"Fatback Reed." The whole circle chuckled. People said all he wanted to do all day was eat fat meat, even as a child, so they called him Fatback. I don't know how he died.

"Aunt Margaret Fuller."

"Aunt Estelle Fuller."

"Cousin Neck Bone."

"Erma Joe Dean."

"Willie Tyson." Granddaddy's other brother.

"Precious Tyson." I frowned because I had never heard that name before. Uncle Roscoe leaned next to me and groaned, "Your daddy's twin sister." I gaped at him. "Close yo' mouth, boy. I'll tell you 'bout her later." I was flabbergasted. Daddy had never even breathed her name before. Ever. I definitely wanted to hear that story. I remember shaking my head woefully and saying to myself, "The secrets we keep."

"Granddaddy Moses Horton."

"Big Mama Izadore Walter."

"Zora Mae Hurston."

"Uncle Well Springs."

"Uncle Jeremiah Moore."

"Aunt Christine Sandidge."

"Cousin John Baldwin."

"Aunt Jessie Bell Sanders."

"Cousin Ella Faye Larsen."

"Uncle Bigger."

"Antionette Morrison."

"Auntie Kay Powell."

It was almost my turn. I didn't know much about the family, so I wasn't sure whose name I was going to call. All the names I remembered best had already been said.

"Grandma Evernessa Green."

"Sloufoot Cunningham," I said, and people immediately burst into laughter.

"What chu know 'bout Sloufoot, boy?" an elder man asked me.

"Nothin' really, sir. I jes' heard people tell stories about him."

"Dat's jes fine," Uncle Roscoe said, rescuing me from the interrogation. "We almost through, so let's keep it goin'."

More names were called and I recorded each one of them. I had pages and pages of names of people I wished I had known. In the stories, they always sounded interesting.

After the last name was called, Uncle Roscoe said, "We gon' bow our heads and pray." He moved from the edge of the circle to the center and bowed down on one knee. "Lawd, we thank You for the gatherin' of jes' a few of yo' humble servants. We thank You fu' life, health, and a reasonable po'tion of strenf. We wouldn't be nothin' without Chu, Lawd! Please bless all dese heayh people under de sound of my voice and don't let no hurt, harm, or danger come upon us. As we travels to and fro, on de dangous highways and byways, keep us safe, Lawd. And until we git togetha again fu' anotha reunion, protect us. All dese things we ask in Your Son Jesus' name, Amen."

"Amen," the crowd responded loudly.

"Now let's eat!" Uncle Roscoe announced. "It's 'bout five o'clock and you niggas act like y'all gon' starve to death! But I don't blame you. Hell, I'm hongry, too!"

There was enough food in the middle of that field to feed everyone in the state of Arkansas. Barbecue ribs, chicken, fish, ham, macaroni and cheese, corn on the cob, collard greens, mustard greens, squash, green beans, black-eyed peas, potato salad, potato pie, peach cobbler, blackberry cobbler, egg custard . . . you name it, we had it. And I mean folks ate! Uncle Roscoe had three plates, one of meats, another of vegetables, and another of desserts. "I'm gon' eat light today," he told me, grinning. "I can't do like I used to."

I got my plate and sat next to Uncle Roscoe, anticipating the story about Aunt Precious, Daddy's twin sister.

"Well, boy, ain't much to tell. When de twins wuz born, both of 'em was healthy and doin' jes' fine. The little girl wuz so pretty. She smiled all de time and no one ever heard her cry. Ever. Now yo' daddy wuz a different story. He didn't do nothin' but cry. Seemed like couldn't nobody figure out what wuz wrong wid him. In de middle of de night he'd just start hollerin' and keep on hollerin' till de sun came up. Precious laid right next to him and never mumbled a sound. While yo' daddy was hollerin' she'd jes' lay there grinnin' like she knew exactly what was goin' on. After a few days, yo' daddy stopped cryin'. Everybody wuz kinda shocked actually. But what really troubled Momma wuz the fact that Precious stopped smiling. All of this happened on de same day. Yo' daddy started smilin' and Precious started cryin'. Every time she would cry, he would laugh. Momma sent me to get Miss Liza, the community healer. Miss Liza came over and studied de twins for a little while. She took dem into de back room and wuz saying somethin', but I couldn't make it out. When she came back into de front room, she was shakin' her head sadly.

Momma asked her what wuz de matter, and at first Miss Liza jes' kept on shakin' her head. I knew it wuz somethin' bad 'cause she looked real pitiful. Miss Liza said, 'De boy is takin' de girl's spirit. She gon' die in a day or two." Then she left. Momma was cryin' real hard. I ran to de field and told Daddy, but he said wasn't nothin' he could do 'bout it, so I came back home and sat wit' Momma. She jes' cried and cried. I went into de back room where de twins wuz and yo' daddy wuz layin' there grinnin' like he had done won a prize. De baby girl was whimperin' and tremblin'. She wuz lookin' at me like she wanted me to do somethin', but I didn't know what to do. I picked her up and held her real close to me and rubbed her back. She quieted down for a minute, but soon's I laid her back down, she started cryin' again. That's when I named her Precious. Momma hadn't named neither one of 'em 'cause she said she jes' didn't imagine she was havin' no two babies. I called her Precious because she was pretty and I really liked her. I told Momma dat I named her Precious and she said dat was fine. 'What you call de boy?' she asked. I told her I ain't thought of no name fu' him so we didn't call him nothin' fu' almost a year.

"Precious died three days later. I woke up and knowed she was already dead. I ran to the little homemade crib and found her layin' stiff as a board. She wasn't smilin'."

"How do you steal somebody's spirit?" I asked, perplexed by the whole story.

"I don't know, son. I don't know," Uncle Roscoe replied and he sucked on a rib bone. He bucked his eyes at me, trying to convey how crazy the whole story was to him, too.

"It's some crazy shit done happened in dis family, boy," he announced, rising to find a napkin to wipe his hands.

I didn't know what to think. Finding out about Daddy as a baby seemed strange. I couldn't imagine he had been anything other than a grown man his whole life. But how did he steal his sister's spirit? Maybe it wasn't that at all, I told myself. Maybe that's simply what old folks said and no one questioned it. Nevertheless, the story left me uneasy.

Uncle Roscoe consoled me, "Ain't no needs in worryin' yo'self 'bout what done happened fifty years ago, boy. Don't nobody know why de Lawd do what He do."

"Uncle Roscoe, do you believe what Miss Liza said? I mean, do you believe Daddy stole Aunt Precious's spirit?"

He didn't say anything at first. He just kept eating and grunting, apparently unsure of whether he should answer me.

"Yeah, I believe it. Some folks come in de world wid dem kinda powers. Everybody don't, but some people do. I believe dat. Jes' like dat time when—"

I tuned Uncle Roscoe out. He had left me with a lot to think about. I always knew Daddy was mean, but I never guessed him to be someone who could take another person's life. Maybe he was too young to know what he was doing. After all, he was a baby. Yet I didn't believe what I was thinking. I studied Daddy across the field, wondering what else, in God's name, I was going to unearth about him.

Just then, Sister approached me and said, "All the kids are getting together to play kickball. Wanna play?" She sounded too excited for me to refuse, so I left my plate half-eaten and ran to join cousins, some of whom I knew I would probably never see again.

The elders were our cheerleaders. "Kick de ball, shit!" they hollered as we tried to show off in front of our families. The weak and prissy—boy or girl—were ridiculed shamelessly.

"Come on, Jamie! Kick dat muthafucka!" said Auntie Pearl, Granddaddy Jake's sister. "If you don't kick dat ball, I'm gon' whip yo' ass!"

We chuckled, but Jamie didn't. Folks said he had always been a shy child who simply would rather be left alone. I didn't see any problem with him, but other folks did, especially his grandmother. She said he was too sorry to be a boy. Wouldn't no woman want no man who can't hold his head up in public, she told him. But Jamie never changed as far as I knew. He and I were the same age, only three days apart, and for most of the family reunion, he only spoke to me. He never acknowledged other folks.

"Did ju hear me, boy?" Auntie Pearl screamed.

"Yes, ma'am," Jamie chirped softly and tried with all his might to kick the ball, although he missed it completely.

"Come here, boy!" Auntie Pearl demanded, hobbling swiftly and awkwardly toward the homemade kicker's mound on knees that people expected to collapse straightway.

"Ain't I done told you to be a man, boy?" She slapped Jamie across the face. "Cut out all dat sissy shit! And stop dat damn cryin'!"

Auntie Pearl didn't believe in coddling children. I avoided her like the plague. Sister said Auntie was sad because all her kids had died and she didn't really have anyone to take care of her. I didn't care about the seed of her discontent; I just knew I didn't want to encounter her if I could help it.

Jamie walked away embarassed and humiliated. I didn't see him again until nightfall, when people were getting ready to leave. He must have gone for a walk in the woods, I concluded, because Sister and I saw him approaching from behind the house. We went to him.

"It's OK, Jamie," Sister said lightly, grabbing his hand. "I think you did fine. Everybody misses sometimes."

"I miss all the time," he mumbled with his head bowed.

"Who cares?" I tried to say boldly but failed. "These people are mean." My words provided no comfort. "Everybody else likes you, man. It's just Auntie Pearl—"

"Why didn't somebody help me then? Huh? If everybody likes me, why didn't somebody help me!" Jamie was angry, hurt, and embarassed.

"I don't know. Who gon' mess with Auntie Pearl?"

Jamie fell silent. He stood there and began to weep again. I felt sorry for him.

"Don't cry, Jamie," Sister sympathized zealously. "You'll get another whippin'."

"I'm gon' get one anyway. I always do. It really don't make no difference."

He cried harder. I embraced him and let him sob on my shoulder until we heard his grandmother calling his name.

"Try to be strong, Jamie," I begged. "You can make it. I know it's hard and all, but you got to hang in there. Don't give up. We can write each other if you want?"

"Yeah! I'll write, too," Sister added.

Jamie smiled a little, giving our hearts temporary relief.

"Thanks, y'all," he said as he wiped tears on his shirtsleeve. "I'll never forget you. Never."

And he never did. We wrote consistently for about a year, and then the letters stopped coming. I don't know what happened to Jamie. When Auntie Pearl died our senior year, folks said, he went to the funeral for five minutes. Busted through the church door, according to Uncle Roscoe, and walked down the aisle to the casket. Jamie stood looking at Auntie Pearl for about ten seconds with absolutely no emotion at all. Then he started laughing real loud, Uncle Roscoe said, and turned and walked out. Someone ran after him, asking how they were supposed to bury Auntie Pearl without an insurance policy. Since he was the next of kin, he should take the responsibility, they said. "I don't give a fuck what y'all do with the bitch," Jamie told his relative. "You can throw her in the ground for all I care!" He left beaming. It was a crying shame, Uncle Roscoe said.

I would have been cracking up! I could imagine Jamie as a grown man finally getting a chance to say what he had been holding a lifetime. Of course, I would have gotten slapped in the mouth for laughing at a funeral, but it would have been worth it. I sure hate I missed that one.

The family reunion ended with Sunday morning worship. The church was full. All the cousins, aunts, and uncles came together to give thanks for the madness we called family. After a few good congregational numbers, Reverend Samuels started whooping and hollering. He gave me a headache. Not only was he saying absolutely nothing, but also he was foaming at the mouth and jumping around like a rabied beast. All he said was, "And early one Sunday morning, de Lawd got up from de grave wit' all power in his hands!" He leaned back and screamed in the microphone as though mimicking Jimi Hendrix in concert. Sister had fallen asleep much earlier, leaving me no one with whom to clown.

Attempting to avoid absolute boredom, I raised my hands and started screaming, "Yes, Lord!" over and over again until I made myself cry. I rolled my eyes into the back of my head and fell on top of whoever was sitting next to me. "Oh, hallelujah, God! Thank ya, Jesus! Glory to God! Hondanna Na Shanda! Kee Bo La Fonda! Hey!" Folks started looking at me crazy. Speaking in tongues was taboo in Swamp Creek and most people's response to it was, "It don't take all of that!" I was clowning hard. I started kicking and screaming like an epileptic as my arms flung open wide and my head jerked back and forth as though my neck were broken. I remember hitting someone pretty hard, but I dared not stop to apologize, for then my Holy Ghost experience would not have appeared genuine. I went on sweating, panting, and screaming. "I love ya, Lord! Can't nobody do me like Jesus! Oh, thank ya, Lord! You sho' a keeper, Lord! You brought me from a mighty long way, Lord! Ke Si Mo Shonda, Wanda Ke Ne Ne Obanda! Ra Fe Lo Lowanda!" I was full of shit like no one would believe. Somebody shoulda whipped my ass right in the middle of that church service! But, instead, people began to holler and shout that I was being possessed by the Holy Ghost! They were thrilled to see someone that young submitting himself to the power of the spirit and not being afraid to let the Lord have His way. I couldn't believe they thought I was serious. I knew ushers would come soon to escort me outside to get some fresh air and cool down a bit. Indeed, that was the aim, for once they left me to recover, I planned to sneak off down the road to the General Store. However, my plan took on complications of its own because people truly thought I was spirit possessed. I continued with the charade, amazed at the power I was calling forth unto myself.

Suddenly a woman stood up and began to interpret my tongues! I was laughing hard and screaming louder to cover it. She said, "Thus saith the Lord, Our God. 'If My people would submit again unto My law, I would bless them tenfold what they could ever imagine. If they would but humble themselves unto My word and hear the voice of My prophets, I would give them the desires of their hearts. Lo, My children, the way of the wicked enticeth the many and causeth all of them to stumble and fall. Hear ye, this day, the word of the Lord and abide'."

The crowd belted out, "Hallelujah!" and, "Amen!" and, "Oh, thank you, Jesus," for the interpretation rendered of my unknown tongues.

I started to stand up and tell her, "Sit down, woman! I ain't said none of that stuff you jes' said. In fact, I ain't said nothin', 'cause I made it all up!" Yet that would have ruined all the fun I was having watching my relatives make complete asses of themselves as they turned my joke into the indisputable Word of God.

The ushers came, picked me up, and carried me outside. I kept breathing hard so that the transition back to normalcy wouldn't seem too abrupt.

"You all right, son?" said one of the ushers, fanning me violently.

"Yes, ma'am. I'm fine," I returned. "I feel a little light-headed. I guess I'd better sit here a minute and get myself back together."

"De Holy Ghost really got on you dis mornin'!"

"Yes, ma'am! It sho' did!"

They left me alone to recover. The minute they were out of sight, I said, "Thank God!" and ran to the General Store to get Sister and me some candy.

When I got back, I knew I was in trouble because church service was over. I hadn't realized I had been gone so long. I walked into the back of the church and started hugging relatives and saying good-bye like I had never left. I could feel Daddy staring at me out of the corner of his eye, but I never turned to face him. On the way home that day, Daddy said, "You don't play wit' God, boy." And that's all he said.

"Yessir," I returned, trembling genuinely this time.

16

I went outside and met Willie James, who was hooking up the hay cutter to the John Deere tractor.

"I get a little help today?" he asked without looking up.

"Uh, sure, but I gotta make a run first. I'll meet you in the field. I won't be long."

Willie James didn't believe me.

"Seriously, I'll be there. I have something important I need to do first. I'll be in front of the old Whitcomb place before eight thirty. Promise. It's seven ten now and you can time me if you want."

Willie James mounted the tractor and said, "Whatever."

I started walking down the road to Ms. Swinton's place. Although I didn't want to upset her, I had some questions only she could answer. Apparently, she, too, was committed to keeping the secret of her maternity away from me, and, because of her illness, I wasn't sure if confronting her was such a good idea, but I persevered, determined to know the full truth. She wasn't going to be around much longer, and I resolved to uncover the details of my conception while I had a chance.

As I rounded the bend in the road leading to her house, I saw a dazzling baby blue Mercedes parked in her front yard. Maybe she has company, I thought, but I hadn't come that far to turn around, so I proceeded to her house and knocked on the front door.

"Yes, come in," a man's voice welcomed far in the distance.

I turned the knob and entered slowly. The house was still and quiet, completely frozen in time. Again I marveled at the books everywhere.

"I'm in the back room," the voice called again.

I followed it and discovered a rather tall, clean-cut, well-dressed young man sitting on Ms. Swinton's bed. He was reading what looked like a journal.

He stood when I entered the room, and smiled broadly, extending his right hand. "Hello, Thomas," he said with a strange familiarity.

"Um . . . hello . . . and how do you know me?" I asked peevishly.

The young man released my hand and chuckled. "Ms. Swinton told me all about you. Every word out of her mouth was Thomas this and Thomas that. She said you'd be coming by, and asked if I'd hang around and wait on you."

"Who are you?" I queried curiously.

The young man beheld me with exuberant hesitation and then revealed, "I'm Ms. Swinton's son."

"You're Ms. Swinton's son?" I bellowed.

"In the flesh. It's a long story, but it's true. I'll explain it to you later." He shook his head sadly, indicating that the story had more complications than he wished to entertain at the moment.

"Where's Ms. Swinton?" I asked, suddenly realizing she was not in the bed.

"Thomas, she passed around ten o'clock last night. She didn't want me to phone anyone, especially you. She said you would come today and that was soon enough."

"Oh no!" I screamed, and collapsed to the floor.

The young man resumed his place on the bed's edge. "Yeah. I was here, though, and everything was pretty nice actually. There was no pain and she said she had no regrets. Well, except one."

I rose slowly from the floor and sat on the bed next to him. Under normal circumstances, I would never have sat on Ms. Swinton's bed if she were not present, but somehow it seemed OK now.

"What was the one regret?" I asked.

"She asked me to stay here and wait on you," he said, ignoring my question. "She knew last night would be the end and made me promise to stay here and tell you everything."

"This is too crazy for me, man."

"I know. You ain't heard the half of it yet."

"What's your name?" I asked after realizing I was having a conversation about my life with a total stranger.

"David," he said rather lightly.

"Maybe I'm tripping or something, David, but you seem to be taking this whole thing rather nonchalantly."

"Death is part of life, Thomas. Plus, I know more than you about the full situation, little brother."

"She told you?"

"Yeah, she told me. Years ago. In fact, I knew when you were born. She said your eyes popped wide open when you came out, like you were searching for something. She knew at that moment you'd be a writer, musician, or some kind of artist. I was living with my dad at the time because Momma wasn't supposed to be a single mother teaching in the rural black South. Hence, I stayed in Detroit. She wanted to marry my father and move back here and have a family, she said, but Daddy wouldn't hear of it. She knew she couldn't come back here with a child as a single woman and teach. Folks didn't accept that lifestyle back in the day, so she decided to leave me with my father."

"Why didn't she stay there with you?"

"Because she said Swamp Creek was calling her and she had to answer. She couldn't get away from it. It didn't make much sense to me then, but I understand it perfectly now."

"She came back here because she had a feeling she was supposed to be here?"

"That's pretty much it, but don't underestimate the strength of a calling. Yearnings of the heart are difficult to ignore. You know what I mean?"

I thought of my own plight. "I know far too well."

Thomas continued, "Momma told me she prayed you'd return, and when you showed up a few days ago, she called me and told me her life was complete. I asked her if she told you everything and she said she couldn't. She wanted to enjoy you the way you always were: smart, handsome, respectful, seeking. She was afraid telling you about her and your father would devastate you and mar her last days with you. She said she owed herself at least a week of peace in her life. I was left behind to do the dirty work."

We both chuckled disingenuously.

"Momma kept journals over the years. Sometimes she would write for hours, it seems, creating ten and twenty-page entries. Your name is everywhere. From the day you were born to the day of your return, Momma recorded it. She was an amazing woman who truly loved to write. Read this one."

David handed me an old torn and battered journal. I had to hold the covers together to keep it from falling apart. The entry was dated January 15, 1965. I read aloud.

" 'Who knows the pain of a mother separated from her child? I wish I could retreat in time and hold Mary's hand as the Romans nail her baby to the cross. His being the Savior of the world surely meant nothing to a mother whose fate was to witness her own son's execution. While the world speaks of his gift of eloquence and his ability to transform water into wine, Mary undoubtedly remembers most his first step and his weight at birth. I wonder, as Jesus' blood was streaming down his side, if Mary even cared that her son had saved other souls. She probably sought desperately for someone to come and save his. And what about her heart after the resurrection? Was the fact that he had died to save the world supposed to compensate for the pain she endured from losing him? What a selfish, thoughtless world that can justify a mother's tragedy simply by arguing that everyone else benefits.

" 'I joined the ranks of Mary yesterday as I watched Cleatis walk slowly through the snow with my baby. The hurt inside my heart is too intense to describe and too deep to find. "That's my baby," I kept whispering, but I can't have him. People would say he didn't come right, that I hadn't been a righteous woman. So I gave him unto a place for safekeeping. I have a bad feeling about this arrangement, but there's nothing more I can do. Having made such a mistake once, I can't ascertain how I did it again. This Achilles' heel just won't give me any peace. Cleatis asked me not to tell the boy what happened between us, and I suppose I won't. It's not logical anyway. I can't explain it to myself. How did I let myself get involved with a twenty-two-year-old former student? Maybe I've been lying to myself about what I need and how badly I want a companion. That lie has certainly forced its own confession.' "

David moved a little closer to me and read along. I felt like I was in the Twilight Zone.

" 'But that's my baby, I keep telling myself. How will he know how much I love him? Who will assure him that his mother contemplated his existence daily? Will others tell him I abandoned him carelessly or thought he was ugly? The future I cannot tell, but I pray earnestly he will grow to be strong and beautiful and certain of himself. Might his joys always keep him in laughter, and might his sorrows be few. I know not how I shall bear this. It seems I have resigned myself to watching him grow without the privilege of nurturing him the right way. I won't get a chance to read to him for hours while he sits on my lap and falls in love with the written word. He may, in fact, never know he comes from a legacy of writers, that he is, in fact, a writer by birth. The best I can hope for is that Cleatis won't kill him if any of my blood announces itself in his character. Oh, God. What shall become of all of this? My baby . . . ' "

David handed me a handkerchief. To think that, all these years, she was watching me and pushing me because I belonged to her was simply overwhelming.

"Read this one," David prompted, handing me a different book.

" 'My son graduated from high school tonight. It's a day I've not anticipated joyfully. He's going to leave; I'm certain of that. I've heard his moans and grumblings about how stifling Swamp Creek is for him. Oh, the days I've wanted to grab him and tell him everything! Maybe the truth would keep him here, I thought. But I made a promise I have to keep. Never did I guess it would be this costly, this painful.

" 'His speech tonight was simply brilliant. He spoke of high standards and convictions of the heart as though he were an old man who had experienced a lifetime. He is absolutely beautiful. Where shall he go? I may never hear from him again after tonight. This must be the price of a wanton love affair. I still can't explain it to myself. Loneliness, maybe. I believe to be alone in the world is the greatest punishment any woman can endure. Cleatis was . . . there. No logic alone can justify my actions. It was the right day and the right time and he . . . appeared. I had asked him to come by and help me mount a bookcase, and somehow, as I read to him, we began to exchange feelings that neither of us premeditated. He stared at me while I read and then touched my face so gently that I melted in response. I laid the book down and rubbed his head, buried in my chest. None of this makes sense to me now, but then it felt right. Or at least it felt good.

" 'I pray the world treats my son with dignity and respect. I've tried frantically to teach him to love himself and to allow people to be the fullness of themselves without judgment. He loves to read! At least I did something right!' "

I chuckled and sniffled along.

" 'He'll probably teach somewhere. He'll be great, too. Charisma, charm, discipline, all the characteristics of a master teacher. I only wish I could be there and watch it all. That's every mother's right! I want to encourage him along the way when he gets discouraged and to fix him coffee and bring it to him as he studies all night for those major college exams. But no, it won't be me. I fear, indeed, it won't be anyone. Thomas is going to have to weather this storm alone. He was conceived by those who *could not give him what he needs. A cloudy origin is his destiny, it seems, yet I pray his life will be filled with uncloudy days. My hope is that he learns to stand firmly and solidly like a tree. He can do it. I know he can. Lord, please help him! Don't let my baby get devoured by a world that never, ever loved a black man. Oh God, I don't know what else to do. I'm putting him into Your hands for safekeeping. And, if it be Your will, if it be at all possible, please let me see him again before I see You.' "*

I couldn't read any more.

"I know this is kinda wild, Thomas, but you deserve to know. Momma wanted it that way." David put his arm around my shoulder and encouraged me to cry freely.

"Hey, man, we brothers, right?" he said as I wiped my tears embarassingly.

"Man, this is crazy," I remarked, rising and pacing the floor. "I come over here looking for Ms. Swinton and discover she's already dead and has left me a brother to serve as a personal messenger? This is too much."

"How you think I felt? I've spent years wondering why Momma had to leave me in Detroit and come down here to nothing. She has another son and I never get a chance to meet my own brother until we come together to bury our mother. This is trippin' me out, too. Believe me."

We looked at each other like two lost bear cubs wondering where, oh where, our mother had gone.

"She told me we'd meet one day. She said it was a long story, but we'd probably have a lot in common. I used to hope we both looked like her so we'd kinda look like each other, too. It's crazy, but I had a lotta thoughts about you over the years. I always wanted a little brother to play with and boss around, and Momma told me I had one, but I couldn't have you. I used to beg her to bring you to Detroit so I could meet you, but she said it wasn't possible. After a while, I stopped hoping. It seemed like a fairy tale anyway; thus I decided maybe you didn't even exist. Now here we are."

We hugged and cried together right there in the middle of Ms. Swinton's bedroom. It was strange, hugging a man intimately I had only met moments earlier, but it also felt very natural. We sat on the floor together and leaned our backs against the bed.

"Your whole life's story is in these journals, Thomas. It might take you a while, but you should sit down and read them carefully. Momma's entire life was obsessed by what you were having for dinner, or what kind of girlfriend you might find, or whether or not you'd become a preacher."

"A preacher?" I asked, startled.

"Yeah. Momma predicted you were going to be a preacher because you talked all the time, she said!"

"No I didn't, man!" I lied. We both laughed.

"She was sure your parents or simply living in Swamp Creek was going to land you in the pulpit."

"I can't believe Ms. Swinton wanted me to be a preacher! She never was one big on church."

"Oh no! She didn't want you to be a preacher. In fact, she prayed you'd never preach, she said. She thought you'd do it because there wasn't much else for a smart black boy to do in a little town like Swamp Creek. She never, ever wanted it for you. She used to tell me preachers were narrow and 'limiting in scope.' That's the phrase she always used. She said she hated the fact most preachers could only see God through the eyes of the Bible and certainly God was bigger than the ideological premise any book could ever contain. She told me she had a dream one time you were in the pulpit preaching and you told the congregation the Bible wasn't even real. It was the creation of writers who got together and decided they were going to write a book about God. Any group of people could do that, you asserted. Wonder what a book about God written by black writers might say? Momma said the church threw you out and told you never to come back. Such rejection is precisely why she hoped you'd never preach."

"That sounds like something I just might say!" I envisioned myself standing before a raised podium, sweating and hollering what I knew to be the truth.

"Are you a preacher?" David pondered.

"No, sir. I never preached. Thank God! I have issues with church dogma and dictates. I probably would have left it years ago, but I love the music. Ain't nothin' like church folks singing."

"Yeah, I agree. I have one of the best choirs in the country at my church."

My entire foot was in my mouth. "You're a preacher?" I asked, hoping he was not.

"Yeah, I am."

"Oh God! I'm sorry, man. I didn't mean to insult your profession."

"Please! Don't apologize. I know what you mean. The church has a few wrinkles here and there to iron out."

"A few?" I offered sarcastically.

"Well, a church is only as holy as the people in it."

"Amen to that." I waved my right hand in the air. "Did you go to seminary?"

"Yeah. I went to the Interdenominational Theological Center in Atlanta."

"What? I went to Clark, right down the street. How funny is that?"

"Wow. Our paths almost crossed. Of course, when I was at ITC you were probably in diapers."

"Incredible," I said in amazement.

"Life is like that sometimes. God is always doin' His own thing."

"Or Her thing."

"Right."

We fell silent. I suppose we were trying to learn from each other and deal with Ms. Swinton's death simultaneously.

"I want to have the funeral as soon as possible. Momma would want it that way. She always said she couldn't comprehend why it took black folk forever to get a body in the ground. I was thinking Saturday?"

"That's fine. I'm scheduled to leave Saturday evening at five o'clock, but, of course, the funeral should be over long before then."

"Are you sure? I don't want to rush you."

"Yeah, it's fine. It's just that . . ."

"What?"

"Your mom, I mean our mom, Ms. Swinton, asked something of me that has really left me troubled."

"What did she ask?"

"She made me promise to take over her job at the school here in Swamp Creek."

"For real?"

"Yeah."

"Did you promise to do it?"

"No, I didn't. In fact, I told her in no uncertain terms I couldn't handle it."

"Why can't you?"

"Excuse me? What do you mean, why can't I?"

"I mean, why can't you? It seems pretty simply to me."

"It ain't simple at all. When I left here after high school, I vowed never to return again. I got back Saturday and this is the first time I've been home since I left."

"Are you serious?" David inquired in stark horror.

"Yes, I'm serious. It's a long story, big brother, but I can't live here. I just can't. And that's what I told Ms. Swinton."

"What did she say?

"She never engaged me. Instead, she went on and on about how great I would be and how all the kids would love me and blah, blah, blah."

"Do what you need to, but maybe you returned for a reason even you don't know."

Vexation prompted me to ask, "What are you saying?"

"I'm saying that maybe taking over the school is something you should think about. You must be a dynamic teacher if Momma implored you to do it. We both know she would only invite the best."

"All that's great, David, but it's more complicated than you could ever imagine."

"As Momma might say, if you can tolerate your own recalcitrance I have no choice."

His reverse psychology made me vehement. I rose to leave.

"Don't go, Thomas," David pleaded sincerely, and grabbed my arm. "I'd like to know about your sister."

The request weakened my resolve to leave and further frazzled my formidable strength. Clearly, Ms. Swinton had told him everything about me. Hearing him speak of Sister left me vulnerable and power-less enough to collapse, again, onto the floor and say, "That's another matter altogether."

"Momma called me and told me when she died. She knew the news would break your heart. She worried about you."

"David, it's asinine. I don't even know where to begin."

"Wherever you like," he said, embracing my hand with his own.

I described how close Sister and I were and detailed, nostalgically, the fun we used to have. I told him how we sang duets in church and mocked people shouting. The butterfly story intrigued him most. Tangentially, I talked for hours.

"Wow. Sounds like she was pretty amazing. How exactly did she die?"

"I don't know! That's why I'm embittered. When I got back on Saturday I saw her grave in our backyard, and I've been perturbed ever since!"

"In the backyard?" David said, bewildered.

"Exactly! Ain't that wild? Man, the entire story is bizarre! I've been trying to determine what happened, but nobody wants to di-vulge information. Everybody's all evasive and hush-hush."

"I'm sorry, Thomas. I wish there was something I could do."

"Thanks, man." Suddenly I discovered hope. "What if Ms. Swin-ton wrote about it in her journal? I mean, maybe she heard something about Sister's death and noted it somewhere."

"Maybe, but I doubt it."

"Why?" I whined.

"Because Momma never wanted to be the source of your hurt. Your past is too painful, she would say. My guess is that she didn't write anything about your sister because she knew that, one day, you'd be reading these journals. She would never write anything that would hurt you. That's a promise she made to herself, I think."

What David said made sense; thus I killed the hope. Anyway, when I thought about it, Ms. Swinton couldn't have known the full truth. Nobody did except Momma and Daddy.

"What if you don't uncover information about your sister before Saturday evening?" David asked, exposing my dilemma.

"I'm history," I offered confidently. "Why would I stay?"

"Because it doesn't make sense to leave before your questions get answered."

"It does if you're in my shoes."

David stared at me pitifully. "Oh, I see."

"For real, man. I'm not staying past Saturday. These last couple of days have been torture for me, and I can't endure much longer."

"Could you live without ever knowing?"

"I don't know. I could if I had to, I suppose."

The smirk on David's face revealed he didn't believe me. "All I'll say is stay long enough to leave with peace, because if anything happens to your folks, the peace you have is all you'll get."

"Amen," I chimed.

David preached on, "Every man's gotta walk his own path and decide how much luggage he can carry. Don't let me convince you to stay. That's a decision only you can make."

"And I've made it. I'd die here, David. I can't stay. I'm flattered Ms. Swinton thought highly of me and I intend to find out what happened to Sister, but I've got to leave here. Sister was the only reason I came back anyway. And even if I find out what happened, why would I stay?"

David glared at me, sensing I was talking more to myself than him. "Again, do whatever you need to."

He rose to his knees and began to place the journals into a cardboard box. I surveyed the room Ms. Swinton had left behind and became engulfed in emptiness, despondence, and agitation made most acute by David's ascension to the role of quintessential big brother.

"What time Saturday?" I stood.

"I don't know. Maybe around noon or one o'clock?"

"That'll work," I heralded, trying not to be melancholy about Ms. Swinton's funeral. "Who has the body?"

"Marshall Brothers."

"Oh, good. They're the best."

While exiting, I noticed an old picture on the wall. "Who's this? Do you know?"

"That's your grandfather."

"What?"

"Yep. That's Granddaddy Swinton. He was a buffalo soldier. The buffalo soldiers were black cowboys who went out west to—"

"Yeah, I know. I have a Ph.D. in black studies."

"Are you serious? You have a Ph.D.?"

"Uh-huh. I graduated last month."

"Did you tell Momma?"

"Yes. I told her the other day when I came by."

"Good. She's at peace then. I'm glad you told her before she died."

I kept marveling at the picture. "Did you ever meet him?"

"Yeah, once. He was the funniest man! All he did was tell stories about the Old West. My father took me to see him when I was about eight. I don't remember him well. I just remember that he was funny. And very dark."

"Really? Darker than this photograph?"

"Much. That picture makes him look light skinned. He said his momma and daddy were full-blooded Africans. You look a bit like him, actually."

"Yeah, right," I chuckled.

"Honestly. He was thin like you and had a wide, flat nose. Look at him good."

I examined the man's profile intensely and suddenly saw myself. "Wow. I see what you mean. This is incredible."

"Told you, didn't I?" David smiled. "Take it with you. I knew him. The picture will help you know him, too."

"No, no. I couldn't do that."

"Why not? Who else wants it?"

"You don't want it?"

"I want you to have it. You need all the pieces of the puzzle you can get. They've been denied to you up to this point, and you deserve them."

I slowly dismounted the black-and-white picture from the wall. It was framed in the antique oval style and had yellowed over the years. I held it out from me and perused it like I had found a treasure.

"Take these, too," David said, handing me the box of journals. "They chronicle your life, so you should have them. You won't really know yourself until you read them, and why not start today?"

David extended a warm smile and dismantled my hesitation. "Go ahead; take them. Under normal circumstances, I might be jealous, and I probably am a little bit, but I know Momma wanted you to have them. Please take them and keep them forever. They're all you'll have of her now."

"Thank you, David," I maundered, unsure of how to express my gratitude.

"It's the least I can do," he assured as I laid the picture on top of the box and embraced it with both arms. "Don't thank me. Thank Momma."

David resumed packing other items in the room, seemingly un-moved by his mother's death. Knowing Ms. Swinton, she had pre-pared him for it.

"I guess I'd better go now. I told my brother I'd meet him hours ago."

"All right. I'm gonna stay around here for the next day or two and pack the house up and finish other last-minute details. Come back and rap with me more if you get a chance."

"I will. I promise." I had turned to leave with what I hoped would not be Pandora's box when David asked, "Do you want to be listed on the obituary as her son?"

The question should have been easily answered, but it was not. "Yes, I do," I reconciled after a moment. "No need to harbor the secret any longer."

"Good," David said, relieved. "Momma would like that."

I got almost to the front door when he announced, "Thomas, I'm glad to finally meet my little brother. I hope we stay in touch."

"Let's promise we will. For Ms. Swin . . . for . . . Momma."

"Deal."

I left jovial and excited that, for the first time since I arrived, my coming home had proven gratifying.

17

When I arrived at the old Whitcomb place, it was after one o'clock and I noticed, either to my chagrin or to my relief, Willie James had almost finished cutting the entire field of hay. Bobbing up and down on the old tractor, he scrutinized me, shaking his head in complete disgust. There was no way I could justify my tardiness. I couldn't tell him I had met my older brother from Detroit and we had spent the morning hours reminiscing about what *our* mother wrote in her journals. First of all, Willie James wouldn't believe me. And second of all, even if he did, the fact remained that he had done all the work in the hay field without me. Either way, my actions confirmed Willie James's notion that I was simply a sorry-ass nigga.

"What happened this time?" he yelled, rounding the corner for the last strip of hay left standing in the field.

"Long story! You wouldn't believe it anyway!" I screamed back. He chuckled and mumbled inaudibly. I stood there and watched the green moody grass Willie James had cut slowly turnin' golden brown in the sun. It was thick. This meant lots of hay bales, which, of course, meant food for Daddy's cows and several large round bales to sell. Maybe Willie James would make a little pocket change, I thought, and come visit me in New York or wherever later in the year, but on second thought, I knew better. Willie James had gotten used to the entire world being contained in Swamp Creek. Anything outside of the ordinary would shift his world too drastically. Even as a child, once Willie James learned a rule, he never apprehended how to accommodate its exception. Like the time Ms. Swinton told him "*i* before *e* except after *c*." He said he understood. He knew if the "*i/e* dilemma" came after any other consonant, the correct spelling was *ie*. One day, on a weekly spelling test, Willie James spelled *seize* "*sieze*," confident the rule had helped him pass the exam. When he got it back and saw that he had misspelled the word, he was dismayed.

"I thought you said *i* comes before *e* except after *c*!" he protested to Ms. Swinton.

"I did say that, Willie James, but there are exceptions to every rule. You must learn both the rules and their exceptions."

"Then the rule ain't no rule at all! You just gotta learn how to spell everything by itself!"

"I guess one could see it that way," Ms. Swinton offered sympathetically.

Willie James decided then that he'd never be a good speller because the rules simply didn't make sense.

I sat on the ground underneath a nearby persimmon tree and waited on him to finish the last lap. Ants were busy gathering food and taking it into their little mound. I picked up a stick and scattered their dirt fortress to see how the ants would react. They panicked. Some ran north and others south as they tried frantically to right the wrong I had committed. I was intrigued by the speed and diligence with which the ants worked to reestablish communal balance and harmony. Only a second or two passed before they slowed once again and resumed their normal living arrangement. Amazingly, they were absolutely unconcerned with the source of their disturbance. They did what they needed to do in order to protect themselves, regardless of who originated the mayhem among them. "Brilliant," I whispered.

"We oughta be like them," Willie James noted, wiping sweat from his face. He had parked the tractor and walked over to where I was sitting without my noticing.

"I didn't see you walk up," I returned, slightly startled.

Willie James peered at me sadly. "At least you see me. Usually people don't see me."

He sat on the ground next to me and leaned back in the grass as he sighed heavily. "I'm tired o' dis shit, man," he said distressfully.

"I feel you," I consoled him.

"You was smart. You got outta here years ago. I don't blame you fu' dat." Willie James patted my shoulder condescendingly.

"You could have left, too. Daddy nem would've been OK without you." My words didn't come out right.

"Yeah, they probably would have, but I never had the balls to leave. Too scared, I suppose."

"Scared of what?"

"Myself. I always knew, if I left, I wasn't comin' back. I stayed here to keep from runnin' so far away I couldn't find my way home."

"I'm not sure I understand."

"You'll understand if you think about it." Willie James started playing with the same anthill.

"I am thinking about it, and I still don't understand. Explain it to me."

"Uhh . . . ," Willie James began demurely, eyes never meeting mine. He had been waiting a lifetime to express the thought, it seemed, and all he wanted was an interested ear. "Remember how we used to cuss Daddy out behind his back and sware when we got eighteen we was gon' leave? I intended to keep that promise. When my eighteenth birthday came round though, I got scared 'cause I hated the place bad enough never to come back if I left. I wasn't confused about my feelings; I jes' couldn't imagine starting life all over again someplace else. See, I always knew I hated this place more than you did. You were jes' mad people didn't love you. If they loved you right, you wouldn't ever have left. Dammit, I actually hated this place. I'm not bullshittin'. I thought you'd come back one day 'cause you cared too much about what Momma nem thought about you, and you and Sister was jes' too close fu' you to leave and neva come home. I ain't neva been close to nobody, so I ain't had nothin' to lose."

He shrugged his shoulders with a contradictory carelessness. "I was always de workhorse. Sunup till sundown, Willie James was sweatin' fu' somebody. I didn't know nothin' else, but I knowed I didn't like it. I didn't have no choice back then."

"We sho' didn't!" I blurted.

"Man, come on, T.L. You ain't neva been one fu' no sweatin'! You dodged hard work every chance you got!" Willie James pursed his lips, daring me to challenge his declaration.

"What? Are you crazy? I worked hard, too, man. Just as hard as anybody else." His assertion of my indolence offended me.

"Yeah, you worked a little bit," he conceded, "but what you did most was read and write or whatever you liked."

"Hell, yeah! That was the only way to survive this madness!"

"You right. Yet when you was readin' or whatever, I was in the field. Day or night."

"Why didn't you do something you liked? At least every now and then?"

"'Cause I ain't neva knowed what I liked. I wasn't great at school, but I didn't know nothin' else to try. I jes' kept workin' 'cause wasn't nothin' else for me to do. At least that's what I thought back then. Now I'm too old to do anything else."

"Why?" I grilled him with too much emphasis.

"'Cause I done fixed my mind to believe I can't do nothin' but farm. I mean, I believe I probably could do somethin', but come on, I done settled into dis damn place, and I ain't goin' nowhere. I know dat."

"Sounds like you don't want to go anywhere. And that's fine," I portended insultingly.

"Dat ain't what I'm sayin', T.L. What I'm sayin' is dat I always wanted to leave, I jes' didn't have nothin' to take wit' me. I couldn't sing, dance, write, or nothin' else, so I had to stay in order to eat."

"You could have learned a trade, Willie James, and done well for yourself. You might have had to struggle for a moment, but you would have made it. Most people do."

"And some don't," he said emphatically. "Dat's what scared me. Ain't no way I was gon' leave here and not make it and have to come back. I would be too ashamed and I would feel like nothin'. I'd die befo' I let Daddy stare me in de face 'cause I failed. He'd really treat me like shit then."

"Sometimes you have to take a chance, man, if you want something badly enough," I said, struggling strenuously to inspire him.

"It ain't dat bad here," Willie James defended himself, avoiding my attempt to make him see otherwise. He demolished the anthill with a stick. "A man can make a livin' anywhere, huh?"

"Some can. And some have to go somewhere else to make theirs."

"You right, li'l brother. You right."

We sat in silence for a while, watching the ants reestablish their community. Truth be known, they simply averted our eyes from each other.

"Sister was pregnant with a boy."

"How you know?" I asked coolly, trying not to rush Willie James's willingness.

"'Cause dat's what she told me. She said you was comin' back to her one way or another and maybe God was sendin' you back through her li'l baby boy. I asked her how she know it was a boy and she said she could feel it."

"My God."

"Yep, she was gon' give birth to a li'l baby boy."

Willie James paused awkwardly and continued investigating the ants for anwers he could not find.

"What happened to the baby, Willie James?" I pressed softly.

"I don't know exactly. Like I tole you de other day, I came home from de field one day and saw the fresh mound o' dirt and wondered what it was. I asked Momma about it when I went in de house and she said, 'Yo' sista died today; we buried her today.' She started cryin.' I said, 'What?' And she said, 'You heard me, boy! Now I got enough on me!' I went outside and stood over the grave and started cryin' a li'l bit myself. I was real sad, T.L. I was confused, too, but I didn't wanna make Momma mo' upset by askin' her mo' questions. I stayed by de grave and stared in de sky all night long. I neva got sleepy and I neva said nothin' to nobody 'bout it. I stared in de sky talkin' to God till de sun come up de next mornin'.

"When I went in de house fu' breakfast, Momma and Daddy was actin' real funny. I didn't say nothin' to neither one o' dem, but I could tell dat somethin' wasn't right. Befo' Daddy left, he said, 'Keep yo' mouf shet, boy,' and went on his way. As scared as I was, dey didn't have to worry 'bout me sayin' nothin'. I did wanna know what happened, though. I jes' decided to keep my eyes and ears open extra hard in case I saw or heard somethin' suspicious.

"When I came home fu' lunch dat day, wasn't nobody home. That was strange 'cause you know Momma don't neva go nowhere. I ain't think much of it till I see her through de kitchen window walkin' through de field like she comin' from back in de woods. She was walkin' kinda fast, you know, kinda nervous-like, so I went out de front do' as she was comin' in de back. She neva knowed I was there 'cause I didn't eat nothin'."

"Where was she coming from?" I frowned, both interested and confused.

"I'm 'bout to tell you dat, man, but you can't say a word to nobody." Willie James awaited my confirmation of secrecy. I nodded.

"When I left out de front, I snuck back into de woods where it looked like she was comin' from. I glanced around fu' a while and didn't see nothin'. Then I noticed one o' Daddy's cows sniffin' some-thin' over by de back fence. I walked over to look and see what de cow was looking at and dat's when I saw de li'l dead baby. It was blue and red and had dried blood all over it. I knowed it was dead 'cause it looked dead. It was real little! I coulda held it in one hand easy. It wasn't wrapped in nothin'. It was jes' layin' on de ground like somebody throwed it out. I was scared 'cause I ain't neva seen nothin' like dat befo'. I bent down and turned it over with a stick and de baby looked like it was smilin'. I dropped de stick and ran like ninety goin' north. I wanted to go tell somebody, but I didn't know who. It was all so crazy dat I thought folks might think I was losin' it. I jes' ran until I got tired and fell out by de creek behind de woods. I was shakin' like a leaf, man, and cryin' 'cause I didn't know what else to do. I knowed Momma had somethin' to do wit' it, but I couldn't put nothin' together dat made sense. After I calmed down a li'l bit, I decided to go back and bury de li'l baby. I knowed it was Sista's. It couldn't o' been nobody else's. But when I got back, de baby was gone."

"What? Are you serious?" I said in total disbelief.

"Yep. It was gone. I looked all around de place where I had saw it, but it was gone. I don't know if Momma came back and got it or if a wild fox or somethin' took it off and ate it or what, but it was gone sho' 'nuff."

"Willie James! You have to be lyin'!"

"Naw I ain't. You de onlyest somebody I done told dis to; now don't say nothin' to nobody 'bout it."

"I won't, Willie James, but this is unreal! You sure you saw a baby?"

"Hell yeah, I'm sure!" Willie James screamed. "I ain't stupid. I know a baby when I see one. And it was a boy, too. When I turned it ova, I saw dat. Sista was right, I said to myself. But I couldn't figure out why somebody had thowed him away."

"Man, I must be going utterly insane!" I said as I rose and paced the earth.

"Nope, ain't nothin' wrong with you. Now, don't go gettin' yo'self all worked up 'cause then you been done said somethin' to somebody and I'll be in a heap o' trouble. Sit down and be cool."

"Be cool? Willie James, this is murder we talkin' 'bout!"

"No, it ain't. We don't know what happened to dat baby. I don't know how it got in dem woods. Since I saw Momma comin' from dat direction, I thought she probably had somethin' to do wit' it. And she probably did, but I don't know what. We can't start accusin' folks 'cause we ain't got no proof o' nothin'. There ain't even no baby no mo'.'"

I resumed my seat on the ground next to Willie James, shaking my head in dismay. "Man, we have to do something! We have to! We can't know about this and go on like we don't!"

"Yes, we can, and dat's exactly what we gon' do. 'Cause, like I said, we don't really know nothin'. I mean, I know what I saw and all, but I can't prove it to nobody."

"Oh, Willie James, please! You know Momma did somethin' to dat baby!" I yelped, sitting only inches away from him.

"Maybe she did!" he hollered back. "But can't neither one o' us prove it. Dat's why we gon' let it be. Now I feel bad about it jes' like you. Believe me I do. But I done thought 'bout dis fu' years now and I ain't come up wit' no way to tell nobody nothin' and make 'em believe me. We gon' keep dis li'l secret between us and dat gon' be dat."

"How can you do that, Willie James?" I gazed at my brother ruefully.

"Do what?"

"Know this information and never say anything about it."

"It ain't hard. You jes' learn to keep yo' mouth shut. Everythang ain't s'pose' to be told noway."

"Some things are supposed to be known!"

"Depends on what it is. A man got to decide what he gon' tell and what he gon' keep. Dis somethin' we both gon' keep."

Willie James stared deep into my eyes to ratify our unspoken agreement.

"OK, OK. I won't say anything. It's not right, though, Willie James. It doesn't make sense not to tell the authorities."

"And who the authorities round here? You know de police in town don't care nothin' 'bout no dead nigga baby!" He swung his arm at an invisible foe. "Ain't no need in even wastin' yo' time wit' dem. I thought about tellin' Daddy 'bout de baby, but you know he know. He know everythang round here. I jes decided to keep it to myself like you gon' do."

Anger, disbelief, and rage battled to control my heart and mind, and none of them would relent.

"De baby had that same mole on his nose like yours," Willie James added after a brief second.

"Really?"

"It's de first thing I noticed when I turned him over. The mole jumped out at me like de monsters in dem scary movies."

"Willie James, come on now! Are you sure you weren't imagining things?"

"Oh, I'm nutty now? I'm tellin' you! He had a mole right on the left side o' his nose. It reminded me of you."

"Momma wins again," I mumbled despondently.

"What's dat suppose to mean?"

"Nothing. Don't worry about it. My own issues, I suppose."

"Maybe I shouldn'ta told you," Willie James suggested sadly.

"Oh no! I wanted to know. You know that. Anything about Sister, please tell me. Don't hesitate."

"Well, dat's 'bout all I know." He folded his lips conclusively. "Except one thing."

"What?"

"T.L., you might be better off not knowin'."

"Man, tell me. Can't nothin' shock me at this point."

"OK, but remember our promise. You can't say nothin' to nobody."

"All right, all right. Tell me!"

Willie James bit his bottom lip, weighing the extent to which he could trust me. "After de day I saw de baby in de woods"—his mouth trembled as he circumvented his better judgment—"I was burning de trash and started smellin' somethin' really foul. I didn't pay much attention to it at first, but then it started smellin' like . . ."

"Like what?"

"Like flesh cookin'. Or somethin'. I took a stick and started fumblin' through de burnin' trash, tryin' to find out what was smellin' like dat. All of a sudden, Momma said, 'What chu lookin' fu'?' I coulda shitted in my pants 'cause I didn't see her walk up on me. She was lookin' a little funny, like she thought I knowed something. I said, 'Nothin'. I was stirrin' up de fire, makin' sure everythang burn good. Dat's all.' She said, 'Well, you go 'head and feed de cows and I'll finish stirrin' de fire.' I didn't want to do dat 'cause then I wouldn't be able to find out what was smellin'. I told Momma I could do both, but she insisted I go feed de cows. I walked away real suspicious, but I acted like everything was normal. I kept lookin' back over my shoulder and she was lookin' at me specially hard, like I better not come back over there. I went on into de barn and fed de cows like I usually do."

"Did you check the trash barrel later?" I queried excitedly.

"Yeah, I did, de next day. But it was squeaky clean."

"What do you mean?"

"I mean, it was clean as a baby's bottom. Momma or somebody had emptied the ashes and washed the barrel out with soap and water."

"Get outta here!"

"No lie. Dat old metal trash barrel was clean enough to eat off of. I gave up after dat. I knowed Momma was hidin' somethin', but she didn't leave no clues behind. I jes' left it alone after that."

"Is she deranged, Willie James? Come on! What's wrong with that woman?"

"I wish I knew, but I don't."

Willie James rubbed his hands together and glanced up at the sun. "I'd betta git dis tractor back home 'fo' Daddy be lookin' fu' me. He know I should be finished by now. He ain't neva been slow." Willie James stood up, brushed off the bottom of his pants, and put his old straw hat back on.

"You wanna ride?" he asked nonchalantly.

"Sure," I said and stood. "But let me ask you one more question, if you don't mind."

Willie James sighed but said, "Help yo'self."

"Do you think Momma came back and got the baby?"

He twisted his mouth and scratched his forehead. "I don't know," he said cautiously.

"I know you don't know, Willie James. I asked you if you *thought* she came back and got the baby."

"If I say yes, dat mean she put de baby dere in de first place. She couldn't come back and git it if she didn't put it dere."

"True," I affirmed.

"I hope you don't git us in no trouble, T.L. I done said a whole lot more than I shoulda said. I thought you should know 'cause you and Sista was close."

"Answer my question, Willie James."

"OK," he stalled, and then said very ardently, "yes. Yes. I think Momma came back and got it 'cause I think she put it dere in de first place. Who else coulda done it? Huh? Who else?"

"You know I don't know."

"It was her. It had to be. But ain't nothin' we can do 'bout it 'cause we ain't got no proof. I didn't see Momma do nothin' 'cept walk out o' de woods. She could say she was doin' anything back in dem woods and I couldn't 'spewt her word."

"Will you take me back there?"

"Back where?" Willie James asked disquietedly.

"Where you saw de baby."

"You don't need me to go back dere. Jes' walk back to de far left corner o' de woods. You been dere befo' without me."

Willie James had no intention of going back there again. He clearly had come to terms with the dreadful experience, at least enough to live from day to day. But I needed him.

"I know, Willie James, but I need to know the exact spot, and you alone can show it to me. Please. This is important."

"It's always 'bout what you need, ain't it? I done told you way mo' than I shoulda told you and still you ain't satisfied. You always was selfish."

"I'm not trying to be selfish, Willie James. I need you to help me out. I don't have anybody else."

"What if Momma or Daddy see us goin' back in de woods together, huh? You think dey ain't gon' know somethin's up?"

"They don't have to know. We can go when they ain't around or when they ain't lookin'."

"And when is that?" Willie James scowled.

"I don't know. We can figure that out. There's got to be some kinda way to get back there without them knowing."

"I'll tell you what, you figure dat out and maybe, jes' maybe, I'll show you where I saw de baby. I ain't makin' no promises, though."

"Fine. I'll think of something. Bet on that."

We climbed onto the tractor and headed home. It had been years since I rode it as a passenger, and it jerked my ass back and forth like an old washing machine spin cycle. Willie James laughed as I held on for dear life. Daddy had bought the tractor used when I was a boy, so it had to be damn near forty years old. "Shit!" I shouted after Willie James hit a large rut in the road. "You tryin' to kill me, man!"

He laughed louder and shook his head, reminiscent of bygone days. "You done fugot how ta ride a tractor, boy?" he mocked. I didn't entertain his words. Instead, I prayed we would hurry and make it home because I awaited the comfort of solid ground.

"Remember dat time I drove dis ole thang to Lucretia Clemmons's party?" Willie James hollered, smiling. The engine coughed loudly, making hearing practically impossible.

"Oh my God! I had forgotten about that! Can you believe you were fool enough to drive a tractor to a party? But you had to go. Nothing was going to keep you from it!"

"Yeah, Lucretia was my girl! She had an ass on her make any man stand up and do right! I was tryin' to court her, but she was actin' stuck-up."

"No, she wasn't! You were too scared to ask her out! You wouldn't even speak to her. She would give you the eye all the time and you went on like you didn't even see her!"

"What? Man, you lost yo' mind! I tried to speak to dat girl, but she acted shy or some shit, so I stopped tryin' to fuck wit' her. Hell, I ain't gon' chase no bitch nowhere!"

"You were definitely chasing her the night of her party!" I was laughing violently and my shoulders were jerking vertically.

"I ain't gon' lie!" Willie James bellowed, turning the big tractor steering wheel toward the left at the fork in the road. "I was tryin' to git me some pussy dat night. Shit! I knew I was gon' git me some."

"Folks said you were clean. That is, until they turned on the lights!" We both laughed uninhibitedly. "What possessed you to take Daddy's advice and drive a tractor to a party?" My voice displayed my bewilderment.

"I don't know, but I ain't neva done it no mo'. I learned my lesson. After I kicked dat nigga's ass fu' callin' me a dust ball, I said fuck it. Ain't no bitch worth all dis energy."

It was time for instigation. "Now what exactly happened, Willie James? I done forgot," I giggled, hoping to incite but not patronize.

"You ain't fugot nothin', nigga! You know exactly what happened!"

"No, I don't!" I roared. "All I remember is what other folks said."

Willie James gaped at me, unsure of whether my question was genuine or I was caricaturing him.

"OK. Here's what happened. I walked into de party and everybody started tellin' Lucretia dat her boyfriend was here. I started feelin' good and gettin' cocky. What I didn't realize is dat ridin' on dis damn tractor at night, I was covered wit' thick, red dust from head to toe."

My laughter caused me to lose my balance, and I almost fell off the tractor. Imagining Willie James grinning while his whole body was red with dust was about to kill me.

"Nigga, you tryin' to make a joke outta somebody!" he alleged cordially.

"No, I'm not. Go ahead." I tried unsuccessfully to hold my laughter.

"I started slow dancin' wit' Lucretia"—Willie James's head rocked from side to side—"and she started sneezin' real bad. She frowned at me and I looked back at her 'cause we couldn't figure out why she was sneezin' all of a sudden. Then, somebody turned on de lights and dat's when Billy Ray Jackson said, 'Oh my God! Look at dat nigga! He look like a black-ass dust ball!' I didn't know what he was talkin 'bout at first, but then everybody started starin' at me, and when I looked at myself I saw dat I was covered in thick dust all over."

"No!" I kept screaming, trying desperately to regain my composure.

"Yeah, it's funny now, but it wasn't funny how I kicked Billy Ray's ass!" Willie James volunteered confidently.

"You didn't kick his ass, Willie James!" I instigated further. "He was three times your size!"

"Dat don't mean nothin'! I jumped ova on dat nigga and started beatin' his ass like he had done stole somethin'! We was rollin' on de floor right in Lucretia's momma's livin' room. She was holl'in' and screamin' fu' us to stop, but I wasn't 'bout to git punked in front o' all those people. I threw him against de wall—"

"Willie James!" I shrieked in disbelief.

"I did! Then I threw him on de floor and jumped on him and started beatin' his chest like Grandma used to grind corn! Dat nigga wasn't gon' git 'way wit' callin' me no fuckin' dust ball in front o' Lucretia and I not do nothin' 'bout it."

"But, Willie James, other people said Billy Ray was on top o' you, smackin' yo' ass like you was his bitch!"

"Oh, fuck you, nigga! You know dat ain't true! I wish dat nigga woulda tried to smack me!"

Tears rolled down my face like bowling balls, merging with the sweat caused by the beaming sun.

"Willie James, I laughed for at least two weeks!"

"I'm glad you found dat shit funny, 'cause I sho' didn't," he said with a straight face. "I didn't speak to Billy Ray again till we was near'bout grown. I saw him in Krogers one day and we looked at each other and both of us busted out laughin' at de same time."

"What is he doin' now?"

"He workin' wit' his daddy down at de paper mill. Ain't nothin' else to do round here but work at de paper mill."

"Whatever happened to Lucretia?" I asked curiously.

"She married a boy from way out in de hills and he took her out dere and kept her barefoot and pregnant!"

"Really?"

"Yep. She got at least six kids and dey say she pregnant again. You oughta see her! Big as a house!"

"Stop lyin'!"

"I'm tellin you! If me and you put our arms together and made a circle she couldn't fit in de middle."

"Willie James!"

"Wait till you see her. She weigh at least three hundred fifty, four hundred pounds," he suggested matter-of-factly.

"Shut up! She used to be the finest girl in Swamp Creek!"

"I know! But she sho' ain't now. She might be de biggest!"

We howled. Lucretia Clemmons's being undesirable vindicated Willie James somehow.

We pulled up in front of the barn and turned the tractor off. Willie James assumed a serious expression and said, "Everythang I done said is between us. Right?"

"Right," I said, praying I'd be able to keep the promise. I must have sounded a bit uncertain, for Willie James huffed and said, "Come on, T.L. Don't say nothin' to nobody. I got to live round here. You don't."

"All right, all right. I won't say anything," I pledged. However, somewhere within, I felt like I was lying.

18

We ate dinner Wednesday evening in delicate, labored serenity. Momma had cooked neck bones, string beans, black-eyed peas, and corn bread. Everything was rather spicy, but Daddy piled salt on his food anyway. It was more habit than taste. The fact that *he* applied the seasoning was what prepared his meal for consumption.

"Look like we might git some rain tonight," Momma announced, breaking the silence.

Daddy scoffed. "De Lawd gon' do whatever de Lawd want to. Don't chu neva thank He ain't." God's intentions was a topic Daddy had always refused to discuss. In fact, his religious rigidity exposed, I believe, Daddy's fragile fear that maybe God wasn't omnipotent.

"I hope it don't rain 'cause I need to git up dat hay 'fo' it get wet," Willie James commented.

"Boy, you don't worry 'bout dat. If it rain, you thank de Good Lawd fu' de rain and go 'head on. De hay'll take care o' itself." Daddy shot Willie James a look of finality.

I didn't say anything; it wouldn't have mattered anyway.

"I want chu boys to walk down dat back fence afta suppa and fix de hole where dem damn cows been tryin' to break out. Take some wire and a couple o' cedar posts wit' chu 'cause you might need to replace dat weak spot right in de back corner. I 'speck y'all better hurry up, too, 'fo' it start thunderin' and lightnin'."

"Cain't dey do dat tomorrow, Cleatis?" Momma asked tremulously.

"Naw, dey cain't, 'cause if it storm, dem cows is gon' git nervous and try to break out. Ain't no tellin' where dey be by mornin'. Y'all hurr'up now."

Willie James and I glanced at each other, thinking the same thing. "We'll handle it, Daddy," I submitted cheerfully. That was a mistake. Willie James kicked me lightly under the table, a sign that I was acting out of the ordinary. I tried to redeem myself by changing the subject.

"Ms. Swinton passed last night," I said, studying the faces around me.

Daddy's head jerked up. He was clearly hurt, yet he dared not express it. Instead, he remarked tranquilly, "Is dat right?"

"Yes, sir. She died sometime before midnight."

"You found her?" Momma asked. I could have sworn I saw a smile.

"No, ma'am. When I got there, her . . . um . . . relatives had already arrived. They told me she had died."

"I didn't know Ms. Swinton had folks. Did you, Cleatis?"

"Yeah, I knowed. Everybody got some folks. Hers is up north somewhere like Detroit or Chicago. We'll see 'em at de fune'." Daddy's susurrant tone assisted his attempt to remain dispassionate.

"When dey gon' have it?" Momma asked with a quiet vengeance.

"Saturday at one," I answered defensively.

"Dat's good; dat's good," she repeated as though the thought brought her satisfaction.

"Dat woman sho' gon' be missed round hyeah. She done taught chillen and chillen's chillen. It's gon' be hard to find another one like dat." Daddy was laying on the guilt trip again, so I kept my eyes focused on my plate. That last bite of black-eyed peas was a lifesaver.

"Maybe de Good Lawd already got somebody else in de makin'. You cain't neva tell 'bout God," Daddy stated.

"Maybe He do," I said, and shot Daddy a kiss-my-ass look.

Suddenly a loud clap of thunder exploded. "Y'all better hurr'up, boys," Daddy urged. "It's gon' storm somethin' terrible, I believe."

We rose from the table and put our plates in the sink. "Willie James, git cho' raincoat, boy. Cain't you see it's gon' rain?" Momma never said a word to me. I took an umbrella anyway I saw leaning against the coatrack, and Willie James and I headed out the door.

The wind was blowing frantically in the cool, dark evening, and although the sky rumbled angrily, the air was actually rather refreshing. I stood still and felt the wind blow on me like one of those huge fans hanging from a factory ceiling. The branches on the trees shook excitedly like one waving at an oblivious friend far in the distance. In the field, the cows lay on the ground completely still as though bracing themselves for the imminent storm. At times, a few of them squinched their eyes when the wind blew hard. Their faces said, "Chile, it's 'bout to storm sho' 'nuff!" The barn door was swinging freely back and forth like a sheet of paper in an upturned notebook. "Go close de barn do'!" Willie James shouted to me, then ran to get the wire and cedar posts. The wind blew him fiercely and caused him to stumble.

After I closed the barn door, we began our descent into the woods. It was beginning to sprinkle.

"We gotta hurry up, T.L.! It's gon' storm bad!"

"You still gotta show me where you saw the baby!"

Willie James ignored me rudely. He lifted the hood of his raincoat onto his head and kept walking as though alone. Another clap of thunder sounded. "Oh, shit!" he clamored.

"I guess God's mad about something," I said, remembering Grandma's philosophy about thunder.

"Let's git dis fence fixed and git de hell back to de house!" Willie James shouted stringently.

The sky was a pretty bluish purple. Clouds moved back and forth, confused or at least unsure of exactly where to settle. A flock of birds hovered overhead, making screeching noises that sounded like frightened children. How amazing nature was, I thought, changing from a breezeless ninety-nine degrees a few hours ago to a whirlwind of beauty and splendor in the rain. "Come on, man!" Willie James yelled some distance ahead of me. I quickened my steps, and soon those tall Arkansas pines, oaks, and cedars engulfed me in darkness. We paused, and Willie James turned on a flashlight. I didn't know he had brought one.

"You got to stay ready to keep from gettin' ready," he said proudly.

"You de man!" I yielded freely.

We walked alongside the fence until we found the weak spot, which would certainly take us more than a few minutes to fix. It was starting to pour.

Willie James pointed with his right foot to a bare spot on the ground. "Take de posthole digger and dig a hole right here!" He had to scream above the sound of the wind, a reality that made it easier for me not to take his orders as demeaning. Remembering my ulterior motive, I obeyed his command.

The ground had not been penetrated by water in years, it seemed. "It's hard as a rock!" I complained, but Willie James dismissed me and I kept digging. Finally, he said, "Dat's good." I leaned against a nearby tree, wondering how much of the moisture on my face was sweat and how much rain. It was pouring down like I had never seen before. Willie James and I glanced at each other to make sure we were all right. "At least we under de trees," he said. "Now take dat cedar post and put it in de hole. Then pack de dirt round it. Pack it real tight!" As I did that, he cut the old barbed wire and strung new wire in its place. It took us at least an hour to repair the fence to what we hoped would be Daddy's satisfaction.

"I 'spect that'll do," Willie James hollered to me as he hammered the last nail in place. "Now let's git outta here!" He started walking briskly toward the house.

"Wait a minute, man!" I protested. "What about showing me where the baby was?" The sound of the water hitting the leaves drowned out the bulk of Willie James's cursing.

"We can do dat anotha time, fool! Don't chu see it's stormin' like hell?"

"Come on, Willie James! We won't get another chance to come back here without Momma being suspicious. It won't take but a minute!"

Willie James shook his head disgustedly and said, "Oh, fuck! I don't know why I ever said anything to you about it. Come on!"

He led me through a thick expanse of overgrown shrubbery until we reached a small grove of young trees. "It was right there," he mumbled, squinching his eyes and pointing with the flashlight. I took a few steps forward to where he was pointing and bent down to see if I could find any clues. I rubbed my right hand on the wet ground, hoping to find anything that might help me make sense of my sister's death.

"Ain't nothin' down there, boy!" Willie James said angrily. He turned the flashlight off and started walking home. After a few steps, he turned and yelled, "You betta come on!"

"There's got to be something here, Willie James!"

"Did you see anything, T.L.? Did you?"

I stood up slowly and followed Willie James back to the house. We walked onto the back porch and took off our wet clothes before we went in.

"You satisfied?" he whispered with one hand on the doorknob.

"No, I'm not," I said with a frown. I couldn't believe Willie James wanted to drop the issue absolutely.

"You may as well be!" he said intensely. "You asked me to show you where I saw the baby, and I did. Ain't nothin' else we can do."

"It's not that simple, Willie James!" I whimpered with the same level of intensity. "I can't just know stuff and act like I don't. I'll never have any peace of mind!"

"You betta learn how to know stuff and keep yo' damn mouf shut. Talkin' too much can git you hurt round here. Dat's all I'm gon' say." And he went in the house. I had no choice but to follow. I couldn't discern if his words were supposed to be a threat or a plea for me to keep the secret he had shared. I decided to be cool.

I took a bath, went into the bedroom, and lay across the bed, listening to the sound of the rain. Water poured off the house like a waterfall. Everyone else either had gone to bed or was about to, so I retrieved one of Ms. Swinton's journals and read for a while.

Sometimes I cannot ascertain if the children are listening. They stare at me with expressions of wonder and then, in an instant, they seem utterly confused. Perhaps I seek too much too soon. I want another DuBois, another Morrison, another Baldwin right away. But, for now, it looks as though I shall have to wait. I beg parents to expose children to books and museums and ideas, but the most these children get is chitlin-cleaning lessons and how to distinguish a possum from an armadillo. It seems so futile sometimes, I hate to guess what would become of them if they were in the hands of a teacher who assumed their inferiority. I know that cleaning hogs and piecing quilts are dignified work and demands a very great level of intelligence. That's why I stay around here. I see the brilliance in the eyes of my students when they arrive early in the morning smelling like cow manure. The problem is that they don't see brilliance. That's why their homework doesn't get completed properly. They, and their parents, equate country with intellectual ineptitude. It's truly strange. The people in Swamp Creek function with the unspoken notion that "real intelligence" is an anomaly in southern, rural places. It's sad. And they teach their children likewise. When the children arrive at school, they prepare to enter a world that has no resemblance to the one in which they live. They can't see that for a poor black woman in Swamp Creek to figure out how to feed six children every day she must be brilliant. Since she cannot afford to frequent the supermarket and since she is too proud to beg, she must find food in places and in ways most people never consider. I have always been completely amazed by such acts of survival, for they demonstrate a level of intelligence about which our children should boast proudly. Instead, they hang their heads low, having concluded that schooling is a gift from the county they simply do not deserve. And, furthermore, they presume it is a gift for which their mental capacity is absolutely unprepared. What a travesty.

"Wow," I mumbled, depressed.

So I continue, day by day, trying mightily to lift the veil of inferiority from before the eyes of my children, only to realize that their parents re-place it every time they return home in the evening. However, I cannot give up. This is my fight, my mission, my purpose. I walk the earth for the sole reason of teaching these children how to recognize their own grandeur, and I will not rest until I've done so.

Cynthia Tyson keeps my spirits high. She is simply a joy and a won-der. She reminds me so much of Tommy Lee that it's rather frightening. I fear, at moments, that I will say too much or let on that I know some-thing. I try desperately to maintain distance, only to fail miserably, I'm afraid. Her eyes are always full of excitement and courage. When I ask the class for a volunteer reader, her hand is first to fly into the air. "Ooh, me! Please! Me!" she begs. I try to disregard her, hoping nervously to find another child confident enough to speak out, but the others sit with low-ered eyes, probably praying that I'll call Cynthia so they can relax. "Pro-ceed, Cynthia," I am usually forced to say. And when she does, she transforms into some kind of literary diva whose debut is on the line. She stands and acts the part as she reads it, complete with theatrical voice variations and body movements. She flings her arms wide and cries and laughs boisterously, as though she stands before a crowd of thousands. Oh, what a joy! Some days, I let her go on for hours as the other children watch through eyes of wonder. But other days, I do not call upon her at all, for I realize Cynthia stands to the other children for what they are not. They seek refuge in her performance, for it means they are saved from the possibility that they, too, could manifest such confidence, such self-belief. They want her to go on and on to ensure they are never called upon to do likewise. Their applause of her reveals this truth. It is almost as if they clap in gratitude for the hiding place Cynthia grants them. They seem to be begging her to return tomorrow and do it again, hoping that her one-woman show will divert my eyes from all of them, at least for the day. And the days I do not comply, the other children are desperate, squeamish, and pitiful. Yet I cannot perpetuate the "one smart nigga" the-

ory, especially not in a place like Swamp Creek. All of the children must know and recognize the manifestation of their own brilliance and the brilliance of their people as well. They cannot be "grateful" for the "exceptional" intelligence of one, as though this is confirmation that there will always be "at least one" smart one in the bunch. Yet this is what their parents believe, making my attempt to counter such a philosophy abortive. Still, I go on, more determined than ever that the power of education will transform the minds of the self-loathing. One day, I shall be heralded as either a great teacher or a fool.

I closed the journal, lay on the bed listening to the rain song, and imagined the battle Ms. Swinton had to fight in order to feel accomplished as a teacher in Swamp Creek. Back when I was in school, we all had to stand and read aloud, whether we wanted to or not. If you couldn't read well, you were jeered and mocked until you could.

Although I rejected the notion, I began to wonder what I would be like as a teacher in Swamp Creek.

"Stand, young man, and recite Langston Hughes's 'Mother to Son' without error," I could hear myself demanding sternly.

"But Dr. Tyson, I . . . um didn't get a chance to learn all of it 'cause I had to chase chickens and—"

"That is no excuse, young man! Your brain must be developed if you are to make something of yourself."

"Yes, sir," the child would probably say, resuming his seat, relieved.

Then I would pace the room and begin to teach about something else, perhaps the Underground Railroad.

"How did people git a train under de ground, Dr. Tyson?" a child might ask curiously.

"It wasn't an actual railroad, children. It was a system of how to journey from the South to the North on foot in order that slave catchers wouldn't find runaway slaves. People's homes were stops along the 'railroad' so the runaways could rest and get food in order to continue their sojourn. It was a very difficult and a very dangerous passage. Some made it, while others did not."

"Did you have to buy a ticket, Dr. Tyson?"

I would chuckle at the innocence of the question and respond with, "No, son, you didn't need a ticket. What you needed was courage, strength, and God. Our people had to run from places like Swamp Creek, Arkansas, all the way to Canada sometimes." I'd show them the distance on a map.

"Wow!" they would exclaim, realizing finally the strength of their own ancestors.

"It was far, yet we did it. That's how you know who you are. You come from the strongest, the bravest, people who ever walked the earth. No one else has ever had to endure the trials and tribulations of the African."

"Was the Underground Railroad right here in Swamp Creek, Dr. Tyson?"

"Yes, it was. Folks say the old Birch place was a hideaway for run-away slaves. Mr. Blue said Old Man Birch had a dungeon under his living room floor, but no one ever knew about it. He kept it covered with a big rug."

"Really?" The children would beam with excitement.

"Mr. Blue said if anybody ever found out about the dungeon, they would have to die."

"Why?" the children might ask simultaneously.

"Because the Underground Railroad was a secret. White folks didn't want us to have our freedom and did everything they could to keep us enslaved. We ran away secretly so slave owners wouldn't try to keep us as slaves for the rest of our lives. It's called the Underground Railroad because it was supposed to be a secret."

"What if somebody found out 'bout Mr. Birch keepin' slaves in dat dungeon?"

"By law, he would have to die. It was illegal for a person to harbor runaway slaves because they were seen as the property of the slave owner. It was a heavy risk, but many of our people took it."

Suddenly I could see the pride on the children's faces that their ancestors had done something morally just and divinely righteous.

"There was a woman named Harriet Tubman who was considered the conductor of the Underground Railroad."

"I thought you said it wasn't no real train," someone would ask, confused.

"It wasn't. She was called the conductor because she made trips back and forth hundreds of times, showing slaves where to run and who to trust along the way. She knew the route better than anyone else, and she spent her whole life helping her brothers and sisters to freedom."

"What if somebody got sick and couldn't run no more?"

"Sometimes Ms. Tubman would leave them, or they might die trying to run. It was not a pleasant journey, children, and many whites would rather Ms. Tubman have been dead because she was stealing precious property. She did what she had to in order to free her people. That's why folks started calling her Moses."

"Like de Moses in de Bible?"

"Yes, just like that one. She took hundreds of men and women north to freedom. She knew the railroad stops and she knew how to tell north from south in the pitch-dark. She knew which roots could be eaten and which could not, and she knew when to lay low in the woods like a rabbit without ever moving. She was an incredible woman with an incredible mission."

"Can we go on de railroad, Dr. Tyson? Can we? Please?"

"I wish we could, but the railroad doesn't exist anymore. Its only purpose was to provide hiding places for runaway slaves. When slavery was abolished, the railroad no longer had a purpose."

"Can we go to the Birch place and see if there really is a dungeon under his living room floor?"

"I don't know, children. The house was abandoned years ago. It's surely about to cave in, and God only knows what creatures are crawling around inside."

"We don't care, Dr. Tyson. We ain't scared! Please take us out dere and show us one o' de stops on de Underground Railroad. Please, Dr. Tyson!"

We close our books and walk out the front door of the school-house, determined to share a piece of the history that has us excited to the bone. We do not speak a word along the way, and we do not entertain fear someone will see us. For the first time in most of their lives, the children walk with a confidence unshakable. I begin to cry as I watch them transform into the ancestors we were studying only moments before. They don't walk like poor country children any-more. They have been endowed with the power of self-love and self-beauty. Their Wal-Mart clothes and Fred's shoes are laughable now as they march toward their past with a zeal almost contagious. People wave along the way, but this time, the children don't ac-knowledge their gestures. In fact, they act completely oblivious. They have only one aim in mind, and that is to see if, in fact, the famous Underground Railroad came through Swamp Creek. I presume that if the children can actually see the dungeon, they will be convinced that their home is sacred, too. They need to verify that slaves ran to Swamp Creek to find safety. It will make their lives and the lives of all their people much more meaningful because then they can speak of themselves as significant contributors to American history.

We march until we get to the house. It has no remarkable features except that it looks dilapidated and fragile. The children stop in front of the shack, looking to me for further instructions.

"I do not want you to be disappointed if there is no dungeon, young people. Sometimes legends do not always prove to be true."

The children remain silently hopeful. They have come seeking something greater than anything I could say to discourage the hunt.

"We must be very careful, for the house is old and not standing se-curely."

Again they stare at me, through me, as though wanting nothing more than to move me out of the way of truth. Seeing my words have no power at that moment, I proceed to lead them onto the porch and into the dust-covered living room of Old Man Birch.

The house is bare, for the most part. An old chair and a battered rug covering the floor are all the room contains. The children step through the door carefully, tiptoeing on a hope that will prayerfully give them joy and meaning. They stare at the rug and wait for me to lift it.

"Children, again, do not be disappointed if we do not find a dungeon. It would not subtract from the reality of the Underground Railroad. The stops along the way might simply have been different from what people said."

The children say nothing. Instead, they stare at the rug and wait.

I bend down and pull it back gently, revealing a trapdoor. The children's eyes grow large. I take a deep breath and lift the wooden door as it squeaks in pain. Below is nothing but darkness and dampness. Some of the children hold each other's hands in fear and excitement.

"Follow me," I say boldly, descending the old staircase. The children follow. The dungeon is larger than any of us had imagined. It is only about five feet high, but it is wider than the entire living room. The children nudge one another with joy and pride as they begin to snicker about having found a lost treasure. Then suddenly, in the depths of the dungeon, a child begins to sing lightly, "Wade in de water, wade in de water, children, wade in de water; God's gonna trouble de water." Others join in. And in the darkness of the dungeon, the children begin to weep and moan as they feel the pain of their ancestors who once rested in this same place. Some of them cry out in agony while others squeeze themselves and rock comfortingly. I wonder whether I should abruptly interrupt the ritual and return the children to the world we once knew or if I should let the spirit have its way. I do the latter and watch the few strips of light sneak through the cracks in the living room floor and cast shadows on the children of those who came here years ago.

Another child begins, "People, get ready; there's a train a-comin'! You don't need no ticket; just get on board!"

And the children keep repeating, "Get on board! Get on board! You don't need no ticket; just get on board!"

I'm crying and can't help it and I'm feeling better than I ever have. "Glory hallelujah, just get on board!" they keep singing. The clapping and the hand waving take me back years and years before I was ever born, and I see my people picking cotton, sweating, and following mules in the field. I see women giving birth without epidurals and men being beaten until the setting of the sun.

The children keep singing, more wildly now than before, "You don't need no ticket! Just get on board!" Some rise and dance what looks like an African victory dance as the spirits completely consume their physical form. It seems like hours before the excitement calms down to a whisper: "Get on board; get on board! You don't need no ticket; just get on board!"

The children are trying desperately to tell me something, I am sure, to free me of some idea or ideology that has kept me bound. I lay hands on each child's head, affirming the power of our journey, and we keep humming the melody as we ascend the old staircase and close the trapdoor behind us. When I raise my head again, the children look like little old people, miniature versions of their own parents and grandparents, who must have some connection to that dungeon in some way. The children smile at me in thanks for giving them a gift that I do not possess. We return the rug to its original place and prepare to leave when a little boy or a little girl or maybe both turn and say, "I love you, Dr. Tyson." All the children follow suit, and I hug them, realizing the children see their own ancestors right before their eyes. I see them, too. The spirits touch their hearts as they mouth, "I love you, too," in a way that weakens my knees and fills my heart with a compassion I never knew before. I stand still and cry as the spirit of my people overwhelms me. The children comfort me this time, telling me that all is well. They rub my head and pat my back as I regain enough composure to continue.

When we return to the schoolroom, they make 100 on their

spelling tests and they want to read aloud—all of them—and they can do long division confidently. I post on the wall in big, bold letters:

"CHILDREN, GET READY! THERE'S A TRAIN A-COMIN'! YOU DON'T NEED NO TICKET; JUST GET ON BOARD!"

The children smile through teary eyes.

19

"Come in," David said with his back toward the door.

"Mornin', big brotha," I said with an overly contrived country accent.

"Mornin'," he returned enthusiastically. "Good to see you. I thought I might not see you again until Saturday. I'm glad you came, though. I have something important to speak with you about."

"No drama, please! I've had enough of that for a lifetime," I declared, shaking my head despairingly.

David laughed out loud. "This is not drama, but it is serious. Have a seat."

The room was practically bare. David, or someone, had removed the books from the shelves and taken most of the living room furniture away. The house felt cold and empty. Goose bumps covered my arms as I wondered what David wanted to speak to me about.

"Coffee?" he offered from the kitchen.

"Yes, please. Black."

"Coming right up," he responded cheerfully.

I sat in a nearby chair. The pretty hardwood floor sparkled as the sun coming through the big east window reflected its brilliance. The hollowness of the room gave me the feeling of a damp, uninhabited cave.

"I've tried to clean out most stuff already, but it's a bigger job than I imagined. I was up till two thirty last night scrubbing floors and packing boxes. Man, this is hard work!" David handed me a yellow and red pastel-colored cup of jet-black coffee.

"I know what you mean. I hate moving. Always have. I'd sooner throw things away than pack them."

"Amen! But, of course, this is Momma's stuff and she'll raise up in that coffin Saturday if I don't handle it right."

The allusion seemed a bit strange, almost morbid, causing me to buck my eyes and furrow my brows.

"Oh, come on, T.L.! It's OK to be light about this. Momma died and that's the will of the Lord. That doesn't mean we have to drag around heavy for the next two days."

"You're right. Unfortunately, I was raised thinking death and funerals are supposed to be solemn, heavy affairs. Thanks for the reminder," I affirmed casually.

"Good," David said, relieved.

I sipped my coffee and waited for him to continue. He simply stared in return.

"What?" I asked apprehensively.

"Oh, nothing," he said lightly.

"Then why are you staring at me?"

"Because, for an instant, you looked like Momma." David smiled above the rim of his cup.

"You think so?" I couldn't even imagine it, but if he thought it I didn't want to ruin his reverie.

"Yeah. It's wild, huh?"

"Too wild for me."

"Naw, nothing's too wild for you. You couldn't have gone as far as you have in life if you weren't an incredibly strong person. I admire you."

"You can't admire me. You don't know me yet."

"Yes, I do. I don't know the specifics of your life, but I know the kind of perseverance you must have manifested in order to move away from here and get not one but three college degrees. I ain't brilliant, but I ain't crazy, either."

We both chuckled.

"OK. What can I say?"

"Nothing. Just let the truth be the truth."

"Easy enough," I said as our small talk began to lose its luster.

"I hope what I'm about to say to you is easy, too."

"Please, Lord, let it be," I mumbled more as a prayer than a response to David.

"I'll say it directly: Momma left all her books to you. All three thousand or so of them."

My mouth dropped. "Are you serious?"

"I'm very serious. It's in her will. I packed most of them last night, but I ran out of boxes. I should have asked you what you wanted to do with them before I touched them, but I knew we'd at least have to move them; therefore, I started packing them up. What do you want to do with them?"

I set my cup on the floor and walked over to the big east window. David kept drinking coffee as though we were deciding whether to eat at McDonald's or Wendy's.

"Just say the word," David said as he drank.

I turned from the window and said, "I don't have the slightest idea! What in the world am I supposed to do with three thousand books?"

"Teach," David said matter-of-factly.

"Oh, don't start that again!"

"Fine. Take them with you back to New York then."

"My studio in New York is half the size of this room or smaller. Even if all my walls were bookshelves, from top to bottom, I wouldn't have enough room for three thousand books."

"I see. I wish I could help you with this one, but I can't. Momma said the books were yours to do with as you determined."

"But I don't have anywhere to keep them!"

David peered at me with the that's-your-problem expression. Then he asked, "Is there room in your dad's house?"

"Are you insane? I can't take the books there! That's too much evidence of Ms. Swinton and Daddy's—"

"Affair? It's OK. Call it what it was."

"Then you know why I wouldn't think of leaving them there. That's out of the question."

"You'd better think of something, because we're both leaving Saturday and these books can't stay here. I'm hoping to rent the place out as soon as possible."

I resumed my place in the chair and began to contemplate what I would do with three thousand books.

"It doesn't make sense to store them anywhere. They wouldn't be useful to anyone, and you know how she was about the utility of knowledge," David said, attempting to help although he definitely was not.

"Yeah, I know," I said, exasperated. "She would trouble my sleep every night if I did that. I wouldn't do that anyway. Maybe I'll donate them to the county library."

"Bad idea."

"Why?" I asked rather loudly.

"Because Momma wanted you to have them. You specifically."

"OK, but if they could be more useful somewhere else—"

"They can't. No one could use them like you can."

"What are you talking about?"

"I'm talking about the fact that Momma knew into whose hands to entrust these books. She also knew exactly what you'd do with them."

"And what is that?"

"I don't know. I said she knew—not me."

"Somebody needs to tell me, because I'm lost," I suggested despondently.

"Naw, you're not lost. You just gotta think about the implications of the gift."

"I'm not following you."

"You will. Think about it."

"I am thinking! And I'm still not following you!" Frustration clouded my words.

"The question is, why would Momma leave *you* her books? Huh?" David was irritating me like a fly buzzing around my ear.

"Because I'm her long-lost son, right?"

"Oh, please! Momma never was into excessive flattery of anyone. You know that. Don't be silly." David moved from his chair with his empty coffee cup and walked toward the kitchen.

"Why do you think she left me the books?" I hollered louder than I needed to.

There was a momentary pause and David reentered the room with a fresh cup of coffee. "You know why. You just don't want to face it." He sat in the chair again and nodded his head up and down confidently.

"Excuse me?" I frowned.

"That's right. You know exactly why Momma left you the books. You just don't want to say it."

"Can we please stop playing this game?" I asked painfully.

"Can we?" David smiled.

"Man, whatever you know, just tell me. I don't have time for all this."

"The question is, what do *you* know? Why would someone who believed in education as much as Momma did leave all her books to you?"

I knew where David was going, and I was trying in vain to avoid it. "Because she knows how much I always loved to read?"

"Wrong."

I sighed heavily. David wasn't going to give up. He was determined to make me say what I didn't want to say.

"All right," I surrendered. "She left me the books because she hoped I would stay in Swamp Creek and teach with them."

"Bingo!"

"But I'm not staying here. She knew that. I told her so!"

"Yeah, I know."

"That's not fair."

"I agree. I don't blame you for not staying here. A man's got to plant himself wherever he feels he can grow. I wouldn't stay here, either."

"Why not?" I asked defensively.

"Because Swamp Creek is forty years behind time. I don't sense activity or life abounding. It appears rather dull and uneventful."

"It's probably not all that bad. I'm sure people have fun and enjoy life in their own little way."

"Then why can't you do the same?" David said, smiling, proud that his reverse psychology was working.

"Because the things I enjoy aren't here. I like southern living, but I also like to go to theaters, concerts, and libraries. Swamp Creek offers none of this."

"That's undoubtedly true, but maybe your job is to bring those things to Swamp Creek."

"You must be joking! It would take a lot more than me to put this place on the map. I'd need about one hundred thousand other folks!"

"Raise them up! What if your legacy here were the seed of a great migration back to Swamp Creek? What if, due to your extraordinary gift of teaching, people from all over the black world came here to give their children the best education possible? Wouldn't that be awesome?"

"No, it wouldn't, because I'm not staying here. And, anyway, you know as well as I do people are not moving to Swamp Creek simply for their children to attend school under my tutelage!"

"OK, that was a bit much, but still your impact could be far-reaching."

"That's true for any teacher anywhere!" I said, feeling like the tide was turning in my favor.

"No, it's not!" he raged emphatically.

"Yes, it is! Any teacher's impact could be far-reaching."

"You don't believe that. You know as well as I do that ninety percent of people in the classroom are not teachers. They're boring as hell, trite, unmotivated, and they do not know how to inspire learning. They want to be teachers, but they don't have the gift."

"What do you mean, 'the gift'?"

"Teaching is not a profession, T.L. It's a spiritual calling. God has ordained some people with the skill to excite the rest of us about learning. These are people whose natural inclination is to search for knowledge and transfer it to the rest of the world in a way that makes us better. Many so-called teachers are smart, but their ability to inspire the rest of us to learn is desperately lacking. Ironically, they think they're teaching."

"Amen. I've had the worst."

"I'm sure you have. You probably sat there the whole time imagining what you'd do if you were the teacher. You thought about how you'd stand on top of the desk instead of sitting in the chair or how you'd tie your students up with ropes to make them feel what being a slave was really like."

"Oh my God! How in the world did you know that?" David's summation of my pedagogical evolution left me uneasy.

"Because you have the gift of teaching. The gift, not the desire or simply the intellectual training, but the gift. And one with the gift would think of these sorts of things. It's not complicated."

"You got me on that one. I used to sit in college classes and wonder why the teachers were so boring! Even then, I imagined a million ways to make the class exciting. I always wondered why teachers didn't imagine them also."

"Because they didn't have the gift of teaching."

"Right, they didn't."

"Yet you do. I can tell it. Momma knew it. That's why she left you all of her books."

"Maybe that is why, but I'm not staying in Swamp Creek. Absolutely not."

"And why not?"

"I've already told you!" I set my coffee cup down, vexed. "I can't breathe here. I feel stifled, unproductive, and hindered. I think it's unfair of you to ask me to stay in a place that makes me feel that way."

"You're right, T.L. I'm sorry. It's only because I can imagine you transforming the children in this little town in a way most people probably can't. In my heart, I want Momma's legacy to live on forever. The Good Lord'll work it out, though."

"Yes, He will," I agreed pleasantly.

We sat in silence as our tempers calmed. I was beginning to like David. He had definitely angered me, but he had also taught me a few things.

"I like you, T.L.," David said suddenly.

"I was thinking the exact thing! We've had our first fight as brothers, huh?"

"Looks that way," David chuckled. "Brothers are supposed to fight."

"No, they're not," I said sadly. "Brothers are supposed to love and honor each other."

"We're on our way," David said.

"We sure are."

With that, David rose to replenish his coffee. When he returned, he asked, "So what good book are you reading these days?"

"I'm in the middle of a book called *Two Thousand Seasons*," I answered vigorously, glad to change the subject.

"What's it about?"

"It's probably the best book I've ever read," I had to say, although that was not his question. "It's about a community of African people whose way of life gets challenged by outsiders. They are forced to leave their own homeland in hopes of preserving their traditions and their sacred cosmology."

"What is their sacred tradition?"

"Armah, the author, calls it 'The Way.' It's a bit complicated, but essentially it's the Law of Reciprocity—the principle that everyone and everything in a community should both give to that community and be sustained by it. As an ideology, reciprocity assures no one gives too much of themselves and no one takes more than his share. It's about communal balance and harmony."

"It's really good?"

"Armah is brilliant! His prose is so lyrical it reads like poetry. I must admit it's a slow read because it's very dense, but every line reflects authorial mastery of language. Some of his phrasing is simply magical."

"Wow. I'll have to read that one. Any time a teacher goes on like that about a book, it's worth checking out."

"Please read it. I promise you'll love it."

"I will."

"You read anything good lately?" I asked in return.

"I'm rereading the Book of Job and it's making me mad as hell."

"Why?" I asked, surprised.

"Because I can't believe God let Satan talk Him into destroying Job's life just to prove a point."

"That story is a literary creation, David. It doesn't reflect the character of the real God. Rather, it's a story about God and man with the purpose of teaching the fruit of endurance and patience and struggle. I never read Job as an indication of what the Divine God might actually do."

"You don't read the Bible literally?"

"Of course not; it's not supposed to be treated as a compilation of factual events. It's a set of combined allegorical stories, just as literary and fictive as any other creative text. The character God in the Bible is someone's perception of what God might do or say. Remember, God didn't write the book."

"Yes, but those who did were inspired by Him," David defended.

"Fine. However, that doesn't mean what they wrote is exactly what God would have written had He or She assumed the pen. Indeed, I would be disappointed if God had written it, for I would've expected more."

"You're on thin ice," he said with an edge of warning.

"Why?" I smiled. "In order for God to have written the Bible, God would have had to embrace the limitations of language. And if God could dwell within such limitations, how could God still be God?"

"That's a good question."

"Anyway, I think it's important to read the character of God in Job as a creation of the writer's imagination, not as a reflection of the Divine Creator. I'm not sure that such an enormous character could even be conceptualized in words."

"Is the Bible the Word of God to you?" David frowned.

"Sure. Yet it's not the only Word of God. God has spoken to everyone on the planet, David, so how could anyone be arrogant enough to suggest that the Bible is the only Word of God? In other words, what makes any text the Word of God? Someone's declaration of it as such, right?"

David surveyed me cautiously and continued listening.

"Who could dispute whether a writer was inspired by God? How can we know what God has said and to whom? It's all a matter of belief. Or better, faith. If you believe it, then it's true."

"It can't be that simple," David said, shaking his head.

"Sure it can. We need, or rather want, God to be complicated in order to rule and control Him. We need for most people to be confused about God and the Bible in order to crown a few scholars as Great Theologians who understand what the rest of us do not. Then we pay them to teach us. If we ever understand the simplicity of God, then God can belong to everyone freely. America fears affording people such religious liberty."

"Why?"

"Because then rules and laws governing people's private lives and their thoughts get dismissed as ridiculous. If every man gets to understand God for himself, then God can be anything, even if the perception appears contradictory to what another man believes. In other words, the control element gets dropped and then any person of any walk of life can be holy because 'holy' becomes self-defined. Interestingly enough, most people need God to be a tyrant in order to believe in Him. It makes Him powerful, majestic, and awe inspiring. I don't think that's how the Divine Creator is, though."

"No?"

"No. I don't think God wants to rule anything. I believe God gave us minds precisely because God didn't want the responsibility of the worth of our lives. He or She gave us life—what we do with it is entirely up to us, and I don't think God really cares one way or the other. I believe God wants us to live the fullness of our spiritual possibilities, but how we do that is up to us."

"Amazing."

"What's amazing?"

"In a matter of moments, you've made me look at God from a totally different perspective. You have the gift of teaching, T.L."

"Not that again!"

"No, I'm serious. I never considered the possibility that the God in the Job story couldn't possibly be the true God. When I do, I get instantly freed from trying to understand what seems like poor judgment on God's part. To see it as a story about God and not a reflection of God makes a lotta sense. Your students will be very lucky."

"I hope so," I said modestly.

"The only other thing you need to try to do is figure out what to do with all these books!"

"I know," I sighed heavily. "I'll figure out something by this evening. Right now I need to go."

"Why? What's the rush?"

"I told my brother I'd give him a hand again today. God knows I don't want to, but it's the least I could do. He's probably half-done by now, so I'd better hurry before I get cussed out. I'll come back by tomorrow."

"All righty, T.L. Thanks."

"For what?" I said as I grabbed hold of the doorknob.

"For the lessons, Mr. Teacher."

20

People began congregating at the Meetin' Tree around sundown. Friday evenings in Swamp Creek were community ritual time, when folks gathered and talked about their week or their children or someone who had died recently, and because Ms. Swinton had just transpired, I knew the tree would be crowded. I had asked David to meet me there at eight, and, sure enough, he was there when I arrived. Daddy was already there, too. He loved to hear the stories other people told, and he loved to share Mr. Blue's grape wine. As long as I can remember, Mr. Blue brought a large jug of that gasoline, as Momma called it, and passed it around like we were having communion service. I always liked Friday nights at the tree because people relinquished their inhibitions freely and shared intimacies otherwise taboo. Folks who were solemn all week laughed easily once they arrived at the tree, for somehow the space released Swamp Creek residents from the confinements and constructs of the world, which told them they were not supposed to have joy. I use to sit under the tree, watch people approach from every direction, and notice how stoic expressions instantly transformed into smiles.

Everyone was there except Momma. She refused to go and watch niggas act a fool, she said. I remember her going to the tree only once when I was young. She arrived dressed like she was going to Sunday morning service. Stockings and all! Folk frowned and asked her where in the world she was going with all those clothes on. Momma murmured, "Ignut niggas," and turned around and went home. People fell out laughing. "Why was Marion dressed like that?" they kept asking. I saw her leave and ran after her. When I caught up, I noticed she was crying. "Momma, you all right?" I asked, completely confused by her tears. "Oh yes, Son. Some dust blew in my eyes. I'll be fine. I'm going home to find some eyedrops." I didn't think much more about it until the following Friday, when Daddy asked Momma if she was coming to the tree. "I can't stand dem stupid-ass niggas," she protested violently. "All dey do is drank liqua and tell lies all night long. I can thank of plenty otha thangs to do wit' my time." Her obvious anguish was apparently meaningless to the rest of us, for we went anyway. Daddy, Willie James, Sister, and I would prance around the house searching for something clean to put on because, come hell or high water, we were going to the tree. Usually we walked out of the house together and never said a word to Momma. She would sit in front of the TV, feigning contentment, but nothing could rival the fun and stories shared at the Meetin' Tree. "She be a'ight," Daddy said one night as we walked. We never talked about Momma's absence from the tree again.

I was excited because I hadn't been to a meetin' in over ten years. Knowing Ms. Swinton's death would resurrect even those who never mingled, I had readied myself for an extraordinary night of clowning, but no amount of preparation could have equipped me for what occurred that Friday night.

David and I sat next to each other after everyone introduced themselves to him. He blended in splendidly and said he felt right at home. Folks told him they were sorry about his momma, and he said, "Why?" Unsure of how to respond, they ignored the reply and took their seats.

Most folk brought their own folding chairs to the meeting. Two or three pews from the church always remained under the tree, rain or shine, serving as the throne of the elders. None of the chairs or pews was arranged in any particular order; people plopped their chairs down wherever they believed the entertainment would be good. One night-light stood some distance away, providing barely enough light for folks to see one another's faces. No one complained, however, for brighter light would have meant more mosquitoes. The darkness also allowed people to relax and relinquish masks without fear of complete exposure.

"What time's de fune' tamorra?" Mr. Blue asked loudly of whoever possessed the knowledge.

"One o'clock sharp," David volunteered with a smile.

"Sharp?" people began stammering. I started laughing.

"What chu mean, sharp?" Ms. Polly frowned like she was offended. "What's du hurry? She goin' somewhere?"

People hollered. You could have heard the laughter for miles. I supposed David realized the wisdom of her reply, for he laughed, too.

"Speakin' of fune's, I 'member dat time Pa'nella and Nila Faye went to Poo Girl's fune'."

"Nigga, dis wuz a lie fifty years ago when you firs' tole it!" yelled Smoked Neck Johnson. The man loved smoked neck bones, even as a baby, Grandma said, so his love became his name.

"No, no. Dis a true story fu' real. Y'all ain't heard 'bout Pa'nella and Nila Faye?" Mr. Blue was chuckling as he surveyed faces unnecessarily. I knew the story would be hilarious.

"I don't thank I heard dat one," people mumbled to encourage Mr. Blue's storytelling gift. Of course, they had heard it before, but the joy was in hearing Mr. Blue tell it.

Folks shifted their chairs around and frowned, pretending they were sick and tired of hearing these lies. This behavior was precisely the prerequisite Mr. Blue needed.

"What happened was, Pa'nella calls Nila Faye and say, 'Girl, ain't you goin' out to de fune'?'"

"And Nila Faye say, 'What fune' you talkin' 'bout?'

" 'Out ta Elizabeth's fune'!' Pa'nella say."

Everybody was either smiling or shaking their heads because we knew this was going to be a good one.

"And Nila Faye say, 'Naw, girl, I ain't goin'. I don't thank I knowed hu'.'

"And Pa'nella went ta frownin' 'cause she know Nila Faye knowed 'Lizabeth. Dey growed up togetha right hyeah in Swamp Creek. She thought dat maybe Nila Faye was havin' a hard time dealin' wit' 'Lizabeth's death, so she didn't push hu' on it too murch. Nila Faye turned right round and said, 'Now I'll go wit' chu if you want me to. I wun't gon' go myself.' Pa'nella say, 'Yeah, girl, come on and go wit' me.' So Nila Faye went."

Mr. Blue was sitting on the edge of one of the church pews. His mouth was trembling from soulful merriment, but he was trying to hold it. Others were looking at him and acting like they couldn't take any more, which, of course, meant that Mr. Blue should proceed.

"So Pa'nella went and picked up Nila Faye and dey went to de fune'. De whole time, Nila Faye sittin' in de back o'de chuch sayin' nothin' to nobody. Folks is holl'in' and fallin' out and carryin' on, but Nila Faye lookin' like ain't nothin' movin' hu' 'cause she don't know no 'Lizabeth. Well, time come to go review de body and Pa'nella ask Nila Faye to walk wit' hu'. Nila Faye say OK 'cause she don't know de woman noway and Pa'nella might get weak and need hu' to lean on. So dey start walkin' toward de casket and folks is touchin' Nila Faye on the arm sayin', 'I'm sorry fu' yo' loss,' and Nila Faye is wonderin' what folks is talkin' 'bout 'cause she ain't loss nothin'. When dey almost gets right in front o'de casket, Nila Faye tells Pa'nella to be strong and know dat de Good Lawd knows 'xactly what He's doin'. Pa'nella shakes hu' head, sayin', 'Sho' you right,' and they walks on.

"When dey gets right in front o'de casket, Nila Faye looks over at de body and folks say she start screamin' like somebody tryin' to kill hu' 'Oh Lawd! Poo Girl! Girl, is dat you? Oh shit, Jesus! I didn't know yo' name wuz no 'Lizabeth, girl! All I eva knowed you by was Poo Girl! Oh shit, Lawd!' "

Folks yelped with laughter. Some faces looked angry because the story was so ridiculously funny. Mr. Blue was wobbling from side to side and shaking like one having an epileptic fit. "Blue, you oughta be 'shame' o' yo'self," Daddy kept repeating every chance he could catch his breath. "Dat woman ain't said all dat!"

"Sho' she said it!" Mr. Blue screamed as he laughed. "I was sittin' right dere! She jes' kept on holl'in', 'Girl, I ain't neva knowed yo' name was 'Lizabeth! Hell! Somebody coulda told me yo' name wuz 'Lizabeth. Girl, you my firs' cousin! Oh shit!" And every time Mr. Blue hollered "shit," people weakened all over again.

I was laughing at other people laughing. Ms. Polly's laugh sounded like a soprano hyena. "Heheheeeeeeeeeeeee!" Every time she laughed I would crack up. People were desperate to hold on to their laughter, knowing it might be a long time coming again.

"Blue, you's a fool!" Daddy said and shook his head in disbelief of the man's antics.

"Cleatis, you don't b'lieve it, do you?" Mr. Blue bucked his eyes as wide as they would stretch. He looked horrified by the mere possibility someone didn't believe his story.

Again, Daddy's expression was exactly what Mr. Blue needed in order to further embellish the tale.

"If you don't b'lieve dat, you sho' ain't gon' b'lieve dis." He stuck out his bottom lip and shook his head from side to side, whetting people's appetite for the remainder of the story. He took a long swig of home brew and said, "You'd think Nila Faye would jes' go 'head on back to hu' seat and git hu'self togetha, but naw, naw." He swallowed another gulp of wine to give our anticipation time to rise.

"What she do, Blue?" Mr. Somebody asked with an impatient excitement. He had acquired the name, Daddy said, because his grandmother sought to build his self-esteem, as a child, by having him repeat, "I am Somebody," over and over again. Actually, because the man was almost ninety years old, his birth name was irrelevant to most folks. The Mr. was the important part.

Mr. Blue continued. "Nila Faye stood at de casket fu' a while and den all of a sudden she hollered, 'Girl, you can't be dead, shit! You owe me fifty dollars!'"

Mr. Blue toppled over with laughter! Mr. Somebody grabbed his cane and took off hobbling toward Uncle James Earl's house, laughing so hard he could barely maintain his balance.

"Blue, you know you lyin'!" folks screamed.

"Cleatis, you know Nila Faye, wit' hu' crazy ass! You know dat bitch li'ble du say anything, don't cha?" asked Mr. Blue insistently.

Daddy told Mr. Blue dat he wasn't in it, but Mr. Blue wouldn't let Daddy go easily. "Shit, you is in it! Dat's yo' cousin, too. Don't act like y'all ain't family. Shiiiiiiiiit! I practically raised all you goddamn niggas!"

No one could dispute him, so we laughed along. After Mr. Somebody returned to his seat, his shoulders continued jerking spasmodically. "Blue, you oughta be 'shame'! You oughta be 'shame'!" he sang repeatedly.

As the evening waned, the crowd grew larger. Mr. Blue kept trying to convince everyone the story was absolutely true until Mr. Somebody said, "I got one even better'n dat! Y'all sho' ain't gon' b'lieve dis hyeah." He spit out a mouthful of tobacco juice and leaned up on his cane to tell his story. He was sitting on the pew next to Mr. Blue.

"I went to visit my cousin down in South Car'lina 'bout five years ago—"

"Stop lyin', nigga!" interrupted Mr. Blue playfully. "Yo' old ass ain't left hyeah in de last thirty years! Who you thank you foolin'?"

"I did go see Cousin Wizerine! Shit! I know where I been! I went right 'fo' we got all dat rain dat year. Shit, I might be old, but I ain't crazy."

Since Mr. Blue wanted to hear the story, he didn't press the matter. Everybody knew Mr. Somebody hadn't been to see anybody in the last five years or even fifteen, but his stories were always good, so he was allowed to proceed.

"Well, like I wuz sayin', I went down to see my cousin in South Car'lina. She and hu' husband live way, way out in de country in a l'il ole bitty place called Sugar Ditch."

When he said this, folks began to mumble and suck their gums.

"I ain't lyin'! Dat's what it's called! Don't blame me! I ain't had nothin' to do wit' namin' de place."

"Go 'head, nigga, shit," said Mr. Blue, the only one with the authority to say what all of us were thinking.

"Dey was gettin' ready fu dere pastor's anniversary program at church, and Cousin Wizerine was picked to be over de program. She decided she gon' put togetha a program like ain't nobody eva seen befo' in life. She take hu' fat ass down to the local college and ask a white German man if he'll come and be de guest speaker fu' de pastor's anniversary program. He got a buncha letters behind his name, so Wizerine thank dat mean he heavy and shit. I guess he tell hu' he'll be glad to do it, 'cause she come home grinnin like a ole bear in a fish house."

Mr. Somebody's antics alone induced chuckling. His eyes, mouth, and hands worked together, like a puppet's, in perfect gestural unity. Accompanied by a squeaky soprano voice far too high for most people's liking, his trembling arthritic hands shaped each word he spoke, forcing others not only to listen but to watch him. Suddenly he leaned back and laughed loudly, and David and I did the same although we didn't know why. The punch line of the story must have overwhelmed Mr. Somebody for a second, we thought, making us more excited to hear it.

"De mornin' of de pastor's anniversay, Wizerine get up and go to hummin' as she cookin' breakfast. She know she 'bout to blow de minds o' de whole community. She so excited 'bout dis German man comin' dat she cook a German chocolate cake in order to take him a piece.

"When we get to church, folk go to snickerin' and whisperin' 'cause hu' nose is 'bout fifty feet up in de air. Plus, she got on canary yellow from head to toe! Hat, gloves, dress, scarf, stockin's, pocket-book, and shoes. Everythang is de exact same loud-ass yellow. She look like goddamn Big Bird, but you couldn't tell hu' nothin'. We walk into de church and see dat de white man done brung a whole group o' white folks wit him, so Wizerine know it's 'bout to be a gred day.

"When it come time to introduce de speaka, Wizerine walk to de podium like a proud-ass peacock and start readin' off de man's 'com-plishments. When she get through wit' dat, she realizes she don't know how to pronounce de man's name proper. His name is 'Fuqua,' pronounced wit' dat guttural sound like most German folk have, but Wizerine didn't know dis. She fumbles around a little bit and then says, 'I would like to present to some and introduce to others Dr . . . um . . . uhru . . . Fucka.'"

That was it! The Meetin' Tree vibrated from all the laughter un-derneath. David's head fell backward as though it were going to drop to the ground as he lost composure and began to cry tears of ecstasy. His arms dropped limp to his side and he gave up the fight for self-control. Mr. Blue fell over on the pew once again, but this time the scream he emitted should have scared even the mosquitoes away. "Stop! Please, stop!" he kept begging, panting and holding his side. "Don't say nothin' else to me long as you live, Somebody!"

The story was far from over. Mr. Somebody sat perfectly still like he didn't know why everyone else was laughing. That's what made the next part riotous.

"No, no. Dat ain't de funny part. Shit. If she woulda stopped there, everythang mighta been all right. But no, no. She got to be high-and-mighty, so she whisper and ask de man who dem folks is wit him and I guess he tell hu' 'cause then she raise hu' head proudly and say, 'He has his three children with him today. The little Fuckas, will you stand and be recognized?' "

"Hahahaha! Hehehe!"

People were on the ground, some clutching their chests, while others simply hollered without shame and wiped tears from their eyes.

"Then, she introduces his wife and turns to go back to hu' seat. Somebody whispers dat she fugot to introduce his momma, so she turns around and hollas, 'Oh yes! And Mother Fucka, would you stand and be recognized!' "

Mr. Somebody couldn't hold it any longer. He dropped his cane and fell onto the pew, vibrating freely. Everyone else was in their own fit of laughter. I had never seen people in Swamp Creek—or anywhere—more full of joy. They slapped one another's leg or arm in disbelief, they leaned on one another like they simply couldn't help it, and they grabbed one another's hands and walked into the land of pleasure together.

I hadn't laughed that hard in years. Either nothing funny ever came along or I never realized that my greatest joy was found in the life I was trying desperately to abandon.

"These are some characters here!" David said finally, huffing for breath. "Are they like this all the time?"

"As far as I know, they are," I said, ashamed I hadn't appreciated them earlier in life.

"I could listen to this stuff forever," he announced.

"Yeah, me, too," I murmured sadly.

"You shoulda seen de niggas in dat chuch fallin' out laughin' at Wizerine!" Mr. Somebody panted rapidly. "You woulda thought de Holy Ghost came ova everybody and knocked dem plumb out!"

The people's laughter rang in the night. It was still hot, but the joy of storytelling cooled the sweat considerably. Folks fanned like they were in church and took deep breaths as they tried hard to recover. "Dat's a clown sho' 'nuff!" Ms. Polly offered. "Somebody Washington?

I wouldn't fool wit' him no kinda way! Not Polly McPheeters! Y'all might fool with Somebody, but I ain't!" Her high-pitched laughter evoked even more from others.

The darkness erased the particulars of people's expressions and made all of us seem like spirits gathered at a tree. Who was cute and who wasn't and who had money and who didn't proved absolutely meaningless. We were all contributors unto a communal joy that was enough to sustain everyone. There must have been at least thirty people gathered at the Meetin' Tree, but together we created enough laughter to go round. As a child, I never noticed how wonderful it was to watch people abandon their daily roles and laugh out loud as they fashioned their own survival in a world prepared to kill them. This was one place and time where the power of white folks was of absolutely no consequence. It was great to see what Swamp Creek folks were like when whites were not our focus; indeed, it was blissful to see us being ourselves without any concern about them.

Truth be told, I fell in love with my home folks that night. The old, the young, the unsure, the desperate, the loud, the soft-spoken all put in their two cents as we constructed, if only temporarily, a world where everyone was free. The differences that disallow unity in America never interrupted our space as we listened to story after story, regardless of who was telling it. What a brilliant way to live, I thought. For the first time in my life, I was glad to be from Swamp Creek.

I told David my thoughts and he said, "Amen! Maybe one day we'll have our own schools and then we can educate our children right. Until we teach ourselves, we will always hate ourselves."

"I know dat's right," I affirmed. "What good is a degree if we can't sit out here like this with our own people and enjoy ourselves? Everybody wants us to acquire education in order to move our people away from our own traditions. We are already in the land of milk and honey because we're black and together!"

"You done said somethin' now, boy," Mr. Blue said and winked at me. I didn't think he had heard the conversation. "If education don' bring us closer together as a people, then it ain't no good. Dat's brain-washin' and white folks is benefittin' as our communities is fallin' apart. You college-degree chil'ren can go to white schools and live in white neighborhoods, and y'all thankin' y'all done progressed. Shit! You done gone straight backward! You know why? 'Cause you love his shit more than you love yo'self. If you got God and yo' own folks, you already got heaven. Ain't nothin' better'n dat! Ain't nothin' to rise to. Shit."

"You teachin' now, Blue," Mr. Somebody chimed in. "Seem like to me education oughta make us love one another mo', but it don't. Dem black teachers and writers talk about each otha like a dog and marry white folks and feel good 'bout knowin' dey ain't neva got to 'sociate wit' us no mo' if dey don't wont to. I wonted to go to school and all, but I'm sho' glad I didn't if dat's how I was gon' be."

"It ain't got to be like dat, though," Mr. Blue countered. "Dat's jes' what happens lots o' times. Learnin' is a good thang when it's done right, and black people could use a whole lot of it. Like take dis boy hyeah for 'xample." He nodded toward me. "He done gone off to school and got a whole buncha degrees, but he can still come home and laugh and talk wit' de rest of us wit'out thankin' he's too good to swat mosquitoes and listen to old nigga stories. Most of 'em don't come out like dat, though. Dat's because dem teachers tell them that dey come to school to better theyselves, which mean dat somethin' was wrong wid them befo' they got there. Yet dey don't need to better theyselves 'cause dey already de best. They jes' need to gather some learnin' in order to fill in what we don't know 'bout ourselves. That'll help all us love one another better and know jes' how good God done been to us. Now dat's what education s'pose' to be fu'. If it don't do dat, you can throw it away, 'cause it ain't no good. Mark my word."

Mr. Blue's profundity commanded attention, causing all laughter to cease. "I betcha dis boy hyeah could tell us a whole lot we don't know 'bout black folks."

Everyone gazed at me expectantly, prepared to receive whatever I had to give. The elder had paved the way and I had no choice but to deliver.

"All right. Um . . . did y'all know that black folks owned slaves?" I stated a bit fearfully.

"Get outta hyeah, boy! Ain't no black folks owned no slaves. Black folks was slaves theyselves!" Mr. Somebody posited.

"Not all of them. There were a few free ones who got rich enough to buy their own slaves."

"Why would they do that?" Ms. Polly asked, genuinely confused.

"For different reasons. Some of them were actually buying their relatives into freedom. They posed as real buyers at the auction, but in actuality they were freeing their kinfolks. They would buy them, take them home, and let them go. It was a masterful way of helping black folks escape from slavery."

"What you sayin' is dat we was trickin' white folks into believin' dat we was really buyin' our own people and treatin' dem like slaves, but what we was really doin' was buyin' 'em and settin 'em free?" Mr. Blue asked.

"Exactly," I said confidently.

"I likes dat kinda shit," he chuckled. "Dey always thankin' dey outsmartin' de black man. Shit, dey de stupid ones."

"Uh-huh," people mumbled.

"Some black owners kept their black slaves as slaves, though. I know it don't sound good, but it's certainly true."

No one said anything. Mr. Blue examined my eyes disappointedly.

"Some black folks simply took advantage of the economic situation at the time. They bought slaves because they had the money, and they worked them in order to make a profit. A book called *Black Masters* highlights several black families that owned slaves whom they worked like any white master would have."

"Now I know you lyin'!" said Mr. Blue disgustedly.

"No, sir, I'm not. I guess they saw slavery as a means by which they could make good money easily. They took advantage of the situation."

"How does a black man own his own people?" Mr. Somebody asked, puzzled.

Before I could answer, Daddy said, "The same way a black man today pay another black man minimum wage 'cause dat's what white folks pay us. He don't value his people no more than white folks do. It ain't hard to understand. If a black boy can kill another black boy ova some goddamn crack, then we sho' oughta understand how a black man can own another one. Same bullshit."

Mr. Somebody tapped his cane on the earth in frustration. "I ain't neva heard tell o' no black man ownin' no slaves. Dat's 'bout de wildest shit I ever heard of."

"It's the truth. South Carolina and Louisiana were the places it happened most."

Mr. Blue shook his head and proclaimed, "See? Now dat's what education s'pose' to do. You s'pose' to learn somethin' dat make you think." He paused. "Well, I'll be damn', a black slave master. I neva woulda dreamed of such a thang."

I couldn't ascertain whether I had said enough or if I should continue. I chose the former because the rule of thumb in the black South is to be silent more than you speak. Various elders spoke simultaneously about what a black slave master might be like, comparing him to a black policeman or a black FBI agent, and then Mr. Somebody changed the subject abruptly.

"Hey, y'all heard dat the last of the Horseman boys died, didn't ya?"

"The who?" people sang in unison.

"The Horseman boys. Y'all didn't know dem?" One could tell by his tone he knew no one knew these individuals. He was simply preparing the groundwork for the ensuing tale.

"Dese folks ain't old 'nough to know 'bout no Horseman boys, man!" said Mr. Blue.

"Well, it was ten of 'em and de last one died last week."

"What about 'em?" somebody asked, taking the bait.

"Y'all don't know 'bout de Horseman brothers?"

Mr. Blue shouted, "I jes' tole yo' ass dat don't nobody know nothin' 'bout no Horseman boys but chu!"

"Who were they?" I asked in an effort not to let Mr. Blue distract Mr. Somebody from the story.

"Dere wuz a woman lived here 'bout sixty years ago named Isabella Redfield. We called her Aunt Taint. She wuz kinda a strange woman, didn't say murch to nobody, but she was nice. She had ten boys and neva did have sex wit' no man."

"Oh, shut up, fool!" Ms. Polly hollered.

"No, dis true! Ain't it, Blue?"

"Dat's what dey say," Mr. Blue confirmed reluctantly.

"Sho' it's true. I was right here. I ain't talkin' 'bout what I heard; I'm talkin' 'bout what I know. De boys did have a daddy, though."

"Dat's why I can't stand a nigga! How dey gon' have a daddy, but de momma ain't neva have sex wit' no man?" Ms. Polly said, feigning outrage.

"'Cause dey daddy wunnit no man. See, looka hyeah," and Mr. Somebody turned up the wine bottle as he got ready to make us believe the unbelievable. "When I was a boy, Momma baked a pie and told me to take it to Aunt Taint. I didn't want to 'cause I was scared o' de woman, but Momma wouldn't o' understood dat, so I went on and took de pie. Momma said de boys' daddy had passed and de least we could do was to take 'em somethin' to eat. I told her I didn't know dey had no daddy, and she told me to mind my business and keep my mouth shut and dat's what I did.

"When I got ova to de house, people wuz everywhere dressed in black. Dat's how I knowed somebody had died. I spoke to everybody real nice, found Aunt Taint, and tole hu' dat Momma had sunt hu' a pie. She said, 'Tell yo' momma I thank hu',' and I turned to go. Jes' then, Henry, the son that was my age, come and asked me if I wanted to go walkin' in de woods wit' him. I didn't 'cause somethin' didn't seem right to me, but I felt sorry fu' him 'cause his daddy had jes' died, so I tole him I'd go. As we wuz walkin', I got up 'nough nerve to ask him how come I ain't neva seen his daddy.

" 'You have,' Henry said.

" 'No, I ain't. I ain't neva seen no man come outta y'all's house,' I said.

" 'He ain't no man,' Henry said.

"Dat shit was way too heavy fu' me to handle; dat's why I didn't say nothin' else.

"Suddenly Henry asked, 'You wanna see Daddy?'

"Dat's when I shoulda took my ass home, but no, no. I was too nosy, so I said, 'Yeah.' And Henry turned and started walkin' back toward de house. I asked him where his daddy was and he said he was 'bout to show me. We got close to de house and I noticed a gred, big ole hole in de middle o' de field.

" 'What's dat fu'?' I asked Henry.

" 'Dat's where we gon' bury Daddy,' Henry said like it ain't mean nothin'.

"Henry kept walkin' till we came to de barn next to de house. 'Daddy's body's in here,' he said. I didn't have no mo' sense but to follow him. It was real dark in dat barn dat day like it was midnight. Henry lit an oil lamp and asked me to hold it while he raked back some hay with a pitchfork.

" 'Momma would probably kill us if she knew we wuz doin' this,' he said nervously.

" 'Leave it 'lone then! I ain't got to know nothin'!' I started walkin' toward de barn do', but Henry wouldn't let me go. He started talkin' to me like he wuz finally gettin' to say somethin he neva got a chance to.

" 'Momma tole us not to worry 'bout what other folks said. She said dat everybody in de world wuz diff'rent and otha folks jes' didn't undastand. I used to tell hu' dat I wanted to be normal like all de otha chil'ren, and she said dat wunnit gon' neva happen 'cause I didn't come in de world like otha folks. I neva undastood what she wuz talkin' 'bout till last year when Momma said I had a right to know de truth. "De truth 'bout what?" I asked her, and she said, "Every boy oughta know his daddy and how he come in de world." Dat's when she tole me everythang.'

"I didn't know what to say. In de lamplight, Henry looked like he wuz 'bout to cry, so I walked over to where he wuz standin', thinkin' dat I wuz 'bout to comfort him. All o' sudden, he bent down and pulled back a big black covering and showed me his daddy."

Mr. Somebody took another hit of wine as the rest of us waited anxiously. Mosquitoes were everywhere, but no one interrupted the tension to swat them.

"What chu see?" Ms. Polly begged.

"I saw de ole field mule laid up dere like he wuz 'sleep. His coat was so black and pretty it looked like silk. Then I noticed, fu' de first time, jes' how much all dem boys looked like . . . dat . . . like de daddy."

"You know dat ain't true, man!" hollered Ms. Polly as everyone else began to laugh.

"Oh, it's true," Mr. Somebody assured, nodding his head. "I saw dis wit' my own eyes. Ain't nobody got to tell me nothin'!" He extended his bottom lip confidently, for no one could dispute his word.

"Do you actually think the mule fathered those boys?" David questioned in utter shock.

"Yep. I know he did. All o' dem boys had dat kinda chin dat stick out too far. Dey voices wuz too deep to be called human. I neva did put two and two together till I saw his daddy out in dat barn de day he died."

"Somebody, you full o' shit!" Mr. Blue accused. "Why is you callin' dat damn horse dem boys' daddy?" He was laughing hard.

"'Cause dat's what he wuz! Henry cried dat day so hard I knew what de truth wuz. I'm tellin' you dat mule wuz dem boys' daddy!"

"Shut up, fool!" and other expressions came from the unbelieving audience, but the rest of us sat there amazed at the mere possibility.

"Lotta strange thangs done happened round here ova de years," Mr. Somebody offered to soften the blow of his story. "Like dat time Emma Jean Sanders birthed dat baby by hu'self."

"What?" I responded a bit too loudly.

"Dat's right. I guess y'all too young to know 'bout Emma Jean, but it's de truf."

David asked, "How in the world can a woman birth a child alone?"

"Most women cain't, but Emma Jean wunnit like no otha woman I eva knowed. She was a short woman, but you talkin' 'bout stout! Dat heifa could lift a square bale o' hay wit' one arm and neva grunt. I'm tellin' you what I seen myself."

Mr. Somebody perused the audience for verifiers and continued with, "One day we wuz all in the cotton field pickin'. It wuz round 'bout Septemba or early Octoba. Emma Jean wuz big as a house. Folks said she looked like she wuz 'bout to bust. But Emma Jean picked cotton dat day like she wuz a natchal-born man. I ain't neva seen nobody pick like dat! Both hu' arms wuz going faster than a octopus in water. I remember watchin' her and sayin', 'My God!'

"When we stopped fu' lunch, Emma Jean said she had to go to de house. Folks asked her if she was all right, and she said, 'Yes.' Said she had to go to the house to git dat baby out o' her. Folks thought she was clownin' so we didn't pay hu' no mind. When it come time fu' us to go back to work, Emma Jean wunnit there. Nobody said much about it, but it wunnit like Emma Jean to miss work. 'Wonder what happened to Emma Jean?' folks started sayin' 'bout one thirty. Then, 'bout two o'clock, Emma Jean come walkin' back to the cotton field, hu' stomach flat as a pancake."

"Get outta here!" Mr. Blue hollered.

"I ain't lyin'! I saw dis myself! She walked up and folks' eyes got big as quarters. My momma asked, 'Girl, what chu done gone and done?' Emma Jean looked round at everybody and said calmly, 'Y'all ain't neva heard of a woman havin' a baby?' Momma said, 'Sho' we done heard o' dat. But we ain't neva heard o' a woman havin' one by hu'self on hu' lunch break.' Emma Jean cackled a little and said, 'Well, you done heard o' it now.' She went back to pickin' cotton de same way she wuz pickin' dat mornin'.'"

"That's amazing," I told Mr. Somebody.

"Not really. Black folks been doin' amazin' thangs since de beginnin' o'time, boy."

"Why don't we do them now?" I asked.

"'Cause we done 'cepted what white folks think 'bout us. And dat ain't much. So we can't do much neitha."

"Amen," Mr. Blue cosigned.

Others told stories and children played until about eleven o'clock. Then the crowd began to thin out. Mr. Somebody rose and said, "I guess I betta be gettin' on back to de po' house. I'll see y'all tomorra at de fune'."

"All righty, Somebody," Mr. Blue responded affectionately. "You need a ride home?"

"Noooooo, nooooo. Walkin' good fu' a old man. I been walkin' all dese years. Ain't no need in stoppin' now."

I was surprised that a ninety-year-old man could walk such distances in the pitch-dark. He lived at least three miles from the Meetin' Tree, down a long dirt road that had absolutely no lights. As he walked away, his body disappeared slowly into the abyss like a mystical being with spiritual powers of levitation. I wondered about the story of Mr. Somebody's life—the things he had seen, the things he had done, the things that had made him cynical about young black folks. I made a mental note not to leave Swamp Creek until I sat at the feet of this man, who lived during a time when black people were amazing and knew it.

The opportunity to ask about Sister's death never materialized, so I decided not to force it. People's awkward smiles were a sign they sought to circumvent the topic like one avoids a contagious disease. I left the tree, however, realizing my coming home was because, in all my academic pursuits, I had missed the most critical lesson any student can learn—that transforming the world begins with love of one's own people.

21

Daddy walked home ahead of Willie James and me without ever having said a word to either of us. He surged from the church pew and proclaimed simply, "I'm gone." Clearly he didn't want company, so everyone honored his unspoken request for solitude.

Willie James and I walked David home, then cut across the backwoods to our house. Midway, Willie James said, "Dem ole men is crazy, huh?"

"Yeah, but they're wise, too," I told myself more than him. "They lived in a time when black people had no choice but to believe in each other. I like the stories myself."

"I like de stories, too, but I don't b'lieve none o' 'em."

"Why not?"

"'Cause they ain't real."

"How you know?"

"'Cause they ain't. All that stuff 'bout a horse and a woman having kids? Come on, man. You know dat shit ain't real."

"No, I don't know that. When we were kids, I would have agreed with you, but I've grown to understand that reality is culturally determined." I forgot where I was for a moment.

"What?"

"In other words, what's real and what's not real is defined by a people's world view. African people once believed that everything is possible. Mr. Somebody, Mr. Blue, Miss Emma Jean . . . these folks are Africans and don't know it. What was real in their youth is a little broader than what is real to us."

"OK. You de book man."

We walked on with nothing but the full moon to guide our way. Its illustrious shine, coupled with the radiance of the stars, made the night feel cozy and serene like a planetarium. Suddenly Willie James asked, "So you leavin' tomorrow?"

"Yep. I gotta go. I have to find a job."

"You ain't gotta go if you don't want to."

I was caught off guard.

"Dis is yo' home. You don't neva have to leave yo' home 'less you wants to."

"I honestly have to go, Willie James. I need to start looking for a professorship somewhere."

"You ain't got to 'xplain nothin' to me. I understand. I'd be leavin', too, if I was you."

"What does that mean?"

"Nothin'. It jes' mean dat you left here for good reason and I'm sho' you got good reason to leave again."

I couldn't figure out what Willie James was trying to imply. He wanted to tell me something, say some final words, but instead he said, "She was going to name the baby after you."

"What?"

"Tommy Lee Tyson Junior. Dat's what she started callin' de baby soon as she knowed she was pregnant."

"Get outta here," was all I could mutter.

"She wuz happy, T.L. She pranced around all day like de Lawd had jes give' hu' evalastin' life. Sometimes I'd see hu' from a distance and she'd be singin' at de top o' hu' lungs dat song y'all used to sing together."

" 'Uncloudy Day,' " I yielded.

"Yep. Dat's it. She'd have hu' head thrown back and go to hollerin', 'Oh, they tell me of a home / where my loved ones have gone.' I'd stop, close my eyes, and listen till she finished and I'd wonder where in de world you was."

He paused and studied me intensely. I lowered my eyes in shame.

"When she got pregnant, we agreed to name de baby after you."

"I'm glad she asked you what you thought."

"She didn't have no choice. It was my baby, too."

"What?" I screamed.

"Don't act so surprised. When you left here, she didn't have nobody, and I neva did; that's why we went to each other. We didn't mean to have sex, though. She jes' came to sleep in my bed one night 'cause she was missin' you, she said, and she asked me to hold her like you used to do. I didn't know how to do dat, so she showed me. It felt good to have somebody dat close to me. I pulled her closer and she didn't stop me. She was cryin' and I was cryin', too. But it felt . . . right. I ain't neva knowed what love feel like, but I felt love right then. I asked her if she wanted me to stop and she squeezed me harder."

I was in total shock. "Are you serious, man?" My fists balled in anger.

Willie James kept speaking. "We wunnit thinkin' of babies or condoms or nothin' like dat. We wuz jes' free to love one another. When I released, I knew we had created life. I felt it. I shook all over and started mumblin', 'No, oh no,' but Sister smiled and rubbed my head as she kept on holdin' me."

"Willie James, are you sick? That was yo' sister!"

"She was yo' sista, too, and y'all made love all de time."

"I neva had sex with Sister! Have you lost your fuckin' mind?"

"I neva said y'all had sex. I said y'all made love. You did it all de time. And all I could do was sit by and watch. All dat laughin' and lovin', and all I eva did was work. Nobody wanted to laugh wit' me, so I thought I jes' wasn't good enough to love nobody. When Sister came to me dat night, I felt like I could love somebody for de first time in my life. I knew dat, really, she wanted you, but even as a substitute I felt like I was somebody, T.L., 'cause somebody came to me, *me*, for once."

"But she didn't come to you to have sex, man! This shit is immoral, not to mention illegal!" My bottom lip quivered.

"So why ain't it immoral and illegal to live a life without ever bein' loved? Huh? Tell me dat."

I had no answer.

"See, you can judge me 'cause you've always had all de stuff necessary to make you a righteous man. You wuz smart and good-looking and people believed in you. Sister thought you wuz God and Daddy always knew you wuz sharper than he is. That's why he beat you like that. Jes' so you wouldn't ever know how smart you really were and come to realize that you didn't have to obey him 'cause half de stuff he wuz sayin' didn't make no sense noway. He wuz scared dat you'd be bigger than him.

"But didn't nobody ever fear me 'cause nobody thought I'd ever be nothin'. I wuz de family workhorse. But who wants to be known fu' workin' like a goddamn mule? Dat don't leave nobody feelin' good 'bout deself. I wanted to be smart and to love somebody, too. So when Sister came to me dat night I gave her everything I had. I completely opened myself to being loved by somebody else. It felt great." Willie James was crying. I saw a tear glisten in the moonlight on his cheek.

"You can judge me if you want to. I don't care 'cause I ain't sorry fu' nothin'. I might not eva git a chance to feel dat feelin' again, and I ain't gon' let you take dat joy away from me. I ain't had but one my whole life. Don't I deserve at least one joy?"

"Yes, Willie James," I said, trying not to unleash my seething rage. "But your joy ain't supposed to be at Sister's expense."

"It wunnit at Sister's expense. She brought de joy to me. I didn't go to her. She came in my bed and asked me to hold her and as one thing led to another—"

"Stop it! You know dat shit is sick!"

"Why is it sick when somebody else do de same thang you did? Y'all laid in de bed and giggled for years as I laid there listenin' to you, hopin' dat, one day, I'd get invited to laugh along. That day neva came 'cause you wuz so damn selfish. It neva crossed yo' mind to include me in de fun."

"What the hell is wrong with you? You were the oldest! It was your job to give love to the younger ones."

"Don't bullshit me, T.L. You can't give nothin' you neva had. And tell de truth, you wunnit waited on me to bring you nothin' 'cause you neva thought I had nothin' to bring."

My silence confirmed his conclusion.

"It's all right 'cause dat's what everybody thought. But it ain't true. I didn't realize this till me and Sister created life."

"Willie James, you need help, man. This is abnormal and psychotic. It ain't right."

"There you go again, judgin' me."

"Willie James, this ain't about me judging you! This is about you having sex with my sister!"

"Dat's why you mad, T.L. 'cause, in your eyes, I had sex with *your* sister. Not our sister. She belonged to you, and you belonged to her. Dat's why you came back here in de first place. To get *your* sister. You didn't come back to see me or anybody else for dat matter."

We stood statuesque in the darkness of night, listening to the crickets sing an unknown song. "I'm sorry, Willie James, for not loving you the way I should have," I offered genuinely. "I never knew the way you felt."

"Don't worry 'bout it. I'll be a'ight. I jes' thought you should know dat de baby Sister wuz carryin' wuz mine, too. Dat's why you came back. To find out 'bout her. I wuz jes' tellin' you befo' you leave tomorrow."

Willie James ignored my trauma and started walking again, moving like a stealth deer through the woods. I ran after him.

"How did she die, Willie James?" I risked asking again. Since he was in truth mode, I tried to get all the information I could. He seemed not to have heard me, so I repeated myself, "How did she—"

"I heard you, man," he retorted abruptly. Then, without notice, he swiveled and yelled, "Momma did it!" and fell to the ground in agony.

"Oh my God," I whispered as I consoled him.

"She did it, T.L. I saw her. I been lyin' to you 'cause Daddy told me he'd kill me if I eva told anybody." Willie James was wailing. "I can't hold it no mo'! You really wanna know what happened to Sister? Fine! I'll tell you. All I got to lose is my life."

Ironically, I wanted him to pause a moment and think about what he was proposing to do, but I certainly wasn't going to stop him.

"Some o' de stuff I told you, T.L., was a lie, but I'ma tell you de truth now." Willie James sighed, "I came home for lunch from de field dat day and sat at de table eatin'. Momma was actin' kinda nervous-like, but I didn't really pay it much 'tention. I asked her where Sister was, and she said she was in de back room layin' down 'cause she didn't feel good. I told Momma I'd go check on her, but soon as I said it she snapped back at me wit', 'Don't chu go in dere, boy. I said she wuz sick. Let de girl be.' I frowned at Momma a li'l bit 'cause she yelled at me way louder than she needed to. I didn't go in de room. At least not then."

Willie James had recomposed himself enough to rise and sit on a nearby tree stump. I sat next to him, our sides touching from shoulder to ankle. He breathed heavily, comprehending fully the price of his confession, but he pressed on.

"I finished my lunch and acted like I was goin' back to de field, but, instead, I got down by de bend in de road and parked de tractor in de woods. Then I snuck back to de house. Momma was hangin' up clothes, so I went round to Sister's bedroom window and peeked in. She wunnit there."

"She wasn't sick in the bed as Momma had said?" I queried, wild-eyed.

"Nope. She wunnit nowhere in de room. I tried to figure out how to get in de house witout Momma seein' me, but I knowed not to try it. I tiptoed round de house, lookin' in every window, but I couldn't find Sister. I gave up after a while and went back to get de tractor. When I put it in gear to drive off, somethin' tole me to look in de barn. I cain't really explain it, but I heard somethin' in my head say"—Willie James lowered his voice to authenticate the one he had heard—"'Look in de barn.' So I turned de engine off again and walked through de backwoods to de barn. Dat's where I firs' seed de baby." Willie James moaned in sorrow and desolation. "It was hid under some hay and blood was all round it. It scared me so bad I started shakin' and didn't know what to do. I still didn't see Sister, but I knowed it was hu' baby. It was a boy and he was dead. His arms was stretched out like he wanted somebody to pick him up and he was blue. De umbilical cord was still on him and he had scratches all over his little body. Tears started runnin' down my face 'cause I was scared to death. I kept askin' myself what to do, but nothin' came to me. Suddenly I heard Momma shoutin' at somebody and dey was walkin' toward de barn. I hid behind a coupla hay bales and lay still. Dat's when I see Momma and Sister bust through de do' fightin'."

"What?"

"Dey was screamin' 'cause Sister wanted hu' baby and Momma tole hu' she couldn't have him. Blood was all ova Sister's dress and she was real weak, but she was fightin' wit' everything she had. Momma was jes' too powerful. She throwed Sister on de ground and tied hu' hands behind hu' back. Still, Sister wunnit givin' up. She kicked Momma real hard in de chest and Momma fell back on de garden hoe, cuttin' hu' arm pretty bad. When Momma got up, she had a look on hu' face, T.L., like I ain't neva seen. She was breathin' hard and cussin' like drunk old men. Sister kept mumblin', 'I want my baby; I want my baby,' and Momma kept sayin', 'Hell naw!' Momma stood ova Sister's bloody, weak body again and Sister spit in hu' face. I knowed Momma was gon' do somethin' bad. Ain't no way she was gon' take dat. But what she did blowed my mind."

Willie James shook and rubbed his head simultaneously. I put my arm around his shoulder, hoping to comfort him. "Daddy's gon' kill me," he muttered softly.

"No, he's not," I assured him timidly. We both knew I couldn't promise anything about Daddy's actions.

"T.L., please don't tell nobody what I'm sayin'. This is gon' make you madder than a wet hen, but you got to promise not to say nothin'. I'm tellin' you, Daddy'll kill me."

Afraid to enter such a covenant, I did so nonetheless. "I won't tell a soul, Willie James. I promise."

He gazed into my eyes, searching for the truth of my words, and continued, "Momma took dat hoe and started choppin' at Sister like she was uprootin' weeds. Sister dodged her pretty good, but then Sister's strength failed. Momma struck hu' leg first. The blood squirted out like juice from a orange when you bite it too hard, and Sister hollered out in pain."

"Why didn't you help her, Willie James?" I cried in confusion.

"'Cause fear had me paralyzed. I tried to move, really I did, but my whole body was stiff like a stone. I couldn't even scream. Everything wuz happenin' so fast dat my brain couldn't process it fast enough. I was cryin' and shakin', but I jes' couldn't move." Willie James lamented loudly, "You woulda been proud o' Sister, T.L. She was fightin' like a wild woman and she jes' had a baby. She grabbed the sharp end of the hoe and hu' and Momma tussled in a frenzy till Momma got it 'way from hu' and started beatin' hu' wit' it. Momma kept yellin' stuff I couldn't make out 'cept de line, 'You ain't bringin' dat boy back here! I swear fo' God you ain't. I done put dat behind me and I be goddamn if you gon' make me suffer it again.' I heard dat loud and clear.

"I knowed Sister was either hurt real bad or dead 'cause she wunnit movin' no mo'. Momma fell on de ground next to her and started cryin' somethin' awful. It didn't make no sense to me. She started apologizin' fu' bein' a bad momma and fu' havin' to do what she jes' did, but she couldn't help it, she said. De baby looked too much like you, and she wunnit gon' neva deal wit' dat again. I didn't know exactly what she meant, but I guessed it had somethin' to do wit' you not bein' hu nachel-born son. I neva knowed she resented you like dat."

I leaned my head back and studied the heavens, unsure if I wanted to hear the rest or run and call the police.

"Anyway, Momma snapped back to hu' regular mean self and ran in de house. I didn't know what she was doin' or how long she was gonna be gone. I tried to move again, I sware I did, but I jes' couldn't. I didn't know nothin' else to do but cry and hold myself real tight. Momma come back what seem like a second later and wrapped Sister in a big white sheet. She didn't do nothin' wit' de baby. Then, she took de shovel and ran out de barn frantically. Dat's when my bones thawed and I ran to Sister's body and unwrapped it real fast. I thought she was dead, but she wunnit. I wuz bawlin' and holdin' hu' tight and tellin' hu' how much I loved hu'. De only thing she said wuz, 'Tell T.L. I love him.' Then hu' head fell back and I knowed she was gone. I put de sheet back ova hu' face and bleated like a young lamb at slaughter. I was helpless, hopeless, and too confused to know what to do. But I knowed fu' sho' I didn't want Momma to know I had seen hu'. I wuz gon' do somethin', I promised myself, but I didn't know what. No police would believe my story, and I didn't have nobody else to tell.

"I grabbed de baby and took off runnin' for de woods. Momma didn't see me 'cause she was too busy diggin' Sister's grave. At least I think she didn't see me. I don't think I ever ran dat fast in my life. I had de baby in one arm and a little garden shovel in de otha. When I got back in de woods behind de barn, I rocked de little boy and hummed nursery rhymes as I rubbed his dead body. I hugged him and thought about you and wuz mad 'cause I didn't know where to find you and I needed you bad dat day. My tears fell on de crown o' his head as I trembled and sang all at de same time. Then I remembered de tractor parked down de lane from de house and told myself I'd betta hurry befo' somebody see it and know somethin' ain't right.

"I laid my son on de ground real gentle-like and dug a little grave where I found a soft spot underneath some old leaves. I couldn't hardly see fu' cryin' and my hands kept droppin' de shovel 'cause I was so nervous. But after a coupla minutes, I had a hole dug and laid de baby in it and covered him up. I put de leaves back over de spot and said a prayer and left."

"Where exactly did you bury him?" My curiousity got the better of my terror.

Willie James scrutinized my face. "I ain't gon' tell dat, T.L. I promised myself I wunnit gon' neva tell nobody and I'm gon' keep dat promise."

As he was obviously resolute in his self-commitment, I pushed no further.

"I wanted somethin' dat wuz jes' between me and my son. Since I couldn't share his life, de least I could do, I said to myself, was to give him a proper burial. I promised him sweet rest by tellin' him dat nobody would ever disturb him again. I intend to keep dat promise."

"What about seeing him on the ground that day back in the woods? How did that happen?"

"I don't know. But I did see him. I was in shock 'cause I knowed fu' sho' dat I had jes' buried him myself. I thought maybe a coyote or somethin' had smelled him and dug him up, but it wouldn't have left him there. It woulda ate him or drug him away, right?"

Thinking the question rhetorical, I returned only a stare.

"I picked him up and cradled him in my arms again. I felt worse than I ever felt in my life. I had done made a promise to my son, and somethin' or somebody proved to me dat I didn't have no control ova his life anyway. I went back to de place where I buried him and it looked untouched. I didn't see no animal tracks and the leaves didn't look rustled. I thought I was losing my mind, T.L."

"You were!" I said.

"Well, to get it back again, I cremated him myself. I wunnit gon' let nothin' disturb my son's peace again, if I could help it."

I was standing before him, staring into his eyes, searching incessantly for the logic that justified his psychopathic behavior.

"Don't look down at me, man!" he reproached me. "What else could I do? I had made a promise and I had to keep it. What's wrong wit' dat?"

"The whole thing is sick!" I foamed hysterically. "You made a promise to a dead baby whom you and your own sister had conceived! Of course, she was murdered by her mother as her brother watched in frozen horror. Then—"

Willie James rebuked my sarcasm, "Don't talk to me like I ain't got no sense, boy. The story is more complicated than I can explain. You make it sound like it ain't nothin', but it is!"

"Yes, it is serious, Willie James! But you don't have the right to cremate a body simply because you want to!"

"I didn't want to!" he yelled violently, and swung his arms in the dark night. "I had to! This was my son and I had made a promise!"

"How do you make a promise to a dead baby?"

"Easy! I was talkin' to his spirit. You should understand dat."

"I do understand that, Willie James, but I don't understand how you cremate a body on your own recognizance."

"Your own what?" He appeared insulted.

I circumvented the explanation by rewording, "I don't understand how you decide to do that and simply do it."

"You did it all the time, T.L. Like when you left Swamp Creek. You jes' up and decided to leave and you left. I don't remember you makin' no announcement or askin' anybody else if they agreed or not."

"That's different," I argued weakly.

"How? It looks like de same thang to me. You make a decision you think is right and you stand by it. Others ain't got to agree."

He was right. Even as I thought of how peacefully I had left home after high school, I knew that if someone had protested, their words would have been meaningless vanity.

"So I made a decision for my son and I don't regret it. In fact, I'm glad about it 'cause now can't nobody mess with him."

"Then what were you smelling at the trash barrel that day?"

"I lied about that, T.L. It was Momma who smelled somethin' and she asked me what wuz burnin' and I told her I had throwed a coupla dead rats from de barn onto de fire. She gave me a funny look and walked away. Everything I told you befo' was jes' to git you off my back. Now, I ain't got to lie no more."

An owl perched itself on a tree limb about thirty feet from where we were standing. It examined us, rotating its head slowly, seemingly assessing whether we were too big to carry away. Then it spread its wings and flew toward us like a warplane.

"Whoa!" we shouted simultaneously. The owl ascended quickly and disappeared.

Willie James said pensively, "Grandma used to say that when you see an owl it's really a dead person comin' to talk to you. Maybe dat was Sister or de little baby boy."

"Maybe," I repeated doubtfully, "but if it were either of them, I sure wish they had told us something to help make sense of all this."

"It ain't gon' neva make sense. Not completely. We too far gone round here to make complete sense. Everybody a li'l abnormal, includin' you."

I chuckled at the naked truth.

"We jes' gotta do de bes' we can wit' what we got left. I know all dis sound real stupid to you, but it ain't. I been carryin' dis fu' years and it finally make sense to me."

"How?"

"'Cause lonely, desperate people do desperate things. Ain't nothin' worse than livin' a life you know don't mean nothin' to nobody. You keep askin' yo'self what you here fu', and you don't neva come up wit' nothin'. I think that's why Sister came to my bed dat night.

She wanted to create life, T.L. After you left, hu' life lost all its
meanin' and she faced de truth dat she might live in Swamp Creek
foreva and die wit'out anybody eva knowin' she had been on de earth.
Dat's a bad feelin', to come to de earth and leave wit'out anybody eva
noticin'. What I'm sayin' is dat everybody in de world is tryin' to figure out how to be remembered. Some people write songs so radio sta-
tions and musicians can still play them long after dey gone, and some
people build buildings and name them after theyselves 'cause dey
know de buildin' is gon' last longer than they are, and some people
write books so others can read them hundreds of years after dey gone
and de author's pleasure is knowin' dat they life don't neva stop influ-
encin' otha lives. But round here, what wuz Sister gon' do to make
people remember hu'? The only thing she could think of was givin'
life to somebody else. Then, someone would be grateful to hu' foreva.
I guess dat's why I didn't stop hu', too. I didn't have nothin' to leave
de world. Farmin' ain't nothin' dat nobody care 'bout and drivin' trac-
tors ain't no special skill. I wanted to touch at least one person's life,
T.L. Dat's what everybody want, I think."

I sighed deeply and fought to receive my brother's words amicably.
In the midst of his insanity, I began to understand my family's dys-
functional sensibility and why we were all determined, ultimately, to
abandon our origin.

"Sister meant a lot to you, and I know dat, but she didn't mean
more than yo' own life. Nothin' wuz more important to you than
makin' de world recognize your presence. Dat's why you left here, although it broke yo' heart to leave Sister. You wunnit gon' let nothin'
or nobody keep you from makin' de world hear what you had to say.
And you wuz willin' to leave motha, fatha, sista, and brotha to leave
dat mark on de world. Good!" Willie James smiled at me. "Jes' understand dat me and Sista wanted to do de same thang. We wanted to be
important to somebody and to know dat somebody would actually be
moved if we wunnit here. De onlyest way to do dat wuz to create
somethin' de world didn't already have, and dat's what we did."

"Oh, Willie James," I said exhaustively, and reached for his hand. To my surprise, he didn't resist.

"I know; I know," he repeated, rotating his head slowly. "It's de best we knowed to do."

"Do you think Momma knew the baby was yours?"

"She mighta knowed."

"How? You think Sister told her?"

"No. Sista would neva have told her. The night we made life, I thought I heard footsteps in de hallway. I closed my eyes and tried to listen real hard, but I didn't hear anything more. But I could have sworn I heard footsteps. I told Sista the next day, but she said she didn't hear anything, so I forgot about it. Then, one day, Daddy told Momma dat a mouse had got in de house. She said, 'I know. I know everythang dat go on in dis house.' She threw me a threatening look. I got nervous, but I tried not to show it. She wuz definitely tellin' me somethin'. You know how Momma do."

"Yeah, I know."

"Don't tell nobody what I'm tellin you, T.L. Ain't no tellin' what's li'ble to happen to me. It jes' don't make sense fu' you to come all dis way afta all dese years and leave here not knowin'. Now you know."

He started walking again, but I grabbed his arm and stopped him. "What about Daddy? Didn't he ever say anything about all this?"

"Nope. Notta word. At least not to me. Maybe him and Momma talked about it, but I didn't hear Daddy say nothin' 'bout it."

"Did you ever ask him?"

"Ask him what?"

"Ask him about Sista's death?"

"Yeah. One time. We wuz feedin' de cows one evenin' and I got up de courage to ask him about it. He told me not to neva mention dat to him no mo' and I obeyed him."

"Daddy knows something, Willie James."

"I know he do. He got to. He don't let nothin' happen round dis place 'less he know 'bout it."

"Big brother, this is madness."

"You tellin' me?" Willie James said, squeezing my hand tighter. "I been carryin' all dis shit round wit' me fu' years. It done near 'bout drove me outta my mind. I'm glad somebody else know 'bout it now, though. Hell, I don't care no more, T.L. Momma nem can do whatever dey want to to me. I'm tired o' bein' scared o' dem and I ain't gon' do it no mo'."

Willie James released my hand and sobbed freely into both of his own; I massaged the nape of his neck and cried along. "We'll make it, Willie James. Somehow, we'll make it."

"Yeah, I hope so." He lifted his head and wiped away his tears.

He looked different to me in the moonlight. His face had an innocence of which the daylight robbed him. For the first time in my life, I saw the core of Willie James's heart. It was caring, sensitive, and compassionate. I supposed I hadn't seen it before because those kinds of hearts in a southern black man either get destroyed or are masked thoroughly. The darkness of the night, ironically, assisted in his heart's exposure and allowed him to express its contents unashamed. The darkness also reminded us of the temporal nature of comfort zones, for we knew that, as morning approached, the routine of our regular lives awaited our embracing like a newborn child its mother.

Willie James's head, like Christ's on the cross, hung in a submission and humility that forbade reprimand. He was willing to die for his convictions, for the weight of the truth had forced him to tell it, and he simply refused to carry the guilt I was fashioning for him. He kept breathing sighs of relief, glad the lies were over. I stood beside him as the moon and stars glowed effervescently above our heads. It was nice, actually, just my brother and me, in the middle of the universe together, without other eyes limiting the intensity of our sharing. I was still livid about him and Sister, but for some reason, my anger abated. Maybe I felt sorry for Willie James and what he never had. Such neglect didn't justify what had happened, but it did explain it. We knew we couldn't stay in the woods long because

Momma would get suspicious, but neither of us wanted to disturb this tranquillity we had discovered. Once again, I extended my hand toward Willie James and he smiled and grabbed it. We laughed simultaneously, knowing that, to the outside world, this scene would probably have appeared ridiculous. To us, it was divine.

"Sing the song for me, please," Willie James begged. "Please. I need to hear it one more time."

My brother's face expressed a longing I could not refuse. For the first time ever, a member of my own family extended to me the opportunity to share in his healing. I cleared my throat and sang richly:

> "Oh, they tell me of a home
> Far beyond the skies;
> Oh they tell me of a home,
> Far, far away;
> Oh they tell me of a home
> Where no storm clouds rise;
> Oh, they tell me of an uncloudy day!"

Willie James's hands, like a drowning victim's, waved freely in the air. His head was flung back and swaying with a sensual rhythm accented most perfectly by the moans of pleasure his throat emitted. Tears flowed down his cheeks, shimmering in the moonlight like icicles on a sunny winter afternoon. He was free. I sang the second verse more boisterously:

> "Oh, they tell me of a King,
> In his beauty there;
> And they tell me that mine eyes
> Shall behold where he sits
> On the throne that is whiter than snow
> In the city that is made of gold!
> Oh, they tell me of an uncloudy day!"

My big brother was gone. He was in a land and a place I had never been before. His arms were stretched toward the heavens and, with closed eyes and a soft whimper, he danced through a spiritual zone unfamiliar to me. I held him in my arms and rocked him in my bosom like church folks begged Abraham to do, hoping our openness was also the birth of our lifelong intimacy. "Oh, they tell me of an uncloudy day!" I repeated, purging our souls of familial hatred and freeing ourselves to dream. I wasn't singing loudly anymore; I was singing earnestly. I had never felt the song so passionately, probably because I had never sung it to one whose heart lay vulnerable before me. I loved my brother that moment in a way unexplainable.

"Wow," Willie James said once he calmed, studying my face for clues about how to sing someone into ecstasy. "I always did like dat song. Every time I hear it, I start imaginin' a place where de sun shines all de time and everybody treat everybody else real nice."

"I wish it wasn't imaginary," I said as we began to walk again.

The house appeared in the distance after a few minutes. We slowed our steps together, savoring the last precious moment.

"Take care of yo'self, little brother," Willie James said painfully without eye contact.

A faint smile forced itself upon me. "I will, big brother."

"I'll neva forgit tonight. It wuz a long time comin'. I'm glad you came home 'cause now I'm free." He examined the night like an ex-con who had forgotten what it looked like.

"I'm glad you're free, too, Willie James. More than you know."

We hugged tightly. "Thanks for all the info," I whispered in his ear.

Willie James nodded and winked at me. "Do somethin' with it," he muttered. "Write a book or somethin'. Jes' don't tell nobody I told you nothin'. Lord Jesus, don't put my name in it nowhere!"

"Don't worry. Nobody'll know anything. I promise."

"Thanks, T.L."

"No, thank *you*, Willie James." We walked the last few steps in perfect harmony.

22

I awakened Saturday morning at the crack of dawn while everyone else was still asleep. It must have been four thirty or five, for Daddy would already have been awake had it been a half hour later. I went to the bathroom and splashed my face because I had nothing else to do. Returning to my room quietly, I clicked on the night lamp and sat on the bed's edge, staring at the beige linoleum floor. I wanted desperately to sleep, yet everything about my return—Ms. Swinton's request, David's unexpected entry into my life, Willie James's heinous confession—converged into an insomia I couldn't shake. We were about to bury my own mother when, a few days ago, I didn't even know she was my mother. I loved her, but knowing I once had lived in her womb bonded me to Ms. Swinton inseperably. All those books were a sign of how much she believed in me, but I didn't know what to do with them. I'd have to conceive a plan, however, since I couldn't leave them in Arkansas and I definitely couldn't transport them to my miniature New York apartment. Ms. Swinton would surely haunt me if I didn't make good use of her literary legacy.

I leaned over the side of the bed and retrieved one of her journals from my suitcase.

Dear Diary,

I've had more than I can take. Teaching in Swamp Creek has exhausted me beyond repair, it seems. Children don't want to learn anymore. I go to school day after day, hoping at least a few get inspired, only to return home in the evenings frazzled, dejected, and overwhelmed. The days of the good student seem past now. No one wants to read anything other than what they must, and no one strives frantically for the A. I miss T.L. That boy would read anything he could get his hands on. I remember the excitement on his face when I gave him Go Tell It on the Mountain *for his birthday. That's the kind of student I long to teach, but I think they're extinct now. Kids come to school tired, cranky, and having done no homework at all. We went wrong somewhere as a people. Children weren't allowed such parameters in the black community once upon a time. Clearly, parents are to blame. We stopped insisting on discipline and character and, instead, granted our youth the choice to do nothing, and most of them took it. Hence, I shouldn't expect much, I'm afraid. Yet I'm a teacher—not a babysitter. I love to discover, argue, analyze, debate, write, think, reason. Unfortunately, my students care little for any of these "useless" activities. All they want to do is play new video games or watch idiotic sitcoms on television. I'm worried about the future of the black brain trust. From where will our next George Washington Carver come? Who will write our stories when Toni Code Bambara, James Baldwin, John Killens, and Gwendolyn Brooks retire? Out of thirty years of teaching, I know I should be more encouraged, more hopeful, but I just don't see the prospects. Honestly, I want T.L. back. I need a class of students who'd stay up late to finish a good book or revise a paper four times to assure its perfection. I need a guarantee that what I'm doing is not in vain. A teacher's life boasts few rewards; thus the best we can hope for is an exemplary student. I guess I've had my one.*

I thought Cynthia Tyson might be another, but it didn't work out that way. After T.L. left, she lost her motivation, her academic spunk. He meant the world to her, and I think she felt abandoned by him. He left in May of 1983, and when school started in the fall, her usual flair and drive were gone. I asked her what was wrong, and she said, "I'm

fine, Ms. Swinton. Just a little lonely." I hugged her reassuringly and told
her not to worry about Thomas. She smiled, but my words did not heal
her heart. Cynthia stopped raising her hand in class and she started mak-
ing Bs on assignments without complaint. I invited her to come see me if
she needed to talk, but she never did. I knew what she needed. I just
didn't know how to tell her that T.L. wasn't coming back. He's gone for
good and I know it. I'll never get to tell him I'm his mother and he'll
never know how much Cynthia loves him unless he reads these pages one
day. I can only hope for as much.

Clutching the journal to my chest, I gazed at the ceiling. Sister's
depression saddened my heart and caused me to reevaluate the wisdom of my decision ever to leave. Had I known then what I know
now, I would have taken her with me. Momma and Daddy's response
I could have ignored. I would have loved Sister, sent her to school,
and dressed her in pretty things. Her hair would have been neat and
she would have been the envy of all her girlfriends. But I never imagined my decision would disrupt Sister's peace like Ms. Swinton described. In hindsight, I felt selfish and egocentric. Yet at the time, I
thought I was saving my life.

Guilt was seeking my attention, and I simply refused to acknowl-
edge it. Instead, I went and took a bath, returned to my room, and began to pack my things. Unsure of how much time I'd have between
the burial and the five o'clock bus, I decided to take my luggage to the
funeral just to be safe. Plus, David and I needed time after the funeral
to decide what I would do with those books.

"What time you leavin'?"

I glanced up, surprised, and saw Daddy standing in the doorway. I
didn't know how long he'd been watching me.

"Uh . . . sometime after the funeral. Around five or so." My hands
trembled like a man on the way to his execution.

"Oh. OK," Daddy droned, and glared at me. He didn't move,
which meant he had more to say. I wished he would say it quickly and
leave.

"Who told you 'bout Ms. Swinton?" he asked rather matter-of-factly.

"Oh! David told me she died late—"

"That ain't what I mean."

I started to ask Daddy what he meant, but patronizing him wasn't ever a wise thing. "I just . . . figured it out," I said tremulously.

"How?" Daddy was still standing in the doorway. Sitting on the bed in nothing but my underwear, I felt more vulnerable in his presence than I ever had before.

"How?" he repeated more turbulently.

I had no choice but to tell Daddy the truth, especially since I couldn't compose a good lie fast enough. "I overheard you and Momma talking about it the other night. I mean . . . I didn't hear everything, but I heard enough to figure it out." My courage, like steam from a boiling pot, was escaping me quickly, but I had to ask, "How'd you know I knew?"

" 'Cause you too cool 'bout everythang." He paused and continued more humbly, "You walkin' round here like you know 'xactly what done happened in de last ten years, but you don't. You really don't."

"You wanna fill me in?" I sounded like a smart-ass brat.

"You 'bout to leave, so it wouldn't do no good nohow." Again, Daddy didn't move, so I didn't, either. "It ain't what I meant," he started explaining. "I was goin' over there for somethin' totally diff'rent, but one thang led to anotha and then you came. She couldn't teach no school wit' a baby out o' wedlock, so I told her I'd raise you myself. She wanted you, though. She wanted you bad, and de best way she could have you wuz to teach you. That way, she could shape yo' mind, she said, and give you all de learnin' you might need to make somethin' outta yo'self. She did de best she could, boy."

"I'm not mad at Ms. Swinton, Daddy," I said and resumed packing. "She's dead now, and nothing else really matters."

"Dat's how I know you mad. You tryin' to fugit even befo' you know de whole story. Even still, yo' heart don't neva fugit hurt. Don't chu neva fugit dat. Hurt'll wait on you a lifetime to face it, but it sho' ain't gon' disappear. I don't want chu to leave hyeah today wit' a whole lotta hatred in yo' heart, boy. It'll kill ya."

Daddy's massive form in the doorway kept me anxious. Had he turned and left abruptly, I would have been relieved. I was starting to feel like I might cry, and I had vowed not to shed tears that day, even at the funeral. However, Daddy always managed to dismantle my peace before I had it built completely.

"Ain't no tellin' when you might git back dis way, boy, so I'ma tell you a few thangs while I got a chance."

He sat beside me on the bed, barging his way into my intimate space.

"She wanted me to give you somethin' if she never saw you again. I promised her I would."

Daddy handed me an envelope. I opened it slowly, not wanting to discover another truth unknown.

"Wow," I said. "Is this me?"

"Yeah. It's you all right," Daddy snickered. "She musta took dat picture de day you wuz born. I ain't neva seed no newborn baby grin. You wuz diff'rent."

"How?" I asked enthusiastically.

"You wuz always laughin'. When de midwife slapped yo' ass, you started grinnin'. She said you looked at her and neva did cry. She thought it was a little strange 'cause babies is s'pose' to cry, but you neva did. She told Ms. Swinton dat you wuz gon' be somethin' special 'cause couldn't nobody take yo' joy away. I guess dat's why Ms. Swinton took dat picture—jes' in case you eva lost yo' joy, de picture would be proof dat all de joy you need you wuz born wit'."

I was too overwhelmed to speak. In the picture, the baby's eyes were really big and the smile on his face was subtle but detectable. I couldn't believe it was me.

"Yeah, dat's you," Daddy said, reading my mind. "The day I went to git you, Ms. Swinton cried like a baby. She kept sayin' how unfair de world is and how wrong it is fu' somebody to take a baby 'way from his momma. I told her it wuz de best thang 'cause if word got out, she would lose hu' job and hu' reputation, too. She said she didn't care, but I knowed she did. She had to. Teachin' was all she had and it meant de world to hu'. I couldn't let hu' give up all dat. Too many chil'ren woulda suffa. Dis community ain't mucha nothin' wit'out dat woman teachin' dese po' black chil'ren how to love they-self. We couldn't lose dat. So I told hu' I'd raise you myself and she could see you every day and any otha time she wanted to. She didn't like it, but she went 'long wit' it. Befo' she let me take you, she took dat picture."

"My God," I mumbled as I kept examining the photograph.

"She wuz quite a woman, boy. She woulda gave hu' life fu' you. In some ways, dat's 'xactly what she did."

Daddy leaned over my shoulder and looked at the picture again. "You always did have a big mouth." We both snickered. "And you neva did cry—till you came here."

I frowned at Daddy, confused.

"The day I picked you up to bring you home, you looked at me and frowned somethin' awful. I asked her what wuz wrong wit' chu and she said she didn't know. Ms. Swinton had bundled you up like you wuz de baby Jesus born in de manger. It was real cold, I remember. I had brought a blanket, too, and we put dat round yo' li'l rump. And soon as I started walkin' out de door, you started whinin'. I thought you wuz still cold or somethin', but dat wunnit it."

"What was it?" I asked, knowing the answer.

"You neva did wanna come wit' me. Neva did. I tried to kiss you, hug you, and sing to you, but didn't nothin' make you feel betta. You wanted yo' momma, and couldn't nothin' else substitute. Especially Marion. Every time she looked at you, you'd go ta holl'in' and screamin'. She said she wuz gon' raise you, but dat she didn't have to love you. She said dat wuz my job. Me and Ms. Swinton."

"Oh, dat's why Momma never loved me."

"I guess so," Daddy confirmed, nodding his head. "She wuz doin' me a favor by 'lowin' you to live in dis house. I asked hu' to help me raise you, 'long wit' de rest of de chil'ren, and she said she would only if—" And Daddy stopped abruptly. He glanced out the window into the darkness of the early morning, then finished, "—only if I would have one more baby."

"You didn't want any more?" I inquired.

"Hell no, I didn't. I didn't wont no mo' after Willie James. Then Shelia, Scooter, and you come 'long, and I really didn't want no mo'. But de ole lady said she wanted another girl. Shelia died not too long befo' you wuz born, and she wanted hu' little girl back. I told hu' I didn't want anotha mouth to feed, but she said she wouldn't take you if she couldn't have her li'l girl, too. We tried and tried and it seemed like she jes' wasn't gon' have no mo' babies. Then, one day, I come home and she tell me she pregnant. I started prayin' right then dat it was a girl so we wouldn't have to have no mo' babies, and sure 'nough it was.

"Yet dat ain't what I'm here to talk 'bout. I wanna finish tellin' you 'bout yo' momma befo' we bury her."

"Thanks, Dad," was all I could think to say.

"No need to thank a man fu' what he oughta do. I owe you and yo' momma this." Daddy reached for the picture. "She followed me all de way home de day I brung you here. I told her it was a bad idea, but she said she needed to know dat you wuz somewhere warm and safe. She put on a coat and followed me all de way through de woods. She didn't want people seein' her, so she lagged behind a bit, hidin' in bushes and trees. Right befo' I got home, she asked me if she could hold you one mo' time. I told her it was cold and I needed to git you in somewhere warm, but she begged me real hard to let her hold you one last time. We moved behind some trees and I put you in her arms. She lifted all those covers and you started smilin' again. Dat's when I knowed fu' sho' dat you didn't wanna come, but we didn't have no choice. At least dat's what we thought back then. Now I ain't sho' 'bout dat decision."

"Why?"

"'Cause once I took you back from Ms. Swinton and brought you on home, I ain't neva seen dat smile again. If you woulda stayed wit' hu,' you mighta smiled fu' a lifetime. I don't know fu' sho', but my guess is dat you woulda been a lot happier. I know ain't nothin' I can do 'bout it now, but at least I can tell you 'bout de time when you wuz happy. I wish I could give you dat time back, but I can't."

Daddy returned the picture. "She used to see you at church and you would jump and kick till I thought folks was gon' guess de truth. Any time you saw her, you would go ta grinnin' and laughin' like you had done seen de Good Lawd. Marion couldn't stand it. She neva would hold you, change yo' diapers, feed you, or nothin'. I couldn't blame her, though. You wuz de evidence dat I had done messed up real bad. Since I couldn't neva make her see dat you wasn't de mistake, she always treated you like you wuz. I know. I saw it all. I jes' couldn't say nothin' 'bout it 'cause it wuz all my fault."

Daddy's openness startled me. My cold hatred for him was transmuting into something warm, like love or respect. It was the last thing I expected to happen before I left Swamp Creek again.

"I did de best I could wit' what I had, T.L. Ain't nothin' I can do now to make yo' life no betta 'xcept make sho' you know dat yo' momma loved you and neva woulda gave you away if she coulda kept you. But she couldn't. She cried all de time 'bout not havin' you and she kept you afta school much as she could jes' to git all de time wit' you dat she could. Don't be mad wit' her, Son. De cards she got she played good."

"I'm not mad at her, Daddy," I wept.

"Then what chu cryin' fu'?"

"Because I wish I could have had you two together."

"Dat wunnit gon' happen."

"I know; I know. It would have been nice, though, to come home to a mother and . . . um . . . a father who loved me." I hesitated. "You're a good man, sir."

Daddy's glazed eyes looked away.

"I never understood you, Daddy. You always seemed a little, um, mean. I didn't know, all the while, you were trying to make a life for me—and catching hell doing it. Thanks, old man."

"I ain't done nothin', boy," Daddy said, patting my shoulder lovingly. "What kinda life did I give you? One where I made you hate everything and everybody in Swamp Creek? That ain't no kinda life. That's worse than death. I prayed dat de Lawd would give me de courage to tell de truth and let you go, but I neva got dat courage. I wouldn't o' told you now, but you found out anyway. Dat wuz de Good Lawd's way o' tellin' me dat He wasn't gon' let dis shit go on forever. I wanted to tell you. Really I did. I jes' couldn't find de right time. All dis bullshit happen wit' cho' sista and, well, too much wuz goin' on at de same time.

"Now you know 'bout cho' momma." Daddy rose to leave but stopped in the doorway again. "Don't neva fugit dat woman. She wuz special, boy. It's gon' be a long time befo' you meet anotha one like her." He turned, closed the door behind him and walked away.

"Wow," I uttered and toppled onto the bed overwhelmed. Daddy had exposed a side of himself I thought nonexistent. He apparently had loved Ms. Swinton; however, I think he was telling me he loved me, too. Imagining him kissing and hugging me was both comforting and incomprehensible.

I left the house before Momma finished cooking breakfast. I told her I was going to help David with some last-minute details concerning the funeral. She shrugged her shoulders.

23

"Hey, little brother!" David's loud, rapturous greeting warmed my heart.

"Wow. What's gotten into you?" I asked, giggling.

"I just realized something," he said boisterously, and began pacing the sparkling wood floor. "Momma went the way she wanted to—in her own house, with her sons finally united. What more could she ask for?"

"A lot," I asserted pessimistically.

David's face lost its luster. "Like what?"

"Like the right to have both her sons her whole life!"

"Oh, T.L," he mumbled sadly, "that wasn't a right. It would have been a privilege certainly, but Momma had no right to hope for that."

"Why not?" I asked.

"Because the act of sleeping with your father was wrong. He was married and she knew it. Did Momma ever apologize to your mother?"

"No, I'm sure she didn't," I said slowly, understanding David's point more than I wanted to.

"That's why she had no right to have you. If she had done everything conceivably possible to correct the infraction, then maybe we could argue for her rights. Otherwise, she got the best deal." David smiled cautiously.

"I never thought of it that way."

"I see," he said, and we walked onto the front porch and sat on the steps together. "Your mother is the one who has an arguable right. She was dishonored and disrespected by your father and our mother, and no one found it necessary to redress the issue? The world was supposed to accept their behavior simply because of who my mother or your father was in the community? That's a lotta gall."

"I swear I never thought about it that way."

"Then you must not have liked her very much."

My cackle confirmed his conclusion. "And she didn't like me, either."

"How could she?"

"Because she was my mother, for Christ's sake!"

"And whose decision was that? Forced motherhood is surely not very fun."

"She was already a mother!"

"Yes, but to children she bore!"

"You have a point," I yielded calmly.

"It would be wrong of us to ask your mother for righteousness and integrity when neither your father nor my mother, it seems, was willing to offer the same."

"That's true," I submitted.

"People here have an image of my mother that's strange to me." David glanced around the front yard arbitrarily. "I didn't like her much as a kid. I wanted to be with her and she would never come get me. I thought she didn't love me." He picked up a dead leaf and began to shred it. "My dad was nice, but he wasn't nurturing, and I knew my mother would be if I could just get to her. Yet I couldn't. She wouldn't let me come here and she hardly ever came to Detroit. After you were born, I relinquished the hope. She was so excited about how cute you were and how brilliant you were going to be that I knew I'd never have my mother. I was disappointed at first—probably down-right mad—but then I adjusted."

"I'm sorry, David," I said compassionately.

"No need. I know Momma did the best she could for both of us. That's why I love her so." He buried his face in the palms of his hands. It was a short cry. "Oh, I have no regrets. God does all things well. I just wish I had been closer to her."

I supplied tissue found in my pants pocket. "She was great, David. Brilliant, beautiful, proud, and committed to black people."

"Yeah, I know. Some days I wished she had abandoned everything and come to get me. But I understand now." His bloodshot eyes con-trasted with his big, broad smile. "So, did you find out more about your sister?"

I almost told him everything. "Not really," I lied. "My brother told me some stuff, but nothing really substantive. I'm OK with it now. What could I do about it anyway?"

David stared at me unbelievingly. I changed the subject.

"Man, I had the wildest conversation with my father this morn-ing," I announced enthusiastically. David invited me inside for break-fast and I followed without hesitation. I sat at a small oval kitchen table in front of a pretty bay window. The morning was bright and welcoming, and I knew it would be hot later.

"What did y'all talk about?" David's back turned toward me of-fered a sense of comfort and distance. The smell of smoked ham and fried potatoes and onions was encouraging, too.

"He told me how him and Ms. Swin—Momma got together. He told me how much she loved me, and he gave me a baby picture of myself that she took on the day I was born."

I handed the picture to David. "Oh my God! Look at the smile on your face!"

"I know. That's the whole thing! I'm not smiling in any of the childhood pictures my parents have. I always wondered why I look mean and depressed in all my baby pictures, and now I get this one and I'm smiling like I'm in heaven."

"Maybe you were," David said lightly, scrambling eggs in the black cast-iron skillet.

"Yeah, maybe I was. Then Daddy took me and I went to hell."

"Not necessarily. I'm sure there's more than one heaven."

"What?" I asked, angry that David was disturbing my analogy.

"Maybe God was sending you to a different kind of heaven." David put the eggs and the ham on the table without looking at me directly. He returned to the refrigerator for jelly and orange juice and then said abruptly, "Part of our job here is to make a heaven for ourselves. All of us get enough hell to be depressed about it for a lifetime. That's the challenge. To turn hurt and pain into joy unspeakable."

David closed the refrigerator door and sat down at the table, nodding his head affirmatively. "Yeah, yeah," he kept mumbling aloud as he stared out the window. Then he snapped back with, "The goal of each life is to see if we can become God. To see if you can take your hell and make heaven out of it."

"I like your philosophy," I said, reaching for the ham. "It leaves the power of your destiny in your own hands instead of waiting to see if you pleased an omniscient God. I feel you, big brother," I smacked.

"You ready for the funeral?" David asked.

"I'm a little jittery, to tell you the truth."

"Why?"

"Because our parents' secrets and deception are about to get announced today. In public."

David rose and put on a coffeepot. "Great! Why would that make you nervous?"

"I don't know. Maybe I don't want people to be uneasy. Or maybe I don't want to be embarrassed."

"About what?"

"The truth of my existence. Who my momma is and all that."

David returned to his seat. "You don't think folks already know?"

"Yeah. My brother Willie James knew. Yet how could everybody know?"

"I don't know," David said, surveying me. "Sometimes little towns like this have big mouths. People might not be surprised at all. And if they don't know, who cares? They're about to know! It's not your mistake or your shortcoming we're talking about anyway."

"I know, but I'm the fruit of the error. I don't want Momma to be gossiped about like a scandalous whore after she's gone."

David laughed heartily. "You can't control what people say. All you can do is offer the truth and see what others do with it."

"Maybe I fear people's judgments," I said, searching for the seed of my discontent.

"Then you've already judged yourself. How can other people's judgments harm you unless you value their opinion more than you value your own?" David peered at me disappointedly. "Love yourself, T.L. Other people's love for you is optional. It's not the other way around."

He rose, retrieved two cups from the cupboard, and filled them with coffee. "If you're not careful, you'll defame Momma's name by being ashamed of what she and your father did," he said, handing me a white coffee mug. "If there's any shame to carry, they must bear it—not you. Your job is to see if you can recover the joy you had in the beginning."

"Amen." I perused the picture again.

"She left that to remind you that your joy is within you. Somehow she knew you'd need it."

"A lot has happened in my life, David. Getting that original joy back could take a lifetime."

"Yeah, or it could take a day, depending on what you can relinquish and what you can grab hold of."

"Man, you always preachin'!" I said jokingly.

"That's my job!" David refreshed my coffee. "The bottom line is that when a boy becomes a man, he must purge himself of all the garbage he collected in childhood. Hurt, disappointment, fear, pain. All those things represent what we collect as we search for happiness. Ironically, the happiness is usually never found because we collect too much other stuff along the way. The journey gets weighed down by baggage and we stop our forward movement after a while, never to resume. We think where we are is as good as it gets, and we make our home somewhere in the middle of this wilderness, having convinced ourselves that true happiness is an illusion. It isn't. We simply lost sight of the original goal."

"So I have to drop all the hurt and pain in order to discover the joy I set out with in the beginning?"

"Not drop it. Transform it. Hurt and pain were guideposts you encountered on your way to ultimate peace. They were not the end result of the journey. Be clear about this."

"Such a transformation can't be simple. Or easy."

"Sure it can. Most people hold on to hurt and pain because it's all we have. But if people knew better, who wouldn't trade that stuff for joy? Few people know the release of one is the beginning of the other."

I didn't say anything. I just kept drinking coffee, imagining my life trauma-free and unburdened.

"It's a little scary, I admit," David confessed. "Still, it's a cleansing ritual every life must perform. Only then can love and happiness flourish in your heart. It's your turn."

"Yes, it is," I said emphatically and leaped up.

"Did I offend you?" David asked with a worried expression.

"Not at all. You didn't offend me one bit," I hollered behind myself as I ran out of the front door. I knew what I had to do.

24

"Daddy, can I speak with you please?" I asked as soon as I arrived back home. He and Momma were sitting at the kitchen table although they had obviously finished eating.

"This is important. Please?"

Daddy stood and followed me out to the barn. He wasn't curious, nervous, or apprehensive. Actually, he appeared rather expectant.

My original courage had turned to mush. Yet I was determined to move forward in search of that joy that had once been mine.

"Daddy . . . I . . . um . . ."

"Spit it out, boy," he said impatiently, then sat on an upturned five-gallon bucket. His voice further unsettled me, but I knew if I didn't speak then, I would be voiceless for the rest of my life.

"I never really understood you, Daddy. Not until today." Sweat beads gathered at my temples. "You gave me an understanding of Ms. Swinton that keeps me from being angry with her for a lifetime. That showed me you really do have"—my voice cracked—"a heart. You always seemed withdrawn to me as a child, and, in fact, I never saw you express love to anyone. I thought that meant you didn't have feelings like everyone else, but when you came to me this morning, I saw that

that wasn't true. Daddy, I never knew you loved people. I never guessed you spent your whole life protecting me and trying to make a home for me, especially when Momma didn't want me. You could have sent me away to make life easier for yourself and your marriage, but you didn't because you . . . wanted me, I think."

Daddy bowed his head but never said a word.

I had to get it all out. "It's funny what kids don't understand, huh? I thought you were mean because that's just how you were. I know better now, Daddy. You did the best you could and I appreciate it. I'm sorry for ever judging you."

I stood there in utter fear. I was glad I had spoken, yet Daddy's silence crippled my courage. Too far out on the limb to come back, I continued, "I suppose I've been arrogant my whole life. I thought my life was the hardest of any human being, but Lord knows I wouldn't trade mine for yours. Of all your children, you really only had Willie James all these years."

"Naw, I didn't have him, either," Daddy admitted. "He only stayed round hyeah 'cause he didn't have nowhere to go."

"Daddy, I didn't know the whole story. Your story. I made a lot of wrong assumptions and I left here thinking I hated you. I didn't hate you, though. I hated the life I saw you live. The only thing you cared about was work. We never did any family stuff together and we were always scraping just to eat, and I knew back then I wanted more."

"I wanted mo', too," Daddy interjected quickly, raising his head.

"I know that now, Daddy. I know. However, back then I couldn't see anything but my own hurt and pain. Nobody explained to me how to live a life; thus I took it upon myself to build a fence around my heart and my life because I couldn't take it anymore. I couldn't see anything beautiful about this place, so I left it in search of a home. But life has taught me that a man doesn't get to choose his home. God gives him a home, a birthplace, and He doesn't ever let him forget it belongs to him. He can choose anywhere to live and call it home, but each of us has a place to which we must return if we are to know ourselves. You know what I mean, Daddy?"

I was shaking like a wet dog in winter. Daddy nodded his head congenially and said, "Yeah, I know what chu mean, boy."

"I don't wanna leave today the way I came. That baby picture Ms. Swinton left for me showed me something about myself."

"Like what?" Daddy asked.

"Like my joy is my own. Situations in life can distract a person from being able to see their joy, but the situations cannot ever take the joy away. In our fragile, naive understanding of life, we give our joy to people and things we fear. This means we can take it back, too. I need to do that today."

Looking up completely, Daddy asked, "You sayin' I took it?"

"No, not at all. I'm saying I gave it away to things and people in Swamp Creek years ago. You, Momma, Ms. Swinton, Sister, the church. Everything. I tried to find happiness in my relationship with all of you, but it's taken me a lifetime to realize that happiness is not something you find. It's something you create whether other folks want it or not."

"How? How you gon' have joy if don't nobody want it but chu, boy?"

"By finding joy within yourself first. Then, if others choose to share it, great. If they don't, it was yours to begin with. There's nothing to lose."

"How do a person find dat joy within theyself?"

"By realizing nothing and no one is more beautiful than they are. It's something a person must believe. Other people are certainly as beautiful, but never more beautiful. Every human being gets the same amount of potential to be like God, Daddy. The result depends on how much each of us manifests in our lifetime. The picture Momma took showed me I don't have to live in fear and dread, because that's not the way God made me. When you came to me this morning and showed me a side of yourself I had never seen before, I realized I am what I determine day by day. I don't have to be tomorrow what I am today unless I concede power over my being unto other people. I don't intend to do that anymore."

I rubbed my hands uneasily. "Daddy, I, um—"

"I love you, too, boy," he said quickly, rescuing the weight from my chest. My eyes met his and suddenly my head was buried in Daddy's bosom. His enormous grip around my back felt safe and uninhibited. We were holding on to each other for dear life. I didn't let go and Daddy didn't, either, for quite some time, and then he said, "Guess we betta be gettin' ready fu' dis fune'."

Our arms loosened and we stood there awkwardly, wondering what two grown black men do after they decide, for the first time, to express their love for each other.

"Daddy?" Pause. "Thanks."

He dropped his head ashamedly and asked, "Fu' what?"

"For giving your best."

"That's all I got, Son. That's all I got." He turned quickly and walked back toward the house. I could have sworn I saw him wipe his eyes.

25

When I exited the limousine, I heard the choir singing:

> "Je—sus keep . . . me near . . . the cross;
> There's—a pre—cious foun . . . tain;
> Free—to all—a heal-ing stream
> Flows, from Cal-v'ry's moun . . . tain."

This same verse was repeated until the deacons opened the big double doors of the church, welcoming the casket and the procession following it. Then the choir bellowed the chorus:

> "In . . . n the cross!! In . . . n . . . the cross!
> Be . . . my glo . . . ry e . . . ver,
> Til . . . my rap . . . tured soul . . . shall fi . . . nd
> Resssst, beyond . . . the ri . . . ver."

Packed like bales of hay in a barn, folks were fanning deliriously, and when I stepped into the church I understood why. It had to be a hundred degrees or better. Somebody had forgotten to turn on the little window units the night before, and now they were doing no good at all.

"Praise de Lawd, church!" Reverend Dawson declared loudly, trying to steer the congregation's attention away from the sweltering heat. "It's hotter'n dis somewhere else!"

"Amen!" people shouted.

I frowned. Everything in black folks' lives was a celebration of the lesser of two evils. We never got the best, and that didn't bother us because we always stayed one step away from the worst.

Glancing around, I saw people everywhere. Some were standing along the walls and others were sitting in chairs placed at the ends of overcrowded pews. Some people's clothing suggested they had traveled from places like Chicago and Kansas City, while others had obviously walked in from the fields. Most people had once been a student of Ms. Swinton's, I assumed, and they were there both to pay their respects and to find out anything about her they didn't already know. Black folks were good for keeping secrets all the way to the grave. When I was young, I remember going to people's funerals with Grandma, a funeral hopper, and finding out things about them I had never known. Like the time we buried Miss Ella Faye. I always thought she was a loner who never got married for one reason or another. Yet at the funeral, I read her obituary and saw she had nine children by three different husbands! "Close yo' mouf, boy," Grandma whispered to me as I read. "Dat ain't nona yo' business."

After the funeral, I asked Grandma why no one knew about Miss Ella Faye.

"Everybody knowed 'bout Ella Faye, boy. Folks jes' don't talk about otha folks' business."

With a puzzled expression, I asked, "How come I ain't neva met nona her kids or any o' dem husbands?"

" 'Cause," and Grandma hesitated. Then she must have decided that dead folks don't mind you talkin' 'bout they business. " 'Cause

Ella Faye ain't neva wanted no chil'ren or no husband. She gave 'em all away."

"What?"

"You heard me, boy. She got married three times and had three chillen each time. Said she jes' wanted to see what de kids would look like. De menfolks said dey wanted babies and she had 'em and gave 'em to 'em. They neva told her they needed her to want 'em. When she got tired of 'em, she told dem husbands to take dem damn kids and leave hu' alone!" Grandma laughed thunderously. "Lawd, Ella Faye was a mess! She wuz so pretty dat near'bout every man round dis place wanted hu,' but dey neva asked hu' if she wanted dem for more than a night or two. She showed 'em!" I snickered, too, thinking about a woman in Swamp Creek with that kind of disposition.

"Ain't nobody done mo' fu' dis community than Ms. Swinton!" Reverend Dawson screamed, interrupting my recollection. "You gon' be hard-pressed to find another woman that brilliant, disciplined, and upright."

"Amen," people hollered.

"Near 'bout everybody here done got at least one whippin' from Ms. Swinton and then another one when you got home! Hallelujah!"

"I know dat's right! Uh-huh! Amen! Sho' ya right!" the congregation responded.

"But it made us betta," Reverend Dawson reminded.

"Yes, it did."

"Ms. Swinton wunnit gon' rest till she believed in hu' heart dat you had done learned somethin'. Y'all remember! You bet not come to school wit'out cho' homework!" Reverend Dawson bucked his eyes and searched for witnesses to confirm his testimony. "I remember one time when I came to school and hadn't got my lesson out. Ms. Swinton grabbed my hand and walked me all de way home and told my folks not to send me back to hu' classroom wit'out my work done. Daddy and Momma was hot about it, but Ms. Swinton wunnit to be played wit', so they said, 'Yes, ma'am', and I got de beatin' of my life. I bet I didn't come to school wit'out my work done no mo'!"

The congregation laughed and remembered simultaneously. A few mumbled their own tales quickly, trying to top Reverend Dawson's.

"She was a woman of conviction! A woman of standard!" Reverend Dawson whooped. "She believed in a thang bein' done right!"

"Yes, she did!" folks said.

"And you talkin' 'bout could read! I always said she shoulda been in Hollywood somewhere. I used to love storytellin' time at school 'cause I would stare hu' in de face and let hu' soft voice soothe me all over. I didn't really care what she was readin' 'long as she was reading out loud. And de books!"

"I mean!" Daddy echoed from the deacons' corner.

"I went to hu' house one day and when I walked in, I coulda fell out!" Reverend Dawson feigned fainting. "I ain't neva seen dat many books in nobody's house. I hadn't neva been to no library befo', so I hadn't neva seen dat many books in no one place at one time. Lookin' stupid, I went from shelf to shelf readin' titles I hadn't neva hear of befo' and wonderin' how any human bein' could possibly read all dem books!

"'You done read all dese books, Ms. Swinton?' I asked in amazement.

"'There may be a few I've missed,' she said and smiled at me.

"'Wow! You's a real smart lady!' I said.

"'Not you is, son, you are,' she corrected.

"We laughed about my bad grammar as I kept shakin' my head in wonder that one lady owned a million books."

David glanced at me and I knew what he was thinking. Somehow, someway, I had to do something with those books. I squirmed in my seat, frustrated with the responsibility and too annoyed by it to grieve.

Reverend Dawson finished his eulogy and everyone read the obituary silently:

Ms. Carolyn Swinton was born the fourth child to the late Jimmy and Frances Swinton on June 4, 1923, in Swamp Creek, Arkansas. Ms. Swinton went home to glory on the evening of June 18, 1993.

Ms. Swinton was a pioneer in the field of education and was extremely devoted to the school in Swamp Creek where she taught for more than 40 years. She was also a devoted Christian and member of the St. Matthew No. 3 Baptist Church in Swamp Creek, Arkansas. She faithfully served her church as a member of the Sunday school teaching staff, a member of the No. 2 adult choir, and a past coordinator of the summer Vacation Bible School.

Ms. Swinton was a product of the same school in which she taught, having started her formal education in Swamp Creek School. She went on to receive her teaching diploma at Philander Smith College in Little Rock, Arkansas. She graduated with highest honors and went on to receive a master's degree in education from the University of Arkansas at Little Rock. She began teaching at the Swamp Creek school in 1948 and taught until her untimely death.

Ms. Swinton loved and cherished the children she taught, accepting nothing but excellence from them. Yet, above all things, she loved the Lord with all her heart, soul, and mind. She lived the Bible instead of preaching it, and her favorite phrase was "I'd rather see a sermon than hear one any day." She now rests with the Lord and walks the streets of gold, teaching children in heaven how to be their best.

Professor, as she was affectionately called, will surely be missed by the many lives she touched and the many hearts she enriched. Her insistence upon the best and her demand for quality have kept Swamp Creek alive for the past 40 years. It will take someone with very large feet to fill her shoes. She will certainly be missed.

Ms. Swinton leaves to celebrate her legacy Mr. David F. Gladstone, son, of Detroit, Michigan; Mr. Thomas Lee Tyson, son, of
New York, New York; and a host of cousins, family, and friends.

"I didn't know she had a master's degree," I leaned over and whispered to David.

"Yeah. She probably got it in the last couple of years while you
were away." David winked at me.

"Why are you winking at me?"

"Because Momma's life resembles yours more and more every day,
huh?" He smiled.

The choir rose and sang "Soon and Very Soon, We Are Goin' to
See the Kang." Mr. Blue chimed in from the amen corner, and by the
second verse the entire church was singing along. It was beautiful. I
closed my eyes and listened to those black angels sing this song of
warning and celebration. I imagined Ms. Swinton approaching the
Gates of Heaven and the angels bowing slightly as she entered. Children cheer and shout while they watch her walk majestically around
the kingdom in amazement at its beauty. A golden stool is where Ms.
Swinton sits, fashioned by God Himself, and she smiles at all the
children as they play at her feet, wanting nothing more than a little
attention and affirmation from the Master Teacher. I begin to cry and
this time I know why.

"I know I might be outta order, church, but I wanna ask T.L. if
he'll come on up and have a word or two. I heard he's leavin' us today
and I want him to leave us wit' somethin' to chew on."

"Amen!"

I could not deny Reverend Dawson's pleading eyes. He had certainly caught me off guard, as tears rolled down my cheeks, but I
quickly wiped them away and rose to a thunderous applause. I had
not the slightest idea what I would say, but it had to be good. Folks
were seeking to be impressed by my college education although had I
lived there currently, they'd hate me for the same. I had to deliver.

The podium was my comforter as I said, "First giving honor to

God, Who is the head of my life, to Pastor Dawson, pulpit guests, members, and friends. I am both sad and glad. Ms. Swinton was first and foremost my mother."

I don't know what compelled me to say that. It was the first thing that came to my mind, so I offered it. What surprised me, though, was that nobody else was the least bit surprised.

"She loved me and taught me practically everything I know. She and my folks." I glimpsed Daddy, and he stared in return, indicating that I should go on. "When I was a little boy, Ms. Swinton told me I could be anything I wanted to be. The secret to success, she said, was I had to believe it first. I asked her how to believe, and she told me something I've never forgotten." I began to cry again, but I tried to hold it together. "She said you should never dream about being a thing. Just be it. Simply stand up and be it. I told her I wanted to be a teacher just like she was, and she said, 'Then teach.'

" 'Who?' I asked.

"And she said, 'Anybody who'll listen.' I told her I was a child and nobody thought they could learn anything from a child. And Ms. Swinton said, 'Then teach the birds in the sky. And the rabbits and the squirrels. Teach the trees, flowers, and the wind.'

" 'How do you do that?' I asked naively.

" 'By assuming they hear you and understand your words. Assume their intelligence, T.L. Treat them as you would like to be treated. Let them know you are open to understanding their world and you want to share yours with them. Believe they all have a heart and a desire to know the true meaning of life. Love them hard enough to weep about it, and value the possibility of their perspective enough to seek it diligently. Only then can you call yourself a teacher. A teacher teaches everybody and everything he encounters. A teacher believes that everything seeks to know and to understand everything else. He is the medium through which this universal miracle shall occur.'

"Ms. Swinton changed my life that day. She opened up a world of possibilities that I would never have conceived. Swamp Creek transformed into the Garden of Eden as she took the ordinary things in my life and showed me how to find the extraordinary things about them. She showed me that teaching is a spiritual calling, not an intellectual occupation. I had forgotten that lesson until my brother David reminded me about it yesterday. The utility of education is the element most pseudoteachers miss, Ms. Swinton always suggested, and she made me realize that if anyone ever had a true teacher, their lives were definitely changed. A teacher does that to a student. Always."

"You betta talk, boy!" Ms. Polly declared.

"Amen! Amen!" others joined in.

"And now, I'm the teacher. It's my turn to transform children's lives and to insist they love themselves although they may never have done so. I must be the one who buys the books and reads them feverishly in search of new concepts and ideas that will intrigue the lost. I suppose I don't have many to buy, though, because Ms. Swinton left me all of hers!"

"Is dat right?" Reverend Dawson exclaimed behind me.

"Yes, sir, it is. My promise to Ms. Swinton and all of you is that I will use them to make other lives better. If I can be even a portion of what she was, then my living shall not be in vain."

The crowd roared as I took my seat. I was trembling, both from adrenaline and the pain of letting Ms. Swinton go.

"Whooooooooooooooo-whee!" Reverend Dawson shrieked. "Dat's what education'll do fu' ya!"

I tuned him and the rest of the congregation out and hung my head and cried. David put his arm around my shoulder, and I was grateful for his touch. I didn't care who saw me that day. That was my mother lying before me and I didn't know how to let her go. I began to wave my arms and shake my head violently. "It's all right, little brother. It's all right," David said. It wasn't all right. I would never get another chance to speak about her or to her, and I needed to make the most of the moment. I rose suddenly, teary eyed, and began to sing, "If I can heeelp somebody . . . as I travel along . . . if I can cheer somebody . . . with a word or a song . . . if I can shoooow somebody he's traveling . . . wrong . . . then my living shall not be in vain!"

People were screaming and falling out all around me. I was purging my soul.

"Then my living . . . shall not . . . be in vain!!!!! Oh, oh, then my living . . . shall not be in vain. . . . If I can heeeeelp somebody as I travel . . . along, then my living! . . . then my living! . . . then my living . . . shall noooot beeeeeeeeeeeeeee in vaaaaaaain!"

Ms. Polly was running up and down the aisle by the time I finished the song. Several folks were shouting, and others were holding them. The majority of the congregation were standing and clapping their hands, declaring, "Sang, boy!" and, "Amen!" and, "Hallelujah!" Yet I wasn't doing it for the praise. I needed some way of turning pain into joy. I remembered the old folks doing it when I was a child, and I knew I could do it, too. I felt a lot better.

After the cheering settled a bit and the ushers carried Ms. Polly out, Reverend Dawson returned to the podium. "Dat was all right! Whoooo-wheeeee! I mean dat was all right! If yo' soul don't feel no betta after dat, den you don't know de Lawd at all!"

"Amen!"

"We now gon' have some words from David Gladstone, Ms. Swinton's oldest boy."

David surged and went to the podium confidently. He had prepared an outline to assist him since he knew he was on the program to speak.

"I am pleased to discover that many people knew my mother intimately and loved her dearly," he began. "She was an incredible woman, by any standard. I believe a person's life celebrates her more than anyone else ever could, and Momma's life certainly spoke volumes. She loved her work, she loved her kids, and she loved her Lord. She wasn't big on shouting and other open declarations of praise, but in her private space she gave God His due. Momma used to call me and ask me to pray for her to have the strength to carry on, especially on nights when her thoughts of T.L. threatened to overwhelm her. She would talk about how much she loved him and how she wanted nothing but the best for him. She used to say her baby was somewhere out in the world alone and needed his mother's prayers to protect him. Yet she often feared her prayers were insufficient. Her only wish was to see him before she died, and the Good Lord made sure she got what she wanted.

"I thank all of you for your prayers, flowers, phone calls, and especially for honoring my mother and allowing her gift of teaching to bloom among you. Your testimony of her greatness comforts my heart beyond what any of you could ever know." His voice cracked as he concluded, "I used to dread the idea of coming down to this little place in the middle of Arkansas. Now I know why Momma stayed. There were people here whom she loved dearly and would have given her life for. I'm glad to know the feeling was mutual."

David resumed his seat, and I squeezed his hand affirmingly. It was almost over.

Reverend Dawson asked the congregation to rise for the recessional. The choir began to sing "Goin' Up Yonder" as the funeral directors slowly wheeled the casket out of the church. David and I walked side by side, both of us crying lightly and humming to steady our nerves. I noticed Momma examining me expressionlessly when I walked out of the church. She should be relieved, I thought. The truth was out, so no need to hide anymore. Maybe there was pain in her heart that no one knew anything about. Yet, I couldn't worry about Momma right then. I had some things to do before I left Swamp Creek.

The burial was quick and nondramatic. Reverend Dawson read the Scripture that says "man that is born of a woman" and then prayed a short prayer. He asked if anyone had anything they wanted to say, but no one responded. Therefore, he said, "Ashes to ashes, dust to dust," and the casket began to descend into the earth. I felt helpless. There was nothing else I could do to honor Ms. Swinton, no way to tell her how much she meant to me, no way to let her know how much I appreciated the sacrifice she had made in giving me up.

"That's that," David said softly after he crumbled a handful of dirt onto the casket.

"Yep," I mumbled inaudibly. We started walking back down the road toward the church.

"Today's gonna be a scorcher, huh?" David was trying to make small talk to ease my pain.

"It might."

"T.L., don't hold on to pain. Let it go."

"How am I supposed to do that?" I snapped.

"There's no magical formula, my brother. You have to take everything in your life as a lesson instead of as punishment. You have to try to see how every event makes you better. Once you get the lesson, you let it go."

"And what's the lesson of this?" I screamed.

"That's for you to determine," David stated boldly. "I'm sure it has at least something to do with your gift of teaching."

"Not that again!"

"You couldn't get away from it if you tried. Teaching's the reason you're on the planet. Your gift is your reason for existence. Everything that happens in a person's life is somehow related to his spiritual gift. Exactly how is your job to figure out."

I didn't say anything more. I wasn't thinking rationally and I was too upset to do any real intellectual work. David was right, though. I knew that much. And, to be honest, I probably didn't want to know the connection between everything and this teaching gift for fear of where it might land me.

As though telepathic, David said, "Don't be afraid of the truth, T.L. It will always leave you better. Always. It might not seem that way at first, but trust me. The truth will set you free."

I could smell fried chicken as we approached the church. I knew the kitchen would be humming with excitement, laughter, and good food. No matter how great the pain or how incredible the loss, the food at funerals was always incredible.

"What time do you leave today?" David asked when we reached the entrance to the church kitchen.

"I'ma catch the five o'clock bus in front of the Meetin' Tree."

"What are you gonna do with the books?"

I hesitated. "I don't know. I just don't know."

"I was thinking. Since now it looks like I'm gonna be here another day or two, packing up the rest of Momma's things, I can ship them to you if you want me to. It could be expensive, though."

"I don't know, David. I'd have to get a bigger apartment first, and that would take longer than a day or two."

"Well, you'd better figure out something quick. It's already three thirty." And with that, David lightly pushed me into the church kitchen.

People were laughing loudly in spite of the tragedy of Ms. Swinton's passing. Their uproarious voices made me much lighter about the situation.

"Sho 'am sorry 'bout cho' momma!" Mr. Blue said, placing a hand on my shoulder. "She was a greeeeat woman, dat's fu' sho'!"

"Thanks, Mr. Blue." I smiled.

David and I sat at the head family table as church mothers served the feast. You would have thought we were at the Welcome Table in the kingdom of God with all the food they set before us. We ate good, too. Maybe hurt creates appetite and a need to fill one's self with something substantial. Mr. Blue sat across from me—he always sat at the head table, regardless of what family it was. I took a chance and asked him, "How long have you known Ms. Swinton was my momma, Mr. Blue?"

I had to wait for a response, for he was sucking on a drumstick. "All yo' life," he said calmly, and kept on chewing. "I thought that was why you left heayh. Folks said you got mad at yo' daddy fu' what he done and just ran off one day."

"That's not true. I didn't even know she was my momma until a few days ago."

"Sometime what folk thank they know ain't so. I sho' is sorry you had to find out thisa way."

"Why didn't you tell me? A long time ago?"

Mr. Blue smirked and said, "It wunnit nonna my business and nonna my place to be talkin' 'bout yo' daddy to you. I knowed 'bout it, but I wunnit s'pose' to talk 'bout it. Dat's why I didn't say nothin'.'"

"How did you know?"

Mr. Blue gaped at me and pierced his eyes but said nothing. He kept smacking on chicken bones and collard greens and glancing at me occasionally like I was supposed to understand his thoughts without him speaking them.

After we ate, I asked David if he would step outside for a moment.

"What time is it?" I asked.

"Four ten," he said. "You must have come up with an idea."

"I think I have, if you'll agree to it."

"Let's hear it."

"Here's the plan: Leave the books in the house until I find a bigger apartment. I'll come back and get them myself. I know you plan to rent the house out, but if you put the books in one of the back rooms, they shouldn't be in the way. What do you think?"

David observed me sternly and said, "No deal. You can't get away that easily."

"What do you mean, get away?"

"The books are supposed to be with you. They're not supposed to be boxed up."

"I'm not abandoning them! I'm going to find a bigger place so I'll have somewhere to keep them. I would literally have no room if I took them home. Plus, I can't take thousands of books on a Greyhound bus! I'm gonna have to ship them whenever I move them."

"Fine. Maybe I overreacted. I don't want those books to go to waste, sitting in boxes in Momma's old house."

"They're not going to go to waste, David. I wouldn't do that."

"OK, T.L.," David said suspiciously.

"What's the problem?"

"Thinking you're gonna come back here soon leaves me doubtful. Swamp Creek is not a place you visit often, to say the least."

"That's not fair."

"Sorry. That was a low blow. But, T.L., you've got to promise me you'll come get those books as soon as you can."

"I promise, David. You have my word."

"Fine. I'll leave 'em in the spare bedroom and you come get them as soon as you can. And I mean as soon as you can!"

"I promise!" I said confidently.

Willie James walked up as David and I were finishing our conversation and said, "Daddy's lookin' fu' you."

"Tell him I'll be there in a minute." Willie James walked away.

David frowned and declared, "T.L., you won't want to come back to this place a few months from now. Tell yourself the truth, man."

"I know," I sighed. "But I'll have to now."

"That's my fear, brotherman. I know your intentions are good and all, but I'm afraid once you leave this place this time, you're never coming back. And Momma's books won't be enough to bring you."

I studied David's eyes as I tried to convince myself I would make another trip to Swamp Creek within a few months. The thought exasperated me.

"I'm telling you. I don't know about this. If you leave those books here forever, Momma gon' be mad about it!"

"Yeah, I know." I plopped down on the steps in front of the kitchen door and dropped my head into my hands.

"Look. As long as you promise to come back, it's cool with me if you leave the books. Don't leave them forever. Please."

"All right, David. I won't. I ain't got no choice."

"Yes, you do. We don't have time for that conversation right now, though. You got a bus to catch."

"I know," I said excitedly. "Let's promise to stay in touch, big brother."

"Absolutely. I wouldn't have it any other way."

We hugged tightly and exchanged phone numbers and addresses. I felt sad leaving David. I had truly grown to love him.

"I'd better go see what Daddy wants. Take care of yourself, OK?"

"Count on it, T.L."

We gawked at each other awkwardly for a second.

"You need a ride to the big tree?"

"Naw. Daddy'll drop me on his way home. Thanks, though. I'll phone you from New York."

"Please do. I'd like to know you're home, safe and sound."

We embraced again and I heard Daddy call my name.

"I gotta go."

"I love you, T.L."

"Love you, too, David. Talk to you soon."

I bumped into Daddy as I rounded the corner of the church.

"You ready to go?" he asked me.

"Yessir. I think I am."

"Let's go get yo' stuff from de house and then—"

"I put it in the truck this morning before I left. I didn't know how long everything was going to last, so I thought I'd better bring my bags to be on the safe side."

"I see," Daddy said disappointedly. "It's gettin' close to five, so you'd betta git on out dere jes' in case de bus is a li'l early."

"I'm ready whenever you are. Just let me say by to Willie James. I'll be out in a second."

I found him sitting on the back pew of the church, glaring out of the window. He appeared depressed.

"Big brother, I gotta go," I said, interrupting his thoughts.

He turned suddenly, unashamed of his tears. "Please stay, T.L. Please." His voice shimmered.

"I wish I could, Willie James, but I can't. I got to get back."

"Please, T.L." He grabbed my hand, and my fingers buckled in pain. "I ain't got nobody."

"You got yo'self, Willie James," I suggested weakly while struggling to free my hand.

He finally let go. "Then at least write, OK?"

"I will. I promise."

Willie James stood and hugged me sensually. He lay his head on my shoulder and allowed himself to melt into my embrace. Then he blinked bloodshot eyes at me and said simply, "See ya."

"See ya," I returned, and left. I was trying to stay light about everything, but Willie James was not helping.

I bumped into Momma as I rushed through the church kitchen. We froze awkwardly, staring at each other like strangers.

"Bye, Momma," I said coyly, trying hard not to feel anything for her.

"Take care," she returned as I stepped around her. "And take this with you."

She handed me the picture of the butterfly I had painted for Willie James years ago. "It made him cry 'cause it reminded him of you, so I took it down. I thought you'd want it if you ever came back."

Momma hung her head and walked away.

"Thanks," I mumbled genuinely, disturbed by what appeared to be an act of kindness from one whom I thought incapable.

I ran to the truck and hopped in. "Ready to go!"

"You sho'?" Daddy asked, starting the engine.

"Yessir. I don't think I've forgotten anything."

"Ain't nothin' else you need to do? Or say?"

I froze. "I don't think so."

"All righty, then. Guess you betta be goin'."

We started down the road. I knew Daddy had something on his mind, but I didn't want to pry. Hence, I sat timidly, praying he'd let me off at the Meetin' Tree and just go on home.

That didn't happen. In fact, he pulled off the highway, parked the truck under the tree, and turned off the engine.

"I sho' do hate it's gotta be like dis," he said after a minute or two. "A man and his boy oughta be able to do bettern we doin'."

I was dumbfounded.

"You done found out a whole lotta stuff since last Sad'dy, and most of it's done made you madder than a wet hen. I jes wanna say I'm sho' is sorry, boy."

Tears welled in my eyes but I held them.

"Ain't nobody's life perfect, son, but yours coulda been a lot betta if I had been a betta man back then. I jes' want chu to know dat I'm sorry. Dat's all."

Every time I tried to speak, I got choked up. I wished Daddy had just dropped me off. Leaving would have been so much easier.

He started the engine again, a sign he was ready to leave. "De bus ain't gon' be long now. It's nearbout five o'clock."

"Daddy . . . um . . . take care of yourself," I mumbled as I wept. "You've been a good father and I appreciate it." That's all I could get out.

"You take care o' yo'self, too, boy, ya hear?"

"Yessir," I said, recomposing myself. I got out of the truck and lifted my bags from the back. I walked to the driver's side and reached my hand out to shake Daddy's. He clutched my hand so tightly I could feel his energy run up my arm and into my chest. When I glimpsed Daddy's eyes, I noticed they were glazed over with tears.

"Come back sooner," he whispered and tried to smile.

"I will, Daddy. I will."

He turned his head away and drove off slowly. I sat on the bench underneath the tree and cried like a baby. I never realized before how much I loved that man.

The bus came a few moments later. It was just as hot that day as the day I had arrived.

"Hey there, young fella!" the driver said as I boarded. "I thought you mighta died from a heatstroke." He laughed.

"No, sir. I'm still kickin'," I said, rumbling through my bag, trying to find my ticket. In so doing, I discovered a strange note written in Momma's impeccable penmanship:

I didn't hate you.

"Damn!" I sputtered aloud.

"Is everything all right, son?" the driver asked.

"Um, yessir. Here's the ticket." I dropped it on the floor and the driver retrieved it.

"You seem nervous 'bout somethin'. You sho' you all right?"

"Yessir," I said as I began to move down the aisle toward a seat.

"Don't let nothin' worry you too bad, boy. My daddy passed last Sunday—had a heart attack in his sleep, they say—and I promised myself after we buried him that I wasn't gon' let nothin' worry me too bad."

I stood in the aisle and felt a cold shiver go all over me. "Shit," I mumbled when I found a seat and sat down. I kept reading the one line over and over again as though hoping it would disappear. I only made myself more upset. Momma always had the last word, and now I felt like crap for leaving Swamp Creek—again. "But did you love me?" I asked aloud in response to the note. Peering out of the big bus window, I saw a field of butterflies dancing wildly in the air. Their movements were frantic, as though trying to remind me of something important I had forgotten. I ran to the front of the bus.

"Let me off, please," I begged the driver.

"Excuse me?" he said, looking up at me, confused.

"Let me off. Now."

He didn't understand.

"Please, sir. Let me off. Please!" I was screaming.

"OK, OK. You sho' is determined 'bout somethin'!" The bus driver pulled to the side of the road. "It's got to be at least two or three miles back to that big tree, son. You gon' walk in all dis heat?"

"The ancestors did it," I proclaimed.

He opened the big door and, as I exited, he said, "Take care o' yo'-self."

"I will," I returned. "I'm sorry to hear about your father."

"Thank you, son. Jes' be glad yours is still in the land of the living. Take care now."

The bus pulled away. I surveyed those thousands of butterflies dancing, though now very gracefully.

"I'll jes' keep Ms. Swinton's books right where they are," I said aloud as the heat wave greeted me again. "That house can't be too expensive, can it, Mr. Butterfly?" A beautiful yellow and black one rested on my shoulder. "David'll be glad to sell it to me, I'm sure."

I was trying to talk myself into believing what I had just done. It was right, but I still couldn't believe it.

"Never say never," I chuckled, then took a deep breath, grabbed both bags, and began to walk home in the midst of a warm, uncloudy day.